VANISHED

First edition. May 28, 2024.

Copyright © 2024 Kay Doherty.

ISBN: 978-1954265073

Written by Kay Doherty.

Dedication

For my youngest brother, Kevin, who harassed me constantly over the past decade or more to finish this book. Here it is – you frustrating butt nugget.

Acknowledgements

Thank you to my parents, Pat and Mike, for their assistance with storyline and grammar. Thank you to my husband, Michael, for his help with word choice, descriptions, and the odd looks when I asked him which sentence sounded better. Thank you to my younger brother, Tim, for his assistance with architecture, building materials, and terrain. Finally, thank you to my coworker, Ming "Frank" Wu, for his help with all my "what if" and "how about" questions.

I never would have finished this novel without all of you.

This is a novel I thought would never see the light of day. It had so many massive problems, plot holes, and situations that just weren't realistic that the inside of a trunk was the best outcome I could imagine. With the help of family and friends over several years and countless revisions, I finally feel like Vanished *might* be worthy of publication and I truly hope it is enjoyed.

Thank you all for reading.

Books by this Author
Contemporary Romances
Blind Date
Only You
Wounded Heart

Paranormal Romances
Sugar Cookies & Mistletoe
Hearts of Fire
Hearts of Blood
Hearts of Magic
Hearts of Destiny
Beck's Wolf
Beck's Pack

Paranormal Mysteries
Vanished

VANISHED

CHAPTER ONE

"Wow," Shane breathed. "Kind of creepy."

Standing outside the decaying hulk of Crystal Creek Hotel, he stared in both awe and dread. The beautiful, snow-capped Colorado Rockies rose majestically behind the relic, but not even a mountain could diminish the grandeur of the five-story building. Dirt-encrusted glass windows stared out like empty eyes over the surrounding forest and dirt parking lot where Shane's feet had grown roots. The area was silent except for the occasional chirp of birds and the ambient whoosh of the river that cascaded over the cliff in a gorgeous waterfall. The rumble of vehicles on the bridge echoed among the rocks and crevices. The two-lane road ran along the south side of the hotel connecting the western slope to the eastern plains by way of a suspension bridge that spanned the canyon at the back side of the hotel.

Shane studied the architectural design. The size and beauty of the building was impressive for this area. Built in the Gothic style, it had a gabled roofline and rounded windows on the top two floors; though the fifth floor was recessed and barely visible from the parking lot. Chimneys and spires rose up at random locations giving the façade a jagged appearance that closely mimicked the rocky landscape surrounding it. An old forest and thick underbrush bordered the grounds, blocking the view of the river and highway. The result was a spooky, secluded feeling. Shane wondered how much time had passed since people had actually stayed here. The place had clearly been abandoned for decades.

The front had an expansive, covered porch and several balconies on the upper floors had stunning views of the surrounding mountains, but had long-since lost their railings and the bricks were disintegrating. Dried leaves, dead tree branches, and litter blew across the lot on a cold breeze to pile up against railing posts and along the crumbling foundation. A few of the windows on the main floor were missing glass panes, and one of the two wooden entry doors was split up the middle. Shane was enthralled. He could imagine what the hotel looked like when it was new – majestic and beautiful.

"Incredible, isn't it?"

Shane jumped at the deep voice behind him, barely managing to suppress an undignified squeal. He had been so focused on the hotel he hadn't heard his friend approach. Shane glanced around the lot, but only saw his beat-up hatchback with Bella's nose plastered to the back window. The German Shepherd looked massive inside the small car. Luke's sedan was nowhere to be seen and Shane frowned at his friend. Luke was rarely seen wearing anything but a suit and tie, but today he was dressed for comfort in slacks, dark button-down shirt, and well-worn loafers. His dark brown hair was short and perfectly styled. Mirrored sunglasses and a windbreaker completed the ensemble. The glasses reflected the setting sun's rays. Long shadows cast by the hotel slowly crept across the dirt and gravel lot.

"Don't do that, Luke," Shane said.

"Sorry. Forgot how jumpy you can be," Luke said with an amused smile that made Shane want to slap him.

"Sneaking up on people has that effect."

"Right."

"And my anxiety goes through the roof every time you call," Shane said.

Luke shifted the folder he carried from one hand to the other in a nervous gesture. He pointed a finger at Shane.

"Your hair is different. Is it lighter?" Luke asked.

Shane ran his fingers through his short blond spikes. "Needed a change."

Luke smiled and nodded. Shane's past had left him with the urge to control whatever he could in his life and Luke understood that. Shane noticed Luke looked everywhere but at him and nervously kicked a toe into the dirt repeatedly. He had a pretty good idea what had prompted Luke to call him and ask him to come all the way up here, but he wanted to hear Luke say it.

"Why am I here?"

Bella started whining from the car. Both men turned to see the dog jumping back and forth between the front and back seats in excitement. Luke glanced around the area. Shane couldn't stop the grin. The poor guy was never sure of things when Shane and Bella were around. Shane didn't see an immediate reason for Bella's activity and figured she was just tired of being stuck in the car. Shane was amused by the way Luke scanned his surroundings, acting every bit the cop he used to be. Luke faced the direction of the highway putting Shane and the forest behind him so he missed Shane stiffen with tension.

Movement among the trees along the southern edge of the property held Shane's attention. When he looked directly at the disturbance, he saw nothing. But if he shifted his gaze slightly to the side, he could see it with his peripheral vision. A woman paced in small circles, wringing her hands together. The foliage and underbrush beneath her feet made no sound. Shane glanced away with a groan. Luke spun on his heel.

"What? What's wrong?" Luke asked.

"It's haunted," Shane answered, feeling a chill that had nothing to do with the cooling temperatures.

Luke's brows drew down and his forehead creased. Shane watched Bella jump back and forth in the car, her movements closely mimicking the circles the ghost woman walked. The dog wasn't showing teeth or growling. That was always a good sign that the ghost was benign. She was probably nothing more than a memory loop forever stuck on replay.

"Should I be concerned about this?" Luke asked and motioned toward Bella.

"No. The ghost is harmless. Bella just wants to get out to look," Shane answered.

He had hoped his words would put his friend at ease, but Luke looked unconvinced. Luke Holmestead was an ex-cop turned private detective. He'd left the force mere months after closing the case that had forged their friendship. Luke knew Shane was psychic and that he and Bella could see ghosts, but that didn't mean he was comfortable with it. Shane suspected his psychic ability was the very reason he was standing outside this derelict hotel.

"Tell me why I'm here, Luke," Shane pressed and watched Luke go from wary to professional in an instant.

"Several years ago a lot of people went missing," Luke said, gripping the folder in his hand tighter. Shane was curious as to what that folder might contain. "We need your help to find them."

"That sounds like a job the cops should be doing," Shane pointed out.

"It's currently a cold case with the department. One of the families hired us to help locate their family member. If we find anything useful, we'll give it to the authorities," Luke explained.

"Okay, but a private investigator can only do so much. You can't make arrests," Shane said. He was stating the obvious, but he felt Luke might need the reminder. Luke shrugged, unfazed.

"Come inside. We'll go over everything with you," Luke said and walked toward the hotel, leaving Shane alone in the lot.

"We?" Shane mumbled.

For as long as they'd known each other, Luke had always worked alone. His preference for the one-man show had frequently landed him in hot water with his superiors in the police department. He was a lone wolf and while that was perfectly acceptable as a P.I., he still occasionally crossed lines that put him in direct conflict with the very cops he used to work with. The fact Luke was working with someone else on this case was disturbing.

Shane walked around his car to the back and opened the hatch. Bella jumped over the seats, tail wagging, and ready to sniff the world outside her makeshift prison. Shane expected the dog to take off toward the grass where the ghost circled. Instead, she ran full speed toward the highway. A short metal and wood bridge just wide enough for a single car spanned the creek connecting the lot to the road. The highway beyond might only be two lanes this far into the mountains, but it was still dangerous. To say nothing of the river swollen with snow melt and the sheer, one-hundred-foot drop off.

"Bella," Shane yelled and ran after the animal.

He knew full well that he would never catch the damn dog. She was bred to run fast. Shane's heart raced unsteadily as Bella reached the bridge. Bella had been given to him as a puppy three years ago by his best friend, Kendra "Kennie" Marks. Because of his unique circumstances, Shane was more attached to Bella that most people could understand.

"Bella, no," Shane bellowed.

An ear-splitting whistle stopped Shane and Bella in their tracks. Bella turned back toward the hotel, ears perked while Shane breathed in relief that she was no longer headed toward danger. He looked over his shoulder at the hotel veranda where a man he didn't recognize stood. From Shane's position he couldn't make out the other man's facial features, but he appeared to be wearing a suit. He was tall and stood back within the deepening shadows. The man slapped his hands on his thighs in the universal dog language Bella understood. She ran back across the gravel lot towards the hotel. With Bella's attention now safely diverted, Shane walked back to his car, rolling his neck and shoulders to ease the tension.

He removed his jacket from the car and slammed the hatch, shoving the keys into his pocket. There was no need to lock the thing out here in the middle of nowhere. Even in the city no one would steal the clunker. The sun was well on its way to setting behind the mountains and the wind made it feel colder than it was. Mid-October in Colorado was hard to dress for. While the daytime temperatures hovered in the 60s, the nights could get quite chilly. Shane cautiously ascended the pitted concrete steps to the porch. He found Bella nosing through a pile of dried leaves and trash and snapped his fingers.

"Come, Bella."

The shepherd snapped to attention and pressed into Shane's leg, tail down. He scratched behind her ears to show his appreciation and pushed the heavy wooden door open. The hinges creaked loudly and echoed through the expansive lobby. Bella brushed past and immediately began sniffing the perimeter. Piles of debris were scattered about. A few pieces of decaying furniture were pushed against the walls. Bella dived nose first into one of the trash heaps, spreading it around with her huge paws.

Shane glanced up at the vaulted ceiling where a massive brass and crystal chandelier hung. Rotting wooden beams jutted out of the once-white ceiling. A grand staircase leading to the upper floors was directly across the lobby from the front doors. To the right of the stairs was an elevator. To the left was the reception desk. The same wall had two massive fireplaces on either end large enough for a grown man to stand inside. All the walls had holes in the plaster exposing the brick beneath. Doors at each end of the rectangular lobby led to other rooms. Several dirt-covered windows overlooked the porch and allowed a meager amount of light into the room.

Luke leaned a hip against the reception desk, holding his upper body weight on an elbow. The file he'd been carrying was now on the desktop by his hand. Beside him was another man who had his back to Shane. The man leaned onto both elbows on the desk but was gesturing animatedly with his hands. He and Luke were speaking in harsh whispers. There was no way the two men were unaware of Shane's entry but he didn't want to interrupt what was clearly an argument. Instead, he decided to examine the room more closely.

Concrete foundation could be seen through threadbare red and black carpet. Entire patches were missing in some spots and the exposed concrete had become blackened. Strips of wallpaper had peeled and rolled down to the floor. Chunks of plaster littered the floor where it had fallen from the ceiling or walls. Ornately carved crown molding still adorned the wall-ceiling juncture. The doors to the left were closed, but the doors to the right stood open offering an unobstructed view of tin ceiling panels stacked in the middle of the otherwise empty room. Shane contemplated their existence; they were so out of place. He pulled his jacket closed across his chest to ward of the chill slowly seeping into his bones. He glanced back to the reception desk to see the two men had stopped arguing and were now watching him.

"This must have been a beautiful place," Shane said as he joined the men at the desk.

Shane was accustomed to getting odd looks Luke still shot one his way on occasion but the look coming from the other man made Shane nervous and self-conscious. The man stood with arms crossed and brows furrowed but was otherwise nice to look at. Handsome features, longish dark blond hair swept back off his face in soft waves. He was dressed more relaxed than Luke in khakis, a polo shirt, and suit coat. In the impending darkness, Shane couldn't tell the color of his eyes, but his gaze had a hard edge to it. Something told Shane this man could smell bullshit a mile away. Luke picked up the folder and motioned Shane closer. He gestured to the other man with a tilt of his chin.

"Shane, this is a friend of mine, Dominic Masters. Masters, this is Shane Cayli."

"Mr. Masters," Shane said in greeting.

Shane didn't particularly want to shake hands with a stranger, especially one he found disturbing, but manners hammered into him by his mother had him extending a hand. After a quick and overt head-to-toe sweep of Shane's body, Masters took the offered hand in a firm grip. In addition to his good looks, Masters also seemed calculating and distant.

"Just call me Masters," he said and released Shane's hand. "Always Masters."

Shane nodded and stepped back. He ran his fingers through his hair then straightened his jacket. He lowered his arms and shoved his hands in his pockets when he realized he was fidgeting. Masters' perusal had left Shane feeling uncomfortable and edgy. Shane managed to hold Masters' gaze for several more seconds out of sheer force of will before looking at Luke. Luke's brows were lowered as he stared at Masters, but as soon as he caught Shane watching him, he smiled.

"Let's head to the dining room. There's a table and chairs there we can use," Masters said.

His words were said with such authority it never occurred to Shane or Luke to object. Masters headed toward the elevator clearly expecting the others would follow him. Luke sidled up to Shane's side and leaned in to whisper in his ear as they crossed the room.

"I told Masters I was bringing you in, but I didn't tell him you were psychic until a few minutes ago. He doesn't exactly approve because he doesn't believe in psychics."

That was nothing new. Luke smiled and shrugged his shoulders when Shane rolled his eyes. People's disbelief in things supernatural was one of the reasons Shane had chosen not to advertise he was psychic. He kept his ability quiet because he didn't like to be insulted and ostracized. It was people like Luke that made Shane willing to take a risk and help people. Shane abruptly stopped and called Bella. He'd been so caught up in Masters, he'd temporarily forgotten about the dog. Bella trotted over to him and he curled his fingers around her collar. He found the men waiting for them by the elevator. Masters was sliding the gate back and forth, making it screech in the track.

"I'm not getting on that thing," Shane said firmly.

Luke laughed while Masters shot Shane an irritated glance.

"It's doesn't work. There's no electricity," Luke said and waved the folder to indicate the room with a shake of his head.

Masters took a few steps and disappeared around a wall, followed by Luke. Shane followed more slowly to find there was a narrow, dark staircase situated behind the elevator bank. Ignoring his mild embarrassment at appearing to be an idiot in front of Masters, he released Bella's collar. She bounded up the steps behind Luke. Shane moved up the stairs more slowly, uncertain of his footing in the near complete darkness. At the top of the stairs, Shane's earlier embarrassment was forgotten as he was greeted with a spectacular view of the mountains.

The wall directly across the room was floor-to-ceiling windows. Extending past the French doors was a cobblestone terrace surrounded by wrought iron railings twisted into complicated fleur-de-lis patterns. The canyon extended along the back of the hotel, the creek cascading over the edge of the cliff in a rainbow of mist. The setting sun painted the sky in deep blues, bright oranges, and soft pinks; the sun glinted off the metal buttresses and cables of the bridge in bright yellow spears. It was one of the most breathtaking sunsets Shane had seen and he smiled at the serene vision. It was a shame this place was condemned.

A flashlight clicked on and the glare reflecting off the windows reminded him there were others in the room. Shane's gaze drifted to Luke and Masters where they stood next to a table with two chairs. Luke cradled the folder to his chest and smiled. Shane grinned back as Masters pulled a chair out and motioned to it.

"Take a seat, Mr. Cayli," Masters ordered.

His tone immediately irritated Shane. He didn't like being ordered around and it was clear that Masters was used to his commands being followed without question. Shane bit back a retort as Masters sat in the second chair and waited. Shane returned his attention to the serenity beyond the glass as he walked to the table and took a seat. Luke took up sentry beside him.

"Pay attention," Luke said with a soft nudge to Shane's shoulder.

Shane reluctantly pulled his gaze away from the view. Masters sat in the chair at an angle with one arm draped over the back. His other arm was stretched out over the table, fingers drumming rhythmically. Shane fought the urge to squirm under Masters' intense scrutiny. His gaze finally slid off Shane to take in the room around them. When Masters finally broke the silence, Shane hung on every word.

"This hotel and its grounds were once owned by Robert Grant. He was a self-made millionaire. He got lucky in the stock market by selling at just the right time. Mr. Grant decided to host a fundraiser in hopes of renovating and reopening Crystal Creek. Several of his friends and business colleagues were invited."

As Masters spoke, Shane glanced around the room. Tables and chairs were shoved against one wall leaving the center of the room empty aside from the table they were using. Dust covered the floor and the only footprints marring the smooth surface were those of Bella and the three men. Shane found Bella sniffing the floor near the stairs.

Across the room behind Masters was a long mahogany bar. Brass poles rose from the floor at regular intervals suggesting they had once been barstools posts, though all the cushions were now missing. Whatever vision Robert Grant had held for this hotel had never come to fruition so he wondered why he was even being told about it. Masters continued speaking and Luke shuffled papers behind him bringing Shane's focus back to his companions.

"At the far end of the bar by the windows is a door leading down to the kitchen," Masters said and pointed in the direction he was referring to. Shane nodded though he couldn't see the door in the increasing darkness. Luke's flashlight beam bounced around erratically with his movements.

"A small, private catering company was hired to prepare and serve the food, but because the party was small, there was only one cook and one waitress present. In the weeks leading up to the fundraiser, Grant made limited and temporary upgrades. He installed electrical here in the dining room and in the kitchen that ran off generators and placed battery-operated lanterns on the porch and throughout the lobby. He also placed a few out on the terrace. Because Grant was a rich man with rich friends two battery-powered security cameras were installed as well. One was placed above the stairs on the porch facing the lot. The other was placed in that corner." Masters hiked a thumb over his shoulder indicating the corner at his back. Shane didn't bother to look. It was too dark in the room at this point to see anything.

"He spent just enough money to get the kitchen in working order and to update the dining room. That's why this room isn't as rundown as the rest of the place."

Shane had been so taken with the view that he hadn't really paid much attention to the room itself. Masters was right; it was definitely modernized with painted walls instead of wallpaper. There were no holes in the walls or ceiling, and the wood flooring was intact and smooth. Shane wondered why Grant would hold the party here. He also hoped the reason Masters was telling him about it would be revealed soon, though Shane now assumed that Robert Grant and Crystal Creek Hotel had something to do with why Luke had asked him here. Once Masters realized Shane wasn't going to speak, he continued.

"As Mr. Grant was new to wealth, he was still quite frugal with his money. He did the minimum necessary to get this place ready for the fundraiser. That includes the security cameras. They were time-lapse cameras, nothing fancy, that he programed to take photos every five minutes." Masters motioned to Luke who placed a photo on the table in front of Shane.

"This was taken at 9:10 p.m." Luke told him.

Pictured was a formal dress party in full swing. Women were dressed in cocktail gowns while the men sported dark suits and ties. The wall of windows behind them was dark but through the glass pots of blooming flowers could be seen suggesting the party had taken place during the spring or summer. All the guests held glasses of wine or snifters of hard liquor. Hors d'oeuvres sat on small tables strategically placed around the edge of the room. The main tables were set for a formal dinner but were untouched. Luke placed a second photo on top of the first.

"This was taken at 9:15," he said.

Shane couldn't reconcile what he was seeing with what he was hearing. It was impossible. The second photo showed an empty dining room. The lights were still on, glasses of alcohol sat on tables, and purses were hanging on the back of chairs. It looked as though everyone had just stepped out of the room momentarily. Luke began placing photo after photo in front of Shane.

"9:20. 9:25. 9:30. They all show the same thing until about 9:45 when the waitress and cook come out of the kitchen. Pictures from that point on captured confusion, the arrival of the cops, and the collection of evidence until the batteries die about 36 hours later," Luke said.

He snatched all the photos off the table and replaced them in the folder he carried. Shane stared at the empty tabletop lost in thought. He couldn't make sense of this, but something in the back of his brain was poking at him, whispering *I get it.* Luke handed Shane another stack of photos that he shifted through numbly. The only thing that changed from one photo to the next was the amount of sunlight coming through the windows or the length of the shadows on the floor. In quite a few pictures, the police were forever captured on film as they processed the scene. Shane's question was, the scene of what? What exactly where the cops investigating? He was about to ask when Masters spoke.

"The initial theory was that the guests left the room to tour the hotel. It was the main reason they were here, after all, to give money to renovate."

"That makes sense," Shane said.

Masters nodded then said, "But they never came back." He leaned his elbows onto the table, turning his palms upward.

"So where did they go?" Shane asked.

"That would be the million-dollar question," Masters said, pointing a finger at Shane. "Or should I say, the multimillion-dollar question since Grant and his friends were each estimated to be worth between seven million and eighteen million." Masters leaned back in his chair causing the wood floor beneath to creak. "There were a total of fifteen people attending the party including Grant, his girlfriend, and thirteen guests. In less than five minutes, all fifteen disappeared without a trace. No one has seen them or heard from them since. There's been no movement on their finances, no ransom demands. Nothing at all. They all just...vanished."

CHAPTER TWO

Shane sat in confused shock. Where had these people gone, and why? How could fifteen of the wealthiest people disappear, and no one know anything? His curiosity was most certainly piqued. Shane loved mysteries, but he wasn't sure why they were telling him about this one. He glanced around the room once more. It was in better shape than the rest of the hotel, but it certainly wasn't new or spectacular. Whatever renovations Grant had made hadn't been done recently.

"How long ago did this happen?" Shane asked quietly.

Luke bent over to take the photos from Shane's hands. "Twelve years," he answered.

Luke slipped the photos back into his folder. Shane stared at the flashlight Luke had set down on the table, but he wasn't truly looking at it. He was replaying everything he'd seen and heard in the past several minutes, letting it all sink in.

"This is why you are here, Mr. Cayli. Holmestead seems to think you can help," Masters said.

Shane kept his head still but shifted his gaze to Masters. The man's tone screamed skeptic. At least now he knew exactly why he was here. They wanted him to find Robert Grant and company. He just didn't know *how* Luke thought he could help. Without looking away from Masters, Shane spoke to his friend.

"What do you want me to do, Luke?"

"Same thing you always do," Luke answered.

Having his suspicions confirmed only made him more anxious. Shane wasn't the typical psychic. He had a modicum of control over his gift, able to increase or decrease the "intensity." When he touched people, and sometimes objects, he would relive whatever memory or emotion carried closest to the surface at the moment of contact. Certain objects would become suffused by a person's strong emotion or intense memory and Shane could pick up on that. The caveat was that he had to know what he was looking for. Here, now, without someone or something to touch, Shane had no idea how to go about doing what Luke asked.

"This case has been cold almost from day one. The cops have exhausted every lead. Masters and I have exhausted every lead. All we have is a wife who wants to know what happened to her husband twelve years ago, this hotel...a rotting, haunted hotel" Luke looked around the room with a soft chuckle "and you."

"It's not haunted," Masters said with an exasperated sigh.

Shane stared at him. "You don't believe in ghosts," he said.

"No, I don't."

"And you don't think I can be of any help."

"No," Masters confirmed.

"I told you about the cases he's assisted on in the past. How do you explain those?" Luke asked. He tossed his folder onto the table lifting a fine cloud of dust illuminated by the flashlight. Masters' chair creaked as he moved his weight in the seat.

"Research, intuition, dumb luck. Take your pick," Masters grumbled.

Shane was accustomed to this type of cynicism and generally he could ignore it but Masters' attitude irritated him for some reason. Call him a fraud to his face, however, and you were asking to get hit. Shane hated being called a liar. For the moment, Masters was stopping just shy of that line. Rather than listen to an argument the two men had obviously had on several occasions, Shane chose to redirect their focus.

"Ok. You've told me you want me to help find these people. Maybe now you can tell me *how* you expect me to do that," Shane said, looking over his shoulder at Luke's shadowed form.

A soft click was followed by a narrow beam of light from across the table. Masters arced it around the room, doing little to illuminate anything, before pointing it at Shane. "Do your psychic thing," he said.

Shane took advantage of the fact Masters could see him and flipped him the bird. Masters scoffed and Luke knocked Shane's hand down. Shane was annoyed that Masters never once moved the beam of light off him.

"You can read objects, right?" Luke asked.

Shane nodded slowly then shrugged. "Sometimes. It depends. Why? You have something?"

"Yes. We have the building," Luke answered.

"You want me to read... the building?" Luke couldn't be serious. Luke wasn't usually one to joke around and Masters looked like he'd break something if he smiled, but what Luke was suggesting was insane. "Do you have any idea what you're asking?"

"Yes, I do. It's a big building with a lot of memories, I know, but it's all we've got. Please, Shane."

Luke put a hand on Shane's shoulder and squeezed. Shane stared at nothing, his eyesight all but obliterated by Masters' flashlight still shining in his face. Shane was not a fan of this suggestion. It would be exhausting and painful, but he already knew he was going to say yes. The decision was made in part because he wanted to know where fifteen people could disappear to where they'd never be found, and partly because he felt he owed it to Luke. The man had saved his life and doing favors like this was how Shane repaid him. Shane blew out a loud breath.

"No promises," he said. "Light up a wall for me."

Shane stood up and hugged himself as Luke pointed his flashlight at the nearest wall. He was growing cold though he knew much of the chill he was feeling came from fear rather than the mountain weather and unheated building. Masters' light stayed on Shane as he walked to the wall.

"Bella," Shane called and snapped his fingers.

He listened to the soft clicking of her nails on the hardwood floor as she heeled. Her large body brushed against his leg and she nosed his palm. Shane stroked her head a few times before slipping his fingers beneath her collar. This was the type of situation where Bella became a service dog. They would maintain physical contact to keep Shane from being completely consumed by the memories. Once images started playing in his mind he would be swept up in them, completely unaware of his surroundings. The real world simply disappeared until the memory ended. Bella became his seeing eye dog and protector. One bark from her and the memory would break, bringing Shane crashing back into reality. It was jarring and disorienting, but sometimes necessary if Shane was in physical danger.

Shane took a deep breath, releasing it out slowly as he allowed the mental walls he'd built around his psychic ability to drop one by one. Warmth flooded his veins, chasing the chill from his bones. He clenched his fingers around Bella's collar and raised his other hand to the wall. He stopped a mere inch away. Once Shane's fingers made contact with the wall, he would be inundated by thousands of memories from the hundreds of people who had once walked these halls. He closed his eyes and thought about the photo showing all the partygoers mere moments before they disappeared. Keeping that image in the forefront of his mind, he braced himself for the inevitable onslaught and flattened his palm against the aging plaster.

Prepared for anything and everything Shane was shocked when he got *nothing*. How was that even possible? He started walking along the wall. Concrete crumbled in spots as his palm slid over it, but that was the only sensation he received. Not one single memory popped into his head. He wasn't even picking up latent emotion. Shane stopped walking and expanded the reach of his ability to a foot away from his body to form a psychic circle hoping he might catch an untethered memory. Not a thing. Bella was alert but calm beside him suggesting she wasn't picking up on anything, either. Shane dropped his hand to his side.

"There's nothing here," Shane said.

"Of course not," Masters mumbled.

"What do you mean there's nothing here? How is that possible? You won't go into a lot of public places because of how much you pick up. Why is this place different?" Luke asked.

"I don't know."

Shane turned to face the men and leaned back against the wall with a shrug, squinting into the brightness of both flashlights pointed at him. Bella pressed her body against his thighs and sat down on his foot. He petted her head and ears absentmindedly. His psychic energy thrummed through his body making him instinctually nervous because he never knew what to expect when he was "live" and not actively giving a reading. He reached behind him and pressed his palm to the wall by his hip just to see. He sighed and let his hand drop. Masters huffed out an exasperated breath.

"Why is this so shocking?" Masters asked. The cynical tone grated Shane's nerves. He really hated the snooty skeptics, but he remained silent. Luke seemed to be oblivious to his partner's attitude.

"It's surprising because a building this size that was used by the public for years should have a shit-ton of memories and emotions locked in the walls for Shane to receive," Luke explained.

"More information might be helpful," Shane said. "I don't really know what these people look like so even if I do come across a memory belonging to one of them from that night I won't know it."

He rubbed his hand along the wall in an upward arc from his hip to his shoulder until he felt the distinct chill of metal. He figured it was the elevator flashing and pulled his hand back. He also pulled his psychic circle back in until all the energy was once again held inside his body.

"Uh huh, and what's wrong with the photos we just showed you?" Masters asked.

Shane shook his head. His annoyance with Masters was escalating, but he tried to keep that from showing in his tone as he answered. "Not specific enough. I couldn't really make out faces because the resolution was grainy. I need face shots, like driver's licenses or personal photographs. Or maybe something one of them owned so I can get a more direct connection to that specific person."

"I'm not sure what I can get for you, Shane. And there's no way we can get our hands on the evidence," Luke said.

Shane wasn't sure if Masters actually scoffed or if his shoe just scuffed across the floor, but the sound had Shane biting his cheek. He was feeling very much on edge and he was pretty sure he would end up slapping Masters if he said one more negative word. Shane rubbed Bella's head and focused his attention on the sound of Luke's voice.

"I don't want evidence. The stuff people wear or take to parties are usually only pulled out for special occasions. I need something that was handled on a regular basis, things they touched daily. That's the kind of thing that will be infused with their life."

Masters' chuckle was heavy with disbelief and Shane couldn't help but give him the finger again. It only made the man laugh harder.

"Knock it off," Luke said to no one specific, though Shane figured it was meant for both him and Masters. "I suppose we could ask Mrs. Roster for something of her husband's," Luke suggested.

"Let's see what we can do," Masters replied. "But we do *not* tell her, or anyone else for that matter, why we need it."

"Fine," said Luke as Shane muttered, "whatever," and rolled his eyes.

Shane hated being put in the public eye so Masters wanting to keep his involvement secret was just fine by him. He'd be damned if he let Masters know that, though. Shane preferred to keep his assistance anonymous because seeing his name and face in papers or on television wasn't something he wanted. It had happened once before and it was an experience Shane never wanted to repeat. Masters stood abruptly and his chair made a grinding sound as it moved across the wooden floor that set Shane's teeth on edge. If the man was doing that on purpose, Shane was going to have to kill him.

"I'll make some calls later," Masters said. "We done here?"

He finally moved his flashlight beam off Shane's face and aimed it at Luke, who raised a hand to block the light, blinking rapidly.

"Christ, Dom," Luke admonished.

Without a word Masters moved toward the stairs. The beam of his flashlight was steady and straight, lighting up the doorway to the stairs, like he had no fear of tripping over something he couldn't see on the floor. Shane would have had the light pointing directly at his toes. He was klutzy on a good day and could easily trip over nothing. Luke's light was pointed at the floor but still several feet ahead of his feet. Shane shook his head. He would have to rely on Bella showing him the way and simply deal with the fact he was going to stumble in the dark. He tightened his fingers around Bella's collar and urged her forward.

As they tentatively made their way toward the stairway Shane began pulling his psychic power back into a tiny ball in his chest and erecting the mental walls to keep it contained. He knew he was succeeding when the warmth dimmed, and the coldness of the room pressed in on him. He shivered. Shane was never more grateful for his meditation habits and Bella's presence as he was the moment his shoulder brushed against the elevator door. A blood-curdling scream erupted in the room and Shane dropped to his knees, covering his ears at the high volume and pitch. He tucked his chin to his chest, yanked Bella closer, and tried to breathe normally. Pain exploded through his head like he'd been hit with a bat. His stomach twisted and lurched.

The scream died as quickly as it had started, but the damage was done. Shane was a wreck. The scream had been loud and terrified, but blessedly brief. Any longer and Shane might have puked or passed out. He came back to his senses a bit at a time. He first noticed Bella's cold, wet nose nudging his face, then her soft whine. Her collar was fisted in his hand and he forced himself to loosen the grip. His fingers tingled as blood rushed back into the digits. Shane reached up and ran a shaky hand over her neck fur. If that scream had affected him this much, it had to have been painful for Bella's sensitive hearing, too.

Shane's head throbbed to the beat of his heart and he tried to calm down so the pain would lessen. He still felt like he had cotton in his ears. A wave of dizziness had him closing his eyes again until it passed. While he tried to breathe slow and deep, he ran a system check. His ability was still safely locked away other than the small amount that always leaked into his system. It was impossible to completely contain something that was as natural to him as breathing. Dialing down his psychic ability allowed him to still see ghosts and hear voices but blocked the more troublesome memories and visions.

It was the only reason he was sane. It had taken years of keeping his distance from people and strict meditation skills guided by Kennie before he was able to be in public places without being rendered comatose by unwanted memories. Without the mental box Shane had carefully constructed he couldn't tell past from present, what was real and what wasn't. He'd have been locked in an institution long ago. Shane still had moments where he looked completely crazy to other people because some ghosts appeared solid and far too alive to be dead.

Several minutes passed before Shane realized Masters was leaning over him. Luke knelt on the floor in front of him trying his best to calm Bella. She was shaking with her tail tucked. Shane pulled her closer to his chest and mumbled comforting words into her ear. He squeezed and rubbed her chest. The motions were meant to be comforting to Bella, but they had the same effect on Shane, bringing his heart rate down and normalizing his breathing.

"Can I touch you?" Luke asked. He spoke in the tone Shane always categorized as brotherly.

"Please don't." Shane winced at the rawness in his throat and swallowed.

"Are you okay, now?"

Shane grunted in response. He was okay as far as the vision being gone, but the aftereffects would set in soon which meant he was not okay. Having a vision was like drinking too much and the aftereffects were the hangover.

"One of you want to tell me what just happened," Masters said from his position beside Shane.

Shane felt a hand on his upper arm and another at his lower back, gently urging him to stand. He allowed himself to be helped to his feet before pulling away from Masters' firm touch. He didn't want to inadvertently read the man. Bella stayed pressed against Shane's legs and he grabbed her collar. He was still a bit unsteady on his feet.

"Didn't you hear that?" Shane asked.

"All I heard was you screaming and the damn dog barking," Masters said.

"I screamed?" Shane asked. He massaged his throat. Screaming explained the pain, but he didn't remember doing it.

"I've heard you scream before so, yes, it was you," Luke said, calm and quiet as usual.

The reason behind Luke recognizing Shane's screams was not something Shane wanted to think about right now. It had been the first case Shane had ever assisted Luke with, the case that had thrown them into each other's lives, and it was a case best shoved into the deepest, darkest corner never to be revisited as far as Shane was concerned.

So, he'd experienced a memory that dropped him to his knees and tore a scream from him. That was concerning and confusing. Why the hell did the elevator have a memory attached to it when the rest of the room was a void? It made no sense. Shane pushed the oddity to the back of his mind for future consideration. His head was throbbing too much to concentrate on that and his ears were ringing. He was extremely tired and wanted nothing more than to sleep for a day or two.

"I'm better now. Can we leave?" Shane asked. He hooked his hand into Bella's collar and took a tentative step forward. His legs were shaky, but they would carry his weight and get him to the car.

"Yeah, this way," Luke said.

CHAPTER THREE

Shane followed the sound of Luke's footsteps and the bouncing beam of his flashlight to the stairwell and down the steps to the lobby. Masters brought up the rear, keeping his beam of light on the backs of Luke's shoes. He stayed close enough to Shane that Shane felt his heat behind him, but he never got close enough that they touched. As they got closer to the front door Shane's fatigue lifted a bit and he was able to think a little more clearly.

"Any idea what happened in the elevator?" Shane asked.

"When?" Luke asked as they carefully made their way through the debris and litter on the lobby floor. It was much harder in the dark.

Shane shook his head at the ridiculousness of Luke's question. It didn't matter when. Shane didn't have the capability to figure out timelines. Everything meshed together unless there was something distinct marking the memory as coming from a certain timeframe.

"You know that doesn't matter, Luke. Anytime since the damn thing was installed," Shane snapped.

Fatigue and a throbbing headache were making him short-tempered. Luke sighed. They'd been through enough together for him to understand Shane's current mental state.

"I don't know, Shane. I'll look into it if you want," Luke said. He opened the door and motioned for Shane and Masters to exit first.

"No, it's fine. Morbid curiosity," Shane mumbled as he passed his friend.

The three men filed out onto the porch and Shane inhaled a lungful of fresh, cool mountain air. The temperature change went a long way to alleviating his lethargy. There was enough sunlight left outside that the flashlights were unnecessary. Luke tucked his small flashlight back into his pocket. Shane squinted as his headache amped up in intensity for a moment before settling down to a constant throb again. The wind had picked up while they were inside and Shane was temporarily blinded by leaves and dirt being kicked up as he descended the cracked concrete stairs to the gravel lot. He released Bella's collar so he could open the car door for her. Luke stood on the other side of the car watching him, probably assessing his suitability to drive. Masters came down the stairs and began walking across the lot toward the bridge. A large truck rumbled down the highway, reminding Shane of Bella's perilous dash across the lot earlier.

"Mr. Masters," Shane called. Masters stopped and turned to face him. Shane didn't have the best opinion of the man, but he'd quite possibly saved Bella from becoming roadkill. "Thank you for saving Bella."

Masters slid a hand into his pocket and pulled out a hotel key. "No idea what you're talking about." He turned away and continued toward the bridge.

"Earlier, before I came inside, you whistled to keep Bella from running onto the highway," Shane yelled at the man's back. Luke's forehead creased as Masters looked back over his shoulder.

"Wasn't me," he yelled back, not breaking his stride.

Shane looked at Luke, remembering the man he'd seen was wearing a suit, and shook his head. "It wasn't you."

"No," Luke agreed. "Listen. Dom...Masters takes a while to warm up to people, especially people like you."

"People like me," Shane repeated with a scoff.

Luke rapped his knuckles on the roof of Shane's car. "He'll get used to you. I booked us rooms across the road at the Thunderhawk Motel. Get checked in, eat something, and tuck in for the night. I know you're not feeling well. Masters and I will make some calls and see if we can get you something more to work with tomorrow."

Luke turned and headed for the bridge to the highway. Thunderhawk Motel must be literally right across the road if both men walked to Crystal Creek. Shane watched Luke leave and contemplated whether or not he wanted Masters to get used to him. He believed in Masters "warming up" about as much as Masters believed in Shane's psychic ability, which was not at all.

Shane realized he had wanted to prove Masters wrong tonight and part of his irritability came from his failure to do so. The other part of his irritability came from the fact that he even cared what Masters thought. He wasn't ten years old anymore trying to impress the cute boy next door. After a lifetime of dealing with non-believers, his parents and brothers leading the charge, he should know how pointless it was to try to change a cynical mind.

Bella whined from the driver's seat taking Shane's thoughts back to her mad dash. He was disturbed but not at all surprised Masters hadn't been the man on the porch. Crystal Creek was haunted after all. Shane slid his gaze across the lot and forest surrounding the property. It made no sense to him that a place could be populated by ghosts, but not have a single memory or emotion attached to it. That never happened. Ghosts *were* memories; they *were* emotions. Through his peripheral vision Shane could see slight wisps of movement among the trees and a soft fog-like substance hung in the air over the river. The female ghost he'd seen earlier had dissipated and everything seemed calm.

A man entered Shane's vision walking down the road that led further into the mountains beyond the hotel. According to the No Trespassing sign at the edge of the gravel lot it was private property farther back. Shane wasn't sure yet if this man was real or an apparition, but he did know that he wouldn't want Crystal Creek Hotel for a neighbor. Shane looked directly at the man as he drew closer. He didn't disappear from sight like many ghosts did when Shane looked directly at them which was the first sign the man was alive.

Shane had forgotten about the car door being open until Bella pushed past him at a dead run for the man. He really needed to focus more on that dog since this was the second time tonight, he was forced to chase her. At least this time she was running toward a person instead of speeding cars. The stranger bent at the waist and petted Bella behind the ears. Shane left the car door open and joined Bella and the man, shoes crunching loudly on the gravel. He wondered if the man always walked around in this area or if his appearance had anything to do with their little visit.

"I'm sorry," Shane said as he approached the man. "I really should have her on a leash."

"It's fine, son."

The man straightened from rubbing Bella's head to look at Shane. The man's white hair stuck up in a disheveled mess and Shane couldn't help but think the man looked to have been electrocuted. Wrinkles creased his weathered skin. Thin laugh lines surrounded his intelligent blue eyes. The same manners that had him extending his hand to Masters earlier, now had him extending his hand to this man without thought.

"I'm Shane. This is Bella."

"Name's Drake."

The man took Shane's hand in a firm grip. Shane regretted offering it immediately. His psychic power still thrummed through his body, barely contained, and he knew better than to touch someone in that state. Unless, of course, that's what the person had paid for. Shane made good money doing psychic readings at the shop he owned with Kennie. Crimson Moon was a metaphysical shop. They had come up with the idea back in college during business classes. Kennie and her girlfriend at the time, Layla, had started tossing ideas around. By the time they graduated, Layla had moved on, but Kennie and Shane had a business plan and enough start-up capital to make it a reality.

Drake was not a paying customer and Shane felt it was rude to randomly read people without consent, but that was exactly what happened. Shane fought to keep his smile in place and his tone conversational as he pulled his hand free. The nanosecond of memory that had invaded his brain had been warm, happy, and filled with love. Shane pushed the snapshot of memory away and focused on Drake. Shane hadn't been grounded by Bella and he was uncertain how much time he'd lost. Judging by Drake's furrowing brow and look of confusion, Shane hadn't lost any time at all this go around. He let out a breath through his smile.

"You all right?" Drake asked.

"Yes. I'm just very tired and have a headache. Long day."

Shane rubbed his neck to emphasize the point. He had one bitch of a migraine setting in. Another gust of wind kicked up dirt and gravel, and Shane shielded his eyes with a hand. Drake's gaze never wavered.

"People don't usually come 'round here. What brings you?" Drake asked. His suspicious tone confirmed for Shane that Drake lived nearby and this visit was prompted by their presence. Shane erred on the side of caution whenever answering questions regarding cases he was assisting on, but he did try to stick as close to the truth as possible.

"I'm researching Crystal Creek Hotel and all the strange things that have happened here."

Shane waited to see if Drake would start talking. It was his experience that people with stories liked to tell them and the hope their story would make it into a book or documentary typically loosened their tongues. Not so with Drake. He remained silent and continued to hold Shane's gaze. It was unnerving.

"Have you lived around here long? Maybe you can tell me about the place, some of the things that happened inside?" Shane prompted. Drake's steely blue gaze never wavered.

"A lot of things happened inside," Drake finally answered, though it wasn't an answer at all. Shane was getting irritated, but he had to admit he wasn't surprised. This guy was seriously suspicious and they were both treading carefully. Shane decided to be a little more direct in hopes of getting the man to open up.

"I've heard stories of people disappearing and a disturbing story about the elevator," Shane said, watching Drake's expression closely for any change. He had no idea if the elevator situation was disturbing or not, but with a scream like that he assumed whatever had happened had not been pleasant. Drake's expression gave away nothing and his response gave only slightly more.

"Disappearances, unexplained accidents, murders." Drake shrugged. Shane was beginning to feel like a bug on a pin under Drake's unrelenting gaze.

"Was the elevator one of those unexplained accidents?" Shane pressed. He'd told Luke not to bother finding out what happened, but he really was curious.

"Nah. That was plain stupidity. Elevator's out for years, but some broad...excuse me, some lady in real estate decides to get on it. Cable snapped supposedly." Drake quickly sliced his hand across his throat in a severing motion and shook his head.

Shane suppressed a shudder. He was correct in his assumption the elevator story would be disturbing. The woman was most likely killed on impact when the elevator slammed into the ground floor. It certainly explained the brief, terrorized scream he'd experienced. It would take mere seconds for the elevator to come to an abrupt halt. Shane was extremely grateful he hadn't received that memory. He looked back to the hotel, noting its obvious dilapidated state.

"How long has it been empty?" Shane asked.

"Decades," Drake answered with a small shrug. "Been rotting longer than it was ever in use. Should have been torn down long ago. Some places shouldn't exist after such evil."

Shane darted his gaze back to Drake. That was an interesting thing to say. The man stared at the hotel in disgust, a stubborn set to his jaw.

"Have you ever seen anything you can't explain or experienced something inside?" Shane asked.

Drake's eyes flashed with something akin to fear, but he masked it quickly. It was enough for Shane to know he had definitely seen or experienced things here.

"Stay out of there, boy. Ain't nothing but trouble inside those walls." Drake cast one more scornful glance at the hotel before heading back the way he came. "Good luck, son," he yelled back without turning.

Shane watched as the man disappeared farther down the road into the trees. He was a mixed bag of emotions, but curiosity was definitely at the top. Bella roamed around a bush, sniffing the ground with rapt attention.

"Bella, come girl. Papa's tired."

Shane clapped his hands and Bella snapped to attention. He began walking back toward the car and Bella bounded past him, into the open car door, and sat down in the passenger seat. Her panting had already fogged up the passenger-side window by the time Shane eased into the car and shut the door. He rolled down the window so Bella could hang her head out, cranked the heat up to combat the cooling temperatures, and edged the car around the circular drive toward the bridge. He eased off the gas and took one last look at the massive structure behind them. Shane wasn't sure what he expected to see. The place was nothing but a darkening mass of decaying wood and brick built at the edge of a mountain cliff. It was the kind of place that spawned ghost stories and horror movies. It still bothered him that the grounds would be so active when the interior was a virtual black hole.

Bella jumped to her feet and started barking. Shane's head snapped back to the front windshield and he slammed the brake pedal to the floor. He hadn't been driving fast, but a thin cloud of dust still wafted up around the car, illuminated by the headlights. Shane blinked and tightened his fists on the steering wheel. Dirt wasn't the only thing being lit up by the headlights. He breathed deeply as adrenaline caused the throbbing in his head to spike severely, bringing blurry vision and nausea with it. He swallowed convulsively against the urge to vomit.

Standing in the center of his car's engine block was a well-dressed, dark-haired man. He was a very well-defined apparition and Shane recognized him as the man who'd whistled for Bella earlier that evening. Seeing the man's body essentially cut in half by the front of the car made Shane sick to his stomach even though he knew the man wasn't solid, or alive. Shane was mesmerized by the fact that he was holding the gaze of a ghost that was cognizant. The ghost's gaze slid to Bella then back to Shane. He nodded once then dissipated like smoke.

The entire encounter was disturbing, from the fact that the ghost could apparently materialize when and where it wanted to the fact that it *knew* it could materialize when and where it wanted. If the ghost was capable of speech or kinetic energy he would be classified as a poltergeist. Shane already knew the thing could whistle. A poltergeist was the last thing he needed, but in all honesty, he couldn't say he was surprised to run across one here.

Shaky, nauseous, and a little freaked out, Shane rested his forehead against the steering wheel for a moment. His head hurt, he was hungry, he was exhausted, and it was only after seven in the evening according to the dashboard clock. Bella pressed her cold nose against his neck and Shane lifted his head again. He rubbed Bella's tummy with the back of his hand until he felt steady enough to drive. At least he didn't have far to go. Shane eased the car across the bridge, leaving Crystal Creek and all its ghosts behind him.

CHAPTER FOUR

Thunderhawk Motel was quaint and small, with only eight individual cabins. The main building was larger and had a shingle hanging outside above the door stating it was the office. Attached to the back of the building was a small house. Except for Luke's blue Ford and a vintage red Beetle, and Shane's poor excuse for a vehicle, the parking lot was empty. The dirt lot was dimly lit by weak bulbs above each of the cabin doors while a brighter spotlight cast light across the front façade of the motel office.

The lot wasn't large and Shane parked beside Luke's sedan. He assumed that Luke would have booked two cabins next to each other but even if he hadn't, it was a short walk across the lot to any of the cabins. He got out of the car, told Bella to stay, and closed the door before she could disobey and take off again. Ignoring the Shepherd's plaintive whining he could hear through the car window, Shane walked into the office. As Shane pushed through the door, wooden chimes overhead clunked, announcing his arrival.

Inside the office was larger than it appeared from outside, but it was crammed full of Native American art, guidebooks, information pamphlets on just about every activity in the state, and anything else a traveler might find they needed. The counter sat directly ahead and bisected the room. On one side was a gift shop and on the other was a general store with a little of everything from grocery items and medication to motor oil and sunglasses. Near the entrance and surrounding the desk were racks of maps, cards, and magnets. Behind the counter was a door that stood half open to reveal a cozy living room beyond. The low drone of a television could be heard, but it wasn't so loud that whoever was inside wouldn't have heard Shane come in.

Shane swallowed hard as an incredibly built, deeply tanned man stepped through the door behind the desk. His jeans and blue T-shirt were well worn and fit snuggly on his muscular physique. Thick leather bands adorned his wrists. The man's long, dark brown hair was secured at his nape and hung to his waist. Shane had a hard time looking away from his dark brown eyes and handsome, sharp features.

"What can I help you with?"

The man's voice was deep and sounded a tinge annoyed at being interrupted during his show. It didn't matter to Shane's libido and he felt the warmth of arousal rising. The man was gorgeous, and Shane would love to run his hands through the man's hair and over the chiseled abs visible beneath the tight T-shirt. The man's gaze never left Shane's face and Shane was careful to do the same. Shane wasn't eager for a confrontation with a guy twice his size who was obviously straight, especially not in his current state. Shane offered a pleasant smile.

"I'm checking in," Shane said.

He glanced over at the grocery side of the office. He could feel the man's eyes still on him. A shelf of antacids caught his attention and Shane remembered he needed medication for his headache and something to help him sleep. He pointed to the shelves as he turned back to the counter. The man pulled a thick binder and box of keys from beneath the counter before their gazes connected again.

"Do you carry sleep aids and pain killers?"

The man nodded. "Next to the allergy medicine, second row over," he answered. He motioned to the section with his chin and Shane walked over to the shelving. "Staying one night?"

Shane found what he was looking for among bottles of antihistamine and motion sickness pills. He picked up a box of nighttime pain reliever hoping to treat both his problems with one pill and walked back to the counter to finish checking in.

"I don't know how long we're staying. I'm part of Luke Holmestead's group."

"Must be the one they were arguing about," the man mumbled and replaced the binder and box of keys beneath the counter. He picked up a key that was tucked beside the register and held it out to Shane. Shane took it with a raised brow. "Paid up for two nights. Cabin eight, other end of the lot. It's the only one big enough for you and the dog."

It hadn't even occurred to Shane to ask if the motel allowed dogs and he fought back a wave of embarrassment. He was off his game tonight. At least Luke had thought of Bella when he'd made the reservations. Shane would thank him for that later. He took the key with one hand as he rubbed his neck with the other. His headache was steadily getting worse, the muscles in his neck and shoulders tensing.

"Thank you. I'm sure we'll be comfortable. I need to grab a few more things and then I'll get out of here," Shane said, offering another weak smile.

Mentioning Bella reminded him he needed to feed her, which then reminded him he needed to eat himself. He made his way through the aisles one at a time, picking up what he needed as he went – a can of dog food, a ham and cheese sandwich from the cooler, and a couple bottles of water. Shane took the items back to the counter and placed them beside the bottle of pain medication he'd grabbed before.

As the man rang up the purchases Shane noticed a book of local ghost stories on a rotating rack a short distance away in the gift shop area. He walked over and snagged it, handing it across the counter to be tallied with the other items. Shane would have a hard time reading it with the headache he currently had and the stories would no doubt make it harder for him to sleep, but he was interested to see who and what the local community thought was haunting these hills.

Shane watched the muscles of the man's chest and arms bunch and flex as he bagged everything. Shane handed him cash with another smile and accepted the change. He was extremely careful not to make physical contact for a number of reasons, foremost being that he couldn't handle another psychic hit right now. He'd be rendered unconscious for sure, especially with Bella out in the car. Shane lifted the bag off the counter and the man lowered to his elbows, watching as Shane headed for the door. He could feel the heat of the man's gaze boring into his back. Before opening the door Shane abruptly turned around. He was wasting a perfectly good opportunity to gather information.

"I'm sorry. What's your name?" Shane asked.

"Eric Thunderhawk."

Shane nodded and introduced himself. "Shane Cayli. Can I ask you something?"

Thunderhawk gave a barely perceptible nod which Shane took as a noncommittal response. He may or may not get the information he was after.

"Do you know anything about the hotel across the highway?" Shane asked and Thunderhawk glanced in the direction of Crystal Creek before returning his attention to Shane.

"I know to stay away from it and so should you. Nothing good ever happens there."

Thunderhawk straightened, turned, and disappeared through the door to his living room. He pushed the door closed behind him, but Shane didn't hear it latch. The office hours stated it would be open for another hour so Thunderhawk would make sure he could hear people coming and going. Shane opened the door and exited to the clunking of the chimes. He was getting frustrated. So far two people had refused to talk to him about Crystal Creek Hotel despite it being obvious they knew something. If everyone was so secretive about the place it was no wonder those fifteen people had never been found. It made Shane wonder what they were hiding.

As he walked the short distance to his car and whining dog, he thought about the hauntings taking place across the road. There were at least three different types of ghosts there. Some manifested as smoke, some were memory loops, and one in particular was very much aware of what he was and of his surroundings. The woman in the elevator only manifested as sound. But there were no memories, and Shane didn't understand that. He couldn't figure out how ghosts could exist without some kind of memory lancing through them or the area around them. He had more questions than answers. Shane never understood how Luke could work blind like this, but Luke loved it. Shane's head pounded and it wasn't just from exerting his psychic energy.

Shane set his bag of goods on the roof of the car. He opened the car door and pushed past an eager Bella to snag her leash from the middle console. He hooked it to her collar and then let her out of the car. He closed the door, grabbed the bag from the roof, and then dragged Bella to the back of the car so he could pull his overnight bag from the cargo area. Luke had told Shane to pack enough for three nights, but he'd only packed clothing and his laptop. Shane had decided to keep things light and buy things for himself and Bella as the need arose.

Cabin eight was on the far end of the parking lot, but it wasn't a huge distance so Shane decided to leave the car where it was and walk. The area surrounding the cabin was darker than the rest of the cabins because it stood the farthest distance from the office's floodlight. The dim bulb above the cabin's door did little to chase away the shadows. The wind was gusty and growing colder as the nighttime temperature dropped. The weatherman on the news this morning had mentioned a cold front was expected to move through in the next few days, but forecasts weren't exact. Predicting Colorado weather seemed to be half science, half pure luck as far as Shane was concerned. As such, Shane had packed layers and an emergency bag should his crappy car get stuck somewhere.

The door to the cabin was weathered and it took a strong turn of the key before it unlocked with a thud. Shane pushed open the door and released Bella to enter the room ahead of him. He shifted the bags into one hand and fumbled around with his other until he found the switch to turn the lights on. Bella had already made herself at home on the dull green loveseat, panting happily with her front paws dangling over the armrest. Shane kicked the door closed and dropped his overnight bag on the floor. He shuffled to the other end of the coffee table and put his grocery bag on the small desk. If this was the big cabin, he'd hate to see the cabins Luke and Masters ended up with. They probably had to shoehorn themselves in.

Shane took a quick five-second tour of his accommodations. The log cabin was only big enough to boast a bathroom with a standing shower, the sitting room, and a bedroom. The log furniture was too big for the space it occupied and the only solid colors in the room were the dull and faded dark green sofa and the red bedspread on the queen-size bed. The rugs and curtains were various designs and colors, and the shower curtain was decorated with one massive Kokopelli in the center.

The coffee table sat in the middle of the room allowing for very little space to move about the room. Shane had no doubt his shin would become intimately acquainted with that table at some point in the middle of the night should he have to pee. The bathroom was long and skinny. The bedroom was cramped with the queen-size bed and an armoire in the back corner. A couple of feet smaller and the bedroom would have been nothing but mattress.

Shane tugged on one of Bella's paws as he passed. He pulled his laptop and Bella's travel dish from his overnight bag and then tossed the bag on the bed. He took the computer and bowl to the desk and sat down. While the computer booted up he peeked through the curtain on the window to assess his view. At night, there wasn't one. There was nothing giving off light on that side of the cabin so all he could see was darkness. He'd have to wait until morning to see if he had a view of the mountains or the valley. Shane let the curtain fall back into place.

One at a time he pulled the items from the grocery bag. He opened the can of dog food and dumped it into Bella's bowl. He placed the bowl on the floor by the wall. Bella would eat it when she felt like it. He dropped the book of ghost stories onto the coffee table for future reading. Tonight, he wanted to do some Internet research on Robert Grant. Shane wanted to find out where Grant had lived, how he'd made his fortune, and most importantly, how he'd come to own Crystal Creek Hotel. Shane was no real estate mogul, but he was certain buying a dilapidated building no one went near wasn't the greatest financial decision.

Shane typed Grant's name into the search engine and scrolled through the list of results. When it came to helping Luke with cases, knowledge was power. In this particular case, it was essential because so far he'd been unable to offer anything else. Shane hoped he would stumble across something that would allow him to pick up a memory from the missing man. Probably nothing would change Masters' opinion of his abilities, but he wanted to give Luke something to work with. He found an old article about Grant and clicked the link. As he read, he shrugged off his jacket, letting it fall across the back of the chair.

Bella lifted her head and stared at the door, alert and whining softly. Shane sat motionless and listened. He didn't hear anything but Bella's massive ears were much more sensitive, so something was out there making noise. Up here in the wilderness it could be anything from a mouse to an axe murderer. A soft knock sounded on the door and Bella ran to it, pressing her nose to the seam of the door and huffing. She was no longer on alert so Shane moved to the door, pushing the dog aside, and opened it to find Luke standing on the stone step.

"You haven't learned a damn thing, have you?" Luke asked.

He stepped into the room and closed the door behind him. Shane raised an eyebrow at his friend and returned to the desk. Bella pushed past Luke's legs and reclaimed her spot on the loveseat. If Luke wanted to sit, he would have to fight Bella for a cushion. Luke glanced around the room with a thoughtful expression.

"Your cabin is bigger," Luke said.

"So I'm told. What haven't I learned?"

"You should always ask who's at the door before you open it. I could've been a homophobic killer."

"There's no one out here except us. Even if there was, how would they know I was gay?"

"You have a rainbow equality bumper sticker on your car."

"The car's parked in front of cabin three if I remember correctly," Shane said. This was an old argument between them, and it would end the same way it always did. Neither of them was right or wrong, and they both knew it.

"I admit it's a remote possibility, but still...don't take chances."

Luke ran his fingers through his dark brown hair and then smoothed it down again. Luke always wanted to look his best. He dressed more like a banker or CEO than the private investigator he was. Though Shane admittedly had no clue how a private investigator should look. Perhaps Luke and Masters were the norm, rather than the exception Shane made them out to be.

"I don't understand why you're so protective of me," Shane mumbled as he rubbed his palms together in his lap.

Luke sat on the edge of the coffee table facing him. The tight space caused their knees to brush against each other. Shane shifted away as Luke rested his elbows on his knees and looked intently at him.

"You don't? I asked you to spy on your fiancé and he tried to kill you when he found out. He got to you before I could -"

"Of course, he did," Shane interrupted. "I lived with him. And I spied because I chose to. I wanted to prove he was innocent."

"I never should have asked. You were in a dangerous situation and didn't even know it, and I made it worse by asking for your help."

Shane shook his head. He had attempted to prove his ex-fiancé, Brent, was innocent of the murders he was suspected of, but instead, he'd ended up becoming Brent's final victim. It had been a time in Shane's life when he refused to acknowledge that he was psychic. He'd finally perfected erecting the mental box the year before and had shoved his ability tightly into it, buried as deep in his psyche as he could manage.

If he'd allowed his ability to flow freely, he would have seen what Brent was doing. It was an old regret and hindsight was 20/20. Shane had believed Brent was innocent of everything Luke, a Littleton PD detective at the time, suspected him of, and therefore never realized the danger he was in. But Brent had been guilty and attempted to kill Shane for betraying him. Luke had gotten to him just in time, preventing Shane from bleeding out from the wounds.

Shane's eyes burned with tears he refused to let fall. He was done crying over all of that. Luke had saved his life and Shane was making the best out of the second change. Shane pushed all unpleasant memories aside and distracted himself by opening the ham and cheese sandwich he'd bought for dinner. He wasn't hungry, but Shane would force it down. He needed to keep his strength up and put something solid in his stomach so the pain killer he planned to take later wouldn't make him nauseous.

"What brings you here? I know you didn't come by just to dredge up the past," Shane said taking a big bite of stale bread and flavorless meat.

"Right."

Luke leaned back and pulled a small manila envelope from the inside pocket of his jacket. He tossed it on the desk beside Shane's laptop. Shane swallowed the dry bite of food and picked up the envelope. He opened it and dumped the contents out onto the desk.

"That's some information on Robert Grant I photocopied for you. I think there's some information about his girlfriend in there, too. The names of all the guests are listed, some notes on our investigation so far, and a few photos. When I left Masters, he said he was working on something else, but he didn't tell me what."

Shane thumbed through the contents. The papers had been folded in half around the photos. Since photos were of more use to Shane than notes and lists, he looked over those first. The picture on top was of a beautiful young woman with brown hair and cat-shaped eyes. She had an exotic beauty that would have pulled men to her like moths to flame. The next photo had Shane hyperventilating. He had known the hotel was haunted so he shouldn't have been surprised. Shane lowered his head between his knees, feeling a little lightheaded. Luke leaned in close, but didn't touch him.

"I don't know what sent you into a panic attack, but I'm right here. You're not alone," Luke said softly, but firmly into Shane's ear.

"I should've known. I don't know why I didn't. Maybe the headache...or..." Shane whispered to himself. He shook his head at his own idiocy.

"Shane, man, you're rambling. What should you have known?"

Shane lifted his head and looked into Luke's eyes. The concern and sympathy he saw there was calming and comforting. "I'm okay," Shane said. "I'm okay."

"Good. Now tell me what happened."

Shane flipped the picture he still held around so Luke could see it. "I hit this guy with my car.".

"What?" Luke asked, straightening. He looked at the photo in Shane's hand then back at Shane's face. "You hit Robert Grant? That's not.... I'm pretty sure he's dead," Luke stammered.

"Oh, believe me, he is definitely dead," Shane said.

Luke shook his head. "Okay. You obviously need to eat some more and get some sleep. We can talk tomorrow." Luke rose to his feet and headed for the door.

"Can you tell me where he lived?" Shane asked and Luke looked at him over his shoulder. "I've been looking online, but I haven't had much luck. Is it in the notes you gave me?"

"The addresses are in the notes, but the property has been sold since Grant lived there. He had a huge estate in the Cherry Hills area. From what Masters and I can gather, though, he spent most of his time living here...I mean, there," Luke said with a jerk of his head in the direction of Crystal Creek Hotel.

"You've got to be kidding me," Shane said, horrified. "He lived in the hotel? Why in God's name...?"

Luke chuckled. "No. He lived in the caretaker's cottage behind the hotel."

"Still awful. Can you get me in?"

"Get you into what, the cottage? Of course, I can get you in," Luke answered, clearly insulted.

Luke didn't like people questioning his abilities any more than Shane liked people questioning his. Shane offered his friend an apologetic smile then stood up and grabbed his jacket off the back of the chair. He joined Luke at the door, but Luke didn't move to leave. Bella lifted her head expectantly.

"What are you doing?"

"You said you could get me in," Shane said, looking at Luke in confusion. Hadn't they just discussed this?

"Shit, Shane, I didn't think you meant now. It's dark as sin out there."

Luke was obviously not excited by the idea and Shane's newfound resolve was wavering already. He wanted to see where Robert Grant had lived, see if there were memories there that could link to his disappearance, but he had to do it before he lost his nerve. Especially since it meant returning to the grounds of Crystal Creek Hotel and releasing his psychic energy again. It was now or never. Luke stared at him the same way most people did when he told them he was psychic, like he was completely insane. Shane reached around Luke to open the door and Luke gave a resigned sigh.

"Fine! I'll take you." Luke knocked Shane's arm, forcing his hand off the door handle. "Just...give me a minute to get some stuff out of the car."

CHAPTER FIVE

Shane smiled as Luke opened the door and walked out. He'd won the battle, but he didn't feel triumphant. He was a little freaked out and already regretting the decision to go back to the hotel tonight. Or ever again. Bella rubbed against Shane's leg and he lowered his hand to pet her as Luke walked across the lot to his sedan. Shane found Bella's leash still attached to her collar. He'd forgotten to take it off when they entered the room which worked in his favor. He deliberately left the room lights on in the room as he closed the door. If he was going to be facing down ghosts and God knew what else, he didn't want to come back to a dark room. Shane pulled on one sleeve of his jacket, noticing the door automatically locked behind him, before shrugging on the other sleeve. He'd have to be careful never to leave the room without his key which Shane had tucked into his front pocket.

Luke slammed the car's trunk as Shane joined him and handed him a small yellow flashlight. Luke carried a much larger, spotlight-type flashlight with the handle on top. He turned it on, testing the strength of the beam by shining it in various directions. Shane did the same because the last thing he wanted was to find himself along with a nonfunctioning flashlight. Once Luke was satisfied everything was in working order, he started across the lot toward the highway and Crystal Creek Hotel. Shane kept a tight grip on Bella's leash and stayed close to Luke. The walk was quiet with nothing but the crunching of gravel beneath their feet and Bella's happy panting.

Clouds had blown in, obscuring the moon's meager light, and there was a constant cold, gusty wind. Shane used the time to tamp down his psychic power as much as possible. He wanted to keep the possibility of surprise visions to a minimum. He suffered a mixture of excitement and terror at the idea of running into Grant's poltergeist again. It would solve everything if Robert Grant could just tell him where he was, but things were never that easy. Shane took only a small measure of comfort from the fact that Luke wasn't as calm as he appeared, he was simply more practiced at hiding it.

Shane kept his thin beam of light pointed at the ground directly in front of his feet, looking up every few steps to make sure Luke was still nearby. He was putting a lot of faith in Luke knowing where he was going and not walking them all off the cliff. Shane also hoped Bella's night vision would keep him from stepping in a hole and breaking an ankle because the flashlight he held did little to illuminate his surroundings. Shane cursed under his breath as he tripped over a tree root. He really should have thought this visit through a lot more.

Luke led them across the steel and wood bridge, the gravel hotel lot where Shane had seen Grant twice, and then around the far side of the hotel toward the cliff. Thick trees encroached on the path and Shane batted limbs away from his face repeatedly. To his right was the oppressive dark shadow of the five-story hotel. He could barely make out the outline of the building and a few trees when he looked directly up toward the sky. Otherwise, it was just dark and eerily quiet. There was no scurry of small animals and the rustling of leaves was due only to the wind. At the sound of Luke's voice, Shane looked at Luke's bouncing light a few feet ahead.

"The two of you are awfully quiet back there. Guess that means I'm not walking through any ghosts. I mean, not that they could hurt me, or anything."

Shane scoffed. Insubstantial ghosts were incapable of hurting people; there wasn't enough left of their spirit to cause harm but they could certainly make a person go insane. Poltergeists like Robert Grant, however, could certainly hurt someone if they had enough strength to push them down the stairs or throw something. Shane had yet to experience something like that and really hoped to avoid such a thing, but this case was feeling more and more like he was going to have that kind of experience at any given moment.

Luke's shoes crunched over dead leaves and gravel, mumbling under his breath about allowing Shane to manipulate him into things. He hadn't even had to try hard before Luke acquiesced. Pansy. The things Shane convinced Luke to do went well beyond the call of duty. Shane was younger and knew Luke thought of him as the baby brother he needed to protect, but even Shane knew that was a lousy reason for them to be traipsing around condemned property in the dark looking for...what? Ghosts?

After Shane told him about driving through Robert Grant's spirit in the parking lot, Luke had been on edge, glancing around nervously as they crossed the dirt lot. Luke clearly did not want to be there, but once Shane got something into his head, it was hard to dissuade him. If Luke hadn't agreed to accompany him, he would have come by himself while he still had the nerve. All the things that could happen if Shane tried walking around an unfamiliar area, in the dark, with ghosts and memories floating around willy-nilly was what likely spurred Luke to grudgingly agree to take Shane to the caretaker's cottage.

Under normal circumstances, Shane would have agreed with Luke's suggestion to wait until morning when the sun was up, but these weren't normal circumstances. Shane became a determined, stubborn ass when he set his mind to something. A puzzle had been placed in front of him and he would stop at nothing to solve it, not just for his own peace of mind, but for that of the families affected.

"I need a drink," Luke muttered making Shane smile.

Luke stopped and aimed his flashlight at the screened porch of a small house. Shane stared at the caretaker's cottage and tried to decide how he was feeling at that moment. Sometimes he would suffer vulnerability, feel naïve or invincible. Sometimes he wanted to run and hide, or crumble on the spot, while other times he could stand tall and take on the world. There were also those times when he would freeze like a deer in headlights, too terrified to move. He hated those moments the most.

What had he been thinking? He should be in bed with Bella tucked in close; instead, he'd been awake searching for information on their primary missing person. When Shane found out Grant had lived on the property, he'd been eager to get back to Crystal Creek to have another look. Shane stopped beside Luke and swung his light over the covered porch in front of them. Bella nudged her way between them and sat. Luke pointed his flashlight at Shane's face, probably to see his reaction to the creepy old house. Shane squinted and stuck out his tongue. Luke chuckled and moved the light back to the porch.

"What do you think you'll pick up in there?" Luke asked. "In fact, what did you pick up when Masters touched you?"

Shane was confused. "He touched me?"

"When he helped you to your feet by the elevator," Luke reminded him.

"Oh, yeah. Nothing. I was too distracted, I guess. My head hurt like a bitch right then and my ears were ringing."

"Interesting," Luke said thoughtfully.

"I guess," Shane sighed. He arced his beam of light over the screened porch, uncertain what he was looking for.

"You okay?" Luke asked.

"It's dark, cold, and I'm a psychic standing on property known to have paranormal activity. Yeah. I'm great."

Luke chuckled at Shane's sarcastic response. The man knew all too well that Shane frequently covered up fear, anxiety, or discomfort with sarcasm. He wanted to grab onto Luke for support, but he didn't want to inadvertently read his memories. Shane had no control over which memory he received. He just grabbed the one closest to the surface and it was frequently not one he wanted. Shane had only touched Luke once and learned Luke had a mistress *and* a pregnant wife. Their friendship had been put to the test but was salvaged when Luke took the high road, told his wife about the affair, and made amends.

Luke walked up to the screen door of the porch and pulled it open. Years of neglect had it squeaking on its hinges but it opened easily. He stepped onto the concrete landing and took the few steps to the front door. Luke had told Shane he could get him inside, but he didn't have a key so they would technically be breaking in. Shane figured it didn't matter given the state the place was in. One solid kick and the wood door gave way. Luke moved to the side and motioned for Shane and Bella to enter the house ahead of him.

"Turn your flashlight off. Let the ghosties come out and play," Shane said as he passed.

"Shit," Luke muttered as he clicked off the light.

The cottage wasn't at all what Shane had expected. For one, when he thought of cottages, they were smaller than this. This was a house built along the side and back of the hotel. It wasn't visible from the highway or the hotel parking lot. Shane knew there was a cliff back here somewhere, but it was invisible in the dark and that terrified him. It would be far too easy to unknowingly walk off the edge. Where the hotel had once been grand and elegant, the caretaker's house had been meant for function and comfort.

The house was single-story, log-built with a screened porch across the entire front that looked like it had been added on later. The concrete addition stood out against the original log construction. The concrete was cracking and crumbling in spots, pulled away from the house by about an inch, and the screen enclosure was fraying and torn in multiple places.

The front door opened into a large open room that smelled of mold and dirt. He wouldn't be surprised to find the floors beneath the windows to be wet and rotting. The house had a cold, dampness to it. Shane's scalp tingled and he loosened his hold on Bella's leash to see if the dog would roam. She stayed pressed tightly against his leg.

That was a bad sign.

Shane moved deeper into the room, noticing the crown molding and stained-glass windows were still intact. The glass was dull and weathered now, but it would have been beautiful back in the day with the sun peeking through. It was an artistic addition Shane found odd considering they were in the middle of the forest. It never ceased to amaze him the ways rich people chose to display their wealth. Another reason the screened-in concrete porch didn't fit it felt like a cheap afterthought slapped onto the front of the house.

Shane pointed his light at the floor. It was made of large wooden planks and seemed to run through the entire house. The dust covering the floor was undisturbed. A stone fireplace sat inside one wall and the ceiling had exposed beams similar to the hotel lobby. Unlike the hotel where piles of trash and debris could be found, the caretaker's cottage was completely empty. If Robert Grant had lived here, someone had come along after his disappearance and removed everything. Shane's hope that he would find something of Grant's here evaporated into thin, stale air.

"You could have told me the place was empty before we came over here," Shane said, as he curled his fingers into Bella's collar and led her toward the hall.

"Really? That would have dissuaded you from this little excursion?"

Shane stopped and thought about that. "Probably not," he admitted. "I still would have wanted to see the place. Satisfy my own curiosity."

"But would it have stopped you from coming *tonight*?"

"Maybe, but we're here now so onward we go."

Shane spoke with a conviction he didn't feel; especially when facing a long, dark hallway in a house with creepy vibes. Shane's skin crawled and Bella stayed glued to his leg. He aimed his light down the hall and slowly entered the narrow space, pulling a reluctant Bella with him. Luke's shoes thudded across the wood floor as he followed Shane.

"Don't get too close to me. I'm going to let my ability radiate a little and I don't want to accidentally read you," Shane said without turning around.

"I'll plaster my back to the front door, then, yes?" Luke said and Shane listened as he retreated.

Luke was always concerned about Shane reading him so he had no doubt Luke was pressed against the far living room wall, exactly as he said he would be. A small smile tugged at Shane's lips at the mental image. He aimed his flashlight at the floor to avoid stepping onto rotted boards. Bella was a service dog but catching him if he fell through the floor wasn't something she could do. There was an arched entryway to the left that Shane imagined would have been a dining room. A door on the other side of the dining room led to the kitchen, which could also be accessed by a door in the hallway. Each room was a box and from what Shane knew of housing it had probably been built in the early 1900s.

Directly across from the kitchen door was a bathroom. The tiny room had been completely gutted, right down to the flooring and fixtures. An old mirror hung on the wall at an odd angle just inside the door. It seemed ridiculously out of place considering there was no sink, tub, or toilet. For a brief moment Shane was convinced the reflection was not his own, but when he blinked the sensation of otherness passed.

The foundation was completely missing leaving a hole about a foot deep so if he did fall through the floor, he wouldn't be severely injured. The bathroom smelled strange, not like dirt or rot, and it made Shane's stomach turn. He wondered if Grant had been the one to tear the bathroom up like this. It he had, then he'd had plans to remodel it quickly because it was the only bathroom in the house. Looking across the hall, the kitchen didn't look much better. Appliances were missing and there was a giant hole in the far wall. Shane's face scrunched in confusion. No way was Robert Grant living here with the house in the state it was in. It was completely uninhabitable. Shane filed the information away for future thought and slowly moved down the hall to the next door.

Bella pressed against his leg and whined. Shane aimed the light at her. She was staring straight ahead at a closed door at the end of the hall. He edged them down the hallway slowly. Something was triggering the dog's reaction, but he had yet to pick up on anything. He turned his light into the room on his left. As expected, it was empty, but had a beautiful stained-glass design set into a half-circle adornment above the single window. The glass was dull and he could see the wood plank through the filth.

Here we go, Shane thought as he lowered his defenses and let his ability flow freely. His body temperature rose and the cold of the house became less noticeable to him. He turned off the flashlight and tucked it into his front pocket. Scared to death of what he might see, Shane lifted a shaky hand, palm out, and reached into the room with his psychic power. The first thing he noticed was the faint scent of a man's cologne and the vague sense of someone standing behind him.

"Luke, where are you?"

"Plastered to the front door, as promised." Luke's answer echoed through the cavernous living room, proving he wasn't in the hall with Shane.

"Great," Shane whispered.

He swallowed the fear tickling his senses, clenched Bella's leash, and took one cautious step into the room. The air in the room immediately became thick and oppressive. Shane gulped in a breath as his fight-or-flight switch was tripped and panic exploded.

He'll pay for this. He's not safe anywhere.

The foreign thought whispered through Shane's mind. He wasn't sure how old the memory was or if it had anything to do with Robert Grant's disappearance, but he couldn't focus on it. The longer he stood in the room, the darker it seemed to get and the more he felt he should run. The air almost took on a physical presence as it pressed in on him from all sides. Shane had the insane idea that he was being surrounded and that he needed to get out of the room immediately. Bella yanked on the leash with a loud whine and Shane allowed her to pull him back into the hallway. He sucked the psychic energy back into his fingers and lowered his hand. Once outside the room the panic faded and the air felt lighter, breathable. Normal.

"Everything okay?" Luke asked and Shane squinted against the beam of light suddenly shining on him.

Shane nodded in response, unsure how to truly answer. He wasn't hurt, but his heart was beating like he'd run a marathon and the adrenaline pumping through his system was making him shake. "There's evil in this room. It's angry and it doesn't want me in there."

The beam of light bounced around on the floor at Luke's feet and the soft rustle of movement drifted down the hall. Shane pulled his flashlight out, clicked it on, and aimed it in Luke's direction. The light was small and weak compared to Luke's spotlight and it didn't quite reach Luke.

"What are you doing?" Shane asked.

"Taking notes. You never know if or when this information will tie in down the line."

"Don't put my name down on paper," Shane warned, though Luke was perfectly aware of his preference not to be named in any reports. It was an unnecessary reminder so Luke responded with an annoyed huff. Shane flexed his fingers around Bella's leash to get blood flowing back into the digits. He clicked off his flashlight since it was useless anyway and put it back into his pocket. He needed one hand free. Shane rolled his head to loosen his tense muscles a bit.

"Tell me what you picked up," Luke said.

"Before I entered the room I smelled cologne and felt like someone was standing behind me."

"Is it because of our surroundings that I find that creepy?"

"It could be broad daylight in a crowded room and the sense that someone is behind you when there's no one is always creepy," Shane said.

"Right," Luke breathed. "And the evil?"

Shane tilted his head to the side as he stared ahead into the empty room. "I don't know how to describe that. It made the air feel...heavy. Triggered my run-away-as-fast-as-you-can response."

Shane listened to the scratching of pen on paper as he turned his attention to the closed door at the end of the hall. That door had Bella whining before they'd even stepped into the hallway which had Shane wanting to go anywhere but there. He shored up his courage as Luke turned his flashlight off returning the hall to foreboding darkness. Shane nudged Bella in the direction of the door. The hall ended at this door suggesting the room beyond extended the length of the back of the house. Shane gripped the knob and pushed the door open, extending his palm toward the room.

His psychic ability entered the room a mere second before his foot crossed the threshold and he was knocked to his knees.

CHAPTER SIX

Shane doubled over, clutching his stomach like he'd been gut punched. His chest protested the movement of simple breathing as air sawed in and out of his lungs. Sharp pain lanced through his spine cutting off his breathing all together. Through the paralyzing pain and fear, Shane heard Bella's vicious barking. Coarse fur rubbed across his face as she positioned herself in front of him in a protective manner. He wanted to grab her and get the hell out of the room, but his body was frozen in agony. His ribs suddenly felt like they were being shattered, his shoulders burned sharply as his arms were torn from his body. A scream was ripped from him as he was cut in half at the waist. Tears streamed down his face while the rush of blood in his ears drowned out Bella's barking. Shane was dying. His life blood pulsing out of him to the beat of his heart and he could do nothing to save himself.

Shane was grabbed from behind and lifted. He wanted to fight off his attacker, but his strength was gone. A muscular chest pressed against his back as he was half-carried, half-dragged from the room. The leash in his hand grew taut momentarily before Bella followed, still barking viciously at the room. Shane held onto her leash like a lifeline as they were pulled from danger. Shane gulped in much needed air as he was lowered to the cold hardwood of the living room floor. Slowly, his head cleared and the feeling in all his limbs returned. Bella stood in front of him, her barking echoing in the cavernous room.

"Bella, quiet," yelled Luke from his position beside Shane.

Shane's throat was raw and painful when he swallowed. Bella stopped barking but continued to whine, staring down the hall. She was on high alert and would stay that way until they were away from the house. She would attack anyone she didn't recognize right now. Shane focused on Luke's voice and stroked a hand down Bella's hind leg. Cold from the floor seeped through Shane's jeans and he pulled Bella closer, trying to absorb her heat.

"What the hell just happened? You screamed like you were being murdered," Luke said.

His voice was softer now that Bella wasn't barking, and it quavered a bit from the spike in adrenaline he was no doubt suffering. Shane reigned in his ability, locking it down tightly, and began shivering uncontrollably. The cold that washed over and through him was intense after the blistering heat of the vision. Every muscle burned like he'd been weightlifting for hours, his head pounded to the rhythm of his heartbeat, and the simple movement of petting Bella fatigued him. All he wanted to do was curl into the fetal position and sleep.

"I swear to god, Shane, if you don't start talking right now, I'm taking you off the case." Luke's angry tone jolted him, reminding him that he wasn't alone or in a safe place.

Shane wondered what the whole situation had been like for Luke when Shane suddenly began screaming and Bella erupted into a frenzy. Seeing Shane lost to a terrifying memory was never easy for anyone to see, but their shared past made it worse; old memories encroaching on the new situation.

"I'll be okay in a minute." Shane's throat burned with every word. Hell, even breathing hurt. "I just need to get outside."

Shane groaned in pain as he rolled and tried to push to his feet. The movement caused sharp pain behind his eyes. He was entertaining the idea of crawling out of the house when Luke slid his hands into Shane's armpits and lifted. Once Shane was standing, Luke's arms came around his stomach and chest. Luke didn't allow Shane to even attempt walking. He simply dragged him backward toward the front door. Bella followed but her leash remained taut, tugging her along reluctantly.

The air grew warmer as they moved through the screened porch and out into the darkened wilderness. Shane's shivering lessened slightly as the temperature increased. In hindsight, that should have been a massive red flag. The temperature inside the cottage should not have been colder than outside, but he'd paid it little mind. Luke lowered him to the ground and leaned him against a tree. Shane rested his head against the rough bark as Bella laid against his thigh, still on high alert.

"I'll be right back," Luke said. "I dropped the flashlight in the back room when I grabbed you."

A spike of fear shot through Shane at the thought of Luke going into that bedroom, but he bit back any warnings. Luke wasn't psychic. It was just a cold, dark room in a rundown cottage to regular people. While Luke was gone, Shane breathed in the fresh nighttime air and tried to make his muscles relax. He had no idea what that memory really was, but it had been excruciating. It was the most unpleasant psychic experience Shane had endured to date. It was certainly not something he ever wanted to repeat. If that memory had anything to do with the disappearances they were investigating, Shane would reconsider assisting.

Bella whined and Shane pulled her onto his lap, hugging her and rubbing her tummy affectionately. She was a good dog. He wondered if it had been Bella's aggressive behavior that had alerted Luke to Shane's problem or if Luke had been clueless until Shane started screaming. In the end, it didn't matter. Luke had realized something was wrong and taken action.

Shane shuddered at the thought of what might have happened if Bella and Luke hadn't been with him. He'd been told by several people in the past that he responded to the memories he received in a physical way. He'd once received a memory of someone drowning and had needed resuscitation to get him breathing again. That was the incident that had prompted Kennie to give him Bella.

Luke exited the cabin and Shane's thoughts snapped back to the present. Luke's flashlight beam bounced a bit as Luke came down the stairs. Shane squinted into the light when it landed on him still sitting against the tree with a large German Shepherd draped across his legs. Luke lowered himself to the ground beside Shane. He reached out and ran a hand over Bella's head. Luke moved the beam of light over both Shane and Bella as if looking for something.

"What are you doing?" Shane asked.

"Checking for injuries. You sure as hell screamed like you'd been hurt."

"I'm fine...now," Shane assured him weakly. Luke turned off the flashlight and they sat in the dark, silent.

"Have you had enough time to process the memory?" Luke asked after several minutes. "I walked into the back room and looked around. Usually when Bella goes ape-shit like that I see something; mist, a blur or glow, *something*, but there was nothing in there."

"You didn't notice anything at all?" Shane asked.

"Stank like rot, but other than that? No, nothing."

Shane considered Luke's original question. He had had time to process, but he still didn't understand. He'd catalogued all the sensations and pains he'd suffered, every emotion underlying the event, but he couldn't really make sense of the memory. There had been nothing visual to the memory. Shane's gaze roved over shadows and dark shapes identifying them as the cottage, trees, the looming monstrosity that was Crystal Creek Hotel. Shane thought about the exact pains he felt, and in which order they happened, and tried to put the swirling emotions into the timeline of events. He rolled his head side to side, the bark digging into his scalp.

"I'm struggling with it, but...I think someone was murdered in that room. I felt sad and betrayed and toward the end extremely angry. Whoever it was, their death was painful. I was torn into pieces, hacked apart."

"Hacked?" Luke asked.

"I'd swear I was being cut in half. That my arms were ripped off my body," Shane answered.

He hugged Bella tightly as he fought the urge to puke. Shane often wondered why, of all the psychic powers he could have been born with, he had been gifted with this one. Reading memories was often more painful than not and he hated that he had no true control. Over the years, Shane had reached the conclusion that visual memories were for the living and the physical or emotional ones for the dead. And the memories of the dead were frequently unpleasant. Dying happy and content while still leaving residual energy was an extremely rare occurrence. He nuzzled Bella's furry neck while listening to the scratch of Luke's pen against paper. It was an oddly comforting sound.

"Stop referring to yourself in the memory. Don't use the word 'I.' It creeps me out." Luke said after a moment. "You said the victim felt betrayed which suggests the killer was someone they knew. You also said the victim was dismembered, cut in half..." Luke breathed out.

"It was painful," Shane added unnecessarily.

"Painful," Luke scoffed.

"At first it was like getting punched. I felt like my ribs were being broken, crushed..." Shane held Bella and closed his eyes, searching for the best words in the correct order to describe what he'd experienced so Luke would understand. "It was like...what I would imagine being on the rack to be like. My limbs, the victim's limbs," Shane corrected at Luke's grunt, "were being pulled away from their body to the point they ripped off. Then they were cut in half."

"Jesus," Luke breathed. "And for you to get this memory...it means the person was still alive while they were...um."

Luke audibly swallowed as the horror of what happened in that room, of what Shane experienced, solidified in his brain. Luke finished taking his notes and sighed. Shane rolled his head in Luke's direction and watched his dark shadowed form. Even though it was warmer outside than inside the cottage, it was still winter in the Rockies and Shane shivered. A migraine was building behind his eyes and he closed them hoping to slow the onset.

"You scared the shit out of me," Luke said softly. "Wish I could tell you never to do that again, but you can't control it. Not really."

"Right."

"Any chance the victim was Robert Grant?"

"I don't know," Shane answered. "There was no visual to it. Just pain and emotion." Shane thought more about the memory before shaking his head in the dark. "I don't think so, though. Doesn't fit. The disappearance was quiet, anticlimactic. Dismembering someone is anything but. Besides, they disappeared from the hotel."

"Not necessarily. They were last seen in the hotel, yes, but we don't know where they disappeared from. They walked out of that room and poof, gone; nothing, zilch, nada. It warps the mind how that sort of thing can happen."

A cold breeze kicked up the leaves around them causing Shane's skin to pebble despite his jacket, which was a glorified windbreaker. Shane hadn't expected to be out in the dark and cold encountering ghosts when he'd packed for this trip. He'd brought a thick sweatshirt to wear beneath the jacket, but hadn't thought to put it on before leaving the room. Bella's body produced a little warmth across his thighs and stomach, but the rest of him was getting colder by the minute and the tree root he was sitting on was causing his butt to go numb. Shane eased Bella off his lap and pushed to his feet, using the tree for balance until he was certain his legs would hold.

"You good now?" Luke asked.

"Yes." Shane pulled out his small flashlight and turned it on. Until this moment he'd completely forgotten he had it. "I'm ready to head back. I need a hot shower and about a month's worth of sleep."

The trip back to the motel was much less tense, but Shane struggled putting one foot in front of the other without tripping. He felt like he was walking through dense mud and his muscles protested every little movement. Bella never strayed more than a few inches from his side and Luke walked beside him rather than ahead like before. Shane's ability was locked up tight except for the small amount that was always flowing through his veins. There was very little traffic on the road by the time they made it across the grounds to the bridge. It was eerily silent as they crossed the highway and walked across the lot to Shane's cabin.

He reached into his pocket to pull out the room key, but found it more difficult than expected to get the key into the lock with his uncontrollable shaking. Luke took the key and opened the door for him and then whispered goodnight when Shane squinted in pain against the light spilling from the room. Bella raced into the room, quickly curling up on the sofa.

Shane waved goodbye to Luke and entered the room slowly. He decided to forego the shower in favor of an over-the-counter migraine pill and sleep. He half-assed his way through his nightly routine and burrowed under the covers to get warm, the bedside clock showing they'd been gone only an hour. It felt like more. Bella jumped onto the bed and curled against Shane's lower back, her warmth and proximity offering enough comfort to allow Shane to drift off to sleep.

CHAPTER SEVEN

Shane woke to Bella's soft whines and insistent nudging. His lids scraped across his eyeballs like sandpaper when he rubbed them. He blinked rapidly but got no relief. Bella shoved her head under the blanket and pressed her cold, wet nose to Shane's bare chest. Shane gently shoved the mutt away but she came back licking every inch of exposed skin she could reach. Bella was being extremely persistent which meant she needed outside so Shane threw the covers off and rolled out of bed with a groan. Every muscle in his body was sore. No light filtered in past the curtains meaning Bella had woken him in the middle of the night. He was unsteady on his feet, fighting against the effects of the sleeping pill as he slipped his shoes on and snapped the leash onto Bella's collar.

Shane habitually slept naked but he'd been so cold he'd crawled into bed wearing the flannel pajama pants he'd shoved into his bag last minute. He briefly considered donning a shirt, but he felt feverish so he took Bella outside bare chested. He opened the door and Bella bounded out as far as the leash would allow. Shane remained on the small step outside the door in the dim circle of light and ran a hand through his short sleep-mussed hair while Bella nosed around for the perfect spot to squat. Frigid winter night air cooled Shane's overheated skin and helped pull him from his drug-induced stupor.

He glanced over at the other cabins. A soft glow seeped around the edges of the curtains in cabin four indicating one of the PIs was still awake. He wondered if it was Luke or Masters burning the midnight oil. It was Luke's car parked out front, but Shane's car was still in front of cabin three so vehicle location wasn't really indicative of anything. If cabin four was Luke, it was just as likely he'd fallen asleep on the couch watching TV as it was that he was still up working. Shane didn't know Masters at all. What would keep him awake at night? Was he the kind of man to lose sleep over a case he was working, even one as old as these disappearances, or was he like Luke, able to fall asleep no matter the circumstances.

Shane leaned against the doorframe of his cabin and wrapped an arm around his middle. The chill was beginning to work its way into his body. A breeze rustled the surrounding trees, sending leaves dancing around the lot, carrying with it the sound of muffled whispers. Shane shivered. In the middle of a cold, pitch black night the sound was creepy. He slid his gaze from cabin four to the bridge leading to Crystal Creek Hotel. He expected to see the source of the whispers, but all that greeted him was the glint of steel barely illuminated by the spotlight above Thunderhawk's office door.

There were so many things wrong with Crystal Creek and the surrounding property. At the top of the list was the high level of paranormal activity on the grounds coupled with the complete void he was met with inside the building. Second on the list was the number of violent and horrific events that had taken place. Death happened. Accidents happened. Even murder and disappearances happened. It was the fact that all of those took place in one desolate isolated location that bothered Shane.

His skin pebbled at the memories he had encountered at the caretaker's cottage. Shane was shocked something that horrific could take place and no one knew about it. That murder should have been one of the first things Luke and Masters had stumbled across when researching the hotel. And he knew for a fact they had researched the location and everyone associated with the missing people the moment they took the case.

Bella yanked the leash drawing Shane's attention back to her. She was wandering aimlessly sniffing at everything so Shane pulled her back into the cabin. He snatched his cellphone off the coffee table to check the time – 2:34 a.m. He dropped the phone on top of his overnight bag. The potency of the sleeping pill had worn off, but Shane figured he could still get a few more hours of sleep. Bella had already claimed her spot on the bed and Shane climbed beneath the covers beside her. He draped an arm over her big body and rubbed her belly. The repetitive motion, warmth, and lingering effects of the drug had Shane drifting off in seconds.

What seemed like only minutes later, the high-pitched ring of Shane's cellphone woke him. As soon as he opened his eyes he knew it hadn't been minutes since crawling into bed, it had been hours. Sunlight spilled in through the seams of the curtains. Shane was both annoyed and grateful for being woken. He hated waking up to any kind of noise, but he couldn't be angry. Thankfully the ringing phone brought an abrupt to the nightmare he'd been trapped in.

In the dream, he'd been surrounded by ghosts. Some had been corporeal, some no more than mist, but they crowded around him, begging and pleading without sound. An ever-growing pool of blood with no source spread beneath his feet as flames climbed the walls and danced across the ceiling. Despite the fire, Shane was bone cold. He couldn't escape, couldn't move, and that's what made the dream truly terrifying to him. Nothing scared him more than being trapped, helpless to stop what was happening around him, to him.

The room became silent as the call went to voicemail, but his phone began ringing again immediately. Shane pushed the remnants of the nightmare aside and kicked the blankets off. He crawled to the foot of the bed and flopped onto his stomach. Using one hand on the floor for balance, he grabbed the phone off his bag with the other. Shane didn't recognize the number on the screen but he'd missed three calls from whoever it was. He saw he'd also missed a call from Luke, but he had actually left a message. He swiped the screen to accept the call and put the phone to his ear.

"What?" Shane snapped.

"Where the hell are you?" The caller's voice was annoyed and somewhat familiar.

Shane shook his head in sleepy confusion. "I think you have the wrong number," he said, irritably. The past twenty-four hours had been agonizing for him and he was in no mood to deal with surly strangers.

"I don't have the wrong number, Mr. Cayli."

"Masters?" Shane asked, waking a little more each second. His position hanging over the edge of the bed was causing the blood to rush to his head and his body weight was making his fingers tingle. He slid off the bed with a thump and sat on the floor. He tucked his legs beneath him and began yanking clothes from his bag.

"You had better be in your cabin and not out somewhere wandering," Masters said.

Shane huffed indignantly. The man really was something, thinking he could control Shane's actions. He'd never taken kindly to dictatorial people. Incensed, Shane asked, "What would you do if I was?"

Not that a verbal warning would have stopped Shane from investigating if he'd wanted to, but he hadn't been told he wasn't allowed to explore on his own. He wouldn't have given it a second thought. After a few seconds of silence where Shane listened to Masters breathing, he rolled his eyes and sighed. He held his clothing against his chest and pushed to his feet. He grew bored with the conversation as he made his way into the tiny bathroom. He closed the lid to the toilet and set his clothes down on top then looked at the ceiling with a sigh.

"I'm in my cabin. What do you want?" he asked.

"So, you're deliberately ignoring me," Masters said.

"How you figure?"

"I've been blowing up your phone for the past fifteen minutes," Masters answered.

Masters was irritable this morning and Shane decided it had been him in cabin four, working into the wee hours of the morning. His attitude was making Shane angry. After yesterday's events, he wasn't in the greatest mood himself and he still had a dull ache behind his eyes. He looked at himself in the mirror and cringed. He looked like a rabid raccoon with dark, puffy circles under his eyes. The whites were bloodshot and the sparkle was gone leaving the brown irises dull. Red cheeks and lackluster blond strands hanging limply over his forehead completed the picture. He looked ill. Shane turned on the water and ran a wet hand through his hair, lifting the strands off his face.

"Mr. Cayli —"

"Did it ever occur to you to knock on the door?" Shane asked, interrupting whatever tirade Masters was working up to.

"I did. Twice."

Shane poked his head into the living room and glared at Bella. "You could have barked," he told the dog.

Bella's ears flattened on her head at Shane's tone, then she rolled to her side dismissing him. She was usually a much better guard dog than that, barking at the smallest provocation. Though she hadn't barked when Luke had come to the door last night either. Shane shook his head at the dog's odd behavior before returning to the task of making himself look a little less like death warmed over.

"I could have barked? Fucking unbelievable," Masters said, his exasperation clear.

"I was talking to the dog. What do you want?" Shane asked again.

"I want you outside. Now. We have someplace to be and you're making us late."

"You're going to have to wait a few more minutes. You woke me up and I'm not dressed," Shane told him as he opened his shaving kit and began removing items one-handed. Things would move so much faster if Masters would let him off the phone.

"You have five minutes," Masters said and then disconnected the call.

Shane tossed the phone onto the dining table beside his laptop and returned his full attention to the reflection in the mirror. He loved the shade of blond he'd recently dyed his naturally brown hair, but today it looked dull. He ran his fingers through the rapidly drying strands attempting to make them spike and give a little volume. He splashed cold water on his face and brushed his teeth before dropping his flannel pants to the bathroom floor and getting dressed for the day. He'd just finished pulling on his shirt, smoothing it over his chest, letting it hang loosely over the top of his jeans when his phone chimed with an incoming text. He shoved his feet into his still-tied tennis shoes as he activated the screen to read the message.

Be out here in thirty seconds or I'll break down the door and drag you out. Dressed or not.

"No doubt," Shane muttered and called Masters several unflattering names when he noticed the time.

It was seven in the morning. Masters had made it sound much later and that fact made Shane more irritable. Tucking his wallet and phone into the back pockets of his jeans, he looked around the room wondering if there was anything else he should take. He leashed Bella and headed out the door to meet Masters. The man was standing with his arms and forehead resting on the roof of his Beetle. His back was to Shane and Shane couldn't help but stare at that perfectly toned butt. Shane was a sucker for a firm round ass. Not that he would ever tell Masters that. Shane's shoes crunched in the gravel and Masters straightened as he and Bella drew closer. Masters opened the passenger door and turned to face them, resting a forearm across the top of the door.

Shane practically tripped over his own feet as he finally got a good, well-lit look at the man's face. When they'd met the day before Masters had been in shadow and Shane hadn't been able to tell much beyond the fact that he had classic good looks. In the light of the early morning sun Shane found the man was incredibly handsome with intense blue eyes. If it weren't for all the hard edges, Masters might have been pretty. Instead, he had that whole don't-mess-with-me aura about him turning those pretty-boy looks into rugged handsomeness. His hair was a light shade of brown he wore brushed back in soft waves. He hadn't shaved this morning so an attractive dark stubble dusted his cheeks and jaw. It would have looked unkempt on anyone else, but Masters wore the look well.

Today Masters wore a cream-colored button down with the sleeves rolled to his elbows and tucked into dark brown slacks secured with a thin utilitarian leather belt. His left wrist was adorned with an oversized watch, but he wore no rings or chains and his skin was free of tattoos. If Shane had met him today, he would have thought Masters was a lawyer on his day off. He wore the scowl of a lawyer with his lips thinned and his brows drawn low over narrowed eyes. Shane stopped in front of Masters, allowing Bella to sniff the interior of the car. Masters scowled at the dog.

"You're a very grumpy person," Shane said.

"I didn't sleep well," Masters murmured. "The dog stays," he said more loudly, looking Shane in the eye.

"No." Shane returned Masters' stare.

"Give her to Luke. He'll be questioning people who live around here. He can keep her with him."

"Never going to happen. She stays with me."

Shane watched the anger flash in Masters' eyes. This was a man unaccustomed to being told no. Masters put his hands on his hips and glared daggers at Shane.

"We're wasting time," Shane said sweetly.

He even added an innocent smile, fully aware it would piss Masters off more. Shane nudged Bella's behind so she would jump into the car. He pushed her over the middle console into the back before sliding into the passenger seat. Masters stared into the distance, nostrils flaring and visibly trying to reign in the temper. Shane grabbed the door handle and yanked the door closed before belting himself in. He watched Masters move around the hood of the car to the driver's side, lips moving as he mumbled to himself.

He got in with a muttered "bullshit," secured his own belt, and turned the ignition. He shot Shane an angry look as he threw the car into reverse and gunned it into the empty lot behind them.

CHAPTER EIGHT

Masters maneuvered the Beetle onto the highway in a cloud of dust and gravel. Shane had several questions, one of which was why they weren't helping Luke question the neighbors, but he was more concerned about where Masters was driving them. Luke had told him the night before that Masters was working on something, but Luke hadn't known what. Shane turned to ask and noticed Masters kept glancing in the rearview mirror and cursing under his breath. Shane turned to look out the back window, but there were no vehicles in sight. He stared at Masters until the man caught him looking.

"This is a vintage Beetle," Masters said between clenched teeth.

Shane glanced at Bella lying across the small back seat. She had her nose between her front paws, big brown puppy eyes staring back at him. She was almost too big for the space, but she seemed comfortable enough. Shane reached back and quickly scratched her behind an ear.

"She's lying down. It's fine," Shane said.

"Getting hair and drool everywhere," Masters grumbled.

Shane chose to ignore the comment and changed the subject. "Does Luke know I'm with you? I really don't need another lecture about strangers."

He could already hear Luke's voice in his head. *What were you thinking, getting into a car with a man you know nothing about?* Forget that Luke had introduced them, or that Luke and Masters were friends. That wouldn't even factor into the argument. All that mattered was Luke's perception that Shane had a reckless disregard for his own safety. Luke had been overprotective from the day he'd rescued Shane. Most of the time his concern was appreciated; others it was downright annoying and suffocating.

"He knows," Masters answered, cutting into Shane's thoughts.

Masters maneuvered the car through the twists and turns of the two-lane mountain highway at a faster speed than Shane thought was safe. In about half an hour they would leave the foothills and enter the suburbs of west Denver. Although at this speed, Shane suspected Masters could forego the next turn and just fly them off the mountain. The man dug his phone out of his pocket and Shane averted his eyes out the side window. Masters was now driving with one hand on the wheel, fiddling with his phone with the other, and the speed with which he was approaching other cars made Shane sick to his stomach. If it had been Luke behind the wheel, Shane would have launched into a diatribe about distracted driving at any speed, but kept his mouth shut; instinctively knowing Masters wouldn't appreciate it.

"Jacob, how are you doing?" Masters said into the phone.

Shane turned to stare at him. Masters sounded so pleasant, though it was clear he hadn't expected this Jacob person to answer the phone. Shane was surprised Masters knew how to act civilly. If Shane wasn't looking directly at him, he would never believe the man talking so politely on the phone was the same man who'd yelled at him this morning. His jaw dropped when Masters chuckled and actually smiled without his face breaking. Shane realized he was gaping at the man and snapped his jaw shut. He looked out the front windshield and immediately regretted it. They were dangerously close to the bumper of a slow-moving semi. Masters tugged the wheel and they launched around the truck without Masters stepping on the brake once. Shane's heart leapt into his throat. Never in a million years had he imagined this was the way he would die.

"Sure thing my man," Masters said, continuing the conversation like he hadn't narrowly missed turning them into pancakes. "Listen, tell your mom I'm running a few minutes late, but I'm on my way. Thanks, Jay. See you soon."

Masters disconnected the call and dropped the phone into the center console. Shane closed his eyes, trying not to hyperventilate. Masters had his full attention on the road and both hands on the wheel, but it made no difference in his driving. Shane focused his attention inward by making a list of all the questions he had about Robert Grant, Crystal Creek Hotel, and the strange happenings that occurred there. After giving himself a headache with that, he started on all the questions he had about the caretaker's cottage, which was a considerably smaller list though no less troubling. Finally, Shane's thoughts took him to the nightmare Masters had woken him from this morning and how that might relate to everything else.

Shane rubbed his temples and opened his eyes to see the great expanse of Denver and her urban sprawl directly ahead. They were on the last downhill run out of the foothills and into the suburbs. In this part of town expensive houses could be found dotting the sides of the hills south of the highway. He looked at the homes and not for the first time wondered why anyone would need such a large house. Every one of them had two or three floors, multicar garages, and brick walls surrounding the properties.

Within minutes the highway cut between Littleton and Lakewood where homes were nice, well-maintained with manicured lawns, but were of a more modest size. The trees had begun to turn with the change of seasons, littering the ground with red and brown leaves. Despite the deceptively warm weather, winter was just around the corner and snow might begin to fall at any moment. Mother Nature liked to play games like that; sixty degrees one day with winter storm warnings and snow the next.

Masters turned off the highway and headed south a few miles before turning into a nice neighborhood of beautifully kept houses. The people living in this area of town weren't rich, per se, but had well-paying jobs. The yards were manicured and landscaped; very few allowed to grow unhindered. Shane glanced around as they drove, admiring how each house looked different, unique. He hated cookie-cutter houses, though he supposed they had their place. Masters turned west and pulled to the curb in front of a two-story, custom-built, Victorian-style house. Colorful flowers still lined the sidewalk leading to the house and the grass wasn't yet showing signs of impending winter.

Shane took in the pillared porch and red brick coupled with gray marbled stone of the first floor. Freshly painted gray siding adorned the top floor. The windows and door frames were a dark maroon that complimented the brick of the ground floor. Ever since he was a child leafing through his mother's interior design books this was the kind of house he'd wanted. He imagined rooms with softly-toned wallpaper, hardwood floors, and overstuffed furniture with fluffy throw pillows. Shane no longer knew what the future had in store for him, but he could easily see himself with a husband living in a place just like this.

Masters shifted in the seat and shut off the engine. Shane reluctantly returned his attention to his companion as Bella pushed to her feet to look out the window. Masters sat quietly for a minute glaring into the rearview mirror, but Shane doubted he was watching Bella. He seemed to be thinking about something. Shane was more than ready to get out of Masters' vintage deathtrap, but since he had no idea where they were going, he waited.

Bella shoved her nose between the seats to look out the front windshield and Shane scratched under her collar. He really hoped Masters would give him some clue as to what they were doing in this neighborhood. Shane hated being kept in the dark and trying to act like he knew what was happening. Masters exhaled loudly, twisted in his seat, and pushed Bella back so he could look Shane in the eye.

"All right, here's the story. Stick to it or you're fired."

Shane scoffed at that. "Yeah, sure," he murmured.

He wasn't overly concerned about being fired. Even if Masters managed it, Luke would still pay him for the weekend. There had to be some kind of compensation for the suffering he'd already endured, up to and including his near-death experience with Masters' driving. The amount would be far smaller than originally agreed to, but Shane would require payment just to stick it to Masters.

"Luke told me you're gay," Masters said.

"Yeah, so what?" It was bad enough Masters had a problem with Shane being psychic. If he had a problem with him being gay as well, Masters wouldn't have to fire him. He'd quit.

"I'm bisexual, but I tend more toward women. Learned early on it was bad for business being seen romantically involved with a man."

"Whatever," Shane muttered. He had no idea why Masters was telling him about his sexuality, but he wished he hadn't. Knowing the infuriating man swung his way on occasion didn't help Shane with his ridiculous attraction.

"When we go in there, you're my boyfriend. I'm taking a day off so we can spend time together in the mountains for some R and R and I decided to stop by to introduce you. Understand?"

"That's the cover story?"

"I didn't have time to come up with anything better that would make sense with a damn dog in tow. Besides, it will keep the family off balance and hopefully keep their own questions to a minimum. Now, tell me you understand."

Shane shrugged and shook his head. "You're bisexual, you prefer women above men but for some reason decided I was worth the potential losses to your business so we're out enjoying a beautiful day. Got it. Now, tell me why we're really here?"

Bella once again tried to insert herself between them and Shane gently pushed her back. The car wasn't moving so she was impatient to get out. Shane caught Masters staring at him with an odd expression and he wondered what had brought on the change. If Shane were pressed to pick an emotion, he would have gone with sadness, but in a heartbeat, Masters was able to restore his usual mask of indifference.

"Things between me and this family are complicated," Masters finally answered. "All you need to know is that these people are Megan Granger's sister and brother-in-law. They're raising her son who was placed with them after she disappeared." Masters must have noticed Shane's confusion over exactly who Megan Granger was because he added, "She was dating Robert Grant at the time they went missing."

The pieces fell into place for Shane and he nodded. "Right, right. Is this the family that hired you?"

"No." Masters answered. Shane sighed in frustration. It seemed Masters was deliberately keeping information from him. "Once we're inside, I'll find a way to go upstairs. Megan was living here at the time of her disappearance and her son currently does so maybe something of hers will still be here as well. We'll find something to use for your voodoo and then get the hell out."

Masters suddenly opened his car door and got out. Shane remained in the passenger seat fighting back a fresh wave of anger. He did not perform voodoo. Shane understood Masters was a nonbeliever, but he could keep his skepticism and derisive comments to himself. Kennie, Shane's best friend and business partner, would hand Masters his balls if he ever said something like that to her. Sometimes Shane wished he could be more like her. Everyone knew exactly where they ranked with Miss Kendra Marks. Masters came around the car and pulled open the passenger door. Shane grabbed Bella's leash as she practically pushed him out of the car and immediately began sniffing her new surroundings. Shane stared at Masters until the man met his gaze.

"You're an asshole," he said as Masters depressed the button lock and closed the door, never once breaking eye contact with Shane. He moved into Shane's personal space and Shane fought the urge to step back.

"I have a gun, Mr. Cayli, and I'm not afraid to use it."

"I'd like to see you try," Shane replied and narrowed his eyes.

Masters was trying to intimidate him, and it was working, but Shane would go to hell before letting it show. If Shane wanted to be treated as an equal, he would have to act like it, even though it was completely foreign to him. He'd never met a man as obnoxious and imperious as the one before him so he didn't really know how to handle him. Shane did know that letting Masters continue to treat him badly wasn't the answer. Masters leaned in closer and lowered his voice.

"You do not tell them you're psychic. You don't tell them you're working this case. In fact, just keep your mouth shut. Period. These people are like family to me and I'll be damned if I let you swindle them."

Shane fisted his hands at his side, about to tell Masters where he could stick it, when Masters turned on his heel and stomped up the sidewalk toward the Victorian Shane had been admiring. Shane wanted to scream but settled for stomping his foot against the pavement. He blew out a hard breath and forced his fists to relax. He couldn't very well go into a stranger's home radiating anger. He used the same meditative techniques to calm down that he used to control his ability as he slowly followed Masters to the porch.

CHAPTER NINE

Masters took the steps two at a time and turned to find Shane was still halfway down the walk. Masters put his hands to his hips, looked up at the roof of the porch, and then waved his hand in that get-your-ass-in-gear manner. Shane somehow managed to use those precious few seconds to his advantage and felt he had his emotions under control, despite the fact Masters was still irking him every second they were together.

The sooner they managed to solve this case or acknowledged it would never be solved, the sooner Shane could get back to his life and put this whole unpleasant experience behind him. He was suddenly filled with renewed motivation and hurried up the steps to stand beside Masters. Shane let his gaze slide over Masters head to toe, once again noting that the man was incredibly handsome and sighed. It was a real shame the man had to be so ugly on the inside.

"Took you long enough," Masters muttered. Shane chose to ignore the comment and waited while Masters knocked on the door.

"What do I call you?" Shane asked.

"Masters."

"Seriously? You make your lovers call you by your last name?"

"I don't have 'lovers,' but yes, I would."

"You're a miserable person, aren't you?" Shane asked.

The glare Masters gave him before knocking on the door a second time was answer enough. The man was a closeted gay asshole who didn't date because it was 'bad for business.' He was the type who hated his life but refused to change it. Shane could never live that way, denying who he was every second of every day. Perhaps being psychic had ostracized him to a point where being openly gay didn't seem so extreme. When things had gone south with Brent, Shane's sexuality had been plastered all over the news, but he'd managed to keep his psychic ability hidden from the press.

Crushing depression threatened to overwhelm him. Shane had gone nearly a year without thinking about Brent but the damn man had intruded on his thoughts more than once in the past twenty-four hours. Masters was a closeted homosexual and Shane was a closeted psychic. Neither of them wanted their perceived faults to be made public. Shane's animosity towards Masters eased quite a bit with that understanding, though the guy was still an asshole.

Shane had thought Luke was an asshole after their first meeting, too. Luke had been mean and pushy. He and Luke had so many fights in the beginning because of Luke's attitude. One time Luke had pushed Shane to the point that Shane had taken a swing at him. His knuckles had connected with Luke's jaw in such a way that he'd hurt himself more than Luke, but Shane had successfully made his point. Luke's entire demeanor toward him had changed for the better and they'd been friends ever since.

It had taken a while for Shane to realize that Luke was driven by a strong sense of duty and responsibility to the point that he'd been unconcerned by the fact he was destroying Shane while going after Brent. As he thought back over his interactions with Masters, he noticed Masters exhibited many of the same traits Luke had back then. Maybe beneath the asshole cynic was a protective and honorable man. Shane didn't have to like the man to respect those qualities in him and he wasn't going to put up with his bullshit. They made eye contact just as the door was opened by a lanky teenage boy.

Upon seeing Masters the boy smiled broadly. The kid had dark hair and eyes and was as tall as them at around six feet, but was all bone. He had that gangly look that indicated a recent growth spurt and his weight hadn't yet caught up to his height. Masters gave the kid a genuinely happy smile that crinkled the corners of his eyes. Shane grinned at the change in the surly man. The boy pushed open the glass storm door and Masters pulled him into a quick hug.

"Damn, Jacob, you're getting tall," Masters said with a clap to the kid's shoulder. Jacob stepped back and shrugged. "How's it hanging?"

"It doesn't much, but mom says that's normal for my age," Jacob answered and ran a hand down the front of his jeans.

Masters barked out a short laugh and Shane rolled his eyes as he finally caught Jacob's meaning. He remembered a time when he and his brothers couldn't control when they popped boners, either. Bella pushed between him and Masters, rubbing against his leg and Shane reached down to pet the top of her head.

"Jacob, my man, company," Masters said.

Jacob finally looked at Shane and Bella. "Nice dog," he said and Shane smiled at him. Jacob was a cute kid and once his physical proportions evened out, he would be devastating to adolescent girls citywide. He did a quick once over of Shane then disappeared into the house, leaving them to find their own way in. Masters held the storm door open, ushering Shane and Bella in ahead of him. Shane stopped in the small foyer and told Bella to sit as Masters closed the wood door.

To the right were stairs leading up to the second floor. To the left of the stairs was a hallway leading to the back of the house. Branching off the small entryway was a formal living room furnished in antiques and floral upholstery. On the other side of the entrance was the formal dining room with a dark mahogany table that could seat six. Centered above that was a chandelier that was dripping with crystals. Dozens of tiny rainbows dotted the walls where the sunlight reflected off them. The turret's octagonal shape was seen in the large bay window that overlooked the front lawn. Masters came to stand behind Shane and whispered into his ear.

"Jacob is Megan Granger's son. They moved here when Jacob was born due to financial problems. He was still a baby when she disappeared. Alyssa, Megan's sister, and Alyssa's husband, Ted, legally adopted him when he was five after Megan was declared dead." Masters' hand brushed against Shane's hip as he stepped away.

"Are you related to them?" Shane asked softly.

"No."

"How did you meet them?"

Shane knew he was pressing, but Masters' words and actions curbside followed closely by his familiar exchange with Jacob on the porch had Shane extremely curious. Masters had said they were like family and it was clear he had affection for them. The idea Masters thought Shane would swindle the family still angered him and he wanted to know where Masters' fierce protectiveness came from. They held each other's gazes for a moment and Shane could see the wheels turning behind those striking blue eyes, trying to decide how much to disclose. Masters answered in an equally soft voice.

"I dated their daughter." The same sadness Shane had seen on Masters face in the car made a brief return before a soft feminine voice chased it away.

"Masters, it's been too long."

A short round woman entered the foyer from the center hall. She was quite a bit older than Shane had been expecting with more salt than pepper in her dark brown hair. Her hazel eyes betrayed an exhaustion her expression didn't show. She carried a few extra pounds, had a beautiful face, and a warm demeanor that Shane instantly liked. She wrapped Masters in a hug of familiarity that spoke volumes.

"Liss," he responded softly and planted a quick kiss on her cheek. She beamed up at him like a treasured son who was finally visiting home. After a moment, she turned her friendly attention to Shane and extended her hand in greeting.

"Hello, dear. I'm Alyssa."

"Shane." He shook her hand, careful to keep the touch brief and gentle. The woman smiled broadly and Shane found himself smiling back. She bent down to pet Bella on the head. "This is Bella. She's my service dog."

"It's a pleasure to meet both of you. I must say, I was beginning to think Masters would never move on."

Never one to miss an opportunity for more information, especially on someone as interesting and closed off as Masters, Shane jumped on the unintended opening Alyssa gave him. "Move on from what?" he asked. He noticed Masters had suddenly found his shoes intensely fascinating. Alyssa glanced at Masters with a frown.

"I'm sorry. I thought you would have told him."

Alyssa looped her arm around Masters. His expression was that blank mask Shane was coming to hate. He was very skilled at controlling his emotions. Shane thought he'd gotten a peek at the forces that were driving the man, but suspected Masters considered any show of feelings to be a weakness. Shane considered it humanity and held onto that, hoping it would make dealing with Masters' bullshit a little easier.

"He's a very private person," Shane said, softly. He hadn't actually meant to say the words out loud, but there they were.

"Yes, he is," Alyssa agreed. Her jovial smile had faded a bit, but she stubbornly held onto her manners and friendliness. "Let's sit in the living room."

Shane caught Masters' gaze as Alyssa led them into the antique-laden room, but he wasn't able to decipher what Masters was trying to say with his eyes. He figured it was probably a keep-you-mouth-shut or don't-ask-questions type of look considering their previous conversation in the car. Shane followed behind them, keeping Bella on a very short lead. All he needed was for a wayward wag of the tail to take out an expensive lamp or tea set or something.

Alyssa motioned to the sofa and Shane took a seat. He pulled Bella against his legs and tapped her nose. She laid on the floor and put her nose on Shane's shoe. Alyssa sat in the armchair on the other side of the coffee table. Masters watched Bella obey Shane's silent command as he took a seat beside Shane. The sofa was barely big enough for two grown men to sit side by side and Shane was uncomfortably aware of the mere centimeters separating their thighs.

"Masters dated my daughter." Alyssa's voice pulled Shane's attention away from Masters' close proximity and he nodded.

"He did tell me that."

"She died a few years ago, and I've been worried that he would never recover. He took it hard, blamed himself. But here he is, with you, and I couldn't be more delighted."

Alyssa's tone and the smile on her face were a stark contrast to the heavy melancholy thickening the air. Unpleasant memories were very much in the forefront of Masters' mind and he was entirely too close. Shane tightened his fingers on Bella's leash and shifted toward the armrest of the sofa, putting as much distance between them as he could without drawing attention. Masters wanted Shane to keep his psychic ability under wraps so Shane didn't want to slip into a memory brought on by an accidental brush of knees. Masters eyed him sideways, but said nothing.

"May I ask how she died?" Shane asked Masters. If he was lucky, they would think his actions were discomfort from the topic of conversation. Masters stared into Shane's eyes a moment before answering.

"Car accident," he said simply. Based on the thought he'd put into that answer Shane knew there was more to it than those two simple words. A glance at Alyssa confirmed that suspicion.

"It was three years ago. She was twenty-four," Alyssa added.

Shane didn't know what to say that wouldn't come across insincere so he kept silent. His attention stayed on Alyssa as he idly ran his fingers through

Bella's fur. He needed to remain grounded, especially since Masters only had to move one inch to come into contact with him. Bella picked up on his unease and rose to rest her head on his lap with a soft whine. When Shane lifted his gaze, both his companions watching him; Alyssa with an endearing smile and Masters with a puzzled expression. Shane was grateful when Alyssa took the discussion in a different direction.

"So, what have you been doing with yourself? Taking a break between cases today?" she asked.

"Right in the middle of a case, actually," Masters said.

Alyssa gave him an indulgent smile and shook her head. "Well, I don't know about Shane, but I'm happy to hear you took a day off."

Alyssa turned that sweet smile from Masters to Shane and he smiled back with a nod. "He does take his work seriously," Shane said without hesitation. Men like Masters and Luke *always* took their work seriously and rarely took time off, especially in the middle of an investigation when time was everything.

"Yeah, Liss, about my day off. This visit is the whole 'kill two birds with one stone' kind of thing. I wanted to bring Shane by, but also, the case I'm working on has ties to the family," Masters said.

"I see," Alyssa said. Her smile faltered and her demeanor became more guarded. "Not the social visit I had hoped."

"Not entirely," he admitted.

Alyssa clasped her hands in her lap and sighed. "Out with it, then."

"When Elizabeth and I started dating she told me about Megan. It had always bothered her that her aunt had never been found." Masters watched Alyssa closely.

"It's been twelve years. Just...let it be."

Shane now understood the fatigue this woman displayed. The death of a young daughter and the unresolved disappearance of a sister had to weight heavy even after the passage of so many years. He thought it unusual that Alyssa wanted Masters to leave the case alone. Most families of missing people never gave up and didn't want the police or anyone else to give up either. Like the family who hired Luke and Masters.

"I can't let it go. Megan wasn't the only one who disappeared that night and other families want answers. Why don't you?"

"I do. But I have a son to raise and a life to live, and I can't do that if I keep revisiting things that can't be changed."

Shane had to agree to a point. He wondered which way he would have chosen to go if it'd been one of his brothers who had gone missing. It was one of those things where he thought he'd react one way, but who really knew until it actually happened. Bella whined and pawed at Shane's arm to get his attention. He shushed her, but she did it again.

"I think she needs out," Shane said. He stood and pulled Bella to her feet by the leash. "I'll just take her out front." His hopes of making a quick, smooth escape so Masters could talk his way upstairs were dashed immediately.

"Don't be silly, Shane. Take her to the backyard and let her run around," Alyssa offered motioning toward the hall that led to the back of the house.

Her joviality was back like it had never left. Unpredictable mood swings were something she and Masters had in common, apparently. Not wanting to risk brushing against Masters by squeezing between his legs and coffee table, Shane moved around the back of the sofa. Masters undecipherable gaze followed him as he circled behind. Alyssa rose from the chair and met him at the room's entrance. She started to loop her arm through Shane's, but he stepped away quickly, immediately regretting the move. For once, he was grateful for Masters' take-charge attitude.

"I'm sorry, Liss. I should have warned you he doesn't like to be touched," Masters said as he joined them in the hall.

"Sorry," Shane added softly.

"It's fine. This way," Alyssa assured them with a smile. Shane followed her down the hall, glancing at the family photos that covered the walls on both sides. Masters brought up the rear at a slower pace. Alyssa turned at the end of the hall and tipped her head to the side.

"Do you mind if I ask what it was about Masters that first caught your attention?"

The memory of Masters leaning across Crystal Creek Hotel's reception desk yesterday afternoon flashed through Shane's mind.

"His ass," he blurted and then immediately blushed.

He really needed to work on his brain-to-mouth filter. It failed him so spectacularly at times. Shane hadn't wanted Masters to know he'd checked him out, or that he liked what he saw, but there was no taking it back now. Masters huffed behind him as Alyssa chuckled. Shane was embarrassed, but the woman's laughter was infectious and he smiled again.

Shane followed Alyssa into an expansive open-concept kitchen with wood floors that bled seamlessly into the family room. It was updated with all stainless-steel appliances and marble countertops. In the center of the room was a cooking island with a chopping-block top. In the family room, Jacob was sprawled across a large overstuffed sectional playing a video game on the biggest flat screen Shane had ever seen. It practically covered the entire wall. On the floor in front of the sofa was a large, brightly colored oriental rug. Between the two rooms were French doors that led to the back yard. Shane led Bella to the doors, unclipped her leash, and opened the door for her. A squirrel scampered up the fence and Bella took off across the lawn in hot pursuit.

"Most people compliment my eyes," Masters said from directly behind him. Shane jumped in surprise.

Shane turned to face him, unsure if he was teasing or just stating a fact. He rolled his lips in and bit down, nodding in agreement. He'd already said too much and he wasn't about to add to it by telling Masters he really did have beautiful eyes. Alyssa leaned against the kitchen island a few feet away watching them. Masters stood close, hands in his pockets, looking relaxed but professional reminding Shane they were actively working. Bella barked and Shane glanced over his shoulder to make sure she was doing okay.

The yard wasn't large, but it was landscaped to give the illusion it was bigger. The house was flanked by a greenbelt that could be seen beyond the back fencing. A stone walkway lead from the house down to a gate that offered access to the greenbelt. The walkway branched off midway to lead to a small white gazebo that sat in the back corner of the yard. Flowers lined the walk and the edges of the wood decking. Shane sighed in longing. This house was everything he wanted. Deciding he would turn his admiration of his surroundings to his advantage, he looked at Alyssa.

"I love this house. It's so beautiful. I've always wanted a house like this. Do you mind giving me a tour?"

Masters furrowed his brow and stared hard at Shane as Alyssa straightened. Shane was perfectly aware he was veering away from the original plan, but Masters didn't seem to be trying very hard to get up those stairs. Alyssa took in the glare Masters was giving him and her expression changed to concern.

"I wouldn't mind, but I'm not sure Masters is ready," she said.

The comment confused Shane, especially since Masters had been the one to tell him Megan's things were still up there, but it did seem he had a problem with it. Or maybe the problem he had was *Shane* going upstairs? His posture had stiffened. Shane got as close to Masters as he could without touching him.

"I don't understand," he whispered. "You – "

"I'm good," Masters interrupted at regular volume. He held Shane's gaze a moment longer before looking at Alyssa. "It's your house, Liss, show him around if you want. I'll just tag along."

"I haven't changed anything. Her room is exactly as she left it," Alyssa told him.

"It's not a problem," Masters insisted.

CHAPTER TEN

Shane shoved his hands into his pockets to avoid pressing his palm to Masters' chest. What Shane saw flash in those clear blue eyes had him wanting to wrap himself around the man to offer comfort. Even after three years it was clear that Masters was still broken over Elizabeth's death. Shane stepped back, putting distance between them, and told himself to stay focused on the objective of this visit. Find something of Megan Granger's to read. They had a mass-disappearance case to solve. His own personal curiosity about the man beside him could wait.

Shane averted his gaze to Jacob still lying on the sectional. This family had a lot of intense emotion swirling around them and it made Shane feel uncomfortable and intrusive. He became entranced by the cars on Jacob's video game racing through realistically rendered city streets. Even the squealing of tires and voices of the characters insulting each other was true to life. Jacob grumbled and shook his game control as he took a corner too fast, jumped the median, and his car landed in a lake with a splash. Shane saw Masters move closer in his peripheral vision and Shane slid his gaze back to him. Masters tilted his head toward Alyssa and Shane realized he'd zoned out and missed something.

"I'm sorry?"

Alyssa motioned for them to follow her. "I said I'd be happy to show you around."

Shane was excited by the news. He wanted to do his job and find something of Megan's to work on, but he also couldn't wait to see the rest of his dream house. His hostess made a sweeping gesture of their surroundings with her arm.

"You've pretty much seen the main floor. It's just one giant circle with the stairs and hall in the center. The basement is through that door there, but it's unfinished. We keep all the junk down there."

Shane looked where Alyssa had pointed and noticed a door he'd missed earlier. It was beside the hallway entrance helping bisect the kitchen/family room area by being placed directly across from the French doors to the yard. Alyssa moved toward the hall, but Shane remained rooted in place.

Something in the room had changed and Shane's psychic ability surged forward. His temperature rose and his breathing accelerated. He must have swayed a bit on his feet because Masters lifted a hand toward him, but Shane shook his head adamantly and held his hands up so Masters wouldn't touch him. Both Masters and Alyssa looked at him with concern. Shane was at a loss how to put them at ease since he was concerned himself. He had no idea what was triggering his psychic power.

"Hot flash," Shane croaked, which wasn't entirely a lie; he was getting hotter by the second.

Shane discretely slid his gaze around the kitchen and then to the family room. In the farthest corner of the room near the edge of the flat screen was the faint apparition of a woman. Shane blinked, trying to bring the woman into better focus, but it was like she was shrouded in cheesecloth, blurred and muted. From what Shane could make out, she had long dark hair that hung in curls over her shoulders and wore a red evening gown that brushed the top of her feet. Cold air wafted from the ghost as she stared at Jacob with so much sadness it made Shane want to cry.

Shane swallowed thickly and took a deep breath against the pressure in his chest. This apparition was strong. It reminded him of Robert Grant's ghost at the hotel. She had formed rapidly and the cold coming off her was heavy with emotion. Shane slid his eyes over the other three occupants of the room. None of them seemed to notice there was a presence in the room. Masters and Alyssa were watching him with furrowed brows and the kid continued to play his video game despite the fact the ghost now hovered between him and the television.

"Who are you?" Shane whispered.

Masters scowled and shook his head. "Are you kidding me? I told you who he was when we got here." Masters had stepped closer and lowered his voice, but his annoyance was clear.

Shane took a deep breath and attempted to regain the tenuous control he had over his ability. He couldn't completely tamp it down as long as the ghost was present, but it was his experience that no matter how strong an apparition was, it couldn't maintain physical form for long. Shane closed his eyes, rolled his shoulders, and blew out a breath before opening his eyes to find the female ghost had moved closer to him, and was staring right at him.

Shane shook his head in response to Masters, at a loss how to explain the presence of a ghost to a man who didn't believe in them. A phone tucked into the corner by the refrigerator began ringing and Alyssa walked around the island to answer it. Shane had a brief second to marvel at the fact this family still had a landline before the apparition began moving toward him again, the cold and sadness flowing over him ahead of her. Shane spun on his heels, yanked the French door open, and called for Bella. There was no way he could remain in this house without her. Bella came running across the yard, but slowed as she neared the doorway, the fur on the back of neck puffing out and a low growl emitting from her throat. Shane snapped the leash on her collar and shortened the lead to keep Bella firmly against his thigh.

Shane faced Masters who was now standing with his arms crossed and feet braced apart. Shane cleared his throat. "How about that tour?"

"One moment," Alyssa said, and both Shane and Masters turned to her. She placed a hand over the mouthpiece and smiled. "I'll be a few minutes still. You go ahead and show him around."

Alyssa made a shooing motion with her hand as she resumed her phone conversation. Shane's gaze darted to the female apparition. The ghost was dissipating, growing more transparent, but still feeding Bella's and Shane's distress. Bella stood rigid against Shane's side as the ghost seemed to study them, which Shane found disconcerting. A bone-deep chill had Shane rubbing a palm over his arm and he was unable to suppress the resulting shiver.

"Are you cold?" Masters asked.

"A little. I'll warm up when we get moving."

Masters took the hint and crossed the room with Shane following close behind. Bella stayed glued to his side on high alert until they left the living room and ghost behind, and then she relaxed her tail and lowered her hackles. Toward the front of the house the temperature evened out and Shane relaxed some. Masters headed upstairs quickly, but Shane took his time. Family photographs lined the wall and he looked at each one. The majority were of Jacob at various ages with a few of a pretty blond girl here and there.

Halfway to the second floor was a landing where the stairs did a switchback. The photos hung in this area varied in size and shape in what appeared to be random placement. Shane was fascinated by the little moments captured on film that this family valued enough to display. One picture caught his attention and he leaned in to get a closer look. Shane saw Masters reflected in the glass as he leaned against the railing, arms crossed and waiting. Shane pointed to the photo that had snagged his attention. Luke and another man stood side by side in dress uniform. The older man had an arm over Luke's shoulders and they were smiling at the camera.

"Who is this?"

"Alyssa's husband, Ted. Holmestead was fresh out of the academy when that picture was taken," Masters answered as he joined Shane on the landing. "This is how we met. Ted introduced us at a barbecue a few years back."

Shane grinned over that little piece of history as he pointed at another photo of a woman holding a baby. He already knew the answer, but he asked anyway. "And this?"

"Megan and Jacob. He was three months old there, I think."

Megan in the picture didn't look all that different from Megan the ghost. She must have disappeared not too long after the photo had been taken. The fact that Alyssa referred to Jacob as her son, rather than her nephew, was not lost on Shane and he filed that information away with all the other little bits and pieces he picked up. When he was alone later, he would re-examine everything he'd learned and try to make sense of it.

That pervasive sadness that radiated from Alyssa and Masters once again pressed in on Shane. He turned and saw Masters staring at the wall, eyes distant and full of pain. Shane followed Masters' line of sight to a photograph of Masters and the pretty young blond girl sitting on the gazebo swing. The girl was leaning into Masters and they were laughing, holding hands, looking as though they didn't have a care in the world.

"You should smile more often," Shane said softly. "She's the one you lost?"

"Yes, that's Elizabeth. That picture was taken at her college graduation party."

"She was younger than you?"

Masters nodded, but said nothing. Shane still couldn't shake the feeling there was more to Elizabeth's car accident than Masters was letting on. The man's answers were too short, clipped, and not at all informative, like the man himself. It suddenly struck Shane that Masters might have been in the car at the time of the accident and survived, which would explain some of Masters' reactions and Alyssa's concerns that he wouldn't move on. Masters slipped into a memory that had the corners of his mouth tugging up into a slight smile and Shane made sure to keep his distance.

He hated accidentally reading people and not for the first time wondered how he'd never inadvertently read Brent. He'd lived with the man, constantly touched him, and never gotten a single memory from him. The situation only proved that Shane could manage his ability, but he couldn't really control it. Shane opened his mouth to tell Masters he was ready to continue up the stairs when the front door opened creating a gentle breeze up the stairway. Masters leaned over the railing to see the man who entered and then stepped around Shane and Bella to greet him. The man looked up the steps at them in surprise.

"Masters, sonofabitch, is that really you?" The man's voice was deep, authoritative, and resonated in the open foyer.

Masters grinned and spread his hands. "In the flesh."

"Damn, son, it's been too long."

Alyssa joined the men in the foyer as they shook hands and the older man clapped a hand on Masters' shoulder. Alyssa's infectious smile had returned and her eyes danced as the men greeted each other.

"How've you been, Ted?" Masters asked.

"Finer than frog hair. What brings you here?"

"It's his day off and he brought his boyfriend to meet us," Alyssa answered.

Ted looked startled at that announcement as Alyssa lifted her hand to indicate Shane on the stairwell landing. Fighting a burst of inexplicable nerves, either triggered by Masters' sudden discomfort or the look Ted sent his way, Shane smiled and waved shyly then lowered his hand to rub Bella's ear. Ted's gaze bounced between Shane and Masters, clearly shocked and not bothering to hide it. Masters gestured for Shane to come down the stairs but he didn't want to get too close, so he stopped a few steps from the bottom. The vibe this man was giving off was extremely uncomfortable.

"Shane, this is Ted. Ted, this is my boyfriend, Shane, who really isn't as shy as he's acting," Masters said, watching Shane with narrowed, suspicious eyes.

"Nice to meet you," Shane said. Bella pushed her way between Shane's leg and the banister. "This is Bella."

Ted's shell-shock morphed into something Shane couldn't readily identify, but knew immediately he didn't like. Despite Alyssa's polite acceptance, it had to be jolting for their daughter's ex-boyfriend to show up at their door with a man on his arm. Shane shifted on his feet, more uncomfortable by the second under Ted's intense scrutiny. Masters picked up on it and steered the discussion in a different direction, swirling a finger in the air.

"Shane's always wanted a house like this so I was giving him the two-cent tour. We were just heading upstairs."

"Get on with it, then," Ted grunted and disappeared down the hall.

"Good to see you again," Masters called after him and received a mumbled reply that sounded a lot like, "yeah, sure."

Alyssa went with her husband, asking about his plans for the day, their voices trailing off as they entered the back of the house. Shane had absolutely no doubt that Ted didn't want him here, but was suffering his presence in a show of politeness. The man certainly came across as homophobic. Wanting to end this visit as quickly as possible, Shane raced up the stairs with Bella at his side. At the top of the stairs he stopped and waited for Masters to join them while staring at the cheery pink and yellow flowered wallpaper.

"Main bedroom is at the end of the hall to the right. Jacob's room is directly across from that. Guest rooms are to the left."

Keeping Bella secured against his thigh, Shane headed for the master suite first, more from curiosity than anything to do with the real reason he was here. The room was color coordinated and expensively furnished. There were a million pillows neatly arranged on top of a quilt with a blue and white star pattern in the middle. The room was so perfect it could have been a photo in a country decor magazine and Shane was again reminded of his grandmother's house.

Despite the room's pristine condition Shane got a strong sense of comfort. Everything looked worn and well-used, unlike the parlor downstairs stuffed with fancy antiques. Alyssa was all about appearances and clearly cared about giving a good impression. Not one thing in or outside the house was out of place. Neat and tidy. Shane wasn't much of a housekeeper and clutter reigned supreme in his apartment so he admired Alyssa's ability to maintain her home to this standard.

A sigh of ecstasy escaped his lips when Shane entered the master bath and saw the jacuzzi tub set beneath an octagonal window. On the far wall was a marble-tiled shower. Double sinks set into marbled counter tops ran along one wall and the toilet was hidden from view behind a closed door. Shane left the room wondering how Alyssa and Ted could afford such an amazing house on a cop's salary, especially since it appeared Alyssa was a housewife. Nothing in the master suite set off his psychic ability so he walked across the hall to Jacob's room where he felt an immediate change. Shane took a moment outside the closed door to adjust to the warmth suffusing his body as his ability once again surged forward. Given that Megan was haunting her family, Shane was nervous about what he'd face when he entered the bedroom.

As it turned out, entering Jacob's room wasn't an option. The mess that was missing from the rest of the house had been hidden behind this bedroom door. Shane poked his head in far enough to see a typical teenage boy's room. Posters of basketball stars and Lamborghinis hung on the walls while clothes, DVDs, and video games littered the floor. A few trophies sat on top of the dresser next to the closet. While Shane's apartment was far from clean, he liked to think he was a step above Jacob's chaos. He bet the kid couldn't find his shoes if they weren't already on his feet. Bella pushed her head and shoulders into the room and began nosing around a pair of discarded jeans.

Gooseflesh erupted over his forearms, so Shane pulled Bella out of the room and closed the bedroom door. The last thing he needed right now was for Megan to think he was a threat to her son. Once the door clicked shut, Shane walked back down the hall toward the stairs and the two guest rooms, blatantly ignoring the intensely cold draft biting at his neck. The forced deep and even breathing was making him feel funny and he gripped Bella's leash tighter. Placing one foot in front of the other was difficult given the pull the ghost was exerting. It was clear to him that Megan wanted him to turn around, but he couldn't indulge her right now. He had a job to do and an ever-decreasing amount of time to do it in.

Shane narrowed his focus on his destination, the guest room to his right, and tugged Bella down the hall with him despite her whining and tugging. Masters stepped out of a doorway to his left and Shane yelped in surprise, slamming his back against the wall and glaring at the man. Bella barked once in response to Shane's spike in anxiety, but then quieted. Masters' brow creased in annoyance as he looked from Shane to Bella and back. Shane looked behind Masters to see he'd come out of a small bathroom that was impeccably kept like the rest of the house. It would seem the only room in the house to escape Alyssa's housekeeping was Jacob's personal space.

"Is everything okay?" Alyssa called up the stairs.

"We're good." Masters yelled back. "I just startled him."

Alyssa's laughter floated into the upstairs hallway before receding as she moved away from the base of the stairs. Shane was dealing with ghosts and an asshole PI. Nothing about his current situation amused him in the least. He looked down the hall toward Jacob's room, pleased to see that Megan hadn't materialized despite the humming warmth still coursing through his veins. Masters reached for him and Shane sidestepped away from him, running a hand anxiously through his hair.

"What is wrong with you? You've been acting weird since we got here," Masters whispered.

Shane allowed his heightened emotions to come out in a hissed answer. "First, you don't know me well enough to know if I'm acting outside my norm or not. Second, don't you feel how cold it is right now?"

Masters let out a humorless laugh and shook his head.

"You're right. Silly me. I forgot for a minute you think you're psychic. Crazy is normal for you. It's always cold up here because of the attic access."

Shane narrowed his eyes and forced himself to breathe slowly for an entirely new reason. He was tempted to push Masters down the stairs. Shane turned his attention to the ceiling, located the attic access panel at the far end of the hall, and shook his head. The frigid air he was feeling wasn't caused by a draft from the attic, not only because it wasn't so much a draft as a cold spot, but because it was very prominent and focused in front of Jacob's door.

"It's not a draft from the attic," Shane said, looking directly into Masters' angry eyes. "This house is haunted."

It wasn't unusual for old houses to have drafts, but he knew the difference even if those living in the house didn't. Masters lifted his eyes to the ceiling in obvious exasperation. Shane couldn't understand the man who in one breath called him fraud and in the next helped him explore a house looking for something to spark his psychic ability. It felt stupid and impossible, but Shane wanted to prove this man wrong. He wanted Masters to believe in him, in his ability. Masters fisted his hands at his sides as he leveled his steely, blue gaze on Shane.

Another chill slithered down Shane's spine and he wasn't sure if it was caused by the ghost or Masters until Bella whined. His ability was suddenly so erratic and unpredictable, and he was beginning to think he never really had control — it was concerning. He couldn't get a read while inside the hotel when he should've been overwhelmed, and then he got hit without warning outside. Nothing was going the way he was accustomed to and he was ready to blame that on Masters. The man was seriously messing with his head, and he decided to never accept another case Masters was involved in.

A few feet down the hall Shane stopped near an open bedroom door. Bella's neck fur bristled and she growled, pressing into Shane's thigh and drawing his attention back to Masters. Gray mist coalesced behind him causing Shane's breath to seize in his chest. He wanted to breathe; he tried, but something about this apparition wouldn't allow him to draw air into his lungs. Megan's sad, empty eyes held him transfixed. He stared back at her, afraid to move, until his chest began to burn from lack of oxygen.

Masters crowded him, face creased with concern. "Breathe, Shane."

Eventually, Shane's mind was able to overcome the spectral paralysis allowing his body to draw in much-needed oxygen with a shuddering inhale. Masters reached out, and Shane shook his head, but not before Masters' hands landed on his biceps. Thanks to the overwhelming ghostly presence, he only received the slightest glimpse of Masters' concern that Shane would pass out. Afraid he'd accidentally pick up more, he eased out of Masters' grip. Megan seemed to lose interest in them and floated down the hall toward her son's bedroom.

CHAPTER ELEVEN

"What is wrong with you?" Masters asked, exasperated.

Shane tore his gaze from the now fading spirit to Masters' annoyed face. He was pretty sure the expression was the man's default. He began to shiver from the huge temperature fluctuations his body was experiencing now that his own innate ability and the ghost were receding. He truly hated the let-down period. Masters took a fistful of Shane's shirt, holding him in place, and stepped a little too close for Shane's comfort.

"Focus on breathing normally. You're pale as a ghost."

Shane chuckled at the comparison, given the situation. Masters' narrowed his eyes.

"Have you completely lost it?"

"No." Shane twisted out of Masters' hold, careful not to make skin contact, and crossed his arms for warmth. "I told you the house is haunted. Megan's ghost was right behind you. She's hovering in front of Jacob's bedroom now."

Masters put his hands on his hips. "That's good, I guess, since she *is* the reason we're here."

"I expected an object with a memory attached, not a fully-formed breath-stealing apparition."

"Right," Masters huffed and then glanced over his shoulder. "Well, I don't see her, but you swear she's there so go talk to her."

Shane wanted to slap Masters across his handsome, skeptical face, but he was too cold to unfold his arms. For a psychic who could read memories and see ghosts, Shane really didn't handle fear well. It made him angry. Add a hefty dose of sarcastic disbelief from someone else and he was furious. Bella pressed into his leg reminding him of the job he needed to do. He turned on his heel, shaking his head and muttering under his breath.

You swear she's there. Go talk to her.

What the hell did Masters think Shane was, some kind of psychic medium? Sure, some ghosts could speak, but not all of them and Shane would never encourage that kind of interaction. It was bad enough he had to see them; he did not need their freakish voices in his head, too.

Unfortunately, short of reading Masters, Shane had no idea how to make a believer out of him. The hall was warming up and relief washed over him when he realized he could no longer see Megan at the other end of the hall. She was gone, for the moment.

"Not a fan of that idea, I gather," Masters said as he propped a shoulder against the molding of the doorframe and crossed his arms.

Shane tightened his grip on Bella's leash in preparation for entering the bedroom he was facing. "What the hell do you expect me to do here? Run a damn séance?" he snapped.

"I'm sure we could arrange one."

Shane glared at Masters. Despite the smirk on his face, Shane knew he wasn't joking. The idiot really would arrange a séance just to prove a point. Shane broke eye contact and stepped into the room. The entire room was fresh and overly feminine. Pink lace drapes were pulled open to reveal a red velvet window seat in the bay window overlooking the front lawn. Pink and red heart-shaped pillows were arranged neatly on the cushion. The bedroom was bathed in soft morning sunlight. A full-size bed sat in the middle of the wall to his left covered with a bedspread covered in red, white, and pink roses. Shane immediately knew the woman who'd inhabited the room was sensitive and spirited.

"This wasn't Megan's room," Shane mumbled.

The room was too soft and quiet to be associated with the ghost he'd encountered in the hall and Bella was too calm. Shane choked off a whimper as he moved toward the bedside table, the sudden urge to cry was overwhelming. In sharp contrast to the bright, airy décor of the room, there was a layer of intense sadness that coated it like dust. It permeated the walls and soaked through the floor. Next to the bedside table was a beautiful ornate roll-top desk. Tucked into one corner was a jewelry box with silver handles on the tiny drawers. He unfastened the thin clasp and lifted the lid.

Send In The Clowns filled the room with the disjointed clinks of a child's music box. A bright, multicolored juggler with red, yellow, and blue balls spun in the center. Memories of a similar music box his mother had owned when he was a child made Shane smile even as a tear slid down his cheek. He hummed along with the tune as he slid his fingertips of one hand along the string of pearls coiled inside while absently stroking Bella's ear. Shane gasped, the reason for the sadness becoming clear. He swiped the tear from his cheek before turning to face Masters, the flash of a heartbreaking memory still clear in his mind.

This had been Elizabeth's room.

She had kept a secret from everyone she had loved. Holding Masters' sharp gaze, Shane wondered if she'd taken that secret to the grave or if she had confided in the man she loved. Masters hadn't shifted from his seemingly relaxed pose against the doorframe, his expression blank. He seemed completely unaware that Shane had picked up a psychic reading from his long-dead girlfriend.

"Do you ever break?" Shane asked softly.

"Elucidate."

Shane smiled. He wasn't all that surprised Masters had used a word that was just shy of obsolete. "Do you ever find it impossible to keep everything in? Do you ever just break down and let the emotion bury you?"

Masters glanced around the room and then straightened. "I did once. Come on. Megan's room is across the hall."

Masters stepped into the hall, indicating the way with a sweep of his arm, and Shane ushered Bella across the hall ahead of him. The room he found himself in was the exact opposite of the one they'd just left. Where Elizabeth's room had been bright and airy in color scheme, this room was warm and subdued. The walls were covered in blue wallpaper with thin brown stripes. A dark brown suede comforter was folded over the foot of the bed and brown curtains covered in large blue flowers adorned the window overlooking the back yard. Alyssa was very color-coordinated in her decorating style. The complete lack of emotion stopped Shane's momentum just inside the door. He was knocked forward when Masters walked into the back of him.

"Damn it, Shane, don't stop in front of me like that."

Shane glanced around the room, one-hundred percent certain that Masters was testing him, and he didn't know how to react. The desire to slap him was back full force when Shane spun to face him.

"What the hell are you playing at?"

"What?" Masters crossed his arms over his chest, an imperious look on his face.

"This wasn't Megan's room, is what," Shane bit out. "There's nothing here."

"Room's full of furniture," Masters said, tone low.

"And not one piece of it belonged to Megan. See? I know that, because there's no psychic energy in this room at all. It's a guest room that's rarely used. And you are a liar."

Masters dropped his arms, hands fisting at his sides, as he stepped into Shane's personal space. Bella shuffled to the side with a whine, feeling the increase in tension that always seemed to be snapping just below the surface of every interaction between Shane and Masters.

"Excuse me?"

"You're a liar. You don't believe in my ability, fine, but don't waste my time by sending me in the wrong direction. I could help find Megan and the others if you'd get out of my way."

"I doubt that," Masters said, eyes narrowed and jaw tense.

"You want proof I'm real? I'll give you proof." Shane backed away and pointed to the room across the hall. "That was Elizabeth's room. I'm willing to bet that nothing in there has been changed since the day she died because everything reeks of pain and sadness. Not only because Elizabeth was hurting before she died, but because Alyssa goes in there and cries over the loss of her daughter more often than she'll admit."

Masters' eyes filled with a pain so brief that if Shane hadn't been looking directly into them, he would have missed it, and it stopped his angry tirade before he disclosed Elizabeth's secret. It took a moment of effort, but Shane was able to redirect his thoughts to the task at hand.

"I should have realized it before, and maybe if Megan's ghost hadn't freaked me out, I would have."

"What are you going on about, now?"

Shane stepped around Masters and tugged Bella out into the hall with him. He stared at the spot Megan had last manifested.

"If Jacob was just a baby when Megan moved here, she probably would have kept him in the room with her. After she disappeared, it would have been easier to keep him where he was. As Jacob got older, anything of his mother's would have been packed away to make room for a growing boy. Megan's not connected to a room or an object. She's connected to her son."

Shane closed his eyes and sighed. He really didn't like what he now knew he would have to do. Whispering to himself, he said, "I *do* have to talk to her."

Masters' footsteps followed Shane as he returned to Jacob's room with purpose. Best to get this over with as soon as possible. He had no doubt that Megan would show again, if she'd ever left. The cold spot was still present in the hall, thickest right in front of the door, and Bella pressed against his leg, emitting a sound that crossed between a whine and a growl. He stopped in the middle of the cold spot, gooseflesh dotting his exposed skin, and simply lifted his hand toward the door.

Contact didn't even have to be made before the air began to change, growing thin yet heavy. Shane felt like he was being pressed in on from all sides. Bella must have felt it too because her whines became louder. He stared straight ahead but paid more attention to what was within his peripheral vision. An intense shiver wracked his body as grey mist swirled between his outstretched hand and the door. Once the apparition became more solid, he turned his head and looked into the eyes of a woman who had been dead for over a decade.

Shane took an involuntary step back. This was the closet he had ever allowed himself to be to a cognizant ghost. It was uncomfortable. Once in a while he would step through a ghost that suddenly appeared, but they were simple loops — flashes of memory floating through space that ended quickly. Those apparitions weren't aware of objects or people around them. He would have an icky feeling when that kind of thing happened, but they continued on their way and so did he. There were no lasting effects. This situation was entirely different. This ghost stared directly into his eyes, clearly aware of his presence and his ability to detect her. Megan's expression became pleading, her mouth moving soundlessly as she attempted to communicate with him.

Glancing down the hall, Shane found Masters leaning against the railing of the stairs. He wore an expression of aggravation being suffered in silence. Shane took a deep breath, steeled himself, and returned his attention to the ghost that was minutely closer. He was going to do exactly what Masters had suggested earlier — he was going to talk to Megan — and he absolutely hated the idea. There was only one way that Shane knew of communicating with the dead. He rotated his outstretched hand palm up in invitation, allowing his ability to pour into his fingertips. Shane had the odd dual sensation of fire and ice as Megan's hand slipped into his.

———— *** ————

Frigid cold seeped into her back through the thinly-paneled concrete wall she leaned against. Her butt was already numb from the cold floor of the raised dais that appeared to have been a stage once upon a time. Dust-covered red velvet drapes were pulled to either side and secured to the wall with ornate hooks covered in rust. The scent of mold hung heavy in the stale air. The paneling on the walls was rotting in places and completely crumbling in others. Chunks of concrete and gold tin tiles had fallen from the ceiling and the hardwood floor was cracked beneath piles of dust and debris.

A massive chandelier that must have been magnificent at one time hung from the ceiling at a dangerous angle. Only two bulbs still worked, one of which was blinking erratically, casting the room in meager light and dancing shadows. It was only a matter of time before it went out completely. The final bulb would eventually follow and they would be left in total darkness. Fear rippled up her spine as thoughts of being buried alive tormented her. While they were not technically buried, they were trapped, and she knew they would die here.

Glancing around the room at the people trapped with her she saw men and women of the highest society dressed in their finest suits and gowns, adorned in their most expensive jewelry, reduced to bleeding, sobbing, terror-stricken animals as they faced inevitable death. A few sat with their backs to the walls, like her. Others against the long bar that extended the entire length of one wall. The grand mirror behind it appeared to have once reached all the way to the ceiling. It had long since shattered and shards of glass littered the top of the bar and the floor. Only a few ragged pieces still clung stubbornly to the gilded edging. A woman cowered in the corner, curled into a fetal position. The lighting and position made it difficult to know exactly who she was. She'd not moved in quite a while. No one had. *How many of us are already dead?*

Jackson, a man she thought she knew, a man she thought was Robert's friend, sat just a few feet away still holding the jagged piece of mirror in his hand. Dried blood covered the dirty glass, his fingers, and his clothes, but he continued to mutter to himself. The panic she'd initially felt when they first realized they were locked in, after repeated attempts at bashing in the heavy metal door had failed, surged through her. Every attempt at escape had failed. The panic had soon morphed into gut-wrenching loss. Her whole body tingled as it slowly went numb. She no longer had the strength to move — her muscles too cold and stiff to respond.

She lowered her gaze to the man draped across her lap, her hand still tightly clasped in his suit coat. She had removed it and balled it up, pressing it to his chest attempting to staunch the blood flow. Jackson had cut deep and high, straight into Robert's heart. Being trapped in this room notwithstanding, there would have been no saving him. Her heart seized up painfully in her chest. She loved him but had never told him. Now, he was dead and she would soon follow. She tried to scream, to cry out at the injustice, but nothing happened. Her body was shutting down.

There was no point in fighting. The lightheadedness she had felt from the moment Robert had been stabbed became dizziness. She felt the world tilting sharply to the side. Pain blossomed in her chest as she struggled to breathe. Her lungs ached and her brain screamed for her to take a breath. *Jacob, my sweet baby boy. Mommy loves you.* Her eyes drifted closed as the fatigue pulled her into the darkness of eternal sleep.

***

Shane snapped back to the present as he gasped for air. His chest was on fire, partly from the memory where there was a lack of oxygen, but mostly because a large German shepherd was lying across his body restricting his air flow. He felt the beginnings of a panic attack at having been trapped, holding his dead boyfriend's head in his lap.

No, he thought. *Not me. Megan.*

It had been Megan's last memory and the horror of it made his chest ache for a whole different reason. Rolling to his side to relieve the pressure on his ribs, he found a dark-brown linen-covered thigh in front of his face. It took long seconds for Shane to make sense of his surroundings, regain his bearings, but eventually he remembered the house he was in, saw that Masters was down on one knee, and became aware of Bella growling. Masters must have tried to touch him while he was down, but Bella had been trained to keep people away because piling one memory on top of another wasn't the least bit helpful.

"Don't touch me," Shane rasped out.

"Can't if I wanted to. Your damned mutt tried to bite me."

The clipped tone told Shane that Masters was pissed, but that was apparently the man's natural state of being so Shane ignored it. He had more pressing matters to deal with, like convincing his brain he wasn't on the verge of death and shoving his still-active ability back into the box. Shane slowly maneuvered his body upright as the aftereffects of the memory began to fade and his muscles remembered how to work. Thanks to Megan's memory, Shane had suffered hypothermia and slow suffocation — his entire body hurt. It was a little concerning that the pain in his chest wasn't receding and he wondered how long he'd gone without breathing.

Masters remained kneeling, watching with an expression Shane deciphered as concerned anger, as Shane shuffled across the floor to lean his back against the wall. The memory of having died in this position whipped through his mind and he began to shake. *Megan* had died like this, not him. *Megan*.

CHAPTER TWELVE

Footsteps sounded on the stairs, drawing closer as Alyssa joined them in the upstairs hallway. Shane rubbed his arms with shaky hands. The friction helped a bit, but this cold was bone deep, bleeding into his veins in place of the warmth as he pulled back on his gift. Alyssa stopped beside Shane, becoming a mirror image of Masters, each kneeling on either side of him. Bella whined as she rested her head on Shane's ankles.

"You're so pale, dear. What happened?" Alyssa asked.

Shane was suddenly overwhelmed by the urge to cry. He cupped his palms over his eyes, feeling the slight puffiness, and drew in shuddering breaths. His eyes stung with unshed tears. No matter what he did, he couldn't seem to push away the horrible memory of Megan's last moments. Despite the squeezing pain from the lack of oxygen, Shane wasn't completely certain that Megan hadn't frozen to death.

"Looked to me like he fainted," Masters answered.

Shane shook his head. "Fainted" didn't begin to describe what he'd experienced, but there was no way he was telling Alyssa that he'd just died, trapped inside a concrete bunker with her sister. Instead, he went with his typical, and believable, lie.

"I had a seizure," he said, motioning toward Bella. Most people didn't truly know what service dogs trained for seizures did.

Alyssa proved to be one of them when she muttered, "I see."

Telling people he had seizures and that Bella was a service dog had been Kennie's idea. He'd become incoherent one day, lost to a random memory in the grocery store of all places, and a bystander had mistakenly believed he was witnessing Shane having a grand mal. After Shane's first few professional psychic readings had ended with him being lifted off the floor by Kennie or the client he'd touched, Kennie had presented him with puppy Bella. Shane had learned quickly that Bella worked wonders as a grounding mechanism, keeping him physically and subconsciously aware of the world around him. It had been years since he'd last been overrun completely by a memory. Megan was one hell of a powerful spirit.

Masters extended a hand in an offer of help, but Shane shook his head. Touching that man was the last thing he needed right now. Shane twisted to his knees, got his feet under him, and stood up slowly. He felt weak, unsteady, so he leaned heavily on one shoulder against the wall. Masters and Alyssa rose with him. Alyssa wrung her hands together while Masters slid his into his pockets.

"You okay now?" Masters asked.

The expression Alyssa gave Masters was comical, making Shane smile despite everything going on with his mind and body. "Of course, he's not okay. He just had a seizure."

"I'm sorry to cut the visit short, but I don't feel well. Can we go?" Masters nodded and Shane turned to Alyssa. "Thank you for letting me look around. You have a beautiful home."

Alyssa beamed at the praise. Expecting one of them to reach for him, Shane tugged Bella to him by her leash, using her as a buffer of sorts, and kept her close to him for balance as he shuffled down the hall toward the stairs on stiff legs. Shane focused all his attention on making it down the stairs without falling, leaving Masters and Alyssa to follow. He'd made it to the door before he remembered the manners his parents had instilled in him and he turned to face his hostess.

"I'm going to go say bye to Jacob," Masters said before disappearing down the hall toward the back of the house leaving Shane alone with Alyssa.

Alyssa watched him go with a sad smile. "He's become a hard man, withdrawn and solitary. He used to be far more physically affectionate. Elizabeth's death changed him. But," she said with a clap of her hands and a far more cheerful smile spreading across her face. "He's dating you, now, isn't he? Keep getting him out and enjoying life again. Don't let him hide you away. Have him bring you back for dinner sometime soon."

Masters rejoined them in the foyer, catching Alyssa's final words and looking a bit pained. The mask of indifference Masters wore like a second skin slid effortlessly into place as Alyssa turned to face him. For the first time since arriving, it became apparent to Shane that if it weren't for the case and this family's connection to it, Masters might never have come back to this house. Perhaps for Masters to move on from his loss, he ultimately had to let go of the entire Sylvester family. It was a depressing yet natural occurrence that all involved would eventually accept. Alyssa enveloped Masters in a hug.

As they shared a whispered conversation, Shane led Bella outside to the front yard where he took a deep breath of fresh air and basked in the warmth of the sun hitting his face. In the open expanse of the outdoors the effects of Megan's last memory became less potent allowing Shane to relax.

Bella wanted to explore so Shane allowed her to pull him down the sidewalk. Children were playing down the street, their laughter and screeches echoing through the neighborhood. Across the street a sprinkler spun in circles with rhythmic ticks. So soon after experiencing death, everything felt odd, disconnected. Surreal.

He leaned against Masters' Beetle and reminded himself once again that it hadn't been real. It was just a memory. Despite how it felt, he himself had not actually died. Shane rubbed the back of his neck and then his forehead before dropping his hand to scratch Bella's back right above her tail where she liked it best. A particularly loud childish scream made Shane cringe. He had one hell of a migraine coming on.

Masters ambled down the sidewalk and came to a stop in front of Shane. This time when he lifted his hand to touch Shane, he didn't shy away. Masters smoothed his fingers over the back of Shane's head; the caress feather light. Shane squinted up at Masters as his fingers brushed over a particularly painful spot.

"Does your head hurt? You knocked it on the floor pretty hard."

"Guess that explains why the headache is worse than usual," Shane said, pressing two fingers to his temple.

Masters moved to unlock the passenger door. He waited for Bella to jump in the backseat before assisting Shane into the car. The headache was making him quite unsteady on his feet. Once he was buckled in and Masters had pulled away from the curb, Shane reclined his seat and closed his eyes. The exhaustion was too strong to fight and the movement of the car was making him a bit nauseous.

"Aftereffects of the seizure?" Masters asked.

"Never had one. Seemed like a good excuse for what happened. I'm just very tired and sick to my stomach," Shane mumbled.

"Don't puke in my car."

"Mm' kay."

They had a forty-five-minute drive ahead of them and Shane planned to nap the entire time. He willed his body to relax and slowly the soft purr of the engine lulled him to sleep. What seemed like seconds later, he was snapped awake as Masters slammed on the brakes, hurtling Bella into the back of Shane's seat. Masters had his arm between the seats in an attempt to hold the dog in place, albeit unsuccessfully.

"Sorry."

Shane adjusted his seat upright as Bella settled herself back onto the seat. He looked around trying to figure out what happened while fighting off the drowsiness from his nap and the adrenaline surge upon waking. They were stopped at a construction zone. In the time they'd been visiting the Sylvesters the construction crew had narrowed the two-lane highway to one lane, systematically alternating the westbound traffic with the east-bound. Shane had managed to sleep through the majority of the trip. Thunderhawk Motel was just a few miles further down the road. The westbound traffic was stopped as the eastbound vehicles were given their turn, so Masters threw the Beetle into park for the wait.

"Up for a little conversation?" Masters asked.

Shane rolled his head on the seat to look at Masters. He knew Masters wanted to discuss the events that unfolded at the Sylvester house, but Shane wasn't ready for that. "No," he answered, and was not at all surprised by Masters' response.

"Too bad."

"Why even ask then?" Shane held Masters' hard gaze for a few seconds before diverting his attention out the side window. The mountainside loomed above them; the jagged rocks supposedly being held in place by netting that seemed inconsequential, at best. An illusion of safety.

"Tell me how you met Luke."

That wasn't at all what Shane had been expecting and he glanced at Masters in confusion. A couple of birds caught his attention and Shane watched them flit around the stopped vehicles as he shifted his thought process to the topic of Luke. The birds disappeared over the cliff top leaving Shane without a distraction, so he stared at the construction crew, willing them to hurry up.

"Thought for sure Luke would've told you that already," Shane said.

Masters gave a one-shouldered shrug. "He told me he worked a case during which you were attacked but said the details were yours to give."

A construction worker signaled it was their turn so Masters shifted the car into drive and eased through the construction zone. Shane imagined he would have driven faster than necessary if it weren't for the pace car ahead of them, keeping speeds in the low tens. Masters muttered curses at the inconvenience while Shane thought about what to share and what to keep to himself. The details surrounding his introduction to Luke weren't something he liked to think about. Once they cleared the construction zone and the pace car u-turned, Masters increased his speed and returned to questioning Shane.

"What was his name?" Masters asked.

Shane shot him a glare. He briefly considered feigning ignorance, but Masters was a private investigator. He had no doubt he'd looked Shane up the moment Luke refused to give answers. Shane seriously doubted Masters didn't already have the information he wanted.

"His name was Brent, and I'm fairly certain you already knew that, so why ask?"

"I was attempting conversation—"

"Well, I don't want to talk about it."

"Fine. Let's discuss what just happened at the Sylvester house."

"For fuck's sake," Shane snapped. "Let's not. I have a bitch of a headache, I haven't eaten today, and I don't feel like being interrogated right now."

Shane's relief at seeing the Thunderhawk Motel sign up ahead was short-lived as Masters angrily jerked the car's wheel, launching them into the dirt parking lot much faster than Shane felt comfortable with. He slowed the car just as quickly and slammed the gearshift into park, but he didn't kill the engine. Shane glared at him as Bella pushed to her feet, whining and ready to get out. Luke exited cabin four with a stack of file folders and walked up to the passenger door. Shane was about to open the door to get out when Masters grabbed his arm.

"Luke and I have an errand to run. Get something to eat, take a nap, whatever, but do not leave that room. One of us will come get you later and we *will* discuss what happened."

Shane ignored both men as he got out of the Beetle. Bella followed closely and trotted beside him to the door of the cabin eight, dragging her leash through the dirt. Luke said nothing, testament to how well he knew Shane's moods, as he got into the car with Masters. Shane heard Luke's soft chuckle just as the car door thumped closed and then listened to the dirt and gravel being kicked up by their departure. Shane released the breath he'd been holding, instantly relieved at being away from Masters' prying eyes and probing questions.

Bella pressed her nose to the seam of the door, scratching at the wood and whining while Shane struggled with the stiff lock. When it finally popped open, Bella pushed her way inside excitedly. The dog's actions would have been warning enough if Shane hadn't been fighting a post-psychic headache. As it was, he entered the room and let out a decidedly un-manly scream.

CHAPTER THIRTEEN

Kendra Marks sat on the sofa with her feet tucked beneath her and looking completely out of place in the southwestern-themed room. Her straight black hair hung to her waist and was streaked with purple. Thick black eyeliner and dark red lipstick completed the look and made her blue eyes stand out. She smiled at him wickedly while tapping a blood-red fingernail against her bottle of beer. Bella jumped onto the sofa and rested her head on Kennie's knee. Shane gave the Tarot cards spread out on the coffee table a suspicious glance.

Shane closed and locked the cabin door. "I'm dying to know how you got in here," he said as he sidled his way to the table and flopped down in the chair. His muscles were becoming stiff and sore.

"I picked the lock because that hulk of a man in the office refused to give me a key."

"Of course, he did."

Leave it to Kennie to view common safety and security as an inconvenience. Shane and Kennie had been best friends since high school and had become business partners after college. They'd been an odd pair as teenagers and were still an odd pair as adults. The two of them couldn't be more different, yet they'd been drawn to each other because they were both psychic. Shane's natural curiosity combined with Kennie's impulsiveness and daring landed them in trouble quite often. Together they owned Crimson Moon Gifts, a metaphysical shop where they sold all sorts of new age stuff and offered psychic readings; Shane with his ability to pick up memories and Kennie predicting the future with her Tarot cards.

"Want a beer?" Kennie asked.

Shane eyed the bottle she was holding. "Beer would be good, but I don't have any. Didn't Thunderhawk see you breaking in?"

"You do now. I brought plenty. And he did catch me, but I was trying to get into cabin three. I kicked up a ruckus and Luke heard because he was right next door. He came out and vouched for me, and then he told me you were in cabin eight." Kennie clicked her tongue ring against her teeth in annoyance.

"That's probably why he was laughing earlier. He knew you were in here."

Shane would have to thank the man later with a slap across the face. Kennie pointed to his feet and Shane bent down to find a small cooler under the table. He winced at the painfully high-pitched squeak of the lid and pulled out a bottle. He twisted the cap off and downed half of it in one long pull.

"Why did you bring beer?" he asked. "It's not usually something you drink."

"But you do and I knew you'd need it."

Kennie gracefully slid to the floor between the sofa and the coffee table, unconcerned with the tight fit as she collected the Tarot cards and began shuffling them. Shane sighed and joined Kennie on the floor on the opposite side of the table. Kennie showing up unannounced with her Tarot cards didn't bode well.

"Why do I need it?" Shane asked, nerves spiking as Kennie laid out a few cards and studied them.

While he waited, he finished off his beer and them immediately regretted it. Masters had rushed him out this morning without breakfast and then subjected him to emotional upheaval and physical trauma. He'd slept on the drive back, but it wasn't nearly enough to stem the effects of a beer chugged on an empty stomach. His gut cramped and rolled, and he leaned against the TV stand with a moan.

"I was entertaining myself with the cards this morning and a vision of you intruded. I knew you were out this way, but not exactly where. Decided to just drive and look for that death trap you call a car." Kennie looked at him through heavily-lined lashes. "Do you have any idea how many hotels, motels, B and Bs, and lodges there are out here?"

"Yes," Shane answered with a chuckle.

He'd noticed the same thing while looking for Crystal Creek Hotel the night before. Shane adjusted himself on the floor so he could stretch his legs out beneath the coffee table, the toe of his shoe knocking against the tree stump masquerading as a couch leg.

"You could have saved yourself time and called," he suggested. "That is what phones are for, you know."

Kennie made a noncommittal sound and quirked her lips as she studied the cards on the table. "I don't like them."

Shane glanced down at the cards his friend was staring at so hard. They were arranged into a V formation but they made no sense to him. He didn't have Kennie's gift.

"The cards?" he asked.

"Phones." Kennie rolled her eyes upward to capture Shane's gaze. "He's not what he appears to be."

Shane blinked at her. He'd only had one beer, but he was feeling the effects. Following Kennie's line of thinking was difficult on normal days, and today was as far from normal as possible. He didn't even attempt the feat.

"Who?"

"The handsome blonde investigator."

Shane lifted his brows in surprise. While Kennie had already known he would be working with Luke, she hadn't known about Masters. Hell, even Shane hadn't known about Masters until the previous evening. His first thought was that Kennie had seen Masters just now when he'd swapped Shane and Bella for Luke, but the windows of his cabin didn't face the parking lot.

He shouldn't be surprised. His friend had always had the knack for knowing things she shouldn't. During their senior year of college, Kennie had shown up at Shane's dorm room door with whiskey in hand a full ten minutes *before* Shane's boyfriend called to break up with him.

Kennie smirked at him from the across the table. "Surprised I knew about him?"

Shane gave a one-shoulder shrug and then shook his head. Kennie tapped a blood-red fingernail on one card, and then another, before pressing firmly down on a third.

"You're picking up clues, but they're not what you think. You're looking for the wrong man...or maybe looking for him in the wrong way. I'm not quite sure."

Ignoring the ill-effects of drinking alcohol on an empty stomach, Shane pulled a second beer from the cooler. It was shaping up to be one hell of a case if the past twelve hours were any indication of what he should expect.

He took several deep swallows of the brew before setting the bottle down on the table, careful to keep clear of the cards.

"There's something not quite right about the building," Kennie said.

She shrugged as she leaned her head back onto the couch. Bella snuffled her hair and Kennie gently nudged her nose away. She straightened and picked up her beer, sipping at it, lost in thought.

"It certainly isn't a normal building," Shane agreed, remembering the activity outside and the eerie nothingness of inside. "What was it you said about the detective?"

"That he's not what he appears to be."

"And what exactly does that mean?"

Kennie shrugged in answer before chugging the remainder of her beer. She followed it with a distinctly un-ladylike belch.

"Wow. Felt that one in the floor," Shane said with a smile. It was a half-hearted attempt to lighten the mood.

"Shut up." Kennie chuckled.

"So, is he lying about his profession? Using an alias?" Shane pressed. He needed more information. He let out an exasperated sigh when Kennie shrugged again. "Well...while I enjoy your company, despite the near heart attack you gave me, you are of no help whatsoever."

"Call it as a I see it," Kennie said.

"You didn't see it very clearly, though, did you?" Shane grumbled.

"Like you're any better? Your visions are clear as mud."

Shane couldn't argue that. A person's memories were a biased impression of a moment in time, completely subjective. Their individual version of events. The memories came to him out of context and incomplete. Sometimes Shane would be successful in directing the person's focus onto a specific time period or one particular event, and he would get a decent memory, a sense of the emotions in that moment. If he wasn't successful, he could pick up any memory created during that person's life, whether it be five minutes before walking in the door to something that happened when they were two years old. His psychic gift was random and relatively uncontrollable. Kennie fiddled with the corner of a tarot card.

"I just get the sense he's hiding," she murmured. "But then I get that impression when I read you sometimes or even when I read myself."

"Really?"

"Yeah. It's not that we're truly hiding or even that we're lying. It's more like we're holding something back. Keeping something to ourselves," Kennie explained. "Everyone has secrets. Things we don't want to share."

"Okay. So, my detective isn't telling me everything. No real shock there."

Shane's words dripped sarcasm. From the moment Luke had introduced them, Masters had been testing him, holding information back to see if Shane could figure it out. Anger and annoyance tightened his gut. He noticed Kennie's shit-eating grin and he grew suspicious.

"What?" he asked and then drained the remainder of his second beer.

"*Your* detective?"

Shane groaned as he set his empty bottle on the coffee table. Leave it to his friend to latch onto a minor slip of the tongue. He'd set the bottle on an uneven knot in the wood table and it tipped over, landing on the rug with a soft thump. He ignored it as he mulled over the several missed opportunities to read Masters. Shane had had enough on his plate with Megan's ghost and the heavy emotions he'd picked up in Elizabeth's room that he'd deliberately avoided Masters at every turn. If he'd known ahead of time that Masters was holding information back, he might've made an exception.

"I should have taken his hand," Shane mumbled, staring at the bottle on the floor.

"He wanted to hold hands?"

"No, not like that. He wanted to help me up. I don't think he understands that I can see his memories if I touch him."

"Probably better that he doesn't. That way when you do touch him, he won't be masking his thoughts."

"Maybe."

Shane considered how controlled Masters appeared to be on the outside and wondered if his mind was just as regimented, or if the exterior hid a chaotic interior. God knew, he'd come across more than a few of those people in his life.

"Up from what?" Kennie asked.

Shane looked at his friend confused. "Has your train left the station without me again?"

"No, just switched tracks." She winked at him and then said, "He wanted to help you up from what?"

"Oh. The floor," Shane answered. Kennie smiled wickedly and nodded, crooking those maroon-tipped fingers in a give-me-the-salacious-details manner.

"Kennie."

She ignored his warning tone, braced her elbows on the table and rested her chin in her palms. She batted her heavily made-up blue eyes at him.

"Was he on top?"

Shane groaned. He knew how this conversation would go.

"Did he whip out the handcuffs?"

"Out of the gutter," Shane said with a laugh, knowing it would never happen.

Kennie's mind lived in the gutter. Her dirty, sarcastic humor was the one thing Shane could count on to pull him from a funk. With his depressed mood lifted a bit, he felt more comfortable letting Kennie in on the darkest event of the morning.

"I touched a ghost."

Kennie's expression went from happy to shocked in a second. Shane had never interacted with a ghost on that level before. Until Megan's ghost had touched him, it wasn't something either of them knew he could do. He still wasn't sure how he felt about it. His first instinct was to never repeat the experience and avoid all future possibilities where it could happen. He also knew that if it became necessary or would be beneficial, he would do it again.

"What was it like?" Kennie asked softly.

"The end result was me unconscious on the floor, for starters." Shane rubbed the sore spot on the back of his skull where he'd bumped it on the floor. "It was intense and terrifying."

"I guess now we know Bella can't keep you grounded when it comes to reading dead people. What possessed you to try such a thing, anyway?"

"I honestly didn't think it through. I just...did it."

Kennie leaned forward slightly. She looked like a little kid listening to an exciting bedtime tale. Little did she know it was actually a horror story.

"So, what did you see before you passed out?"

"Her death." Shane swallowed down the nausea those words elicited. "I experienced it. Like I was the one dying. The whole experience was terrifying and...overwhelming. I still feel it, Ken. I still feel like it happened to me instead of her."

"Damn," Kennie whispered. "How did she die?"

"I think she suffocated. There was no air in the room. I couldn't— I mean, *she* couldn't breathe." Shane wrapped his arms around his middle, remembering the chill of the room. "And it was really cold. The concrete was freezing."

"That's amazing."

"It really wasn't."

"Not her death, no. I mean the way the memory completely took over like that. To the point you could feel temperature? And the lack of oxygen? That's incredible. Usually your gift plays the memories like a movie and you're just watching it, but never like you were *actually there.*"

Shane stared at Kennie in disbelief. Why she thought she had to explain how his gift worked...to him...he'd never understand. He was well aware of how he typically received memories. He also knew that Megan's had been different. But so was the presence in the back bedroom of the caretaker's cottage. Shane had experienced that memory as though it were happening to him, rather than someone else, as well. It seemed everything remotely to do with these disappearances was more potent than usual.

"How did it happen?" Kennie asked, pulling Shane out of his unpleasant thoughts.

Shane sighed. He was exhausted on a cellular level. "You have got to start asking complete questions."

"How did this woman end up suffocating?" Kennie asked. "Strangled? Plastic bag over the head? Buried alive?"

"You are seriously macabre, and I don't know. She was in an old, rundown room. It looked like a barroom. It was weird, but Megan knew she was dying."

"Megan?"

"The ghost," Shane clarified. "Her name was Megan Granger. She died twelve years ago."

That was one thing Shane was absolutely certain of. The people he'd been hired to help find had died the night they disappeared. They walked out of that dining room straight to their deaths. He just needed to find out exactly where on the Crystal Creek Hotel property those deaths took place.

"How does someone suffocate in a barroom, Shane? That doesn't make sense."

"I don't know," he mumbled.

Shane couldn't explain how Megan and her companions had suffocated, only that they had. He had experienced it, and it wasn't something he ever wanted to do again. It was horrifying to have your body slowly shut down and be conscious of it; to know you're dying and not being able to do anything about it. Shane shuddered at the memory.

"I feel like I'm missing something," he said.

"There's plenty missing. Despite the power of it, it's still just a memory. A split second in time." Kennie lowered her palm onto the same card she'd been touching when she mentioned the hotel earlier. "There is something so wrong with that building. Everything is surrounded by a dense fog that I can't clear away enough to get a good reading. It's odd, and I don't have a good feeling about it."

Shane closed his eyes and let his body slide slowly down the wood panel of the TV stand until his shoulder hit the floor, and then he adjusted his upper body so he was on his back, waist twisted to the side and legs curled beneath the coffee table. He was hungry, tired, and his head throbbed. He slowed his breathing. Ignoring the rustle of movement in the room with him, he focused on the faint sound of a bird chirping somewhere outside. It was a quick meditation technique that he used often to re-center himself. The ache in his head dulled and his nerves settled a bit.

"Drama Queen," Kennie muttered.

Shane opened his eyes to see Kennie's face directly in front of his. His heart lurched in his chest at the unexpected closeness. She had draped herself over the coffee table on her stomach, balanced on the floor with one hand by his shoulder. She had her knees bent and her feet resting on the sofa near Bella's head. The German shepherd seemed completely uncaring that she was close to getting kicked in the face as she laid there staring at him with those soulful brown eyes.

"Get up," Kennie ordered.

"You first."

Kennie blew him a kiss then awkwardly adjusted her body on the table to once again get her feet on the floor. Shane watched as she humphed and grumped until she was finally sitting on the coffee table.

"Can this room possibly be any smaller?" she griped.

Shane glanced around as he sat up on the floor. "I imagine it could be, but so could the furniture. This stuff is too big for the space."

Kennie nodded her agreement as she reached forward to open the lid of the cooler. The squeak grated against Shane's nerves and did no favors for his headache. She handed him another bottle and then started shoving Bella's bulk to one end of the sofa to make room for herself. The dog shifted a bit, but apparently wasn't too keen on sharing her comfy spot with a human. Kennie gave the shepherd one more shove to the rump as she crossed her ankles on the coffee table.

"All right. Talk me through your mess. What did the room look like?" she asked.

Shane thought about that as he took a swallow of beer and watched Kennie gulp half of hers in one go.

"Well, first off, the hotel these people disappeared in...or from, is in bad shape so the fact the room was dilapidated fits. It was literally crumbling in pieces. It was empty for the most part but it had a bar with a huge mirror behind it and an old chandelier hung in the center of the dining area." Shane sighed and wiped a drop of condensation from the label. "I bet it was quite opulent back in the day."

"Maybe my first question should have been, why are you here? I might be able to help better if I knew what the main objective was."

"Oh, right."

Luke had only told Shane he needed help with a case but hadn't given any additional information so when Shane had taken a few days off from the shop, he'd only told Kennie what he knew he'd be working a case with Luke.

"Years ago, a lot of people went missing from the hotel across the highway. Luke hired me to help find them."

They spent the next several hours discussing the case and Shane's encounters with the ghosts of Megan Granger and Robert Grant. A fellow mystery nut, Kennie was as entranced as Shane with the fact that so many people could disappear so quickly and completely, without a speck of evidence as to where they'd gone or why. By the time Shane had finished relaying all the information he'd gained, they were both well into their fourth beer and had polished off the sandwiches and the bag of nacho chips Kennie had brought. Shane realized he really didn't know all that much, but Kennie wanted every detail he could pull from his head about the memories he'd received. He kept what he'd received inside Elizabeth's room to himself; that memory belonged to Masters. Some memories, because of their intimate or emotional nature, were far too personal to be shared.

"This is such an awesome mystery," Kennie said. "I mean, it's sad and all, but wow. How do fifteen people just walk out of a room and disappear without a trace? And rich people, at that. How does something like that happen? If these people were as rich and powerful as Luke says, you'd think the cops wouldn't ease up, like, ever."

"I don't know," Shane said. "I'd expect the families to keep hounding, but they haven't. Megan Granger's own sister asked Masters to let it be."

"Someone cares. The someone who hired Luke," Kennie pointed out.

Shane nodded his head in agreement.

"Almost feels like there's hush money involved, doesn't it?" Kennie asked, drawing Shane's gaze to her face. "They disappear, but nothing at all is found? It's odd."

"It is."

Shane agreed wholeheartedly that the case was strange. Nothing about it had felt normal, but he'd chalked that up to the location being creepy, the scenario being unusual, and the ghosts being excessively touchy-feely. The idea that the police could be bought didn't sit well with him. He also didn't like the idea that the authorities had simply not cared enough to truly look into the disappearances. What truly bothered him was that either one or both of those ideas might well be true. Shane knew that Luke and Masters would be looking into the missing people's pasts, digging up secrets, and if there was a reason for hush money, they'd find it.

"So, when are we going?" Kennie asked, drawing Shane from his thoughts.

"Where?" he asked.

"To the hotel. We're not going to find these people sitting on our butts drinking beer."

"I was just there last night and didn't find anything. There's a ton of ghost activity outside, but not a thing inside. Except for that ear-piercing scream from the elevator." He'd already told her about Robert haunting the parking lot. "Oh, and there was a horrendous murder inside the caretaker's cottage. Don't go in there," he added.

"Gee. I can see how that was a complete bust."

Shane narrowed his eyes at her sarcasm. That hotel was all wrong and Shane would be just fine if he never set foot inside it again.

"It *was* a bust. I was looking for missing people, not a dismemberment or whatever that was in the elevator or any of that other stuff."

Kennie grabbed the trash can from the bathroom and started putting the empty food wrappers and bottles into it, face tightened in thought.

"Maybe the hotel wasn't helpful because the ghosts aren't actually inside it," she said, replacing the trash can in the bathroom. "Robert's ghost is *outside* and Megan's ghost is at *home*. Who knows where the others are or if they're even ghosts at all. Not everyone who dies becomes one."

"No, but I'm not looking for ghosts. I'm looking for memories, and everyone has those. That hotel should have thousands of memories inside it, and there aren't *any*."

Kennie flopped back down onto the sofa and rested her chin in her hands. "Well, those people disappeared somewhere, and according to Megan's ghost that somewhere is a rundown room and, going off the evidence your detective provided, that room is most likely inside the hotel."

"There's no reason to go back there. Ever," Shane said. The comment was completely ignored by Kennie, assuming she'd even heard it.

"You said it yourself. Suffocation is a horrible way to die. And if Megan's memory shows that all of them died that way... God, Shane. That's an intense memory you should've been able to pick up."

Shane had to agree with that, and he had no idea why he'd not been able to. He understood the point Kennie was trying to make, he just didn't like it. It meant he'd have to go back to Crystal Creek Hotel and that didn't settle well.

"In my defense, I didn't have a clue what I was looking for when I was there the first time. Masters kind of put me on the spot. It wasn't until a few hours ago that I learned they'd suffocated."

Shane groaned as he remembered last night. He'd only walked a narrow path and touched one wall. While those areas had been devoid of memories, Luke and Masters hadn't given him a grand tour of the place. There was a whole lot of the hotel he'd not seen and that meant a lot of memories he'd not opened himself to. There were four more floors and several dozen rooms of dark and creepy he'd yet to explore.

"But you know now and maybe knowing that feeling is all you need in order to locate memories where the feeling is the same," Kennie suggested.

That was not an appealing thought. Shane winced even as he nodded in agreement. They were going back to Crystal Creek Hotel. At least this time he'd be in better company. Kennie was infinitely more understanding, supportive, and fun than Masters could ever hope to be. Shane took pleasure from knowing that Masters would be furious when he and Luke returned from their errand to find Shane wasn't there. Shane would not be at Masters' beck and call. He wasn't going to play by Masters' rules. Luke should've warned his partner about Shane better.

CHAPTER FOURTEEN

Shane's head still throbbed slightly, but the food Kennie had brought with her had helped. He needed a nap, but that would have to wait. They'd barely made it across the wood and metal bridge when Masters' Beetle had pulled into the Thunderhawk lot. It had been interesting trying to get Bella to stay hidden among the underbrush where Shane and Kennie had ducked out of sight. Eventually, Luke and Masters might realize where they were, but they didn't want to get caught just yet. Shane bit his lip when Masters got out of the car and went straight for Shane's cabin.

"Shit."

"Relax," Kennie said from her position hunched down beside him.

"Easy for you to say. You haven't had to deal with the ass," Shane grumbled.

"Can't see him very well. Seems to be nicely dressed. Is he handsome?"

"Gorgeous," Shane answered.

Bella whined at a gray mist that appeared and disappeared, a barely-there ghost that whispered past them. Shane pulled her against him and muzzled her with his hand. Her bark would draw unwanted attention. Masters gave up on Shane's cabin when there was no answer to his knock and went to Luke's where the two men had a discussion before Masters disappeared into his own room. Hopefully, they both thought Shane was sleeping off his psychic hangover.

"Now or never," Kennie said.

They both rose to their feet and hurried toward the hotel. They slowed their pace once they reached the hotel's gravel lot. Kennie took in the massive structure much the same way Shane had the day before. Her mouth hung open in awe and her eyes were huge as she took in the towering hotel. In the early afternoon sunlight, the hotel looked a little less frightening, though Shane could still see it being cast as the location in some horror movie.

They ascended the stairs to the double front doors and stopped at the porch. Kennie ran her fingertips over the brass door handle. Shane took a deep breath and strengthened the containment around his abilities. He was already uncomfortable, feeling tendrils of memories bumping into his psyche. It was strange that he hadn't experienced that feeling the day before.

"What kind of security system is in place?" Kennie asked.

"Are you joking? You are standing in front of the same derelict hotel I am, right?"

Kennie looked around the porch, taking in the piles of debris and the crumbling shutters. "Good point. Okay. Let's do this."

Shane and Kennie placed their hands on the doors and pushed. The wood scraped along the flooring and the hinges squeaked loudly. Kennie walked into the expansive lobby and looked around while Shane stared at the door, trying to remember if it had sounded like that when he'd opened it last night. In the bright light of day nothing seemed to be the same and he was questioning his own memories. This was the first time Shane was uncertain exactly what he'd experienced. It didn't feel good.

Bella pulled on the leash, trying to follow Kennie, so Shane closed the door and let himself be tugged across the lobby. Kennie moved to the center of the room slowly, taking in her surroundings. Shane took the opportunity to look around the room again, overlapping what he'd seen the night before with what he was seeing now and once again imagined the place when it was new.

Shadows still stretched across the floor and walls, but the objects casting them were more easily seen in the hazy light that filtered through the dirty windows. Shane wouldn't have thought it possible, but the place actually looked worse in the light. Smells he hadn't noticed before assailed his nostrils. He recalled the air inside being old and stale, but he didn't remember the cloying scent of rot, mold, and something probably best left unidentified. Shane shuddered at how many small animals might have crawled inside and died over the years. He vowed not to let Bella off her leash again lest she find the carcass of some dead thing somewhere.

"So...this is creepy," Kennie said, voice a dull echo in the room. "But I can still imagine what it was like when it was first built. Colors still bright. Fresh scents and shiny metal."

"I can visualize the image, not the smell. I don't remember the place stinking so much."

"How old do you think it is?"

"I don't know. Not enough of the décor left for me to guess."

"It has that overdone grandiosity of the late 1800s, don't you think? Reminds me of the hotels down in the Springs," Kennie said.

Shane shrugged. "Maybe."

He and Bella followed Kennie as she navigated the piles of leaves, plaster, and wood to the registration desk. She placed her purse on the counter and removed two flashlights. They were small and lightweight and probably wouldn't offer nearly the amount of illumination Shane knew he'd want. If Masters' spotlight hadn't been able to hold back the shadows, these were certain to be useless. Kennie handed one to Shane, looped her purse strap across her chest, and then clicked her flashlight on. As Shane feared, the beam of light did nothing to dispel the shadows they were near. Kennie shrugged and clicked it back off.

"I'm not feeling great about this," Shane said, fidgeting with Bella's leash. "Why did you even bring flashlights?" he asked.

It was a bright, clear mid-October day. Plenty of light to see by filtered in through the dingy windows. They could see fine.

"The cards showed us surrounded by darkness. I took it literally, but maybe it was just metaphoric," Kennie answered.

Shane looked around the room once again. The muted daylight peeked from under the closed double doors at one end of the room. On the other end, where the double doors were opened to the space beyond, the tin ceiling tiles glowed dimly, as did the gilt edging of the elevator. Dust motes could be seen dancing in the air, illuminated by rays of light. Shane refused to think about what they might be breathing in.

"Now that we're at the scene, tell me about the night everyone disappeared," Kennie said.

"Okay. The fundraiser took place at night. Not something I would have done, but Robert Grant did, so whatever," Shane said.

"Was he trying to scare the money from their pockets?"

Shane adored his friend's attempt at humor, but it did nothing to dispel his nerves. He smiled and shook his head. Kennie smiled back at him.

"I assume these people came in the same front door we did. Where were they headed?" Kennie asked.

"There's a dining room at the back of the hotel. That's where the dinner was to take place. There are some narrow stairs, almost like servant access, hidden from view on the other side of the elevator. That's the way Luke and Masters took me so I assume that's the way the guests got there, too."

"I wouldn't make that assumption," Kennie disagreed. "He's having a fundraiser to get money from rich people to renovate. He'd want to show the place off. Servant access stairs wouldn't do that." Kennie turned and pointed behind her. "But the grand staircase would."

Shane took that idea and rolled it around in his head as he glanced back at the main entryway. The floor had been cleared of debris in a much wider path from the doors to the grand staircase, but the walk to the elevator was much more cramped. He turned back to Kennie and nodded in agreement with her assessment.

"Luke and Masters said Robert had the dining room and kitchen wired for electricity so he could do the dinner on site, but they didn't say anything about the entryway. There had to have been some kind of lighting or they wouldn't know where to walk to avoid the piles of trash and debris," Shane said.

"I find it interesting the trash and debris is in piles at all. Inanimate objects don't pile themselves into neat little heaps. He must have cleaned," Kennie stated, hands on hips as she took in the hem of her skirt. "He wouldn't want rich people in expensive clothing wading through dirt and what-all. Look at my skirt."

Shane took in the dark-purple velvet covered in a good layer of dust. He glanced at his own clothing and noticed his jeans and tennis shoes had shared the same fate, though far less noticeable. His clothing could be brushed clean with a swipe of the hand; Kennie's would probably require dry cleaning. Kennie took the first few steps of the grand staircase without hesitation before turning to smile down at Shane. Bella had attempted to follow Kennie and was now tugging at the end of her leash, whining.

With a twitch of her head, Kennie said, "After you."

"What?" Shane squeaked and then cleared his throat. The sound had been slightly embarrassing.

"Let Bella lead," Kennie said. "Dogs are supposed to be great at sensing danger and she's sure-footed. I suggest only stepping where she steps, though. These stairs are a death trap."

Shane took in the staircase one step at a time, following the tight curve that ended overhead at the second floor. The creases and corners of each stair were crowded with dirt, plaster, and cobwebs. What carpeting could be seen underneath was worn thin. One of the stairs about halfway up was completely missing; the rotted boards hanging from each side on bent nails. Shane grumbled under his breath as he joined Kennie and Bella, stopping next to his friend.

"This whole building is a death trap," he informed her.

Kennie shrugged. "Come on, mystic boy, open the box. Let the memory catcher free."

Shane looked at her and wondered if she'd been possessed. Because he'd thought his best friend would never suggest something so dangerous.

"Have you gone completely insane?" Shane snapped. Kennie raised her eyebrows. "There is no way in hell I can navigate these damn stairs and deal with psychic visions at the same time."

"Excuse me, but we could be walking over fifteen dead bodies right now and not even know it because you're buttoned up tighter than a nun's habit. Christ, Shane. You honestly think I'm going to let you fall through a hole?"

Shane huffed and returned his attention to the staircase. Neither Kennie nor Bella had led him wrong so far so he put his trust in them. He let the tight barrier he'd erected around his gift fall away like the eroding walls of Crystal Creek Hotel. Warmth spread through his body making him overly warm. The staircase tilted precariously beneath his feet and he swayed, but Kennie caught his elbow and guided him up the steps.

He was faced with conflicting desires. On one hand, he wanted this visit to be successful so he could return to Luke and Masters with some kind of information that would lead them to the missing people. And in the process, prove to Masters he wasn't a fraud. On the other hand, he was truly terrified of what memories or other ghosts he might encounter. He slid his palm along the thick wooden banister as they carefully ascended, his gift flowing through his fingertips. It was quiet and serene until they neared the second-floor landing; the dam burst and Shane was immersed in a whirlpool of sight, sound, and emotion.

Half lunging, half tripping, Shane took the final two steps and then slammed his back against the wall of the hallway. He pulled on Bella's leash until her body bumped up against his knees. Looping his fingers through her collar, he took deliberate, measured breaths as he attempted to make sense of what was real and what was memory. The leather of Bella's collar was real. The wall at his back was solid. The rest was a swirling mass of overlapping memories. Hundreds of voices were talking at once. Colors and movement made him dizzy and he felt like the world tilted. Shane tried to find something to focus on, but just when he thought he had it, the memory slipped away.

It was comforting and annoying and nauseating that he'd stumbled into the chaos he'd been expecting to find the night before when he'd opened himself to the dining room. Shane cursed himself for allowing the void he'd experienced prior to let him believe the rest of the hotel would be the same. He'd had a false sense of reality and therefore wasn't prepared for the onslaught. Not completely. He pulled back on his gift as much as possible, sliding some of his barriers back into place. He needed to regain at least some control and readjust his expectations before diving back into the murky waters.

The sights and sounds of a dozen decades blurred together to become a dull roar in his head. Shane's ability was almost completely locked down, and still the memories charged at him. Using Bella for balance, he pushed away from the wall, hoping to sever contact and stem the flow, but it had little effect. Kennie passed him as she walked a short distance down the dilapidated hall. Shane was still trying to find his equilibrium. He blinked.

An expensive tuxedo pulled at his shoulders. The tailor hadn't gotten the measurement quite right, but it was too late to get it fixed now. A slender arm looped through his. He smiled at the beautiful blond, covered chest to thigh in silver tassels. She had insisted the flapper dress was the height of fashion. The plush carpet sank beneath his feet with every step and the sconces on the wall cast a dim glow over the patterned wallpaper. Gold-plated numbers adorned each of the dark-wood doors.

Blink.

Her back hurt. This was the eighteenth trip to this floor today. The guests were so demanding and unappreciative, but she needed the money. The linens she carried weren't light, but she'd stacked them as high as possible to decrease the number of times she had to squeeze down the tight servant stairs. Her long, dark fingers were a stark contrast to the white of the sheets. A man bumped her into the wall, but continued on his way without a glance. She glared after the man in his rich clothes and wondered once again what it would take to burn the hotel down. She'd be released from her duty then; able to find work elsewhere.

Blink.

Kennie stood in front of him and he reared back in surprise at her proximity. She held his face in her hands, staring into his eyes. He focused intently on her face, at the thick eyeliner around her blue eyes and the curious tilt to one corner of her mouth. Anything to keep from blinking again. Eventually nature would take over and his eyelids would close of their own accord, but he'd fight it as long as possible. He stroked his fingers over Bella's head and ears.

"Are you back with me now?" Kennie asked.

"For the moment. I hate this. I can't control any of it."

"Keep looking at me. I'll keep my mind clear."

It was then that he realized how Kennie had managed to pull him out of the deluge of memories — she was touching him, skin to skin. Shane sighed in relief. Kennie began walking backward down the hall, tugging Shane along with her by his chin. She remained calm and kept her mind gloriously blank. Bella stuck close to his side.

"Has it ever been this bad before?"

"Only in the beginning before I learned how to box it up. I don't understand what the hell is going on around here. I initiated it yesterday and got nothing except the shadows and low-level ghosts I always pick up on. Now, I'm getting inundated by memories despite the fact I've shut it down."

"You've never been able to completely shut it down. There's always some of it coursing through your veins. That's why you can see the shadows and low-level ghosts all the time. The memories here must be strong enough or just numerous enough to trip that tiny thread of psychic ability."

They moved further down the hall and Shane felt the power behind the memories ebb slightly. Bella moved away a few inches to sniff at some debris on the floor near one of the room doors. Shane kept his attention on Kennie, but his eyes were beginning to burn from forcing them to stay open. He felt the blink coming just seconds before it happened.

The world tilted as she was dipped backwards. The arm wrapped around her waist was just as strong and trustworthy as ever. Joy and nerves warred with each other in her gut, and her heart raced as he bestowed her very first kiss. She would never understand what she had done to deserve the attentions of a wealthy, older man. God knew there were far more beautiful women at the party; certainly more sophisticated and worldly women than herself. But he had chosen her. He'd asked her to dance and hadn't let go of her since. He pulled her closer and she opened her mouth to allow him to deepen the kiss. She threaded her fingers through his salt-and-pepper hair the way she'd seen other girls do, and fantasized about what the remainder of the night might bring.

Shane stumbled as the memory abruptly ended. His brain was convinced he was still tipped backward in a man's arms, but his body was upright and the momentary confusion made him dizzy. For a terrifying moment, he lost his vision and hearing. It was something that happened on rare occasion when the memories overloaded his brain's ability to differentiate sensory input. At least, that was how Shane described it to outsiders. The past few minutes definitely qualified as overload.

He pitched forward again and Kennie grabbed his shoulders to steady him. Bella whined when the movement yanked on her collar. Shane didn't even remember wrapping his hand around it again. The return of his eyesight was only seconds behind his hearing. Attempting to get his bearings, Shane looked at his surroundings to find they were in the dining room where he, Luke and Masters had been the night before. That explained the abrupt end to the memory.

CHAPTER FIFTEEN

The view of the cliff behind the hotel through the floor-to-ceiling windows was just as breathtaking at mid-day as it was with the sun setting behind it. The table and chairs were still situated in the center of the room. Kennie led him to a chair and he eased into it. Shane felt as battered and worn as the hotel. He scratched Bella's ears before releasing a length of leash so she could explore a little. The room was still the void it was before, but for once he was grateful for that because the rest of the hotel was very much alive. Now that Shane knew what to expect, he'd be more prepared when they left this room again. He hoped. He was shocked to learn he'd somehow missed being hit by all of this the first trip out here with Masters and Luke.

"I hate feeling disoriented," Shane murmured. "I still don't understand why this room is void."

"No memories at all?" Kennie asked. "Interesting."

While Shane sat recovering, Kennie wandered around the room. She stepped behind the bar, ducking out of sight momentarily before moving to stand in front the large windows. She took in the landscape behind the hotel and then disappeared through the door Shane had been told led to the kitchen. Shane took the quiet time to erect and strengthen a psychic shield around himself, and then focused his ability down into the palms and fingertips of both hands which would allow some modicum of control.

Shane hadn't encountered psychic activity strong or numerous enough to require this level of protection in years. The shield would take a lot of mental energy to keep up because it was still his ability, just used in a different way. Any amount of effort was worth it to keep the memories infesting the hotel from dropping him on the spot. Shane and Kennie had discovered the shield while experimenting with his ability during college. All he had to do was take the mental box he usually shoved his gift into and with exhalation, imagined the box growing larger, expanding it until he encompassed his entire body. His body hummed with psychic energy as it coursed through his veins. There was no need to hinder the flow because the "box" kept his ability from touching the memories until he was ready. When the time came, he would reach outside the box, allowing the memories to wash over his hand.

Convinced his protection was solidly in place, Shane was ready to take on Crystal Creek.

Kennie crossed the room to stand before Shane. "You are exerting some serious power, mister. I can feel it."

"Because you're brushing up against it. Take a step back."

Shane narrowed his eyes as Kennie complied with an exaggerated step backward.

"So, while I was on a self-guided tour of the creepy kitchen, which is directly beneath us, by the way, I got to thinking —"

"Dangerous thing, that."

"Why throw a fundraiser here? I mean, this isn't exactly the Ritz."

Shane couldn't agree more, but what bothered him more than the chosen location, was that the guests suddenly felt the need to leave. "The guys told me Grant had the fundraiser here because he wanted everyone to see what their money would be used for, but I don't understand why they would leave the one room he'd actually renovated."

"Grand tour of the macabre? Were they into that sort of thing?"

"What sort of thing?"

"The occult. I mean, yes, this hotel is massive and renovating it would cost a small fortune, but if this dude and his rich friends were into macabre, paranormal shit, then a tour of an abandoned, five-story hotel would be *the* number one agenda. The money he needed to make this place habitable would've been secondary."

"Grand tour," Shane mumbled. "That would explain why they all left the room at the same time and we already know why they didn't come back, but it still doesn't tell me *where they are*." Shane's voice was loud and exasperated, echoing off the walls.

"Calm down, dude. Jesus! Obviously, you are not thinking clearly or you would have realized by now that your missing people may have left this room, but they never left this hotel. They died here and their bodies are still somewhere in this building."

Shane held Kennie's gaze as that little seed planted itself deep in his brain. Was it possible the fifteen missing people were still inside the building? How had they not been found during the initial investigation over a decade earlier? Did the police even truly look for them? Shane swallowed thickly around the lump in his throat. Bella rested her head on his knees, sensing his discomfort. Shane rubbed between the dog's ears to comfort both of them. With the back of his hand, he wiped the fine sheen of sweat from his forehead. Psychic energy was pulsing through his body, raising his temperature and making him tired with each passing second.

"We need to get moving. Keeping this shield up is making me hot and tired, and I'm already in for one killer migraine when this little fieldtrip is over."

"Okay." Kennie nodded and spread her arms out to her sides. "They come in here, have cocktails and appetizers before they leave the room *en masse*."

"And take Robert Grant's Grand Tour of the Macabre...assuming that's what happened," Shane added, tilting his head.

"How soon after the disappearance were the cops called?" Kennie asked, hands now on her hips.

"According to the police report Luke gave me, it wasn't until two days later when the CEOs attending this fundraiser didn't show up at their offices for work the following Monday. The report says police searched this entire building but didn't find anything." Shane shook his head again. "If those people are still here, in this hotel, I wonder just how thorough the cops really were."

"In their defense, we haven't been anywhere but the lobby, kitchen, and dining room. Who knows what conditions they were dealing with, or what we may find when we go on our own Grand Tour."

"True. Anyway, they searched homes, businesses, and the cars that were still parked in the lot out front. Even the damn catering truck was still parked at the door to the kitchen out back. Detectives talked to friends, family, and enemies. No leads. No witnesses. The case basically went nowhere. There's probably a lot more to that report, but I was reading it while brushing my teeth before bed and I'd already taken a sleeping pill."

Kennie twisted her long hair on top of her head, heaved a dramatic sigh, and then released her hair to tumble down around shoulders. "The cards said there was something odd about the hotel and, I don't know, I have this overwhelming sense that those people are here, somewhere in this building."

"Without leads or witnesses the case went cold. What I find interesting, among a whole list of other things, is that Megan's family wants to leave it cold."

"Frustrating," she muttered.

Kennie glanced at Shane and then walked around him and Bella, past the elevator, to an entryway Shane hadn't noticed until she disappeared through it. He snaked his fingers beneath Bella's collar and then followed Kennie's lead. During the onslaught, Shane hadn't been able to differentiate between real and remembered, but this time he was able to see the long, narrow hallway connecting the dining room to the main hallway of the hotel. He took his time, taking in the peeling, decayed wallpaper, the worn carpet, and remembered a kiss that had stolen his breath. Shane blinked away the memory that wasn't his and refocused his thoughts onto the task at hand. He stared down at the floor, taking each step carefully. The last thing he needed was to fall through rotted floorboards because he was distracted.

The narrow, doorless hallway only continued for about twenty feet before abruptly widening to the first floor of the hotel with numbered doors on each side. Shane could see the grand staircase railing to the left, three doors down. He glanced over his shoulder at the corridor he'd just exited. The way the rooms were detached from the rest of the hotel made Shane think the dining room and kitchen were an afterthought, slapped onto the side of the hotel haphazardly when it occurred to the construction crew a crucial element had been missed.

The rooms were all but hidden to the back and side. The stairs leading to the dining room had been narrow as well and weren't readily visible from the lobby. The hallway itself gave no indication that it led anywhere guests would want to go, appearing more utilitarian than inviting, and that was assuming anyone ventured that far. Kennie had stopped at the landing of the grand staircase, waiting and watching him.

"Nothing indicates where this funky hallway goes. How did you know it led to the dining room?" Shane asked.

"My amazing powers of deduction," she answered. "You said the servant stairs leading up to the dining room were on the other side of the elevator. The elevator is tucked into that corner just behind you. Now get your butt moving. We have an entire hotel to get through before you collapse from fatigue."

Shane followed Kennie across the landing and down the hall on the other side, stopping every so often for Kennie to stick her head into doorless rooms along the left wall while Shane gave into his own curiosity and did the same with the rooms on the right. He kept Bella's leash short and his hands close to his body. A few shadows and soft white wisps moved among the debris. Some had a malevolent aura to them, but none held the power of the spirits in the caretaker's cottage he'd experienced the day before.

They systematically made their way through the second floor; the entire time Shane puzzled over the fact that the lobby and dining room, two public rooms that should have been overwhelmed with ghostly activity because everyone would have passed through them, were void. It was odd that the individual rooms were more active.

At the end of the hall was another narrow stairwell used by staff and servants to access all the floors of the hotel while remaining largely out of sight. Knowing what he knew of the time period when Crystal Creek was built, the servant stairs would end at a smaller, tighter top floor not visible from the ground where the servants of guests would have lodged while their bosses enjoyed the luxury of the lower floors.

"Let's head back to the main staircase and go to the next floor from there," Shane suggested.

Kennie nodded in agreement and they headed back down the hall. As they neared the main stairs, Shane extended a hand beyond his shield and gently brushed over a few memories created when the hotel was new, filled with light and life. He didn't allow himself to sink into those memories; they weren't the ones he was looking for. He was looking for the memories created when the hotel had already fallen into disrepair. Those were the memories most likely to belong to Robert Grant and the other missing people.

"I wonder what those people saw," Kennie said, her voice distant to Shane's ears. He pulled away from a memory filled with laughter to focus on what was being said to him. Kennie stood as close to the railing as she dared, looking up into the cone the curving staircase created. "Do you think they saw the beauty Crystal Creek used to be or the wreck it's become? Did they see the possibility of what this hotel could become with enough money, time, and dedication?"

"I don't know," Shane answered, though he knew the questions were of the rhetorical variety.

Kennie was musing out loud. Shane's eyes were drawn to the dirty stained-glass window overlooking the landing. The sun was making a valiant effort to push through the grime to paint the stairs in a rainbow of muted colors. The window was a beautiful work of art despite the filth coating the panes. There were similar windows on each of the landings as they explored the third and fourth floors. Shane moved faster through the mid floors, finding the activity was the same as the previous levels. All the memories Shane encountered were from a happier, livelier time in the hotel's history.

The light streaming through the smaller stained-glass window of the fourth floor was far dimmer and Shane wondered if it was due to thicker dirt coating the glass, or if the sun going down. He didn't relish the idea of being inside Crystal Creek after dark. Over the years his experiences with the paranormal seemed to be stronger and less pleasant once darkness fell. The higher they went, the smaller and more cramped the rooms and halls became, but from what he could tell, the rooms were still as luxuriously furnished as the more expansive lower floors.

Kennie followed Shane and Bella up the stairs to the fifth and final floor. There was no stained-glass above the stairs and the hall was noticeably darker than the floors below. Shane attributed the darkness to the incredibly tight spaces the spirits inhabiting this floor were bound to. The memories and apparitions overlapped each other, creating a dense fog of energy Shane was not looking forward to pushing through. Bella pressed against his leg but remained quiet. The energy here was heavy, but Bella wasn't whining so Shane figured it was quantity rather than malevolence creating the darkness swirling before him.

There were more doorways lining the narrow hall, several having the appearance of communal living. The ceiling was lower on this floor as well. If the intent was to hide the fifth floor, the builders had succeeded. Shane had caught a glimpse of the top floor through the trees as he'd driven across the bridge, but it was all but invisible from the lot. The servant stairs that had been discretely hidden behind a wall on the other floors was blatantly visible on this floor, only a plain iron railing demarcating the hole in the floor where the stairs descended.

"This is...claustrophobic," Kennie said. They stood side by side, Bella between them, looking down the hall.

"The floor reserved for *the help*," Shane said. "The guests who stayed in these rooms would have had no illusions as to their status in the world." Or their place among the hierarchy of the hotel.

A small hole in the roof toward the back of the hotel allowed a cool breeze into the cramped space. Shane moved closer to it and breathed in the fresh, clean air. Only then did he notice how heavy and putrid the air in the rest of the hotel had been. Shane's overheated skin pebbled as the much colder air caressed him and he shivered. He pulled his damp T-shirt away from his torso allowing the cold breeze to hit more of his sweat-slick skin. Kennie rubbed Bella's ears and then ventured down the hall a little way while Shane glanced around his immediate area.

Insulation bulged through holes in the walls and piping could be seen where parts of the walls and ceiling had completely disintegrated. He imagined this floor had been low on the maintenance list, the lower floors taking priority, which no doubt contributed to the advanced state of decay he was seeing. Shane reached out and felt the gamut of emotions rolling through the air. A soft white globe of light hovered just inside the room across from him, but the feelings he got from it were benign. Kennie looked back at him as he wiped a trail of sweat from his forehead before it could drip into his eye.

"You look like you're melting. Picking up anything?"

Shane joined her, gently tugging Bella behind him. "I've gotten plenty of memories, but they're all very old, from back when the hotel was still new and occupied by the living. I haven't picked up anything that I would attribute to the missing people."

Together, they moved to the top of the servant stairs. Kennie switched on her flashlight, the beam of light barely cutting through the darkness. It was a black pit of emptiness. A wave of vertigo hit Shane hard and he swayed on his feet. The floor tilted violently and he pitched forward into the railing. Bella pressed into his leg with a low whine that steadily grew into a growl.

Shane blinked down at her, noticing the shepherd's attention was riveted to something behind him.

"Are you okay? What's happening?"

Shane lifted his gaze to see Kennie stood several inches away. Her instinct would've been to grab him, help to steady him, but she had refrained and he was grateful. Shane felt the push against his psyche from whatever entity had decided to join them. His legs were shaking and he was burning up, but he gave Kennie a small smile. He caught slight movement at the edge of his vision and glanced over his shoulder.

CHAPTER SIXTEEN

Robert Grant's ghost was moving down the hall toward him. The closer the ghost got, the dizzier Shane became, and the more he felt like the ground was tilting beneath his feet. Shane gripped the stair rail harder, afraid if he let go, even a little, he would topple down them. On one hand, he was excited to have finally found something linked to the missing people. On the other, he was terrified that Grant's ghost would cause him to lose consciousness the same way Megan's had when she touched him. He clenched his jaws shut as bile burned the back of his throat.

Grant never slowed his forward movement. He stared directly into Shane's eyes before he floated through him and down the stairs, but it gave Shane a fleeting glimpse of memory. He saw Grant leading his guests down this hall and then suggesting they head back to the first floor via the servant stairs. Grant was excited; he'd saved his best discovery for last. The memory was short. So brief, that Shane had no idea exactly what it was Grant was excited to show. As the ghost dematerialized into the darkness of the stairwell, the ill effects Shane felt disappeared. Now, he was freezing and shaking uncontrollably. He pried his fingers from the railing and rubbed the sweat from his eyes.

"Holy fuck," Shane muttered.

The need to vomit hit him hard and there was no holding it back. He released Bella, stumbled to the nearest corner, and heaved up everything he'd eaten for lunch. His guts felt better after the purge, but a migraine now pounded behind his eyes.

"You are seriously pale and feverish, my friend. Do you need help? I could probably clear my mind enough to get close—"

Shane held up a palm. "No. Stay. I'm better now." Shane straightened and Bella came to his side immediately. He grabbed her leash and wrapped it around his hand.

"What happened? You were okay one second and puking the next."

"Robert Grant's ghost just walked through me. While I appreciate the snippet of memory he shared with me, I don't ever want to experience that again. Ever."

"Finally, something to go on." Kennie clapped and smiled, but Shane was too drained to share in her excitement. "I was beginning to think this trip was going to be a dud. What did you see? Did he show you where their bodies are?"

"No. I'm a little concerned he was able to walk through my shield. He's a ghost. He should've rolled off it like all the other memories and spirits have."

"Good point. That is disconcerting. He shouldn't have been able to do that, which is bad, but he gave you a memory to work with, which is good. Yes?"

"Yeah, sure." Shane swallowed against another wave of nausea.

"What was the memory?"

"He was taking them down these stairs."

Shane grimaced. He did not want to follow in Grant's footsteps. The stairwell was dark and narrow, and there was no way in hell he was going to enjoy the trip. Shane still harbored a bit of claustrophobia since experiencing Megan's memory of being trapped. Eventually, that lovely side effect would subside, but it was still too fresh in Shane's mind for him to be comfortable stepping into a deep, black hole in the floor of a dilapidated building.

"Okay. So, we head back downstairs and try to figure out what we missed...I guess."

Kennie was halfway down the hall toward the main staircase before Shane stopped her.

"Wrong stairs," he said.

Kennie turned to face him so slowly it was almost comical. She looked terrified of what he was about to say. He couldn't blame her. He didn't want to go down the servant stairs either, but if it was the way Grant and his guests went, that's the way Shane needed to go, too. The chances of picking up a memory from one of them was much higher if he followed the same path they took, whether he wanted to or not.

Shane pointed. "This way."

He looked down into the dark abyss awaiting them. Bella was glued to his thigh and he took comfort in her trusted, sturdy build. He'd make sure not to let go of Bella's collar until they reached the bottom. It was going to be a tight fit with the dog beside him instead of in front or behind him, but he wanted, and needed, the physical connection.

Shane moved away from the railing as Kennie carefully passed him. Kennie aimed the flashlight right in front of her feet and hesitantly started down the stairs. Shane flicked on his own flashlight and followed, keeping the beam of light on Kennie's back. He didn't want to lose sight of his friend or miss a step and tumble down the stairs.

"These steps are really steep...and tight."

"And dark," Shane added.

There was a dull thunk Shane couldn't identify, but wasn't left to wonder for long.

"Ow! Son of a bitch, that hurt."

"What happened? Are you okay?"

Kennie cussed under her breath. "Watch you head. There's something hanging on the left wall, right at head level."

Shane tipped his head to the right to avoid hitting the same object Kennie had and suddenly had to shield his eyes against the beam from her flashlight. When she moved the light away from his face, he opened his eyes and looked at where she was aiming.

"Is that a sconce for a candle?" she asked, full of disbelief. "Jesus."

"Guess servants didn't merit electricity," Shane mused, though he was just as confused by the sconce. He was pretty sure there had been electricity when the hotel was built. Even if there hadn't been, there was an elevator, so the hotel had been renovated for electricity at some point.

"Why is it so bloody dark in here? The rest of the hotel wasn't like this," Kennie said, nervously.

Shane understood completely. Tight, dark places were something he hated any day of the week and the addition of his claustrophobia only made things worse. The unwelcome idea that they were descending into a tomb filled his brain as they slowly made their way down the steps. His chest constricted, making it hard to breathe. Another wave of dizziness hit him as he made the sharp turn at another small landing.

He tightened his fingers around Bella's leash and leaned back against the wall, the back of his head resting against the cold drywall. A few seconds later, when he tried to straighten himself, the floor felt like it gave way and his knees went weak. He yelled as sharp pain shot through his kneecaps where they connected with unforgiving concrete. The flashlight fell from his fingers and rolled down the steps, sending a single beam of light dancing across the confines of the stairwell. Bella pressed against his chest, giving him something to hold onto until he got his bearings.

"Oh my god, what happened?" Kennie asked from three steps below the landing where Shane knelt.

He blinked against the brightness of her light hitting him in the face. His clothes clung to his body, his limbs were weak, and the energy he was using to keep his psychic shield in place was waning. He really needed to be away from the hotel when that happened or Kennie would be dragging his unconscious body a long way.

"I feel like shit," he said. It was an understatement of massive proportions. He was certain this was what death felt like.

"Do you need to throw up again?"

"No." Shane shook his head slightly but stopped immediately when it made the walls fold in on themselves. He closed his eyes and focused on the solid floor, Bella's fur against his cheek, anything but the dizziness and panic clouding his mind. "I'm feeling claustrophobic and panicky. I can't get enough oxygen and it's making me dizzy. I think I'm going to pass out."

"Awesome!" Kennie's joviality made Shane want to slap her.

"The hell, Kennie? No, it's not."

Shane was positive his ability was killing him. He'd never had his psychic power "on" at this level for more than a few minutes at a time. He didn't know what the repercussions would be. Shane kept his eyes closed in a vain attempt to make the world stop spinning. Kennie brushed against his shield as she joined him on the landing. He opened his eyes to slits and watched Kennie retrieve his flashlight and hook it to Bella's collar. The beam of light bounced on the floor directly in front of Bella's paws.

"Yes, it is. We're looking for people who suffocated, remember?"

Kennie's disembodied voice echoed through the tightly enclosed space. Shane blinked as her words worked their way through his muddled brain and re-evaluated what he was feeling. He didn't recall Megan's memory of suffocating being this intense, but if he was picking up on the group memory, that could account for the severity. His shield was strong, but clearly not impenetrable, as proven by the fact Robert Grant had walked right through it.

Shane pressed his back into the wall and used it to slowly push himself to his feet. The nausea and shakiness were still present but not worsening. If he really was suffering through a memory, the faster he could remove himself from the source, the better. Once he was away from the memory, he could look back at the experience with fresh eyes and analyze it all. For now, he wanted out of this godforsaken concrete tomb. Leaning heavily against the wall, he slid down one step at a time.

One tug on the leash to let Bella know he wanted her attention and Shane issued his command. "Bella, lead."

He immediately felt the shepherd's body press against his leg, angled slightly in front of his knee. When Bella took a step down, Shane felt the shift of her body and stepped down after her. He kept his eyes firmly shut and used the wall to help him maintain balance. The symptoms worsened with each step downward which meant each step brought them closer to the missing people; assuming Kennie was correct in her assessment and Shane's body wasn't simply turning on him. A loud creak echoed loudly through the stairwell and light bathed his eyelids making him squeeze them tighter. It was too bright after the complete darkness he'd been immersed in.

"We're at the bottom," Kennie announced. "And I have no idea where we are."

Shane left the stairwell with Bella leading the way. His chest hurt from lack of oxygen, his heart was beating too hard and fast, and his legs felt like they'd give out on him any second. Bella slowly led him further away from the stairs into what felt like a rather large room. After feeling the confines of the stairs pressing in on him, this room felt expansive and open. A door slammed closed behind him, far closer than he expected, and he felt the shudder in the floor as the sound echoed around them. Shane pulled Bella to a stop when he felt Kennie's energy brush the shield.

"Wow! Now that we're back in sunlight, you really do look like the walking dead," she said.

Shane grunted before taking a massive breath of stale air. The air in the stairwell had been stifling and rank. It wasn't the freshest breath of air he'd ever taken, but it filled his lungs and eased the pain in his chest. He slowly opened his eyes, squinting and blinking, until he'd adjusted to the light.

"Good girl," he murmured to Bella as he scratched the top of her head. She was panting almost as hard as he was. "I'll give you extra treats with dinner tonight," he promised. The dog's ears twitched at the mention of treats and she sat down, looking up at him expectantly.

As the three of them stood in the center of the room, breathing deeply and reorienting themselves, the cloud in Shane's head cleared. He noted that the dizziness and panic had abated almost as soon as he'd exited the stairs. He glanced around the room. Muted, dust-filled sunlight fought through the dirt-encrusted windows adorning one entire wall. He caught a glimpse of a pillar through one corner of a glass pane and came to the conclusion they were at the front of the hotel, but he didn't recognize this room. It must not have been visible from the lobby.

The room had dark paneling and a long wooden bench along the wall to his left. A small raised dais took up the corner behind him. Along the same wall, in the opposite corner, was the door to the stairwell. It had sounded like metal when it slammed shut, but from this side, it appeared to be the same wood paneling as the walls. Three feet down the wall from the stairwell door was an enormous stone fireplace that took up the majority of the wall to Shane's right. The stone mantel jutted out approximately seven feet above the worn wooden floor. All three of them could easily fit inside without having to duck. Across from the far end of the fireplace were closed double doors.

A loud thump over their heads startled a yelp from Shane and Kennie, and a menacing growling bark from Bella. She was alert and ready to attack like the guard dog her breed was known for. Kennie took a frightened step closer to Bella, her eyes riveted to the ceiling.

"What the hell was that?" she whispered.

"I don't know."

"Did you encounter something up there big enough to cause that and not tell me?"

"No." Bella took an aggressive step forward, lowering her head as her growling increased in volume and Shane felt a trickle of fear slide down his back. "Ok, that's not a good sign—"

Shane's words were cut off as a dark, nebulous cloud dropped from the ceiling to land behind Kennie. The apparition dissipated almost immediately, but not before Kennie got a good feel of it and screamed.

"Something's touching me. It's touching me."

Kennie dissolved into a confusion of flying hair and flailing limbs as she brushed frantically at her head and arms in an attempt to dislodge whatever she felt. Shane half expected to see a swarm of bats flying around her the way she was acting. He pushed a calmness he didn't feel into the shield and took one large step toward his friend, encompassing her body quickly within it. His mind was instantly flooded with her panic and a vision of spiders crawling all over her. Shane cringed at the uncomfortable feelings.

"Kennie, be quiet. It's gone now."

Kennie quickly calmed down and the thoughts of fear and spiders were replaced by heated embarrassment. Shane took that as his cue and stepped far enough away to place Kennie on the outside of his psychic shield. Having her inside the shield only worked while her mind was consumed with the present moment. Once she started thinking clearly, Shane would have access to whatever memory decided to replace that fear and he didn't want that. He had enough on his plate without adding his best friend to the mix. Kennie gathered her long hair into one hand at the nape of her neck. She wasn't sweating as heavily as Shane, but there was a fine sheen glistening on her skin. Bella tugged on the leash as she sniffed around a small pile of trash, pawing at it and spreading it around, before shoving her nose back in.

"I don't like this place and I don't want to be here anymore," Kennie said. She released her hair and gave a full-body shiver.

Shane pointed to the double doors. "If I'm guessing right, those doors lead to the lobby.

Kennie rushed to the doors and Shane followed, trying not to smile at the woman's discomfort. They passed through the double doors to find they were, indeed, on the opposite side of the lobby from where they'd started. If the windows in the paneled room had been cleaner, he might have been able to see the parking lot. The skitter of something along the front wall claimed Bella's attention and she pulled on the leash, ready to give chase. It took all the strength Shane had left to keep her away from whatever it was.

Shane dragged the reluctant shepherd to the front door, left ajar by Kennie when she'd stepped outside onto the porch seconds before. He pulled Bella close enough he could grab her collar and control her better. Once outside, he kicked the door closed with one foot before turning around to go down the steps to the gravel. A heavy thump on the decking behind him made Shane spin around where he came face to face with a very pissed off private investigator.

CHAPTER SEVENTEEN

"Don't touch me."

Shane jumped back while yanking the psychic shield back against his body like a second skin. He was in no condition to take on Masters' memories, accidentally or otherwise. Masters narrowed his eyes.

"Hi, honey. How was your day?" Shane asked.

He smiled sweetly and batted his eyelashes, deliberately poking at the bear. He bit his lower lip and swallowed the hysterical laugh he felt bubble up as Masters' scowl deepened. Too much had happened inside the hotel and he was feeling manic and reckless. He didn't want to explore too closely why he got so much enjoyment from Masters' expression.

Movement in the lot drew Shane's gaze to his friend. Luke stood there, one hand on his hip, looking just as annoyed as Masters. Luke's other hand was tightly clasped around Kennie's upper arm. Shane locked eyes with Kennie. She winked at him and then shot a glance at Masters. Shane jumped his gaze back to Masters just as the man reached for him. He took another step back and was stopped by the hotel door behind him, so he changed his momentum to the side. Anything to keep Masters from touching him while his ability was on, snapping around him like a live wire. Masters was about to give chase, but Luke's voice stopped him.

"Best not to touch him if he's active," Luke said.

"Oh, come on. Let him learn the hard way," Kennie said.

Luke glared at her. "You, be quiet."

Kennie pouted. Luke turned his glare onto Shane. Masters rolled his eyes before stepping to the side of the stairs.

"Get back to the motel."

Masters issued the order calmly, but his tone snapped with barely contained anger. Shane coughed out a laugh as he went down the stairs, keeping Bella between him and everyone else. Was this what a nervous breakdown felt like? At the very least, he had succumbed to hysteria. Shane wanted nothing more than to curl into a ball to laugh and cry himself to sleep.

Kennie pried Luke's fingers off her arm and joined Shane as he crossed Crystal Creek Hotel's parking lot toward the bridge. Masters walked past them, taking the lead, while Luke followed behind; probably to make sure Shane and Kennie actually returned to Thunderhawk Motel. If the man only knew how eager the two of them were to do just that.

Without breaking stride, Masters stepped off the bridge and crossed the highway. Either the man didn't care if he got hit by a speeding car or traffic was working in his favor. Shane and Kennie at least looked both ways before stepping onto the asphalt. Luke was close enough to them that he was safe following behind without checking. Shane relaxed his hold on Bella's leash, allowing the dog to pull ahead and explore a little.

Shane detoured to the same patch of grass Bella had used the night before and watched as she sniffed around for a spot to do her business. Kennie followed them but kept glancing back at the other two. Luke stopped near the door to Shane's cabin. Masters walked up to Shane, stopping when Shane moved out of reach. He sighed and held out his hand.

"Give me the room key."

Shane pulled the key from his jeans pocket and handed it over. He breathed in the cool, clean mountain air before he and Kennie followed Masters into his cabin. Bella ran past them, leash trailing behind her, and jumped into the middle of the bed. Shane collapsed onto one end of the sofa. Seconds later, Luke directed Kennie to sit down beside him. Luke closed the door and stood shoulder-to-shoulder with Masters.

Despite Shane's room being the "largest," it was entirely too small for all the testosterone. Kennie and Shane glanced at each other, silently agreeing to wait the investigators out. Masters crossed his arms while glaring at Shane. Luke headed to the only chair and sat down, resting an ankle over his knee. He appeared relaxed and calm compared to Masters, who was wound up tight and ready to snap, anger pulsing off him in waves.

"Care to share?" Luke asked.

"Share what?" Shane asked innocently.

Luke stared at him, letting Shane know without words exactly how displeased he was with that answer. Shane made the mistake of looking back to Masters who took the eye contact as his cue to release his bottled-up fury.

"What the fuck were you thinking?" Masters yelled.

Shane rose unsteadily to his feet and let out all the emotions he'd been carrying around inside him at the hotel. If he hadn't been blocked in by Kennie on one side, Luke on the other, and the coffee table bumping his shins, he would've gotten in Masters' face.

"I was investigating. Last I checked, that was my job," Shane yelled back.

"Running around a condemned building is not investigating. It's a great way to kill yourself, though."

The truth of Masters' words and the overwhelming fatigue blasted the fight out of Shane. He was angry and in no mood to put up with Masters, but he just didn't have it in him at the moment.

"We were careful," he said.

"Careful," Masters repeated. "That entire building is rotted and disintegrating. You don't go into a place like that alone, especially when no one knows where you are."

"Did you think your psychic ability would keep you from falling through the floor?" Luke asked.

"Or the ceiling from collapsing on top of your head?" Masters added.

Head pounding from the migraine and new waves of nausea rolling through his belly, Shane pressed his palms to his temples and sat back down. He folded his legs beneath him and focused on controlling the storm brewing in his gut. Luke and Masters were right, but Shane would never admit it. Seemingly content with the fact he'd made his point and won the argument, Masters fell quiet and leaned against the door.

"It's sweet of you to be so concerned," Kennie said sweetly.

Shane dropped his hands to his lap and looked at her. Her saccharine smile was aimed directly at Masters and Shane wondered if the man knew Kennie was actually being sarcastic. He must have because he scowled at her.

"Who are you?"

"Your boyfriend's BFF," Kennie answered.

"Boyfriend?" Luke asked, genuinely confused.

Realizing Kennie and Masters hadn't actually met, and hoping to avoid having to explain the boyfriend comment to Luke, Shane sighed and did the honors.

"Masters, this is Kennie, best friend and business partner. Kennie, this is Masters, private investigator and the biggest pain in the—"

"Okay," Luke interrupted.

Shane shut up, but continued to hold Masters' narrowed, steely blue gaze.

"Shane."

Slowly and deliberately, Shane looked at Luke, who's anger was far less antagonistic than the raging bull at the door.

"We already searched Crystal Creek, top to bottom. We didn't find anything," Luke said.

"Neither did we," Shane said, somewhat surprised how easily the lie fell from his lips.

Kennie shifted uncomfortably next to him, and he fought the urge to do the same. Luke was observant. If Shane looked the least bit uneasy, Luke would know for certain he was lying. Luke and Masters shared a look, another wordless conversation, before Luke scrubbed a hand down his face.

"Right. That's why you look like shit. All right, fine. Tell me what happened this morning. Masters told me you passed out."

Shane rubbed his tired eyes. Every movement of his body pulling on weak, fatigued muscles. He simply wasn't up for an interrogation. He needed to shut down completely and sleep.

"Luke, please. I'm so exhausted I'm about to pass out. I've dealt with more paranormal activity today than I've ever encountered before. I need a migraine pill and uninterrupted sleep for, like, a week."

Luke huffed his displeasure, but Shane knew he wouldn't push. Shane was prepared for a fight with Masters, but he remained surprisingly quiet. Masters leaned back against the door with his arms folded across his chest. His posture suggested he was relaxed, but his face was lined with tension.

"What about you, Kennie? Anything to tell us?" Luke pressed.

Kennie flattened a palm to her chest. "I wasn't even here this morning."

Shane giggled softly at his friend's deliberate misunderstanding as Masters cursed under his breath. Nothing about the situation was funny, but Shane was wrecked and stupid tired.

"I know these people have been missing for a long time, but we are on a deadline. I don't know what you found, *honey*, but I know you found something because you look like the walking dead and neither of you can lie worth a damn. Stop holding out on us," Masters said. His voice was heavy with his own fatigue and frustration. Shane could sympathize, but he could barely holding his head up. Rather than respond, he let his head fall back against the cushion.

"Clearly, everyone is too tired for this right now," Luke said as he rose to his feet.

Shane cringed inwardly at the disappointment and resignation in his friend's voice. Masters yanked open the cabin door and left without a word or glance. Luke stopped at the open door and looked at them.

"Check out tomorrow morning by eleven and go home. You're done here."

Luke left the room, closing the door behind him. Shane's entire body deflated and he shrunk in on himself. All his energy had been sucked out the door alongside the men. Kennie stood up to lock the door and Shane flopped onto the abandoned cushion. It took a moment for the room to stop spinning with the sudden position change.

"That man does get to you, doesn't he?"

"Says I'm a fraud. Want to hit him with my car," Shane mumbled.

"Your car wouldn't survive the impact and Masters would barely notice the bump."

"Hate him."

"If you say so," Kennie muttered, running her fingers through Shane's messy hair as she passed him. Shane curled up on the sofa, pulling a throw pillow beneath his head, and fell asleep to the sounds of running water coming from the bathroom.

CHAPTER EIGHTEEN

Morning arrived sooner than Shane wanted, but after sleeping on the short sofa all night, he was stiff and it felt good to stretch. The aches and pains throughout his body couldn't be fully attributed to his squished position on the couch, though he'd woken in the same position he'd fallen asleep in. The sun had been out when he'd fallen asleep and it was out now, warping Shane's sense of time. Footsteps scuffled outside the door seconds before he heard Kennie chattering at Bella. She entered the room amidst a flurry of dark red skirt and panting German Shepherd.

"Oh, great! You are still among the living. I wasn't sure with how horrid you look," Kennie said. "You should shower and change clothes. Your boys want us to meet them at Crimson Moon in a few hours."

Shane grunted in response as he went in the bedroom to grab clean clothes. A hot shower sounded amazing. His stomach growled on the way to the bathroom, making Kennie chuckle. Bella ignored Shane completely in favor of the belly rub she was receiving. Shane left the bathroom door open as he started the shower and began undressing.

"How was Luke when you saw him?" he asked.

"Looked fine, but I'm sure he's not happy that you lied to his face. You look like shit, Shane, so he knows something happened."

"Do you think he'll forgive?" Shane spread paste on his toothbrush and cleaned his teeth. His entire mouth felt fuzzy and gross.

"Of course, he will. Your friendship was forged in the fires of hell, literally. You just have to tell him the truth; the *entire* truth."

Shane winced in pain as he stepped beneath the hot water and it hit his sore muscles. His skin was ultra-sensitive, every muscle in his body tight, and his mind was in turmoil. He didn't mind talking through everything with Luke, but he didn't want Masters there. Unfortunately, there was no way around that. Even if Shane asked him to leave, the man wasn't likely to acquiesce. Crimson Moon was Shane's and Kennie's metaphysical store and Luke probably wanted to meet there for privacy, plus Shane would be more comfortable in familiar surroundings, but he couldn't stop wondering what Masters would think of the place given his blatant disbelief.

142

While washing the previous day's grime from his hair and body and wishing he could do the same with his mind, Shane gave himself a little pep talk. By the time he stepped out of the steamy bathroom, he felt somewhat human again. The scent of eggs, bacon, and, most importantly, coffee, wafted through the heavy air once again making his stomach growl. The calories he'd ingested before revisiting Crystal Creek had been forcefully expunged from his body or burned up with the first memory or two he'd encountered. Kennie came out of the bedroom with his suitcase and dropped it by the door.

"I already packed your stuff, except whatever you have in the bathroom. You can toss it in later," she told him. "Sit down and eat first. You still look like you're about to drop from exhaustion."

"Thanks."

Shane picked up a slice of bacon and shoved it in his mouth before turning his attention to his shoes. He'd dressed in faded jeans and a black t-shirt. His favorite oversized sweatshirt was tossed over the arm of the sofa. Kennie saw him looking at it and commented.

"It's cold today. You'll want it."

He nodded as he took a few large bites of the eggs. They were a bit overcooked and dry, but he needed the protein. Additional steam was released as he pulled the top off the coffee cup and he inhaled the rich aroma. He poured all the creamer and sugar that was provided into the cup, stirred, and then set it aside to cool for a few minutes while he pulled the sweatshirt on. Bella whined from her spot on the floor, begging for some of the bacon on the table. Shane put a forkful of egg and half a bacon strip on a napkin and put it in front of Bella's paws. Like the trained dog she was, she waited until Shane's fingers were safely out of bite range before she scarfed the treat down without chewing.

Half an hour later, Shane had finished his breakfast and they loaded up the car for the drive back down the hill. Bella sat in the front passenger seat watching the scenery through the windows while Shane sipped his coffee, heater on high and tunes blasting through the speakers. Kennie was two vehicles ahead of him driving a few miles under the speed limit. After experiencing Masters's chaotic driving, Kennie's puttering was slightly annoying.

Shane couldn't really blame her, though. Kennie had been involved in a car accident while driving through the mountains several years before. A pickup truck had taken a tight curve too fast and hit Kennie's car, pushing it into a guardrail, one wheel dangling precariously over the side of the steep embankment over a river. Being trapped in a car that was teetering over a forty-foot drop had been terrifying. She still had nightmares and was excessively cautious when driving in the mountains. Their traumas were vastly different, but they suffered the effects the same and they were always there for each other when the symptoms flared. Working this case was no different; Kennie was by his side like always.

As his favorite band blasted through the speakers, Shane knocked his thumbs on the steering wheel with the beat and, for the time it took to get home, was able to shut his mind off. He didn't think about old memories or past hurts or missing people. He just existed in the moment but was all too soon pulled from his peaceful bubble.

Shane parked his wreck of a vehicle in the far corner of the tiny parking lot that ran along the backside of Crimson Moon Metaphysical Shop. The store occupied the lower level of the two-story building. The top floor was divided into two apartments – Shane lived in one and Kennie in the other. They had bought the building a few years before. The list price was good and it had everything they needed, including a nice location on a main thoroughfare between downtown Denver and the suburbs to the east. This area was a mix of old houses, newer apartment buildings, and small businesses.

Three other vehicles were parked in the lot. Kennie's car was next to Shane's. The other two SUVs belonged to the part-time employees who ran the store in their absence, Jan and Connie. It was almost time for the midday shift change which explained why both ladies were inside. Eleven-thirty to one was always a busier time for customers, especially during the week. Saturdays and Sundays were more of a steady stream throughout the day. Shane wasn't sure why Luke would want to meet at Crimson Moon during peak hours, but as long as Shane didn't need to assist customers, he would go along with it.

"Doesn't look like the suits are here yet," Kennie said.

Shane lifted the hatchback to grab his bag and had to snatch Bella's leash as she bounded over the back seat.

"Why are you so impatient?" he mumbled to Bella and then asked Kennie, "Did Luke say what it was he wanted to discuss, or maybe why he wanted to meet here?"

"No, but I figure it's one of his old cop interrogation techniques. Familiar places and comfortable surroundings equal looser lips."

"That doesn't sound right. I don't think that's an actual cop thing."

Shane dropped his bag to the ground so he could close the hatchback without releasing his hold on Bella. She was excited to be home so she was tugging on him a lot. A horn honked behind him when he bent down to pick up his bag. He spun around to glare at the offending driver.

"Seriously, Luke?" he yelled as the familiar blue sedan pulled into a parking spot, followed closely by Masters in his Volkswagen. "You're a married man."

Kennie and Shane walked toward the back entrance of the building where they could then enter the storage room of the store. A metal staircase fixed to the outside of the brick building led up to the second-floor apartments. Bella tugged hard toward the stairs, but Shane redirected her to the door of the shop. Luke and Masters joined them seconds later.

"I wasn't honking at your ass, Shane. I was trying to make you jump," Luke said.

Kennie and Shane huffed in response. Shane entered the storage room and unhooked Bella's leash. She immediately ran to her doggie bed where she curled up with her favorite toy – a stuffed squirrel she often carried around by the tail. Shane dropped his bag to the side of the door and gave in to a full-body stretch. He looked over his shoulder when he heard a strangled groan to see Masters glancing around the storage room with an annoyed expression. Shane was struck by the differences between the four of them.

Shane was dressed in jeans and an oversized sweatshirt. Kennie was in a long, flowy skirt and blouse in her usual goth style. Luke had opted for a grey suit today but sans the usual tie. Masters, despite the distasteful expression, looked swoon-worthy in dark jeans and a black leather jacket over a white shirt. It was a shame his personality wasn't as attractive as his appearance. Luke and Kennie had already entered the main part of the store so Shane left the storage room and went to the Divination Room. Masters could find his own way.

Bella trotted into the room, squirrel dangling from her mouth, and laid down beside Shane's chair. He stared at her wondering how she'd gotten out of the storeroom until Masters walked through the heavy, velvet drape separating the Divination Room from the rest of the store. Shane had his answer. It took everything he had not to stare at Masters as he raked a hand through his hair. The shirt he wore pulled tight across his abs and Shane had to look away before Masters caught him staring.

Masters sat across the table from Shane with a bland expression, watching Bella play with her toy. At least that was an improvement, though Shane didn't understand what had caused Masters to be annoyed in the first place. Kennie joined them in the room and placed several sets of Tarot cards on the table before lighting the candles sitting inside old-fashioned silver sconces hung on the walls. Shane swallowed at the recent memories of the truly old sconces hung in the servant stairwell. Kennie turned off the overhead light, allowing the flickering gold flames to illuminate the room.

Shane found the pale glow calming, which he preferred while doing customer readings. Entering the memories of the living could sometimes be touchy, requiring delicate handling, and that was something he did better when he was centered and at ease. Everything in the Divination Room was chosen with very specific purposes in mind.

All five elements – earth, air, water, fire, and spirit – were represented by paintings on the walls and in the objects placed around the room. The white wicker table they were seated at was in the center of the room, four chairs placed around it. A five-shelf white wicker bookcase was tucked into one corner where Kennie kept all the implements she used for her readings. Shane didn't need much for his readings other than a peaceful atmosphere and bravery

Satisfied with her preparations, Kennie sat down and started shuffling a deck of cards. Shane didn't think she planned to do a reading, but rather giving herself something to do. Luke joined them a few minutes later. Shane wanted to ask what he'd been doing, but he didn't get a chance.

"So, this is where you do your witchcraft and voodoo," Masters said.

Kennie stopped shuffling and glared at him.

"No," Shane snapped.

"Crimson Moon is a successful metaphysical shop that happens to be owned by two very real psychics," Kennie said. "Also, because it's clear you're ignorant, Wicca and Voodoo are legitimate religions." She glanced at Shane. "If he's been spouting stupid shit like that to you, I can see why you want to run him down with your car."

Masters huffed, unfazed.

Kennie stood up. "If I'm not needed, I'm going out front. Certainly more pleasurable than being in the same room with *that* one."

She left the room in a flourish of skirts, curtain, and the scent of lavender. Shane envied her. He didn't want to be around Masters either. The man caused too much confusion and Shane was often uncomfortable around him. Luke's gaze bounced between Shane and Masters like he expected them to come to blows any moment.

"Luke," Kennie yelled. "Get out here. I want to read your cards."

Luke shared a glance with Masters before smiling at Shane and then ducking out through the curtain. Shane was surprised Luke was allowing Kennie to read his future; he didn't usually like that. Luke was one-hundred-percent believer, so Kennie's ability made him nervous. Sitting across from Masters in a dark room lit only by candle flames sent Shane back to the dining room of Crystal Creek where Masters and fifteen missing people had first been indelibly lodged beneath his skin, causing an irritating itch he couldn't scratch.

Masters folded his arms on the tabletop. Shane met his gaze with resigned apprehension. Neither of them looked away as Masters leaned in closer.

"Talk. Prove to me you're worth the money we paid."

Shane shook his head. "Say what you mean, Masters. You want me to prove myself, period. Despite everything I've done up to this point, you still don't believe in my ability."

"Not really," Masters said.

At least he was man enough to admit it, not that Shane needed his confirmation. He wasn't exactly sure how to prove himself or where to start with regard to the memories he'd encountered. So many things were floating around his brain. He supposed the best place to start was at the beginning, the reason Shane was here in this situation in the first place – fifteen missing people.

"The missing people suffocated. Except Robert Grant. He was stabbed with something shiny, like broken glass."

"Not helpful information when it doesn't tell me *where* they are. Also, if you're trying to prove psychic ability, give me something I can fact check."

Shane leaned back in his chair with an audible sigh. There was only one way to prove his psychic ability to this man. He'd have to read one of Masters's memories and tell him something he already knew. Shane hoped Masters' pain of losing his love, Elizabeth, had diminished over the past three years or what he was about to do was going to hurt.

"Elizabeth was pregnant," Shane said.

Masters gaze never left Shane's face so Shane saw the pain that flashed through his eyes. Masters clasped his hands together tight enough to make his knuckles white and lifted them to his lips. Shane wanted him to walk out of the room a believer so he went a little farther.

"She cried a lot because she wanted the baby, but she didn't think you did. She thought you would leave her if she told you."

Shane kept his voice soft, knowing his words were painful to hear. Masters averted his gaze to something behind Shane, but Shane wasn't sure he was actually seeing anything. Masters seemed to be lost in his own mind. His throat worked as he swallowed and then he looked at Shane again.

"She did tell me."

"I know."

"How would you know?" Masters asked.

Masters' voice was strained as he lowered his clasped hands back to the tabletop. His entire body was tense, but at least he wasn't being confrontational. Shane wanted to say "I'm psychic, duh," but he shoved the response aside in favor of a more tactful response.

"I touched her necklace. She must have been wearing it when she made the decision to tell you about the baby." Shane tilted his head as he replayed the memory he'd encountered. "Or she was wearing it when she *did* tell you. I'm not exactly sure which, honestly."

Masters shook his head with a huff and Shane realize he still had work to do. He didn't think twice about his next move. Shane released his gift, allowing the heat to flow to his fingertips. Under the guise of sympathy, he reached over the table to touch Masters' tightly clasped hands.

"I'm sorry you lost them," Shane said as he made physical contact. The memory hit him like a solid right hook to the jaw. He realized too late that touching Masters without first connecting with Bella was a mistake of epic proportions.

— —-*****— —-

The muscles of his throat felt like they were ripping open as the scream erupted from his body, torn from the depths of his chest. The sound was drowned out by the screech of brakes and the explosion of metal on metal as the train slammed into the car. Rushing blood pounded in his ears to the rapid beat of his heart. Police cars, some marked, some not, spun out in front of him, coming to rest at odd angles on the road. One wasn't able to stop in time and rear-ended another. The scene was loud and chaotic as the train tipped precariously toward them, derailed, and crashed to the ground in a cloud of dirt and smoke.

He didn't remember leaving his partner's car or how he'd gotten so close to the wreckage. He must have run because he was short of breath, but he couldn't remember the trip. Flames spread from ruptured gas tanks to the nearby grass and brush, sending waves of heat over him. There was a moment of deadly calm, a silence he'd never experienced before, and then there was a burst of frenzied action. The activity around him was a cacophony of background noise and blurry movement. His focus was narrowed with pinpoint accuracy on the remnants of his car and the thin arm he could see sticking out from the twisted wreckage.

Elizabeth.

He had to get to Elizabeth. He stepped forward but strong arms grabbed him from behind, halting his movement. His throat hurt and his eyes burned as his vision grew blurry with tears. He struggled against the arms holding him. Why weren't they helping her? Why wasn't he being allowed to go to her? The area was swarming with cops and firefighters, but no one seemed to be concerned with pulling her from the wreckage. After a moment of struggling, realization seeped into his brain with painful precision. No one was helping her because she was already dead. That knowledge only made him struggle harder. He had to know for sure. He had to see for himself that the only light in his life had been snuffed out.

He was wrestled to the ground and he was proud to note that it had taken three men to succeed in restraining him. He could see their mouths moving, heard the buzz of voices. He even recognized the one closest to him as his partner, Luke Holmestead, but he wasn't giving in easily. He continued to fight. The woman he was going to marry and his unborn child were mangled in the heap of metal that used to be his car. Anger, loss, and guilt seared through his chest, blinded him, deafened him. His chest hurt with every breath he struggled to take, his thoughts incoherent and fuzzy. He was so lost that the sting of a needle in his arm barely registered before the oblivion of drugged unconsciousness welcomed him. Still, he fought.

CHAPTER NINETEEN

Shane slammed back to the present as Masters pulled his hands away. The change was jarring. Masters stared at him with an odd expression on his face and Shane realized he was crying. He swiped the tears away, but couldn't seem to stop the flow. He'd known Masters had endured emotional pain, but he hadn't been prepared for *that*.

Holy fuck!

The memory had been completely unfiltered because Maters had no idea what Shane could do and Shane hadn't given any warning before touching him. Why hadn't he decided to prove his ability in a more benign way? He could have led Masters to a more pleasant, calmer memory if he'd tried. Bella whined and put her head on Shane's thigh.

"What's wrong? Why are you crying?" Masters asked.

"Fuck," Shane breathed. He wiped his face before sliding one palm down his thigh and ruffled Bella's ear with the other. "Proving I'm psychic."

"This" – Masters pointed at him – "Is you proving you're psychic?"

Shane nodded and blew out a breath. "You told me Elizabeth died in a car accident."

"She did."

"Technically, sure, but saying car accident never would have led me to think she was hit by a train."

A myriad of emotions played over Masters's features; shock, sadness, anger, fear, it was all there. Shane wasn't surprised by any of it. Masters was facing a reality he hadn't believed was possible.

"Why do you feel guilty over her death?" Shane asked. From what he'd seen and felt, Masters wasn't to blame.

Masters pushed back from the table and stood up so quickly the chair flew back across the floor, almost tipping over, before it struck the wall. Shane knew his pain was still raw despite the fact Elizabeth had died three years ago. Masters paced along the back wall of the small room occasionally casting Shane an angry glare. He stopped moving when Kennie stormed into the room, Luke close on her heels. Luke leaned a shoulder against the doorjamb, watching Masters.

"What's wrong?" Shane asked Kennie.

"Remember what I told you yesterday? That they were hiding something?"

"Well, I remember you said Masters was hiding something."

Shane glanced at the man in question. He and Luke were having one of their silent conversations. Kennie pulled Shane out of his chair and dragged him to the other side of the room. Bella laid back down under the table. Kennie leaned in close to Shane's ear and whispered.

"Did you read him and find out what it was?"

"Not exactly," he answered.

He didn't know what Kennie had learned, but he doubted it was the same thing as him. She had read Luke, after all. Kennie took a step back, jabbing an angry finger in Luke's direction.

"They were hired to find these people, but they're breaking the law to do it," Kennie said, staring hard at Luke, who huffed in response.

"Technically, so did we," Shane pointed out.

"No, no. We trespassed. A very minor thing compared to them." Kennie pointed at Luke again. "He stole from the cops. He didn't get that case file legally. Cold Case probably doesn't even know the file is missing, but that's not the point. He made us accessories to...to something. I don't even know what, but it's bad."

By the time Kennie was done talking she was fired up and short of breath.

"Calm down," Shane said.

"Why would you tell her something like that?" Masters asked Luke.

"I didn't tell her anything," Luke answered. "How many times do I have to tell you they are psychic?"

Kennie began tapping her foot in agitation and Shane bumped elbows with her. Neither Masters nor Luke seemed too concerned that their secret was out which helped keep Shane calm.

"I trust Luke," Shane said.

"I don't care. You need to get away from this now. If you stay with them, bad things will happen."

Having said her piece, Kennie returned to the main part of the store, leaving the three men in the Divination Room. Shane hugged himself around the waist as a wave of nausea hit him. He glanced between Masters and Luke.

"I'm not feeling well. Can we finish this another day?" he asked.

"No," Masters answered.

Shane closed his eyes and sighed. He should have known that Masters wouldn't let things go so easily. The man was dogged, to say the least.

"You told me the people we're looking for suffocated. How?"

"I don't know."

"Then tell me where they suffocated," Masters pressed.

"If I knew that, they wouldn't still be missing, now would they?" Shane snapped.

He felt terrible and his fatigue was growing exponentially. He was not in the mood to deal with Masters' attitude. Masters scowled and took a menacing step forward that made both Shane and Luke stiffen.

"Do you want to know what I think?"

"Masters," Luke warned.

"You can't tell me anything about those missing people because no one knows what happened so there's no material for you to research. But you can sure as hell research my past, can't you? You managed to find just enough information to throw out a few painful details, add in some tears, and try to reel me right in, huh? Well, that doesn't work on me, sweetheart."

Shane got the impression that Masters was allowing his hurt and shock to run his mouth, but it didn't stop Shane's anger from boiling over. The detective was beyond infuriating.

"Get out before I knock you out," Shane snapped.

Masters started to come at him, but Luke snagged his wrist in a vice grip and yanked him toward the exit. He mumbled something to Masters as they stepped through the tapestry, disappearing from sight. A few seconds later, Shane heard the heavy outer door slam shut but there was still the distinct clicking of shoes on concrete. He was still trying to decide which was stronger, the urge to vomit or cry, when Luke returned to the room looking resigned.

"Thank you for your help so far, Shane, but Kennie is right. You need to stay away now. I don't think there's much else you can do to help."

"Are you firing me?"

"You'll still get paid," Luke said, instead of simply admitting that, yes, Shane was being fired. "I'll admit that my expectations were unreasonable. I thought you'd walk in, touch something, and tell us everything that happened to those people." He laughed humorlessly. "Get some rest. We'll talk later when you don't look and feel like shit."

Luke left the room, the massive tapestry fluttering in his wake. Shane stood rooted to the floor, staring at the large pentagram, uncertain how to feel. Anger was always fast and easy, and therefore usually the first emotion to make itself known. Following close behind was overwhelming grief and guilt that still flowed through his veins, keeping all his nerve endings zinging and his anxiety on the razor's edge. One gentle push and he'd dissolve into full-blown hysterics. Kennie found him standing in the same position when she returned to the room some time later.

"Hmm. I didn't hear them leave," she said.

Shane snapped out of wherever his mind had wandered. "I kicked them out," he said.

"Good for you. I'm headed up. You coming?"

"Yeah. Come, Bella."

Shane followed Kennie into the storeroom and waited while she locked the shop's back door. Bella pushed her stuffed squirrel against Shane's hand. He took it and tossed it up the stairs so the dog would run up ahead of them. He and Kennie said goodnight at the top of the steps and then entered their respective apartments. Shane immediately relaxed, surrounded by the safe and familiar. He hadn't realized how much he'd missed home. He grabbed a beer from the fridge, tucked his feet beneath him on the sofa, and turned on the television. He thumbed through the channels until he found a monster movie marathon and then settled in for a relaxing evening with Bella.

It was the calm before the storm he felt brewing in his subconscious. He would be having nightmares. Masters' memory had been powerful, raw, and vivid, without the dimming that usually came with the passage of time. Masters must dwell on it, replaying the moment over and over, refusing to forget which ultimately resulted in the memory remaining so vibrant. Shane couldn't imagine living that way year after year. He ached for the man. As the TV droned on, Shane's thoughts drifted from Masters to Elizabeth to her family, which inevitably led him back to his encounter with Megan's ghost.

Random pieces of memories, thoughts, and emotions floated disjointedly through his consciousness. He attempted to put them into one coherent, big picture, but the answer to where those people had gone remained elusive. If Luke thought Shane could just walk away from the mystery, he didn't know Shane as well as he thought. Shane wanted to find the missing people so their families would have closure, and he wanted to help Masters, as infuriating as the man was. Shane wasn't naïve enough to believe that giving the Sylvester family closure over Megan's death would help Masters in any way with his own loss, but Shane hoped that by helping them, Masters would find some measure of peace.

CHAPTER TWENTY

As the morning sun rose, so did Shane's conviction. He didn't have a plan, but he wasn't giving up. There had to be something more he could do, despite Luke's assurances he had already provided all the help he could. When Shane thought about the conversations he'd had with Luke and Masters, he believed he hadn't actually told them everything. There were so many small details that he'd overlooked or hadn't thought to share. He hadn't told them everything that had happened during his visit to the hotel a couple of nights before. That trip with Kennie had significantly narrowed down the search area as far as Shane was concerned, but he hadn't told Luke or Masters any of it.

He showered, dressed, and chugged two cups of coffee in record time before heading downstairs to Crimson Moon. He settled Bella in the back foyer with a peanut-butter filled rubber toy, topping off her food and water bowls. Soft harp music played from hidden speakers and welcomed him when he entered the store. The scent of sage and roses filled the air, and Shane happily breathed it in as he searched for Kennie. A few customers were browsing the shelves of books, while another sifted through the greeting cards. Shane slipped behind the counter and sat down at the register. He had yet to see Kennie, but the sound of boxes being moved in the smaller storeroom off the entrance told him where she was.

"Blessed be," Shane called out as one of their regular couples left the store.

The woman waved goodbye with a smile. They were leaving empty-handed this time, but they would be back. A few minutes later, Kennie came out of the storeroom with an armful of candles.

"Here we are," Kennie said as she approached a woman near the candle display along the far wall. "These are a bit darker in color, but they're still lavender scented."

"They seem bigger," the woman stated.

"They are," Kennie agreed. "They fit a bit snuggly in the holders, but they do still fit. We don't actually carry these anymore. This is the last of the stock, but this is all we currently have until the shipment comes in next week. If you want them, I'll sell them to you at half price."

The woman ultimately agreed and Shane rang up her purchases while Kennie worked the floor, checking on the other shoppers. Shane lost himself in comfortable mundane tasks until he glanced at the clock and realized the entire morning had passed. Not once had he thought about missing people, ghosts, or irreverent, infuriating private detectives. Shane's pleasantly normal morning came to an end when Kennie flipped the sign from *Open* to *Closed for Lunch* and locked the door.

"Do I have any readings scheduled this afternoon?" Shane asked.

Kennie joined him in the Divination Room and placed their salads on the table. Bella whined from the back foyer so Shane got up to let her in. He rubbed her ears and poked at his salad as uncomfortable memories from the night before pushed their way into his head.

"Not today or for the rest of the week. I cleared your schedule claiming family emergency because I know you. Luke said he didn't need you anymore, but you aren't done with this case. You won't be able to let it go until it's solved. Honestly, Luke should've known that, too."

"Thank you, and yes, he should."

Shane was blessed to have a friend and business partner who understood him so well. Both he and Kennie were stubborn and, when faced with a mystery, also determined. They would go to great lengths to get answers.

"I did a little research on my own last night and found a few little tidbits about the hotel that may or may not help solve things. Probably a history lesson more than anything," Kennie said.

"I'm listening." Shane stabbed some veggies with his fork and shoved them in his mouth. Any information could be good information.

"The original owner, Herbert Logant, broke ground for the hotel in 1886 but didn't actually start building it until 1888 when they finally got all the materials on site. They had to use horses and wagons because there was no road to the location yet. The highway wasn't built until the mid-1930s when they decided to put a bridge over the gorge to make it faster and easier to access the western slope. Apparently, the hotel took a lot longer to build because Logant kept wanting to add more rooms so they kept building.

The hotel was met with a lot of skepticism and a ton of people were opposed to it being built citing bad location. They were convinced no one would ever visit and the hotel would never make money, but Logant was extremely wealthy and did what he wanted. The doors opened briefly in 1895 but closed when winter came and no one, including Logant, could get to the place. As expected, the hotel bombed."

"Bad location." Shane shook his head. "How did he expect visitors to get to the hotel if there was no road? That hotel is massive and looks to have been extravagant for the times, so he clearly meant for the upper class to stay there. If this guy was so rich, why didn't he build the road, as well? Would've made getting the building materials to the site much easier, too, I would think. What is it with this hotel and the crazy rich people it seems to attract?"

"No idea."

Kennie shoveled a few forkfuls of salad into her mouth. Shane ate his food much slower, lost in thought as he waited for Kennie to swallow and continue.

"The place has had nothing but bad luck since Logant broke ground. Quite a few accidents and materials shortages plagued the first two years. Once they started constructing the hotel, there were five on-site deaths and tons of setbacks due to weather. In 1918, a man rumored to be a small-time mob boss named Julian Pastori bought the hotel and allegedly used it as a front for his illegal activities. In 1933, the hotel was partially destroyed. What we see today is only the front half."

"The front *half*?" Shane asked in disbelief. "My God, exactly how big was the place?"

"I'm guessing twice the size it is now since the article specifically stated half was destroyed," Kennie deadpanned.

"Smartass." Shane chuckled. Kennie smiled and bumped her plastic water bottle against his with a dull thud. "Okay, so share. How was the back half of the hotel destroyed?"

"First things first," Kennie said.

"What?"

"The caretaker's house has some interesting history, too."

"I don't care about the caretaker's house," Shane said quickly. That was a memory he never wanted to revisit.

"You said you felt an evil presence there."

"Yes, but that doesn't mean—"

"It was dismemberment," Kennie interrupted, eyes sparkling.

The macabre always had interested her more than normal. Shane swallowed convulsively to keep the salad he'd eaten in his stomach. He'd suffered a little reflux when he heard the word *dismemberment*. Completely unaware of Shane's fight against vomiting, Kennie bounced in her seat. Memories of malevolent shadows, the coppery taste of blood, and oppressive evil washed over him and he struggled to breathe normally. He really needed to steer the conversation away from that house if he had any hopes of finishing his lunch.

"So, back to the hotel. How was it destroyed?"

"Partially destroyed," Kennie corrected.

"Whatever."

"It was a flood, bad one too from what I read. Crystal Creek Hotel was named for the erroneously classified "creek" that runs through the gorge, but that gorge wasn't nearly as wide in 1933 as it was by 1934. Good thing the bridge wasn't constructed until 1935 or the flood would've taken it out."

Shane hummed in interest as he chewed. Kennie was into Goth and the macabre, but Shane loved natural disasters and psychology. The elements and human mind, and what each was capable of, fascinated him. A massive flood that widened a gorge and destroyed half a building fit that niche perfectly.

"So," Kennie continued. "In 1933, several miles up the canyon, a cloudburst moved in. It dropped a huge amount of rain in very little time. What resulted was a ten-foot-high wall of water that came crashing through the canyon wiping out everything along its banks. It killed thirty people and leveled two towns. After the flashflood, half the hotel was missing and what was left was teetering on the edge of a cliff. Seeing as how the land was now gone, they couldn't exactly rebuild the half that was destroyed so they demolished the parts they had to, walled it off, and then renovated the portion they still had."

"That means the halls and rooms we explored were originally in the middle of the hotel. The halls probably wrapped around the center staircase in a square," Shane thought out loud.

"Maybe. I found some photos from when the place was being built and plenty more from the early 1930s, but nothing from the decades in between. Figure it's because no one with photography equipment could get to it." Kennie shrugged.

"I wonder if that's why I couldn't pick up on anything in the dining room. It's at the back of the hotel so was probably one of the renovated areas. It's too 'new' to have embedded memories."

Shane leaned back. At least he now had an answer to one of his questions. It was one of about a hundred that floated through his head, but it was still an answer; however insignificant it might be to the overall mystery.

Kennie nodded.

"That's *exactly* why," she said. "The part of the hotel that was over the kitchen and dining area was destroyed but the kitchen was mostly intact so they renovated what was damaged and rebuilt the dining room over the kitchen like it previously was. Finished off the exterior to make it look like the hotel had always been that way."

Shane thought about everything Kennie had said, then shook his head. "Something is missing."

"What do you mean?"

"Well, from the history you've shared, very few people if any ever visited the hotel. Even before the flood. But I came across dozens of memories that suggest otherwise."

"The memories you came across are most likely from Crystal Creek's boom days."

Kennie picked up a deck of Tarot cards from the nearby shelf and started shuffling them. Shane stared at the movement of the cards between her fingers as he listened to Kennie speak.

"The hotel was a flop from the time it was built until Julian Pastori bought it. He made the road leading to the hotel wider and easier to traverse in inclement weather. Pastori reopened Crystal Creek Hotel to business in 1919. Fortuitous timing and a good head for business turned the hotel into the place to be for the who's who of Colorado back in the day."

"Timing and business sense, my ass," Shane scoffed. "Pastori was a low-level mobster with a hotel in the middle of nowhere just as Prohibition was starting. He was opportunistic, if anything."

"Exactly. Pastori was a bootlegger, and apparently a rather successful one. The hotel was too far away from any major city center so law enforcement didn't interfere."

"Or were easily paid off if they did," Shane added. He knew a lot of cops were on the take back then. Hell, even the police were patrons of those illicit clubs during Prohibition.

"Not only did location and Prohibition make Julian Pastori a very rich man, it made him a target, as well. His brother, Benji, wanted to be more than Julian's right-hand man. It was never proven, probably not even truly investigated, but in late 1928 Pastori was found in his bedroom cut into pieces." Kennie paused for a moment then added, "The brothers lived in the caretaker's cottage."

Shane scrunched his face. "I guessed as much because that certainly fits with the level of anger, hate, and pure evil I felt in that house. The stench of blood and decay was horrible." Nausea rolled in his gut as he remembered the sensations of being ripped apart. He cleared his throat and then said, "I think Julian might have still been alive when the dismemberment started."

"Oh, God! Seriously?"

"That's what it felt like."

The look of disgust on Kennie's face probably mirrored his own. A few minutes of silence passed before Kennie continued with Crystal Creek's history.

"Anyway, after his brother's death, Benji took over the business except he made a phenomenally bad decision when he took the money made from bootlegging and invested it in the stock market. Do you know why it was a bad idea?"

"Stock market crashed the following year," Shane answered.

"Bingo. The year 1929 was not a good one for Crystal Creek. The hotel suffered one setback after another. The final nail in the coffin was the flood that practically leveled it a few years later. While it was renovated, it was never reopened."

"This history lesson is interesting, but it doesn't help me find Grant and his missing friends." Shane loved history in general, and Crystal Creek's was fascinating, but he needed to stay focused.

"Here's my theory," Kennie said. "What if Grant knew about the hotel's history of bootlegging and took his peeps on a tour of the brewery?"

Shane grunted. "Two things wrong with that theory, well three. First, if he was making his own liquor, he was a moonshiner, not a bootlegger. And it would have been a distillery not a brewery."

Kennie narrowed her eyes at him but said nothing so Shane continued.

"Second, if it was that simple then the party goers would have been found by now and no one has said anything about an on-site distillery."

"Right, because your detectives have been so forthcoming with information, they couldn't have possibly left that out." Kennie's words were heavy with sarcasm and she rolled her eyes.

"Third, the location where I felt the suffocating sensation was on the opposite side of the hotel from the kitchen."

Kennie shrugged. "I agree that it would make sense to have the distillery near the kitchen but that doesn't necessarily mean it was. I can't find any information about where the alcohol was stashed, whether it was bootleg or moonshine."

She stood up and stretched, and then straightened the deck of Tarot cards before replacing them on the shelf. Bella lifted her head, watching Kennie pick up the glasses and leave the room. Shane collected the other dishes and followed. "Stay," he told Bella as he left the Divination Room to join Kennie in the small kitchen behind the coffee bar. Kennie loaded the dishwasher and set it to delayed run.

"Now that I think about it, having the distillery near the kitchen wouldn't make sense. Too easy for the authorities to find it. They would have hidden it or had it offsite, right?" Kennie asked. She leaned back against the counter, tapping her long nails on the Formica surface.

"I don't know, but maybe. I know nothing about what goes into bootlegging or moonshining," Shane answered.

"The cards told me this whole thing revolved around the hotel so that's where I've been focusing my attention. Dog," Kennie said.

Bella trotted out of the Divination Room with a rope toy dangling from her mouth. Shane waited for the Shepherd to come to him so he didn't have to chase her around the store, which happened on occasion when Bella was in the mood to play. Shane snagged her collar and led her back to the foyer. Kennie followed as far as the door and then stopped.

"Hopefully the history lesson pays off. I'll go reopen the store. You go do some more investigating." She waved and then went back into the store, letting the door close with a loud click.

CHAPTER TWENTY-ONE

Investigating wasn't what Shane planned for the afternoon. He wanted to track down Masters and tell him everything he knew. Nerves bubbled up at the thought of facing Masters again, but he would bite the bullet if it meant successfully finding those missing people. He grabbed his coat, put Bella's leash on, and walked her outside. It was a cold day, but the sky was clear and the sun was shining brightly. Shane breathed in the fresh, crisp air and tried to calm his nerves.

He watched Bella scratch at the dirt and sniff around the bushes along the edge of the parking lot. Masters wasn't fond of dogs so if Shane was going to extend an olive branch, it was probably best not to have Bella chewing on it. Resigned and a little afraid, he took Bella back up to the apartment.

A quick internet search on his cell phone resulted in the address for Masters Private Investigations. Shane drove several miles down the road and then parked the car in a paid lot. His thoughts bounced around his head in a jumbled mess while he tried to decide how to repair the damage he'd done the day before. He stood across the street from the brick building housing Masters' PI firm.

Situated in the heart of downtown, the firm was in old warehouse that now contained a mix of shops and restaurants at street level with high-priced apartments on the upper floors. One side of the brick façade still had the original advertisement for the warehouse and the concrete above the main entrance was still engraved with the original business's name. Vehicles and pedestrians clogged the road. The sound of music and the scent of food drifted on the breeze from the pedestrian mall a few blocks away.

Shane pulled out his phone and dialed Masters' number. Once again, the man skipped all pleasantries.

"Mr. Cayli."

"Call me Shane. Listen, I'm across the street. Can I come up?" Shane waited for a response, but after several seconds of silence he began to wonder if Masters had hung up on him. He quickly glanced at the phone screen to see the call was still connected. "Masters?"

"It was too much to ask, wasn't it. You backing off was never going to happen." Masters sounded resigned to the fact Shane was determined to see this case to the end.

"You started it," Shane said. "You dangled this mystery in front of me, asked for my help, and then suddenly told me to go away. I can't stop now. I have to know what happened. I need to know where these people went. Can I please come up? I have some things to tell you."

"Things," Masters repeated with a sigh. "Apartment 410."

Shane disconnected the call and slid his phone back into his pocket. As soon as there was a break in traffic, he darted across the street and entered the building. Once inside, Shane considered the age of the building and decided against the close confines of the elevators, taking the stairs instead. His thighs would burn by the time he got to Masters' apartment, but there was an odd sensation coming from the walls as he walked through the lobby. He didn't want to be someplace he couldn't quickly and easily escape.

Shadows moved in the periphery of his vision, some more substantial in shape and density than others. Shane was never surprised when old buildings had ghosts but he studiously ignored them as he climbed the stairs. As he neared the fourth floor, he became more unsettled. He wished he could blame it on the upcoming conversation with Masters, but his gut told him differently.

He exited the stairwell into the middle of a rundown hallway with water-damaged carpet; the wallpaper was yellowed and peeling in spots. Shane wondered how long ago the warehouse had been turned into apartments and if it had always looked so crappy. The hall obviously hadn't been updated in decades. For the cost of rent in the place, Shane had expected a much nicer interior.

Hovering at the far end of the hall was a dark mass of ghost shadow. He watched it from the corner of his eye as he located the door to 410. Should he knock because this was Masters' home or could he just walk in since it was also a place of business? After a second of deliberation, he decided to do both. Shane rapped his knuckles on the aged wooden door and then grabbed the doorknob to let himself in. As his fingers closed around the brass knob, the ghost shadow launched down the hall and in the blink of an eye, Hell opened up and swallowed him whole.

_____*****___ __

Screams erupted all around him as the hallway was engulfed in flames. Fire licked up the walls and rippled across the ceiling like water. He opened his mouth on a silent scream as his skin bubbled and blistered. His clothing ignited, melding with his burning flesh as acrid smoke and the scent of burned meat seared his nostrils. Watering eyes did nothing to block his vision of others escaping their apartments only to burn alive in the hall beside him.

This memory was different than others Shane had previously experienced. He wasn't lost to it. He was very aware he was inside a memory but was still helpless to stop it. He couldn't extricate himself from it. Even letting go of the doorknob did nothing.

It's not real, he thought to himself.

Shane crumpled to the floor, curling into the fetal position trying to escape the pain. He wanted to scream in agony but his lungs felt like they were turning to ash in his chest.

It's not real. It's not real. It's not real.

In the distance, he heard his name being called, barely audible over the cacophony of screams and crackling flames. He strained to hear it more clearly, tried to respond, but it was all futile. He couldn't make a sound. With great effort, Shane pulled his consciousness away from the horror surrounding him, reminding himself where he was and that he was not truly burning alive.

He was alive and safe. He tried again to scream and managed a whisper. The pain became excruciating, and he wanted nothing more than for the vision to end. Loud creaking and groaning of timber snapping made him look up just as the ceiling crashed down in a cloud of flaming debris. As wood and plaster buried him, he finally found his voice.

"TOUCH ME," he screamed. "TOUCH ME."

_____*****___ __

The vision ended as abruptly as it started when a hand grabbed his. The floor tilted beneath him and he suffered disorientation. Concerned voices surrounded him, too loud in the silence that followed the deafening roar of fire and fear.

"He's fine. Sorry for the disturbance. He's okay now, thank you."

Shane immediately recognized Masters' voice among the others and he pressed himself into the warmth of Masters' body when he was lifted from the floor. His eyelids felt fused together so he didn't try to open them as Masters carried him inside. The thud of the door closing behind them reverberated through his head, making the headache he already had blossom into a full-fledged migraine. Masters placed him on a soft surface and tucked a blanket around his body. Shane shivered violently. The air-conditioned apartment was too cold after the intense heat of the blaze. Masters gently brushed a sweaty strand of hair off Shane's forehead.

"Shane, are you okay?"

Shane swallowed a few times before answering with a faint, "yes."

The word scraped over raw, damaged vocal cords. His throat like he'd swallowed ground glass. Once again, he found himself hating his psychic ability and the way memories affected his physical body. Mind over body was not just a new age concept. For Shane, it was a very painful reality.

He pried open his eyelids, squinting against the harsh glare from three bare bulbs in the ceiling fan overhead, and cursed himself for leaving Bella at home. Masters' hand slid across Shane's stomach as he smoothed out the blanket, making sure Shane was completely covered. Shane moved his gaze leisurely over the room, taking in his surroundings, and trying to dislodge the remaining confusion brought on by the vision.

Shane focused on little things to make sure he was grounded in reality. He noticed the softness and warmth of the blanket. He noticed the calming effect Masters' touch elicited. He noticed the flat screen on the dresser and the overflowing closet next to it. The entire situation suddenly felt too intimate. Shane pushed himself to a sitting position and instantly regretted it as pain exploded behind his eyes. He swallowed down the bile that rose in his throat and squeezed his eyes closed, grabbing his head in both hands. He was certain his skull was splitting open. Shane felt Masters shift on the bed beside him, but he didn't dare open his eyes, yet.

"Why am I on your bed and not the couch?" Shane asked, breathing through the pain.

"I don't have a couch," Masters answered.

"Don't you live here?" Shane was trying to sort out exactly which side of Masters he would see when he finally opened his eyes.

"I do, but the living room doubles as the agency. I don't want clients lingering overlong so I don't make it comfortable."

Shane nodded, because that made sense to him, but he stopped when the motion slammed his brain against his skull. He pushed his legs out from under the blanket to dangle over the side of the bed. Masters stood up to lean against the doorframe. Through the door, Shane could make out the corner of the kitchen counter. He glanced around the bedroom once more, taking notes as he did so. This might be the one and only time he got a glimpse of Masters' private life.

There was a gym bag and tennis shoes on the floor between the closet and dresser suggesting Masters worked out regularly. The closet was small but tidy and organized with suits on one side, jeans in the middle, and shirts on the other side. The room itself was cramped, but not messy. Shane noticed Masters watching him, but his facial expression gave nothing away.

"Can I use your bathroom?"

Masters blinked as though Shane's question startled him out of his own thoughts. He motioned to a closed door next to him.

"Right there. Do you want something to drink? I have water, tea, or scotch if you prefer something stronger."

"On the rocks, please," Shane answered.

He shuffled past Masters into the bathroom. Hard liquor was rarely his alcohol of choice, because he had no tolerance, but after the welcome he'd just endured, he needed it. He closed the bathroom door and instantly felt claustrophobic. The room was tiny. The toilet was snug between the tub and sink to the point that his elbows bumped the shower door on one side and the paper dispenser on the other. His knees were mere inches from the wall in front of him. There were two doors, the one he'd used from the bedroom and another that he suspected was an entry from the living room. It was hard to imagine a man of Masters' size fitting in here.

Shane washed his hands and splashed cold water on his face then smoothed his hands over his hair. He stared at his reflection in the mirror. Dark circles framed his eyes, his brown irises dull. A few strands of hair hung limply over his forehead. Otherwise, he looked pretty good for a man who'd just burned to death.

That whole experience confused him. Ghost shadow was nothing new since he could see ghosts, fully formed or not, even when his gift was boxed up. He did not, however, typically get full memories. The fact that he had dropped into one without initiating his ability bothered him. If that started happening all the time, he would have to change how he interacted with the world. And he would never be able to leave Bella behind again a decision he whole-heartedly regretted

The memory of the fire had been sudden, strong, and very clear. He had no idea who the memory belonged to, or even whether it was from a man or woman. Usually, he would get a sense of age and gender. Even when reading the memories floating around Crystal Creek he'd known if they belonged to a male or female. Another odd trait about the memory was the disorientation he felt once it had ended. Every time he came out of a reading, he was perfectly aware that the memory had not been his, but this time, he couldn't detach himself. It still felt like the memory was his, as though he had lived through the fire and suffered the injuries.

There was also the disturbing knowledge that he'd been able to act, of his own free will, within the memory, rather than simply observe what had already happened. Usually, he would feel how that person felt, do what that person did. Not so with this one. He felt his flesh burning, his lungs being seared by the heat, and the weight of the debris as it buried him. If he hadn't known better, he would've called it a flashback, but that just wasn't possible. He had never been in a fire, and this was the first time he'd ever set foot in this building. Sadly, Shane knew without a doubt the person the memory belonged to had perished in that fire.

He shook off the fear and unease of the whole situation and focused on less dangerous thoughts. Funny how the upcoming discussion with Masters was now the more desirable activity of the day. Masters' muted voice floated through the door leading to the main living area as he started speaking to someone. Shane didn't hear anyone respond so he assumed Masters had taken a phone call even though he hadn't heard a phone ring.

Shane dried his face and hands and then joined Masters in the living room that acted as the P.I. office. Masters was sitting behind a glass-topped metal desk speaking to someone on his cell phone. The wall behind him was painted a dark green while the other three walls of the room were a deep mocha color. There was a desktop, a laptop, and a multi-line phone equipped with voicemail sitting on the desk, but no other office supplies.

Masters placed his elbows on the desk and leaned forward, watching Shane with such scrutiny it made Shane uncomfortable and sent his heart into a wild beat. Turning away from those probing blue eyes, Shane walked around the room, examining the curated image Masters had created. He was fascinated by the wall with the door to the bathroom. On each side of the doorway was a locked glass case. The one to the left was filled with handguns, two rifles and several different knives. Shane recognized a Ka-bar and thought one of the handguns was a Ruger. The case on the right held a myriad of gadgets – a flashlight, binoculars, a fingerprint kit, cameras from various decades, and several sets of handcuffs.

There wasn't a fleck of dust anywhere. Masters was excessively organized and clean. Another glass-topped, black metal desk shoved into the corner by the front door had two Kevlar vests hanging on wall hooks behind it. Everything in the cases appeared antique or collectible versus items Masters used on a daily basis. The impression the items gave off was exactly what Shane would have expected from a private detective's office.

"What's that address again? Got it. No, I'll get this one. Later, Holmes-y boy."

Shane spun to stare at Masters, surprised at the light, teasing tone coming from the man's mouth. Masters disconnected the call and dropped the cell phone on the desk with a clatter. He motioned at the two chairs across the desk from him before spinning in his chair to grab a glass of scotch from the thin liquor cabinet behind him. He placed the glass on the desk in front of Shane and then quickly typed something into his cell phone. The metal chair was hard and cold, quite uncomfortable, just as Masters had said earlier.

He picked up the glass, raised it in salute to Masters, and then downed half of it in one swallow. Liquid heat burned his entire esophagus, sending instant warmth through his body. The resulting relaxation made the pain and shortness of breath caused by the large swig worthwhile. Shane suppressed a cough to the point his eyes began to water. Despite his reaction, the scotch was excellent – smooth and full bodied. He looked up and caught the barest hint of a smile on Masters' face before he wiped it away.

"Too much for you?" Masters asked.

Rather than answer, Shane finished the remainder of the scotch in one swallow. Unfortunately, this time he wasn't able to stop the cough. He blew out a ragged breath and wiped his eyes. Sometimes he was too cocky for his own good and the universe had no problem putting him back in his place.

"You good?"

"Mmhmm. Did you just call Luke 'Holmes-y boy?'" Shane asked.

"You should hear what he calls me sometimes."

"Oh? Do tell."

"Not today."

Masters' amusement faded as he returned his attention to the cell phone in his hand. He tapped the corner of the case on the desk's glass surface. He set the phone facedown and looked directly into Shane's eyes.

"Floor is yours," he said.

Shane couldn't get over how striking Masters' eyes were. He was drawn in by them and before his brain caught up this mouth, he blurted, "Your eyes are so pretty."

"Doesn't take much to get you drunk, does it?"

"Tipsy. Not drunk. Who is the address for?"

"Nothing you need to worry about." Masters leaned back and crossed his ankle over a knee. "Why are you here? What 'things' do you need to tell me?"

"I think it's time you and I swap information."

"Swap?"

"Yeah, you know, a little tit for tat. Give a little, get a little." Shane furrowed his brow, annoyed Masters didn't understand what 'swap' meant.

"I know what you mean. I'm just not sure how useful your information will be."

"Me, either, but honestly, how useful is the information you have? You're no closer to finding them than me, unless you've suddenly had a breakthrough."

Shane crossed his arms over his chest, feeling bold and righteous; nothing like a little scotch to give one courage. Masters narrowed his eyes.

"Fine. You first."

"I learned the reason why I couldn't read the dining room the night we met at the hotel. It's because that room wasn't original to the building. It was added decades later." Shane held Masters' gaze for several quiet minutes. He couldn't tell what the man was thinking.

"And?" Masters finally said.

"And...it's your turn. Tell me something."

"Robert Grant and Megan Granger were engaged to be married," Masters said, appearing bored by the conversation.

While the engagement was new information, it wasn't what Shane had hoped for.

"The other night at Crystal Creek when Kennie and I were exploring, I discovered that Robert and his party took the main staircase to the fourth floor but then took the south wing servant stairs back down." Shane pointed at Masters to indicate it was his turn.

"First, a tour was expected but why the servant stairs? Dark, claustrophobic, and dangerous doesn't make sense. Second, how do you know that's what they did?"

Shane sighed. "Why do you keep asking me how I know things? Robert's ghost showed me. Made me sick as hell doing it, too."

Masters' expression remained blank, not giving the slightest hint to his thoughts. Shane suspected there was still a healthy dose of disbelief and skepticism banging around the man's skull. He admitted to himself that he hadn't actually expected Masters to change his mind in a heartbeat. Shane might have to read him a few more times to make him a believer. Luke had been the same.

"It's your turn to share," Shane reminded him.

Masters nodded once. "Megan was having an affair, but I'll be damned if I can figure out with who. For reasons I'm not going into right now, I suspect she was fooling around with Luke or Ted, but there's no proof. I want to say she'd never hurt her sister like that, but who really knows."

"Ted. Alyssa's husband?" Shane asked. If Megan was having an affair with her brother-in-law while living in the same house as her sister, that was quite a ballsy move. Luke had an affair before so that wasn't as hard to believe. "Do you think Robert knew?"

"No way to know. What I do know is that everyone was against his engagement to Megan. The reasons why aren't clear."

Shane shifted in his seat. If he'd been Megan, with a child and a rich man willing to take care of them both, he wouldn't risk losing him by having an affair. He supposed it was possible Megan was a gold-digger. Plenty of women had married men they didn't love for a lot less. Shane's parents were a classic example; his mother's unexpected pregnancy had pushed them into a marriage that wouldn't have happened otherwise. They divorced shortly after Shane was born. His mother had remarried for love a few years later and by the time Shane was five years old, he had twin half-brothers. Masters voice pulled Shane from his thoughts.

"Just so I understand clearly, Megan is haunting the Sylvester house and Robert is haunting the hotel."

Shane nodded.

"And you've spoken to both of them."

"No," Shane said distractedly. He had touched Megan the traditional way, so to speak, whereas Robert had just drifted through him. The memory made him shudder and made his stomach roll. He really didn't want to repeat either experience.

"I touched Megan's hand and fell into a memory of her suffocating with everyone else in some sort of dining room. Robert just ghosted through me and I caught a brief glimpse of him leading everyone down the servant stairs. The vision didn't last long enough for me to see where they ended up, though."

Shane felt like his thoughts were coming out jumbled and nonsensical. He was struggling with keeping things in order and relaying each memory properly. The scotch was seriously messing with his concentration. Masters continued to stare at him with a blank expression.

"Have I lost you?" Shane asked him.

"Yes and no. I understand the words you're saying but I've missed something. The question now would be is it worth retracing our steps or should we just move on. Since your words are a bit slow, I'm thinking the scotch was a bad idea."

"Not the first mistake I've made during this case."

"No? What was your first mistake?"

"Answering the phone when Luke called."

Masters laughed. Shane was surprised by the sound but smiled. He was pleased Masters had relaxed and found some humor rather than completely freaking out and cutting off all contact with him. Masters rested his elbows on the desk, leaning toward Shane.

"Here's my issue. You tell me they suffocated in a dining room, but not the dining room they disappeared from. Despite the fact you wandered around the hotel, you never found a second dining room so do you see why I'm confused? Honestly, I'm doubtful of everything you say."

"Yes," Shane admitted. "But you have to remember that I'm only getting fragmented memories. I'm seeing the past, not the present, and even then I'm only seeing the past they experienced. I can only tell you what they saw. Megan witnessed Robert being stabbed by one of the other guests, so I know that. She knew she was slowly suffocating, so I know it, too. God, I *felt* her suffocating and let me tell you, that is not something you ever want to go through. It's like your brain knows you need to breathe, but your body can't comply and you're completely aware that you're not breathing and you want to, but you can't so you panic "

"Shane, steady your breathing before you hyperventilate," Masters interrupted.

Shane took deep, measured breaths while getting his thoughts back under control. He blamed the alcohol for his inability to keep the memories at bay, instead allowing them to bleed into reality. He caught Masters staring at him and fidgeted in his seat. He was uncomfortable and tense and so damned tired.

"What are you thinking?" Shane asked.

"Wondering how legitimate you are."

"I'm legit and you know it."

"Is loss of consciousness a side effect of your...psychic gift?" Masters asked, forcing the words out as though saying them aloud was acknowledgement Shane was indeed psychic.

"Not usually, but I've never touched a ghost before so maybe it's something that happens after connecting directly to the dead. Generally, people are alive when I read their memories. I do tend to get lost in memories, though, which is why I normally have Bella with me."

"Your dog?"

Shane nodded. "Touching her keeps me grounded so I can tell memory from reality. Dogs are perfect because their brains work differently. Touching another person would only result in me reading two people at the same time and compounding the problem. Does that make sense?"

"As much as it can, I suppose, except that you've passed out twice since I met you."

"When was the second time?"

Masters pointed to his front door. Shane glanced that direction and then shook his head in confusion when he turned back to Masters.

"You knocked and then screamed. By the time I got the door open, you were on the floor curled up in the fetal position unresponsive. I thought you'd been attacked but there was no one around. Next thing I know, you're screaming and thrashing about, and people were starting to come out of their apartments, so I picked you up and brought you inside."

Shane hadn't realized he was unconscious during the vision. He had certainly felt like he was aware of his surroundings. He remembered hearing Masters talk to other people, being picked up and carried. That was something new. Ever since Luke had introduced the two of them, Shane's psychic ability had gone haywire and he didn't like it. There was a level of comfort in knowing what to expect but that was gone now.

"Kennie said the same thing when I called her – that you were 'lost to a memory.' She said you would come out of it on your own. Since she wasn't too concerned, neither was I. You should give her a call, though; let her know you came out of it okay."

Shane pulled his phone from his back pocket. He was shocked to see two hours had passed. Another wave of nausea hit him as he dialed Kennie. As he waited for the call to connect to Kennie or her voicemail, he let his thoughts come out of his mouth.

"I know better than to leave Bella behind when I go out. Usually when I get lost to a memory I'm completely unaware of my real-life surroundings and that can be dangerous."

When Kennie's voicemail picked up, Shane left a brief message that he was fine and to please feed Bella, and then put his phone back into his pocket.

"How recent was the fire here?" Shane asked.

The expression on Masters' face suggested Shane had sprouted horns. He ran his fingers through his hair just to make sure he wasn't turning into a demon. Eventually, Masters' expression smoothed out and he answered.

"Late 1957, if I remember correctly."

"How many people died?"

Masters furrowed his brow again but didn't hesitate answering. "Seven with a dozen more severely burned. The roof collapsed."

Shane nodded. That jived with what he'd experienced in the hall, but the memory had started as soon as he touched the doorknob. Or was it when the ghost shadow had swept over him. It had happened so fast Shane couldn't remember clearly.

"Did one of the victims live in this apartment?"

"No. This building wasn't apartments back then. Shane—"

"All the bodies were found in the hall. The roof collapsed while they were trying to escape. They didn't have enough time to get out because there were no fire alarms or sprinkler system and the blaze spread incredibly fast. Am I right?"

Masters visibly swallowed and then nodded. If he hadn't believed in Shane's ability before, maybe he did now. Shane glanced around the room while he let the memory recede once again and giving Masters time to assimilate what Shane had told him.

"I never get a pleasant, happy memory, like a trip to the beach or a wedding or kids playing on swings," Shane muttered to himself. "Do you know why I hate this so much, Masters? Why I'm so reluctant to tell you the details of the memory I saw when I touched you?"

Masters shook his head, so Shane continued.

"Because it's awful, that's why. Painful and vivid and horrible. Ever since Luke brought me on this case, I have died twice. Both times were quite unpleasant and it scared me. I don't want to experience memories from the dead anymore and I don't want to relive them by telling you the details. I don't like it."

"But that's what I *need* you to do because only the dead know what the hell happened," Masters said softly, though his annoyance and frustration thickened the air.

Shane wished he could tell Masters what the hell happened, but he didn't know either. He knew the missing people died of suffocation, but he was no closer to knowing the where and why of their deaths. He pounded a fist against his thigh a few times in irritation. Masters sighed.

"Think of it this way – through your suffering you've gleaned important information. We know that Robert took everyone on a tour of the hotel that eventually led to their deaths by suffocation. We didn't know that before. For whatever reason, they've chosen you to be their voices from beyond the grave, so you need to speak for them. Despite what you may think, or what Luke and I have led you to believe, you have been helpful."

The longer Masters spoke the more animated he became, and Shane got a glimpse of another side to the man.

"This is why I love detective work," Masters continued. "Every piece of information is useful. Every little detail, no matter how insignificant it may seem, when placed with the other puzzle pieces in the right order, can give you a snapshot of what happened. We started with the edge pieces, the where and when, and now we're filling in the middle, the how and why. We don't even have to complete the puzzle in order to see the answer. Get enough key pieces and you can figure it out. Eventually, everything you have seen and experienced will make sense."

The joy and satisfaction Masters found in his line of work was clear in his words and actions. Shawn watched as his features smoothed out and lit up. Shane wondered if he, himself, had ever looked so alive when he was working. He doubted it. Shane liked this side of Masters more than the brooding, skeptical one he'd first met. This version of Masters was one Shane could work with.

"So, did you learn anything else while you were risking your life the other night?" Masters asked.

Shane sighed. The no-nonsense professional Masters he was familiar with was back in full force. At least now Shane understood what drove the man and he found his temperament easier to handle. He thought back over everything he and Kennie had discussed and became annoyed at how all of it was jumbled in his head.

"Does information about Crystal Creek's previous owner help?"

"Couldn't begin to tell you. What is it?"

"In the 1920s the hotel was owned by a mob boss and moonshiner. That was the only time Crystal Creek was truly open and operating apparently. His brother chopped him into pieces in 1928. The Depression hit in 1929. Then in 1933, the hotel was partially destroyed on the canyon side by a flash flood. It was rebuilt but never reopened." Shane cocked an eyebrow at Masters.

"Who the hell did you touch to get *that* memory?" Masters asked.

"No one. That was Kennie's research but don't ask me where she went to get the information."

"She probably called the local historical society. That's what I did."

Shane sighed. Masters already knowing about Pastori and Crystal Creek's sordid history deflated him. The buzz he'd gotten from the scotch was wearing off and fatigue was setting in. At least his post-vision headache had dissipated. He and Masters sat in silence for a few moments, lost in their own thoughts.

"Ok." Masters slapped the desk with an open palm loud enough to make Shane jump in surprise. The chair gave a soft squeak as Masters pushed back and stood up. "Let's go. Visiting hours end at eight."

CHAPTER TWENTY-TWO

Masters moved quickly, pulling his jacket off the back of his chair as he went. Shane watched the man in confusion as he donned the jacket and then pulled a folder from the top drawer of the short filing cabinet behind his desk. Masters' movements were rapid, smooth and purposeful. This was a man accustomed to emergencies and being rushed.

"Stop watching my ass and get off yours, Mr. Cayli."

Masters disappeared into the bedroom and Shane slowly stood up, every muscle in his body protesting. His entire body hurt and his cognitive function was noticeably slower than normal. His own light-weight coat was hung on a coatrack by the door and Shane carefully pulled it on. Masters came up behind him and reached past to open the door, his chest brushing against Shane's arm. As Masters stepped out of the apartment ahead of Shane, his eyes were drawn downward to Masters' ass, because now that he'd been told *not* to look, that was all he could do. Blushing, he forcibly looked at the hallway wall and followed Masters out. Shane kept his hands in his pockets as they walked toward the elevator to avoid accidentally touching anything.

"Where are we going?" Shane asked. The elevator doors closed with a ding and began the descent to the lobby.

"Sunnydale Nursing Home."

Shane met Masters' reflective gaze in the metal elevator doors.

"We need to go get Bella on the way. Nursing homes are dangerous territory for me. They're full of people who have nothing to do but relive the past, not to mention the ghost activity that will be present."

"They don't allow dogs inside," Masters said, no doubt trying to dissuade Shane.

"I'll put the service dog vest on her. They'll let her in."

Years ago, when it had become evident that Shane couldn't go many places without Bella, he had bought a camouflage-colored *Service Dog in Training* vest online. The vest allowed him to take Bella pretty much everywhere with little to no questions asked and didn't make him feel overly guilty for the lie. Shane had expected a fight, but Masters drove them to

Shane's apartment in silence. He used the time in the car to catch a quick nap, but it did little to alleviate the heavy fatigue.

Masters waited in the car while Shane went inside to retrieve Bella. He put her in the vest and then taped a short note to Kennie's apartment door letting her know where they were. Shane didn't want his friend to worry when he didn't come home until late. He got Bella situated in the back seat and then climbed into the car himself. Masters peeled out of the lot and into the mid-afternoon traffic with a recklessness that made Shane's heart rate increase.

"Who's at Sunnydale?" Shane asked.

Conversation while driving like a fiend might not be the best idea for Masters, but Shane needed the distraction. His grip on the door's armrest couldn't get any tighter.

"Robert Grant's younger brother, Paul."

Masters kept his eyes on the road as he spoke, which Shane was grateful for, but he still held his breath every time Masters got too close to another vehicle or whipped into another lane. His heart was pounding against his ribs so hard he was convinced it was trying to escape from his body. After his short, perfunctory answer, Masters went quiet again, not offering any further details or commentary. Deciding conversation wasn't going to be the escape he'd hoped for, Shane turned on the radio. He glanced at Masters when the sounds that piped through the car were that of a news program. He didn't know what station he'd expected, but talk radio wasn't it. The serious, predictive inflection of a newscaster's voice filtered through the speakers.

" — burning east of Kenosha pass. The blaze was reported approximately two hours ago and fire crews are arriving on scene. Authorities state they expect the wildfire to grow substantially due to wind gusts from the west. Containment will be difficult due to the weather conditions and surrounding terrain that make it difficult for firefighters to access the remote area. Homes and businesses in the direct path of flames are being evacuated. Several other surrounding areas have been put on alert. At this time the cause of the fire is still unknown."

Shane closed his eyes as the newscaster droned on with the occasional vocal inflection they must have learned in college. After a few minutes, he grew bored and turned the radio off. Silence was preferrable to the boredom and depression the news always caused him. Masters' phone rang. As he pulled it from his pocket, the car swerved a bit in the lane making Shane glare at the man. Masters was a terrible driver and didn't seem to care.

"Holmestead," Masters barked in greeting. Shane found comfort in the fact the man was unfriendly to everyone; it wasn't just him. "I heard. How close is it to the hotel? On my way to visit Grant. Sure. Keep an eye on it and we'll talk tomorrow."

Masters tossed the phone into the cup holder and finally returned his full attention back to the road.. Masters abruptly switched lanes to avoid hitting a stopped car and Shane tamped down a squeal.

"Are you curious about the scream you heard in the elevator?"

Shane struggled to make sense of Masters' question. The scream in the elevator? Slowly, the memory came to him, distant and unreal despite having been only three days before. He remembered distinctly that Masters hadn't believed in Shane's psychic ability at the time. Was his question now a sign that he was beginning to believe?

"Yes, I'm curious. It was unexpected and far more recent than I would've guessed," Shane answered.

"I investigated it a bit. In 1982 a nonprofit organization showed interest in the building, so they asked their real estate agent to work on obtaining it. After taking the board of directors on a tour one afternoon, she realized she'd left her purse on one of the top floors and returned to get it. The rest of the group headed back to town, thinking the agent would return home on her own since she'd driven herself. Two days later, one of the directors reported her missing. The next day her body was found in the elevator shaft, on top of the elevator which was sitting on the basement level."

"How the hell did she end up on top of the elevator?"

"Curiosity killed the cat," Masters said with a smirk that Shane found entirely too sexy for his own good. Shane forced himself to focus on the words rather than the facial expression. What was Masters hinting at? A few seconds later, Masters spoke again. "I honestly don't know. Maybe she thought the elevator worked. She hit the button, the doors opened, and she didn't notice there was no elevator car when she stepped forward."

Plausible and terrible - falling to one's death in such a way. Shane nodded thoughtfully.

"The place was condemned and basically forgotten until Robert Grant bought the property. His lawyers immediately had the state designate the place a historical landmark. Grant had every intention of keeping his renovations as close to the original as possible. All was good until he and his friends disappeared," Masters added.

Shane listened, patiently waiting for him to finish before returning the conversation to an earlier statement. "When you said the elevator was on the basement level, are you referring to the same floor as the kitchen?"

"Yes. There are no doors on that level which leads me to believe it wasn't supposed to go down that far, but there it was. Maybe the cables rusted through and it fell."

"Why would the shaft go down to a level with no access?"

Masters glanced at Shane from the corner of his eye. "How the hell would I know?"

Shane shook his head and muttered, "That place is cursed." He truly believed it. Far too many people had died horrible deaths in and around Crystal Creek Hotel. Demolition would be a blessing.

"Anything else?" Shane asked.

Masters was finally talking and willingly sharing information, and he wanted to take advantage. Plus, the conversation was keeping his mind off Masters' atrocious driving.

"Robert may have been Jacob's father," Masters said. "The timing is right, although it's odd. Megan moved in with her sister after Jacob was born. If he belonged to Robert, why didn't she go to him when she found herself strapped for cash?"

"You told me she was having an affair. Maybe Jacob is the result of that," Shane offered.

"Maybe."

Masters went silent and Shane retreated into his thoughts, returning to memories of the self-tour he and Kennie had taken. They'd visited each floor all the way to the top and when they came down the servant stairs, they exited on the first floor because that's where the stairs ended. Neither of them had looked for access to the basement level or the kitchen at the back.

"I didn't go into the basement," Shane said to himself.

"Why would you?"

Shane glanced at Masters. He was impressed the man could follow his random comments. Luke would have been lost, wondering where Shane's thought process had taken him. Kennie was the only person who could switch tracks quickly and keep up with Shane's disconnected thought processes.

"Because maybe Robert did?" Shane answered. "Have you been down there? Did you see evidence of a distillery?"

"Yes to both questions. One of the walls is brick and clearly not original to the building. Did you see a brick wall in one of your visions?"

"They're not *visions*, exactly, but no. No brick walls. It was like a bunker almost, all concrete."

"A dining room...in a bunker."

"Yeah."

Bella shoved her head between the seats looking for attention. Shane rubbed her chin and then gently pushed her back onto the seat.

"Why are you suddenly talking to me?" Shane asked.

"Ignoring you didn't work. Keeping information secret didn't work. You just decided to go off on your own. So, I'm trying a different strategy."

"Ok. What about a brick wall says distillery to you?"

"My god, Shane, are you incapable of sticking to one topic at a time?" Masters asked, exasperated. "The wall itself doesn't say distillery, but three large stills were found downriver after the flood, among other things like cars, animal carcasses, and a few bodies of people unfortunate enough to get caught by the water."

Masters took a corner much faster than Shane felt necessary. He grabbed the dashboard to steady himself and then glanced over his shoulder to make sure Bella hadn't been tossed about too badly. Masters continued speaking, either unaware or uncaring that he'd just caused trauma to his passengers.

"Julian Pastori was quite the character and very smart. He was a moonshiner and a bootlegger. What he couldn't make, he trafficked in bread trucks. His brother, on the other hand, was stupid as shit. I'm hoping the Grant brothers are the same. This visit will go to hell real quick if Paul turns out to be the smart one."

Masters slowed the car, barely, and pulled into the parking lot of Sunnydale. The nursing home was built in a star pattern, each point three stories tall. The outer walls were painted a shade of cream with reddish-brown shutters framing the windows on all floors. Mature trees and landscaping would have offered a warm and inviting atmosphere in spring and summer months but were currently nothing more than naked branches giving the place a dismal appearance. The moment the car stopped completely, Shane got out and wrapped his arms around the nearest tree trunk.

"Something stationary. I'm so happy to be alive to experience this moment."

The car door slammed and Shane glanced at Masters' perturbed expression.

"Such a smartass," he grumbled as he passed on his way to the entrance.

Bella whined from the passenger seat where she'd jumped after being left alone in the car. Shane released the tree to retrieve her. Once she was out of the car, he jogged to catch up to Masters, convinced the man would wait for no one. Shane found him waiting in the vestibule between the outer and inner doors. He stared down at Bella and then entered the lobby through the sliding doors.

"This should be interesting," Masters muttered.

"Why?" Shane whispered when he caught up, mindful that their voices would carry in the spacious lobby.

The space was cold with a strong scent of antiseptic hanging in the air, and very yellow. The color was painted onto every wall. Yellow fabric with large black and white flowers adorned the furniture placed into small conversation areas. Even the floor was a haphazard pattern of black, white, and yellow tiles. Shane wasn't sure what was worse, institutional gray and green he'd seen in other hospitals, or this hideous overuse of one entirely-too-bright color.

Masters matched Shane's volume when he answered. "Paul suffered a stroke a few years ago. He's nonverbal but has all his mental faculties whereas I doubt you have all of yours."

"Go to hell."

"Already there, babe."

Shane rolled his eyes. "How are we supposed to interrogate someone who's nonverbal?"

Masters opened his mouth to answer but was interrupted by a plump woman in peach-colored scrubs stepping behind the chest-high counter.

"Hello. How can I help you?" She was smiling and trying to be cheery, but Shane could tell it was forced. She was either miserable in her job or was simply an unhappy person.

Masters stepped up to the desk and returned her smile. "We're here to see Paul Grant."

"Mr. Grant is a very ill man and doesn't receive visitors."

The nurse's expression changed to one of sympathy, but the transition wasn't smooth and Shane didn't buy the act. Masters didn't either.

"Which room is he in?" Masters held up his ID for the woman to see and Shane wondered if that trick had worked in the past. Masters wasn't a cop anymore and Shane didn't think private detective badges held the same power as a shield. The nurse didn't seem to be swayed. Shane sighed loudly, drawing the nurse's attention to him.

"Ignore him. He's pushy and used to getting his way." Masters glared at him as Shane shoved him aside. "I'm a friend of the Grant family. Robert used to protect me from Paul's incessant teasing. I haven't seen Paul since Robert's disappearance. I was so young back then I didn't understand what happened. I only recently learned of Paul's stroke and thought I should come by to say hi."

Shane wrapped up his sob story before he went overboard. Masters stared at him, still clearly irritated. Shane would ask for forgiveness for taking over later when they no longer had an audience.

"And this one?" she asked, tilting her head toward Masters.

"My egotistical and very bossy boyfriend," Shane answered without missing a beat assuming it would be best for them to stick to their original story through the entirety of their investigation.

"You should put that leash on *him*."

Shane laughed and then cleared his throat when Masters grunted.

"Sorry. So, what room is Paul in?"

The nurse stared at him for a moment and then sighed. "Do *not* overstay your welcome."

"Most definitely will not," Shane assured her, giving her a two-fingered salute.

"Second floor, room 223. Left off the elevator in that wing." She pointed them in the correct direction and then disappeared back down the hall from where she'd come.

Masters headed down the hallway the nurse had indicated, slipping his ID back into his pocket. Shane wrapped Bella's leash around his hand and tugged her after Masters. They caught up just as the elevator doors opened and Masters stepped inside. By the time Shane managed to coax his hesitant dog inside, the doors began closing. He shot Masters a glare for not holding the doors but the man refused to look at him, standing with his back to the wood-paneled wall.

"What are you so pissy about? I got us in, didn't I?"

Masters grunted in response with a side-eye at Bella. The elevator dinged as it arrived at the second floor and they stepped off into another god-awful yellow hallway. The brass plate hung on the wall opposite the elevator listed room numbers with arrows pointing in each direction. Rooms 220-225 were to the left, as the nurse had told them, and rooms 226-230 were to the right. Shane followed Masters down the hall to the left, letting him locate the room they wanted.

Bella stayed pressed against Shane's thigh while Shane kept himself in the center of the hall, carefully avoiding coming into physical contact with anything. He hadn't encountered any unwanted memories, so far, but he knew they were there. Hovering in the air, lightly plastered to the walls or dangling from the picture frames just waiting for Shane's psychic ability to give them life once again.

CHAPTER TWENTY-THREE

A woman with a strange aura paced at the end of the hallway in front of a large window. A seating area separated her from the rest of the hallway. She stilled and slowly turned her head to stare at Shane. Not liking the looks of her, Shane averted his gaze and rubbed Bella's ears. Masters stopped in front of the door to room 223 and Shane quickly joined him.

Shane leaned in close to Masters ear and whispered, "Do you see her? The woman in front of the window."

Masters glanced both ways down the hall. Shaking his head, he answered, "No one else is in this hallway."

"That's what I was afraid of," Shane mumbled to himself.

Masters knocked on the door once and then entered Paul Grant's room with his usual air of confidence and authority. Risking another look toward the window, Shane noticed the woman was headed toward him and the closer she got, the more certain he was that she was no longer among the living. Shane rushed into the room, yanking Bella along with him and shut the door.

The space Paul Grant now called home was sterile and shockingly white after the intense yellow of the hall. No personal effects or photographs were anywhere in sight. The man himself looked to be nothing more than a shell. His wheelchair was turned to face the single window, though there wasn't much outside worth seeing. Just a large, leafless tree branch that stretched across the skyline. Oxygen tubing ran from Paul's nose to the concentrator whirring a few feet away beside the twin bed. From Shane's vantage point at the door, Paul looked like an emaciated, bald, and much older version of his brother. If Shane hadn't already encountered Robert's ghost, he would have thought this man was him.

A loud scraping sound filled the room as Masters dragged the only chair in the room from its place against the wall and placed it in front of Paul. He sat down facing the man and pinned him with an intimidating glare. At least, it was intimidating to Shane. Paul appeared unfazed.

"Hello, Mr. Grant. My name is Dominic Masters. I'm the detective currently investigating your brother's disappearance."

Shane bit back the automatic desire to correct that faintly misleading introduction and settled on being annoyed Masters was pretending he wasn't standing there. Why hadn't he introduced Shane? He rubbed Bella's head and watched the non-verbal pissing contest taking place in front of him. Bella whined, drawing Paul's attention. Paul's rheumy, dark eyes were filled with intelligence, anger, and pure hatred. It didn't matter if the hate and anger were a side effect of being an intelligent man who could no longer move, speak, and care for himself, or even if it was because they were there to ask about his brother. Shane's blood turned cold and he instinctively pulled Bella closer.

Having all that emotion directed at him made Shane extremely uncomfortable. A chill slithered through his body, but Shane managed not to outwardly show he was affected. His instinct told him not to show weakness. Shane glanced at Masters, but he was still intently watching Paul. He wondered if Masters saw the same evil Shane did.

"I'm going to ask you some questions," Masters said.

Paul's gaze slowly shifted back to Masters. The two of them once again locked into a silent battle of wills. Shane wagered Masters would win and mentally congratulated himself on his guess when Paul looked away first. With Paul's eyes averted, Masters pointed to the bed. Shane quietly moved to where Masters indicated and sat on the edge of the mattress behind Paul's wheelchair. Masters had placed Shane within easy reach of Paul and he thanked every deity he knew that Paul was old and weak. Shane would've never allowed himself to be so close to evil otherwise. He pulled Bella between his legs so he was constantly in contact with her. If Paul truly was mute, he knew why Masters had brought him along, and it was going to be quite unpleasant.

"Do you know where your brother is?" Masters asked.

Paul ignored him, looking out the window at nothing but the tree branch. Shane wondered if he was truly seeing the tree branch or if he had already retreated into his memories. Shane glanced at Masters, lifting a hand toward Paul's back before lowering it back to his leg at Masters' nearly imperceptible shake of the head.

"A body washed up in the river.".

The lie slid off Masters' tongue so smoothly Shane would have believed it if he hadn't known better. A small twitch was the only visible response Paul gave. Masters narrowed his eyes and tilted his head to the side a bit. Paul's tiny movement meant something to him.

"The body belonged to Megan Granger, your brother's girlfriend. I'm sure you remember her."

The air in the oxygen tubing began to wheeze at a faster pace, belying the outward calm Paul was projecting. The information Masters was pretending to share was having some kind of effect. Many thoughts and emotions could cause an increase in breathing. Masters leaned in closer, resting his elbows on his knees, and spoke in a menacing tone.

"I know those people are up there, and I *will* find them."

Paul finally turned his head toward Masters. The stroke had left half of Paul's face paralyzed, but the unaffected side held a malicious grin. Shane's blood formed icicles. Paul knew where his brother was. He knew exactly what had happened to him. But Robert wasn't the only victim. Fourteen other people were missing. Children were left without parents. Families were left wondering what had happened to their loved ones. There was no closure.

The awful man seated in front of Shane had all the answers locked inside his head and the injustice of that settled like a stone in Shane's gut. Shane initiated his ability. The warmth of his power flowing through his body was a welcome change to the bone-deep chill he'd suffered since stepping into the room. Without a second thought, Shane touched Paul's shoulder.

———-***——-

"I don't like this idea. Are you sure it's even yours?" he asked.

"It's mine," Robert assured him. Robert stood with his back to him, stirring the pot of stew he was making for dinner. A few seconds later, he put the spoon down and turned. "Besides, she agreed to do a paternity test after the baby is born."

"So wait until then. Don't do anything stupid." His anger was hot and sharp, all directed at his brother and the bitch he called girlfriend.

"I'm not waiting. I'm changing my will now, Paul. The baby is mine. Megan and I will get married and raise it together."

Robert turned back to the stove, ignoring Paul's fury. Hatred for the whore who had gotten herself pregnant and was forcing his bother into marriage burned inside his chest. His fist tightened, threatening to snap the wineglass in two. Robert sighed and continued speaking.

"It's not like I'm writing the rest of the family out of the will, I'm just decreasing the amount everyone will get so I can secure the financial future of my child. God knows I have plenty of money and property to go around."

"This is insane," Paul bit out.

"I met with the lawyer this morning and signed all the necessary paperwork. I'm going to tell Megan over dinner tonight." Robert took another deep breath and then let it out slowly. "I'm also going to ask her to marry me."

"What about the other guy she's fucking?" Paul asked. His jaw was hurting from how tightly he clenched his teeth.

Robert tossed the spoon aside and spun around. He braced his hands on the countertop, his irritation evident. Well, he could suck it up, because his older brother was angry enough to spit nails.

"She stopped seeing him months ago and he's already married. He can't offer her anything."

"She's a money-grubbing bitch," Paul spit out, stepping closer to Robert. "But you ignore it and turn a blind eye every time she spreads her legs for you."

"Get out," Robert yelled. "She'll be here any minute and I want you gone."

Paul choked out a laugh. "You know it, don't you? You know that sorry ass, cheating fuck of a cop could be the father."

Robert turned his back again, which infuriated Paul even more. How dare his younger brother dismiss him in such a way. At least he could take some pleasure in the fact he'd struck a nerve. Robert's posture was rigid, every movement stiff. Knowing the chances Megan's baby didn't belong to Robert did nothing to alleviate the hate and anger Paul felt towards the woman. She was stealing everything from him. The woman was a gold digger and she wasn't just taking Robert's money; she was taking Paul's share, too.

"I said, get out," Robert spat.

Paul slammed his wineglass on the countertop, shattering the delicate stem and sending wine cascading across the granite.

—— -***—— -

The memory dissipated as Shane pulled his hand back. The fingers of his other hand were fisted around Bella's collar. He forced himself to relax and then gently rubbed behind Bella's ear. Paul turned to glare at Shane over his shoulder and Masters frowned Belatedly, Shane realized the soft touch to Paul's shoulder may have looked like a comforting caress. Shane caught Masters' gaze, willing him to understand. A brief second later, Masters returned his gaze to Paul.

"Where is your brother's body, Mr. Grant?" Masters asked.

Paul narrowed one eye, appearing to be the crazed killer Shane suspected he was. Shane reached out again, but this time decided to touch the back of Paul's chair where the material of the seat met the fabric of the man's clothing. Given the amount of energy pulsing off Paul's body, Shane would have no problem picking up on everything without making physical contact with the man himself. The moment his fingers touched the chair, the memory hit Shane with the force a bomb.

—— -***—— -

His shoulder ached from the uneven door frame he leaned against, watching the activity in the dining room while also remaining out of sight. The electricity was minimal and the entryway he stood in, along with the hallway behind him, was steeped in darkness. The scent of mildew and decay mixed unpleasantly with the scent of new paint and food.

Robert's parties were always elegant and fanciful affairs, even when taking place in a decrepit, condemned building. The party was ridiculously formal despite the filth that surrounded them. Robert wore his favorite tuxedo and the bitch he called a girlfriend stood at his inside, tucked in close with her arm around his waist. The pair made him sick and hostility boiled deep inside him.

"Are you sure this will work?" A deep voice whispered from behind him.

Paul tore his eyes away from the party and glanced over his shoulder at the dark form of his co-conspirator. He couldn't see him clearly due to the heavy darkness, but he didn't need or want to. He hadn't even bothered to learn the man's name. Only the most necessary information had been exchanged between them.

"It'll work." He returned his attention the dining room.

Robert and Megan were talking to different groups of guests, laughing and looking as though there was nothing they enjoyed more. Paul felt his companion move closer.

"How do you know he'll take them down there?"

"Because I know," Paul snapped. "He's a history buff and loves this damn building. He'll definitely show it off. He thinks I've come to terms with his decision and that I've done my part." He scoffed at his younger brother's idiocy. "I haven't wasted one damned second on this shit hole. Lock is still broken but by the time he realizes it, it'll be too late."

He didn't bother telling the other man he also hadn't unblocked the air vent or turned it on. The less information he shared, the better.

"There are more guests than I expected. Will he take all of them with him? We can't risk one of them being able to help before we're ready."

"Jesus, fucking relax. Aren't cops supposed to be calm under pressure?"

"I'm calm enough."

"Look at her," Paul said. "She fucked you and then dumped you for a man with deeper pockets stupid enough to fall for her lies. He has your woman and your son, and every penny of *my* money."

If it hadn't been for Paul cleaning up his younger brother's messes all these years, Robert wouldn't be as well off as he was. That money was much as his as it was Robert's.

"You haven't given me any proof the kid is mine and remind me again how trapping them in this hellhole is going to help with anything."

"The brat is yours. She did a paternity test and my idiot brother sure as shit ain't the daddy. He knows it, too, but will he change the will back? No. Says the kid needs a father and apparently you don't count." Paul said. He ground his teeth in fury. No matter what Paul said or did, Robert refused to see reason. "If Robert dies, everything goes to that bitch and her boy. But, if he goes missing and no one can prove if he's dead or alive, the money gets split three ways between me and them."

Paul had shared all of this with his co-conspirator before, but he hadn't told the other man everything. He deliberately left out the detail that if Megan disappeared, too, all the money came to Paul. He also left out the fact that he had no intention of freeing these people once they were trapped. His companion had only agreed to assist when given the guarantee that Megan and the others would be released after a day or two. Paul knew he wouldn't have gotten the cop to help if he'd admitted all these people were going to die.

The cop hadn't seemed to have a problem with Robert dying, which was supposed to happen by the hand of a guest Paul had blackmailed. Paul had no intention of releasing the photos of the man having sex with an underaged girl – Paul had screwed her himself – but he had no problem using them to get what he wanted. Paul smiled as it got closer to time for the tour. Soon, he would be getting everything that was rightfully his.

"I don't care about the kid or the money. I just want Megan back."

"Plan to leave your wife, do you."

Paul listened to the man shift his weight from foot to foot behind him. His attention was drawn back to the party by Robert's booming laughter.

"She'll never leave him for you, not when she's got it made. And be honest, my friend. You'll never leave your wife for a lying slut. You just get a rush out of sticking your dick in other women behind your wife's back -"

— —-***— —-

Shane snapped out of the memory, breathing hard and once again clenching Bella's collar. It wasn't until Masters tugged on his hand that Shane realized why he'd come out of the memory the way he had. Masters had pulled his hand off Paul's wheelchair. Masters's touch was scalding against Shane's icy skin. His ability was still pumping through every inch of his body so he yanked free of Masters's grip. The last thing he needed was for Masters's memories to intrude and confuse things.

If Masters misunderstood anything, Shane would explain in the car. Shane shivered as he made eye contact with Paul. His predatory gaze slid over

Shane's body, head to toe, making Shane feel slimy. This man had killed his own brother and fourteen other innocent people, then conspired with a cop to cover it up. Shane stood up and shuffled toward the door, pushing Bella ahead of him with his knees. He couldn't leave the room fast enough.

"Thanks for the lively conversation. Please, don't get up. We know the way out," Masters said, exiting the room behind Shane.

Despite his intense fatigue and weak muscles, Shane grinned at Masters' blatant insult. Shane didn't have to look at Paul to know the jabs hit the mark. Knowing what he did now, Shane knew Paul was infuriated by the hand fate dealt him and Masters had successfully rubbed his face in it.

Shane turned at the sound of the door closing and then jumped back, plastering his back to the wall just in time to avoid becoming one with the female ghost wandering the hallway. The ghost passed right through Masters who stared at Shane like he'd gone insane. When Masters didn't react to the apparition at all, Shane knew he was completely unaware of her. Shane carefully pushed off the wall and using one hand on the railing for balance, he shuffled toward the elevator.

Pain exploded behind his eyes followed by a wave of nausea. Shane pulled Bella against his leg and hooked his fingers into the handle on the back of her vest.

"Lead," he instructed.

He closed his eyes, knowing Bella wouldn't let him trip or walk into anything. Behind him was the thumping of Masters footsteps muted by the blood rushing through his ears. He wavered on his feet as dizziness threatened to drop him. Using what strength he had left, Shane shoved his ability back into the protective mental box. His temperature dropped even more and his muscles stiffened as he tried to stay upright. Masters' voice floated to him through dense mental fog.

"Can I touch you? You don't look like you'll make it out of here without help."

Certain that if he opened his mouth, he would vomit, Shane only nodded. His ability was locked down and if he did pick up on anything Masters projected, it would likely result in unconsciousness again, which Shane would happily accept. His tongue felt like it was coated in wool and his throat hurt. Nausea sat at the top of his esophagus threatening to open the gates at the slightest provocation. Masters slid one arm around Shane's waist and used his other hand to hold Shane's upper arm, helping redistribute Shane's weight. Bella stayed pressed against his leg on the opposite side.

"Service dog in training," Masters mumbled, pressing the down button on the elevator. "Seems like she's already trained."

"Mmhmm," Shaned hummed in response.

The elevator dinged on arrival and Masters guided Shane into the car. Bella was less hesitant this time, stepping in alongside Shane. As the doors slid closed, Shane sent a silent prayer that the shuddering movement wouldn't make him puke. They arrived at the first floor without incident but as they entered the hallway, Masters pulled Shane closer and whispered in his ear.

"Look upset."

Shane wanted to laugh. Did he not already look like he'd survived the apocalypse? He felt like he had. Shane lowered his head to Masters's shoulder and sniffled.

"Uh, is everything okay?" a woman asked as Masters led Shane across the lobby.

"He's fine. Harder than he thought seeing his old friend in such a state," Masters answered.

Once outside, Masters relaxed his grip and Shane took in a lungful of fresh, clean air. The cool temperature did no favors for Shane's already chilled body, but it did wonders for his mind. The nausea, dizziness, and lightheadedness eased up with every step he took toward the car. Masters warm arm around his waist was a stark contrast to the cold evening air.

Shane leaned heavily against Masters as he ushered Bella into the back seat. Masters helped Shane into the car, making sure he didn't bump his head or fall back out, before closing the door and making his way to the driver's side. Masters turned the car on and cranked up the heat. Shane wasn't *that* cold, but he appreciated the gesture. He rested his head back and closed his eyes.

"Why did you ask before touching me?"

"Kennie told me to. When I spoke to her earlier she told me that and to not touch you immediately after you do your thing and to keep you warm. She did not, however, say why."

"Because my ability is active. If you touch too soon, I can accidentally read you. It makes me warm and the longer I use it, the hotter I get. When I lock it down, the resulting drop in body temperature is too much."

Masters reversed out of the parking spot and drove away from the nursing home. Shane was happily unaware of his driving with his eyes closed, but he was constantly assaulted by Paul's memories and everything he'd learned. He was disgusted by the man. He was angered by the fact that Paul had killed fifteen people out of greed and, due to his poor health and lack of proof, he would likely never pay for his horrific crime.

Shane took some small satisfaction that Paul was confined to a wheelchair, stuck in a dismal nursing home, dependent on oxygen and other people to do the most basic things for him all while being lucid enough to know there wasn't a damned thing he could do about any of it. Shane hoped the asshole was miserable. He still didn't know where Robert and the others were. Paul had an accomplice, the man Megan had an affair with, but the man's name hadn't been part of the memory so Shane didn't know who he was. The man's voice tickled the back of Shane's mind with faint familiarity. He had nothing substantial to share with Masters.

With the heater warming him and the onslaught of tragedy he had witnessed over the last few days, Shane's fatigue and emotions overwhelmed him. Unable to keep it all in anymore, he let the tears fall.

"I was wondering what kind of fallout I would be dealing with. You've been entirely too quiet," Masters said. He slid a hand behind Shane's head and massaged the tired muscles of his neck. "But I think I prefer the fighting and fainting to the crying."

Shane wiped the tears from his cheeks with the back of his hand. "Too much—" He cleared his throat and blew out a rough breath. "He killed them."

"I suspected as much. Did you see him do it?" Masters squeezed Shane's neck one more time then returned his hand to the steering wheel.

"No. he didn't kill them so much as he put them in a situation that would kill them." Shane cracked an eye to peek at Masters. "Did that make sense?"

"Sadly, it did."

Shane grunted. "What led you to suspect him?"

"Money. Only a few months after Robert's disappearance, Paul started selling off his brother's properties keeping only two – the mansion Paul moved into almost immediately and Crystal Creek Hotel. Six years after the disappearance, Paul pushed to have Robert declared dead so he could, quote, bury him and move on, unquote. Two years after that, he succeeded. According to Robert's last will and testament all of his wealth was to be split between Megan and their children, and Paul. Problem with that was Paul had already drained his brother's assets so even if Megan and her kids could claim it, there was nothing left for them."

"How much money are we talking about?" Shane asked, his discomfort and sadness all but forgotten.

"Thirty-six million. By the time Robert was declared dead, Paul had blown through most of it. The last one million is currently being used to pay his medical bills."

"That's a lot of money that could've paid for college and stuff," Shane mumbled. He was depressed to realize that Jacob was probably one of the children mentioned in Robert's will. He was convinced Paul knew who Megan's son was but had said nothing to avoid losing half his ill-gotten fortune to a child.

"Hell, the fact he didn't sell the hotel was enough for me to suspect him," Masters continued. "Whenever authorities asked Paul about it, he claimed to be holding onto it out of sentiment because his brother loved the place and he couldn't bear to part with it."

"Bullshit. He hated that place and he hated his brother. He kept it because he didn't want anyone to find the bodies."

"Considering no one has found any bodies yet I don't think he has anything to worry about."

"But you told him a body *was* found," Shane pointed out. "He must be shitting himself thinking one of his victims was found and identified."

"I'm sure he is."

Shane collected his thoughts as Masters turned into the underground parking garage of his apartment building. Masters shut the engine off, but neither of them made an immediate move to get out of the car.

"If he had sold Crystal Creek and it was subsequently torn down, would his victims have been found?"

"It's possible. Bodies have been found at demolition and construction sites before. But Robert had the place designated a historical landmark so new owners wouldn't be allowed to tear it down no matter what shape it's in." Masters patted Shane's thigh. "Let's go inside."

They both got out of the car and Shane grabbed Bella's leash. They followed Masters into the building and then onto the elevator. Shane stared at their reflections in the doors as they ascended. Masters was looking down at Bella with a frown. The man really seemed to have an aversion to dogs.

"New owners could renovate, though," Shane said, drawing Masters's attention away from Bella. "The room Robert died in was found while planning to renovate. I don't think a search party would look at the structure of a building the same way an architect would."

"Paul must be a genius to mastermind something like this. There were a lot of variables that had to work out just right for things to end the way he wanted them to, though I'm certain his current paralyzed state wasn't part of his plan."

"Jacob's father helped. He was a cop."

Shane rolled his neck and shoulders as the elevator shuddered to a stop and the doors opened. He and Bella stepped out, but Masters stared at him until the doors began to close again and then he rushed off.

"What? Why are you staring at me like that?" Shane asked.

"Want to tell me how you know who Jacob's father is? Megan never told anyone."

They stopped in front of Masters's apartment door. From the corner of his eye, Shane watched the looming cloud of darkness bouncing around the end of the hall that had sucked him into a raging inferno. Masters unlocked the door and pushed it open, gesturing for Shane to enter first. Masters's cell phone started ringing and he pulled it out to check the caller ID. He glanced at Shane unhooking Bella's leash and vest, and walked into the bedroom to take the call, closing the door as he answered. Shane sat down in the chair behind Masters's desk and put his head down on his arms. He was so damned tired. He had so much to tell Masters but no energy to do it. Bella curled up next to his feet and he fell asleep listening to the deep rumble of Masters's voice in the other room.

CHAPTER TWENTY-FOUR

Shane woke to an unfamiliar pinging. He was warm and comfortable beneath a heavy blanket and the reassuring weight of Bella's head on his leg. A deep voice began cursing next to him and Shane's eyes flew open. The bed shook and the warmth at his back moved away. He didn't get the enjoyment of a slow climb to awareness, it slammed into him with a jolt. He glanced behind him and confirmed his suspicions – he was in bed with Masters. He closed his eyes, hoping Masters wouldn't realize he was awake just yet.

He replayed the events from the night before but couldn't recall walking into Masters's bedroom and climbing into bed with him. Shane's mind raced trying to find a way out of the awkward situation. He adjusted his legs beneath the blanket and realized he was wearing significantly less clothing than he remembered, too. He'd been fully clothed, coat and all, when he'd drifted off sitting at Masters's desk. Bella lifted her head when Shane moved and then dropped it back down once he stilled again.

Masters answered the phone with a sleepy, "What? No, I'm up...noon is fine...No, I'll pick Shane up on the way."

Shane had a moment of silly giddiness at the way his name sounded in Masters's sleepy voice. His grin was wiped off his face a second later with Masters's next words.

"Bullshit. You're just jealous he's sleeping with me."

All pretense of sleep was gone. Shane rolled over to stare at Masters who sat on the edge of the bed wearing nothing but boxer shorts. His gaze slid over Masters's bare back and arms, and then down the dips and contours of his defined muscles as Masters placed the cell phone back on the side table and turned toward Shane. He folded one knee in front of him on the mattress and then placed the back of his hand to Shane's forehead.

"Good. Fever is gone."

Shane gently pushed Masters's hand away and glanced at the phone, eyebrows listed in question.

"Holmestead wants to meet for lunch to discuss the case. I tried to cover the fact you spent the night with me but he's at the shop and Kennie told him you were here."

"How did Kennie know?"

If Kennie suspected he'd spent with the night with a man, especially Masters, she would have been blowing up his phone but he'd received no calls or texts.

"Apparently you left a note on her door."

Shane pulled the blankets over his face and groaned. He'd completely forgotten he'd taped a note to her front door the day before. It would've been one thing if Luke and Kennie had just *suspected* where he'd been, but Masters had confirmed to both of them that Shane had spent the night in his bed. He wondered if Masters had deliberately misled Luke by not telling him Shane had been unconscious the entire time. Luke and Kennie were going to razz him something fierce later.

He was embarrassed and annoyed. He wanted to kick Masters's ass, not only for stripping him down to his boxers, but for creating a situation Shane wouldn't be able to talk his way out of. Maybe he would lie and say he'd slept on the floor. Masters stood up and pulled on a T-shirt, but the thin, worn fabric did nothing to hide his muscular physique. The man looked amazing. Shane fisted the blanket and forced himself to meet the man's gaze.

"What exactly happened last night?" Shane asked.

"You fell asleep and I couldn't wake you, probably because of the fever. So, I carried you in here, undressed you, and sated all my wicked sexual desires with your unconscious body."

Shane rolled his eyes and swung his feet to the floor, pushing himself up slowly. Every muscle in his body hurt and his bladder screamed for relief. Like a distressed damsel in the movies, he wrapped the blanket around his exposed skin.

"I believe everything except you having your way with me."

He stood up and pulled the blanket off the bed, intent on keeping it wrapped around his near-naked body. Masters chuckled and Shane glanced back at him in time to see the man's gaze drift over him top to bottom.

"I've already seen it all, babe."

Why did Shane find that deep timbre so damn sexy? His heart rate increased and he felt the blush rise from his neck to cascade over his face. He dropped the blanket on the floor and rushed into the bathroom, slamming the door behind him. He was annoyed that Masters let his friends think they were sleeping together, but he wasn't angry. He wasn't even all that horrified at finding himself mostly naked in bed with the man. There was a knock on the second door leading to the living room and Masters called out from the other side.

"I put your clothes on the bed and shut the bedroom door. Take a shower but make it quick. I need to take one, too."

"Fine. Can you take Bella outside to pee?" Shane yelled back.

"No. I gave her a pee thing in the living room."

What the hell was a pee thing? Despite Masters' order to be quick, Shane took his time showering, letting the hot water massage away some of the soreness and tension. When his fingers resembled prunes, he stepped out and wrapped a towel around his waist. He hadn't brought any clothing into the bathroom with him except for his boxers, and he wasn't keen on wearing those a second day in row. He cracked the door to peek into the bedroom.

When he saw the room was empty, he walked to the bed where his folded clothes had been placed. The second door between the bathroom and living room opened and closed, and then the sound of the shower being turned on filtered into the room. Trusting that Masters was beneath the spray and not likely to walk in on him, Shane dressed in his day-old clothes, sans underwear, as quickly as possible. With a sigh, he folded his boxers and stuffed them into a pocket. He slipped on one shoe and then the other as he shuffled out of the room.

Bella was curled up against the door but jumped to her feet as soon as Shane opened it, whining the way she did when she needed outside. He grabbed her vest and put it on her, and then attached the leash. His gaze moved to the corner by Masters's desk where a potty training pad for puppies was laid out, the so-called pee thing Shane suspected, with a large wet patch in the center of it. Bella had actually used it which surprised him.

Shane hadn't bought a pad like that for her in years, always preferring to take her outside to do her business. The smell wasn't overwhelming, but it was noticeable so Shane folded it up and tossed it in the kitchen trash. Bella wasn't whining to go out as he'd thought but was probably hungry instead so Shane started going through the cabinets in search of food he could share with the dog and caffeine. He huffed a few minutes later when his search turned up neither. Did Masters not require sustenance?

The sound of the shower cut off so Shane sat down at Masters' desk to wait for him. They were having breakfast elsewhere. *Make that lunch,* he thought when he glanced at the time on his phone. It was already half past ten; factor in the time it took for Masters to dress and drive them to wherever they were meeting Luke, and it would be lunchtime. Bella trotted over to him with her leash in her mouth and then laid on the floor beside his chair. He reached down to pet her head. The beeping effect he'd assigned to Kennie's text messages drew his attention.

Meeting at the Grey Goose. We'll get our margarita on.

Shane smiled as he sent the simple reply of *okay.*

The Grey Goose was a Mexican restaurant that he and Kennie only went to when they wanted to get drunk. The food was mediocre, but the drinks were strong and cheap. He leaned back in the chair as he opened the app for his favorite news station to see what was going on in the world. The headline "Forest Fire Spreading Fast" caught his attention and he clicked on the link to the article.

According to the report, the fire had started in a campground located twelve miles northwest of Crystal Creek Hotel. The previously hot, dry summer coupled with the beetle kill was giving the fire plenty of fuel despite the colder temperatures. There hadn't been any snowfall yet and apparently the hope of moisture to help control the flames wasn't expected. Winds were pushing the fire west, but that could change any moment putting many homes and businesses, including Thunderhawk and Crystal Creek, in imminent danger.

The despair Shane felt after visiting Paul at the nursing home deepened with the knowledge that his search for those missing people may never be resolved if a forest fire destroyed the hotel and incinerated their bodies. Robert, Megan, and their friends deserved to be found. Paul deserved to pay for his crimes. And the families of the victims deserved closure.

When Shane first answered Luke's pleas for help, he'd thought he had all the time in the world to find Robert and the others. Now, he felt time was running out. The sand in the hourglass was slipping from beneath his feet. He set his phone on the desk and cradled his head in his hands.

Masters came out of the bedroom wearing dark brown slacks and a deep blue button-down shirt that complimented his eyes. He raked a hand through his damp hair, but stopped when he noticed Shane staring at him. Masters glanced down at Shane's phone where the photo of bright orange flames that accompanied the article could be seen.

"Why do you look so depressed? Are you going to cry again?"

"I am and I might. Everything is going wrong." Shane picked up the phone and closed the article. "I can't find these people. I know Paul killed them with a cop who is supposed to help people, but I can't prove it. And now there's a fire that's going to destroy everything, not that it would necessarily be a bad thing. That building *needs* to be destroyed. I don't know what to do. There are no tangible clues. To top it all off, I spent the night in your bed and there's no coffee."

Shane stopped talking when he realized he was rambling and spewing disjointed thoughts. Masters stared for a moment before sighing and taking a seat in the chair across the desk from Shane.

"Okay. First, I'll buy you coffee at the restaurant. I don't drink it so of course I don't have any. Second, we do have clues. They're just trapped in here." Masters thumped Shane on the forehead and Shane rubbed away the soreness.

"I can't make sense of what's in my head, though."

"That's my job. I just need to figure out how to get the relevant information out of you. I've never worked with someone like you; someone who can get into people's minds and see things."

"Except everything I see is out of context. It's like walking into a theatre in the middle of a movie, watching a few minutes of it before walking out again, and then trying to guess what the movie is about so I can explain it to someone else. It's exhausting."

"So, watch the bits of movie available to you and then tell me what you saw. Let me help figure out what the movie was about. Chances are good I've seen different segments of the same movie. Holmestead may have seen different parts than both of us. Perhaps between the three of us, we'll have seen enough to make sense of the plot. We don't know how it started, and we won't know every second that occurred in the middle, but if we figure out what went down in the last scene, right before the movie ended, we'll have enough for a synopsis."

Shane stared at the dark screen of his phone, lost in thought. Masters had a point. There were so many horrible images in Shane's head. Maybe if he shared those horrors, it would not only help with solving the case, but would help him keep his sanity. After all, they now had a limited window of time before all hope was lost amidst the flames currently ravaging the mountainside.

CHAPTER TWENTY-FIVE

The Grey Goose boasted itself to be a fine dining establishment serving traditional Mexican cuisine, but the menu was typical Tex-Mex that was tolerable, served by waitstaff wearing outrageously colored costumes and forced smiles. A mariachi band played from a small stage near the bar where a few patrons were already drunk despite the early hour. Masters and Shane followed the hostess to the back of the restaurant where Kennie and Luke were already seated in a booth, munching on chips and salsa. Shane slid onto the bench seat beside Kennie. She winked at him, waggling her eyebrows. Shane ignored her and picked up a menu. Masters sat beside Luke on the other side of the table.

Within seconds of sitting down, a young woman in a neon pink, green, and orange dress with ruffles came to the table to take their order. Shane tried not to openly cringe at the outfit and forced himself to look the waitress in the eye. They each placed their orders then Shane watched Miss Ruffles disappear into the kitchen. He fiddled with the edge of the tablecloth while he waited for someone else to start the conversation. Luke had requested this meeting so Shane expected him to begin the discussion. As the silence dragged on, Shane turned to Kennie.

"Why did Luke bring you? Didn't you tell me to stay away from them?" he whispered.

Kennie whispered back, "I'm curious, what can I say?"

At that moment, Luke finally decided to speak. He made brief eye contact with Shane before looking at Masters.

"So, did you learn anything by visiting Paul Grant?"

"I don't know yet," Masters answered. "But I'm sure there was some illuminating information."

"Illuminating?" Luke scoffed. "How can information from a nonverbal man be illuminating? Now that I think about it, how did you get information from him at all?"

Masters drank some of his iced tea, glancing at Shane over the glass, before answering. "I took him with me."

Luke's eyes narrowed as he glared at Masters, but Masters didn't seem to notice. Or if he did, he didn't care. The longer Luke stared, the redder his face got and his jaw ticked from grinding his teeth. The man was pissed.

"You did what?" he gritted out.

Shane and Kennie glanced at each other. It was unusual to see the typically reserved Luke so outwardly angry. Seconds later, Luke erupted.

"Have you lost your damned mind? You took Shane to visit a psychotic killer?"

Several diners looked their direction and Shane lifted his hand to wave in apology. Kennie kicked Luke's leg under the table. The simultaneous actions had the desired effect because when Luke spoke next his volume was closer to normal.

"That man is probably responsible for the deaths of fifteen people and you dangled a psychic in front of him. If he finds out, he'll think Shane read his mind. Paul is paralyzed and mute, but he isn't stupid, Dom. Plus, if our suspicions are correct and he had an accomplice, then you've made Shane a target."

"I did not make him a target," Masters said. "Paul doesn't know his name or that he's psychic because I never introduced him. Shane touched him once, but no words were spoken."

"He saw his face and he was with you. Paul will assume Shane is your partner and that may be enough."

Shane had seen Luke's anger before, but not quite to this severity. The idea that Paul might find him and kill him made his stomach roll. The man had killed his own brother. He wouldn't even think twice about taking Shane's life.

"You're first name is Dom?" Kennie asked.

"You'll call me Masters like everyone else," he answered.

Kennie shrugged and Masters slid his gaze to Shane. His anxiety was ramping up. Shane forced himself to breath slow and evenly, telling himself the whole time that Paul didn't know his name. He wouldn't be able to find him. Shane glanced from Masters to Luke. It was time to divulge some secrets

"Paul did kill those people. He considered them collateral damage, loose ends, whatever, but his main targets were his brother and Megan. He wanted the money."

"We guessed as much but somehow Paul was never considered a suspect by authorities," Luke said.

Shane opened his mouth to explain why, but Masters beat him to it.

"Because his accomplice was a cop."

Everyone fell silent as Miss Ruffles placed their food on the table and another waiter refilled their drinks. Conversation took a back seat as they all dug into their food. Shane and Masters hadn't eaten before heading to the restaurant and apparently neither had Luke and Kennie. Shane didn't know if he preferred the uncomfortable conversation about dirty cops and homicidal millionaires or the silence that allowed his mind to ruminate on all the ways Paul Grant could find out who he was and have him killed. The food settled in his stomach like a rock. Inevitably thinking about Paul led Shane down a terrifying hole of memories featuring his ex-fiancé, Brent.

He was transported back in time to a cold and filthy walk-in freezer tucked into the back of an abandoned meat packing plant. While engaged to Shane, Brent had kidnapped, sexually assaulted, tortured and murdered four women. Then there was the torture he'd put Shane through when he'd learned Shane was helping the police catch him. Brent had drugged him, stripped him naked, and chained him to a cold, steel table. Even now, Shane could feel the icy metal against his back and the iron cuffs cutting into his skin as he struggled to avoid the pain inflicted by knives, cigarettes, and teeth. The kind, charming, successful businessman Shane had loved and planned to marry transformed before his eyes into a madman he didn't know.

After all the heinous acts Brent had committed against Shane he'd had the gall to whisper "I love you" seconds before he pulled out a knife and began slowly cutting Shane's throat. Shane would have died on that table, slowly bleeding to death from the stab wounds scattered over his body, if Luke's bullet hadn't dropped Brent where he stood. Luke and several other officers rushed to Shane's side, some working to free his limbs from the shackles while others put pressure on his wounds. He still remembered the heat of Luke's hand on his throat as Luke tried to stop the bleeding without choking him. The whispered words of encouragement that he was strong, he'd survive, he still had so much to live for. Eventually, the pain, fear, and blood loss became too much, and Shane had lost consciousness.

Shane came out of the memory in stages. First he noticed he was breathing hard and fast, and the food he had eaten was threatening to leave his body. He cradled his head in his hands, trying to catch his breath and hoping his heart didn't give out from the erratic pounding. Dizziness and lightheadedness threated to drop him to the floor. Voices battled to be heard over the rush of blood pumping through his ears as several hands forced him to turn in his seat, shoving his head between his knees. One cool hand settled on the back of his neck while another gently rubbed up and down his back.

The hand on his neck moved away to be replaced by two more cupping his face. His head was lifted until he was eye to eye with Luke who was kneeling on the floor in front of him. Luke was talking to him, but Shane couldn't make out the words. He focused on the movement of Luke's lips until his heart and lungs resumed a more normal rhythm, and the dull roar that had rendered him temporarily deaf lessened.

"–understand me? You are safe. No one is hurting you. No one will hurt you again. Take deep breaths and try to calm down," Luke said.

Shane nodded and Luke relaxed. Shane felt a glass of water against the palm of his hand. He glanced at Masters as he took the water. Shane would be embarrassed about his flashback later, but for now he needed to get a grip. He sat up, raked his hair back off his forehead, and gulped down several swallows of cold water. Luke pulled the glass away from Shane's mouth.

"Sip it, Shane. Don't gulp or you'll pass out. Remember the last time?" he said.

"I'm better," Shane told him.

"Paul is paralyzed. He can't come after you," Masters said, drawing Shane's attention to him.

Masters sat on the edge of the booth cushion, one elbow on the table and one on the back of the bench seat. Shane was kind of disappointed that he'd missed Masters being shoved out of the booth by Luke. Did Masters move quickly enough on his own or did he land on his ass on the floor? Luke stood up and Shane twisted around to sit in the booth properly. Kennie was still massaging his neck and back, adjusting with him as he moved.

"That's not what the episode was about," Shane told Masters.

Luke nudged Masters further into the booth and sat down. Kennie rested her chin on Shane's shoulder, hugging him around the waist.

"Are you really okay?" she asked. "Were you thinking about *him*?"

Shane nodded. "I'm really okay. Just a nasty flashback. Sorry."

"Nothing to apologize for," Luke said.

Masters was the only one at the table who didn't know about Shane's past. He furrowed his brow but remained silent. After they finished eating, the table was cleared and the check settled using the business account of Masters Private Investigations. For the duration of the meal, Kennie had successfully kept the conversation solidly on Crystal Creek Hotel's history.

As they left the restaurant, the discussion turned to what the next step in the investigation should be. Kennie stuck close to Shane all the way to Masters's car. A wink and hug later, Luke drove Kennie back to Crimson Moon so she could open the store. Luke said he had a lead he wanted to follow but refused to share what that lead was. After Shane's flashback, Luke had been withdrawn and quiet.

Masters took Shane back to his apartment where he'd left Bella. Neither of them spoke the entire drive and Shane got the sense Masters was biting his tongue. He glanced at Masters's profile and debated telling him about Brent. Remembering how he had invaded Masters's privacy by reading him without his permission, Shane decided to share. He waited until Masters put the car in park and turned off the engine.

"My ex-fiancé tried to kill me."

Even after so many years had passed, it was difficult for Shane to admit. Masters turned to look at Shane. Shane closed his eyes and took a deep breath. *In for a penny, in for a pound,* he thought, and then blurted out an abridged version of his trauma.

"He kidnapped, raped, and murdered four women. Luke asked for my help and I said yes. Brent found out so he tortured, raped, and stabbed me. He was cutting my throat when Luke shot him. When Luke said I might be a target, I had a flashback."

Shane shook out the heaviness in his arms, hoping it would decrease the tingling in his fingers. Even the quick and ugly version of his past made his neck and shoulders instantly tight. Suddenly needing to move, Shane got out of the car and headed to the elevators. Masters caught up to him as he pushed the call button. Shane had one simple desire – to retrieve Bella from Masters's apartment and go home. Once on the elevator, Masters broke his silence.

"Thank you for telling me. I know it's not easy to do. I also know you're not in the best frame of mind at the moment, but I need you to do something for me."

"What?" Shane asked.

"That fire is burning far too close to Crystal Creek. If our missing people are still on site, then we are running out of time so...I want to interrogate you."

"Interrogate me, how? I get confused easily when I'm recalling memories that aren't my own."

"Hypnotism, guided imagery, call it what you want, but I'll put you into a state of deep relaxation and guide you through the memories with pointed questions directed at the information I want. The way we've been going about this with you pulling up the memories and trying to regurgitate information you think will be helpful has done nothing but create more confusion. I will have to deduce some information but let's try it and see."

CHAPTER TWENTY-SIX

Masters unlocked the door and they were greeted by an excited German Shephard. Shane ruffled the dog's fur and then reached down to rub her belly. He glanced at the potty pad Masters had put down for her before leaving to see it was dry. A quick check of the apartment didn't reveal any doggy accidents.

"Where did you get those potty pads from?" Shane asked. When he'd been searching for coffee he hadn't seen any of the blue pads stashed away.

"Borrowed a few from my neighbor down the hall. She has a bulldog with a weak bladder. After putting you to bed last night, I knocked on her door and told her I had a visiting mutt. She gave me six of them, I think. Go lay down on the bed."

Shane stiffened. "Why?"

While he liked the idea of getting back in bed with Masters, it was the last thing he should do. Images of Masters' smooth, muscular back and arms had jumped, unbidden, into his head at inopportune moments all morning only firmly displaced by the horrible memories of Brent. Shane liked the idea of having Masters' skin pressed against his. He felt his face flush with heat and thanked the heavens that Masters had turned away.

"I'm tired of picking you up off the floor. I've had to do it three times already. It will also be easier for you to relax if you're comfortable," Masters answered.

His words were the dose of reality Shane needed to get his rampant libido under control. It was all work to Masters. He wasn't attracted to Shane the same way Shane was to him. Masters rolled one of the office chairs into the bedroom. Shane followed and climbed onto the bed, stretching out on his back, hands resting on his stomach. Bella jumped on the bed and curled up against his thigh. Out of nervous habit, Shane placed a hand on the dog's side. Pushing all thoughts from his mind of Brent's vile actions and Masters' sexy physique, Shane focused on relaxing one muscle group at a time starting with his shoulders and working his way down to his feet. Masters sat in the chair, frowning at Bella on the bed, but not saying anything.

"I'm taking myself down," Shane said. "Kennie taught me how to self-hypnotize when I was still mastering my ability. When it looks like I'm asleep, that's when I'm ready."

"Okay." Masters picked up a notepad and pen from the dresser behind him.

Shane closed his eyes and regulated his breathing. With every exhalation, he relaxed his muscles further. He imagined a white room devoid of decoration or furniture. The walls of the created room would soon be the theatre screens that played all the horrible memories he had experienced. He had the oddest combination of feeling lighter than air, floating on the wind, while also growing heavier, sinking into the mattress like a stone. Inside Shane's silent, white room Masters's voice echoed.

"Are you ready?"

"Yes," Shane breathed. As deeply relaxed as he was, forcing his tongue to work was difficult.

"I've never done this before – questioned a person about someone else's memories. I apologize for any fuck up that may occur."

Shane smiled lazily as he laid on the floor in his white room. He was comfortable and warm, and as ready as he could be to relive unpleasant memories.

"I'll start with simple questions we already know the answers to so you can get accustomed to pulling up the memory at will and homing in on specific aspects of it. My hope is that you'll *see* the answers."

"Got it."

Shane dimmed the brightness within the white room like a real theatre preparing for the movie to start. While self-hypnotizing wasn't new to him, using the walls of his meditation space as a way to view memories in this way, was. If he was successful, he would have a whole new way of helping law enforcement with future cases.

"How did Robert Grant die?"

Masters's voice was low and soothing. Shane allowed Megan's memory to seep into the room around him. Once again, Shane found himself leaning against a cold wall, Robert's head in his lap. He watched his fingers twitch around the suit coat he held. His eyes moved over the blood-covered concrete floor. Jackson had cut deep and high, straight into Robert's heart.

The man now sat a few feet away, outside the reach of the spreading pool of blood, muttering to himself.

"Jackson stabbed him with a piece of glass," Shane answered. "At least, that's what Megan believed. The memory I have doesn't show the stabbing itself."

"He didn't suffocate?"

"No. Megan is the only one I'm certain died of suffocation. I'm only guessing when I say the others did, too."

"What gave Megan the impression Robert had been stabbed?"

"It's a memory, Masters. She didn't have the impression of him being stabbed. She witnessed it. It's just not part of the memory I received."

Shane's body stiffened and his chest started to ache. Megan was dying and he was suffering the effects of the suffocation. His fingers gripped Bella's fur as he forced the memory to stop playing.

"What was Robert stabbed with?"

Masters's voice cut through Shane's discomfort and gave him something else to focus on. He took a breath as the tightness in his chest eased. Shane glanced at the walls of his room, studying the parts of the concrete room within Megan's sight. When he pulled himself out of the memory and became an observer, it was easier to make sense of what he was seeing and hearing.

"Piece of glass, maybe part of the mirror. Jackson is sitting close to Megan muttering that he didn't want to - it wasn't his fault or something along those lines. Megan couldn't hear him clearly. She was too focused on losing Robert and never seeing her son again. She knew that even if they got out of that room, Robert would still be dead. Maybe Jackson was the inside man Paul was talking about."

There was a soft scratching sound coming from Masters that Shane thought was pen against paper. "We'll come back to the accomplices later. Did Robert know he wasn't Jacob's father?"

Shane let Megan's sad memory fade to be replaced by Paul's hate-filled one. Shane had to take a moment to acclimate to the sudden and uncomfortable change in emotion. Goosebumps erupted across his skin. Megan's memory had been warm and filled with love that was slowly overpowered by the aching need to breathe. In stark comparison, Paul's memories were cold and filled with an evil that made Shane want to distance himself as much as possible. The scene of Paul and Robert talking in the kitchen played around him and Shane recognized the location as the caretaker's cottage. It was satisfying to see what the house had looked like while inhabited versus the stripped shell he'd first experienced. He shivered as he searched for the answer to Masters's question.

"Not at first. He found out later, on the night of party when they disappeared. Paul mentioned to his accomplice that the paternity test proved Jacob didn't belong to Robert. Paul made it sound like Robert knew and didn't care."

Shane's body was starting to hurt from the intense shivering. A heavy weight was eased over his body and then unseen hands tapped against his sides. He smiled as he realized Masters had tucked a blanket around him. Shane's shivering eased with the added warmth but didn't completely subside. Cold emanating from within was hard to quell. Another heavier blanket was tucked around his lower legs and feet. There was a creak of springs as Masters returned to the chair.

"This isn't going the way I had hoped. I'm not getting many definite answers, just a lot of maybes and conjecture."

"Welcome to my world."

"Relax a minute. Let me think."

"Don't take too long. Paul's memories are frigid. It's unpleasant holding onto them."

"Robert changed his will to include Megan and Jacob. Did Paul know about it?"

"Yes. Robert told him."

"When?"

"No idea. Memories don't come with a timestamp. I can tell you it was after Megan got pregnant but before the paternity test. Robert changed the will before he knew Jacob wasn't his, though he did know it was a possibility."

Masters sighed. "Good way to piss off big brother."

"That is a masterpiece of understatement. Paul was more than angry."

The gentle whisp of Masters turning pages in his notebook filtered through Shane's consciousness. "You mentioned before someone named Jackson might be an inside man. Explain that."

"It's another guess," Shane admitted. "Paul blackmailed someone at the party to kill Robert. He had photos of a sexual indiscretion." Shane kept that part of the memory abbreviated. He didn't want to revisit what the two men had done with the underaged girl. Why were there so many vile people in the world?

"So, we know Paul planned to kill his brother, but how did he kill the others? You said before that Paul created the circumstances that lead to their deaths. What did he do?"

Shane played Paul's memory from before the partygoers went missing. He listened closely to the words Paul spoke, but nothing either of the men said gave Shane any clues to how Paul had suffocated fourteen people. He huffed in frustration, his fingers curling into fists. Bella's whine reminded him he had her fur in his hand and he instantly relaxed his fingers.

"I don't know."

"I'm not sure why, but I think you *do* know," Masters said.

Shane shook his head. The bed dipped as Masters sat beside his hip. When he spoke again, his voice was much closer to Shane's ear. Masters' warm breath caressed his cheek. Shane found the sensation comforting and he relaxed, heat finally seeped into the recesses of his mind where Paul's evil pooled.

"What memories do you have?"

Masters's question caught Shane off guard. "What do you mean?"

"I've never asked what any of the memories are about and you've never told me. You were either unconscious or being outright stubborn. So, tell me. What parts of these people's lives do you have access to?"

Shane cleared the images frozen on his internal movie theatre, returning the room to the warm, white meditation space he preferred. After a moment of recentering himself, Shane answered.

"Megan's memory is of her death. Robert's memory was of him leading his friends down the servant stairs during the tour. Because I touched Paul twice, I got two memories from him. One was a conversation he had with Robert about the will. The other was the conversation he had with his accomplice at the fundraiser before everyone disappeared."

"And you can recall the memories at will?"

"Yes."

"The conversation Paul had with his accomplice paraphrase what he said, what he did, and what he saw."

Shane flexed his fingers along Bella's side as he once again pulled the memory to the forefront of his mind. As the memory played in front of him, he told Masters what he was seeing.

"Paul is in the hallway outside the dining room. The one we were in when you asked for my help," Shane clarified to avoid any confusion as to which dining room he was referring to. "His accomplice is behind him in the dark so his face isn't visible, but his voice seems familiar. Paul says Robert never should have trusted him to fix things. The air vent is still blocked and the lock is still broken."

"An air vent suggests an enclosed space. Locks indicate a door in an intact room. Crystal Creek Hotel is falling apart so I can't imagine an air tight room being inside it." Masters murmured to himself. "What did the accomplice say?"

"Not much, but he was on board with Robert's murder because he wanted Megan back. He didn't know Paul planned to kill everyone at the party, including Megan. Paul wasn't leaving any loose ends."

A cold shudder worked down Shane's spine and into his limbs. That bone-deep chill he had every time he pulled up Paul's memories grew more uncomfortable the longer he kept them in front of him.

"Describe the room Megan and the others died in," Masters instructed.

Shane was more than happy to ditch Paul's icy memories. Megan's memories of suffocating to death were only marginally better than Paul's homicidal hatred, but they were significantly warmer. Masters' questions had Shane jumping from one memory to another in a pattern that seemed random, but the order of questions must make sense to Masters. The cold dissipated and Shane was filled with warmth as Megan's memories once again took center stage.

He appreciated the heat but didn't like the instant chest tightness. This entire exercise was nothing more than Shane repeatedly replacing one type of pain with another. He'd sleep for a week when this was done. The blankets covering his body became too hot and heavy and his chest hurt with the effort it took to breathe. Sweat broke out on his forehead. Masters brushed Shane's hair off his forehead, fingers lingering at his temple.

"Are you okay? Do we need to stop?"

"Too hot," Shane croaked.

The blankets were immediately removed. A soft thud came from the floor where they landed. The cool air was welcome for a few seconds until the chest tightness and shallow breathing threatened to bring on another panic attack. Shane reminded himself he was safe in a bedroom with Masters, not actually suffocating to death in a dark pit. His breathing sped up. Masters clasped Shane's hand and gently massaged his fingers.

"Relax. You're safe," Masters whispered.

With great effort, Shane released the tension tightening every muscle in his body a little at a time though he never achieved the full relaxation he'd started with. At least his breathing returned to a somewhat normal rate. Masters caressed Shane's face with one hand while massaging Shane's fingers with the other. The motions were both grounding and comforting. Shane only had a moment to comprehend the fact he wasn't getting any of Masters' memories from the skin-to-skin contact before Masters' voice interrupted the thought.

"Do you feel better?"

"A little. Can we try to finish this quickly?"

"Describe the room. Start in one corner and work your way around in a circle."

"Doesn't work that way," Shane said. "I can only see what Megan saw in that moment."

"Do your best."

Shane allowed Megan's memory to play out, making the conscious effort to ignore what he felt physically and focus on what he could see and hear.

"It's a dining room. There's a bar along one wall with a huge broken mirror behind it. There's a chandelier that's too big for the room. All the tables and chairs are piled up in a corner. Megan and Robert are on an elevated platform that I think is a stage. The room is tiny but seems to be in a better state than the rest of the hotel. Things are crumbling, but not to the same extent."

Shane fell silent as he continued to observe the room through Megan's eyes. Something was wrong with what he was seeing, but he couldn't identify exactly what. As the intense discomfort from lack of air closed in on him, he shifted on the bed and instinctively rubbed Bella's body. Shane played the memory again from the beginning but still the wrongness of the room prodded him.

"Damn," he whispered.

"What's wrong," Masters asked, cupping Shane's cheek.

"I don't know; that's the problem. Something is wrong with the room they died in, but I can't figure out what it is."

"When I was a cop I learned that sometimes what suspects *don't* say can be just as important as what they *do*. If your brain is telling you something is off, pay closer attention. Look, listen, smell, and feel everything around you. The answer is there. Don't rush this; I'm not going anywhere. Let yourself live in the moment."

Shane's chest tightened. Not because of the memory, but because he was about to give himself over to it completely.

"The only way for me to truly live in a memory is to allow myself to get lost in it," he told Masters.

The very idea scared him. He had survived the first time Megan's memory had overcome him so he figured he could do it again, but he'd never willingly lost himself inside someone else's memory.

"How do I bring you out of it if I need to?" Masters asked.

"You can't. I'll automatically come out of it when it runs its course. Don't touch me until I tell you to."

Shane gave Bella's leg a rub before clasping his hands together on his stomach. He let his meditation room slip away to be replaced completely by Megan's memory. He was no longer lying on Masters' bed, disconnected from the memory as an observer. He was Megan. And he was dying. This time, he paid attention to every little thing. He felt the cold. He smelled the dirt and mold. He heard the muffled, subdued movements of those around him. He saw the room dancing in shadow from the flickering of the bulbs.

Before he could finish out Megan's memory, Shane's own consciousness took over, throwing flashes of Paul's memories mixed with Shane's personal conversations with Kennie, Masters and Luke, threading them into Megan's memory. Shane's eyes snapped open and his body stiffened as he became aware of reality like a cold bucket of water had been thrown over him. He slammed into the bed beneath him. Masters stood up and looked down at him. Shane slowly moved his gaze from the ceiling fan above him to Masters's face.

"I don't know what to do. You didn't pass out," Masters said.

Shane heard the sarcasm but couldn't react to it. He had come out of the memory far too easily, but he would examine that oddity later. His mind had snagged on something so strange that it couldn't possibly be true. The missing people had died in a concrete room, but –

"Where is the door?" Shane mumbled.

"What?" Masters eased onto the bed beside Shane, careful not to make contact.

"In Paul's memory, he mentioned the lock being broken, and you said that indicates a door, and of course they had to get into the room somehow. As she was dying, Megan had a fleeting thought about trying to break down the *metal door* and then there was the comment made by Paul's accomplice about *going down there*."

Masters grinned. "Nicely done, Mr. Cayli."

He got off the bed and picked up his pad and pen. As Masters jotted notes down, Shane brought his awareness back to his body. The bedroom was overly warm and bright after having been immersed in Megan's cold, dimly lit memory.

"Are we done?" Shane asked. He wiggled his toes and fingers, slowly waking up his body one muscle at a time. He stiffly reached for Bella to pet her flank. She stretched out along his side, offering her belly for a rub. "Did I remember anything helpful?"

"Yes, and yes," Masters answered.

Shane grunted. It didn't seem to him that he'd offered anything remotely helpful. He'd only given bits and pieces of random memories. Not for the first time, Shane wished he could give the memories to someone else so they could see things for themselves, rather than Shane trying to relay what was in his head. He had the same desire every time he worked with Luke. Masters smacked Shane's knee with his notebook, drawing Shane's attention.

"Our missing people are in an underground room on the south side of the hotel," Masters said as he turned to leave the room.

Shane was shocked by the declaration. Stiff and sore, he managed to get off the bed and follow Masters into the living room. Bella jumped down with a thump and trotted along beside him. He sat down in the office chair at Masters's desk with a grunt of pain. His muscles objected to every move.

"How the hell did you come up with that?" Shane asked.

Masters pulled a glass from one of the kitchen cabinets and filled it with water. He handed it to Shane as he sat down on the opposite side of the desk.

"I told you, Mr. Cayli, puzzle pieces."

Shane used both hands to lift the glass to his mouth. He drank the water in big gulps, not stopping to breathe until the glass was empty. He hadn't realized he was thirsty, but it was all he could think about. His limbs were heavy and his muscles slow to respond. He had expected more pain, but the headache that typically followed his visions was noticeably absent. Shane made a mental note to try reliving memories like this again to see if the migraines were caused by the memories themselves or the activation of his ability. He hadn't needed to initiate his ability during Masters' interrogation. He'd simply been recalling memories he'd already received.

"Let's get you home," Masters said.

CHAPTER TWENTY-SEVEN

Masters took the empty glass from Shane and placed it in the dishwasher. Shane was tired, but that was nothing new. Sluggishly moving on autopilot, steeped in a mental fog, Shane leashed Bella and followed Masters to his car. Masters opened the door and practically shoved Bella into the back seat before making sure Shane got in without hitting his head. Shane's uncooperative body made him clumsy and he flopped onto the seat. He closed his eyes as Masters drove out of the parking garage and joined the early evening traffic.

Images of a burning car and mangled train pushed into Shane's head. He opened his eyes to look at the man behind the wheel. One of Masters's hands was on the gear shift, his knuckles gently brushing against Shane's thigh. Shane adjusted on the seat enough to break contact.

"Will you tell me what happened to Elizabeth?" Shane asked.

He kept his voice soft. He was curious but he knew he was poking a painful wound. Masters's grip on the wheel tightened. He cursed but never took his eyes off the road. Several minutes passed and Shane thought Masters wouldn't share, but then he started speaking, filling the car with his smooth, deep voice.

"She worked in social services while I was still a cop. That's how we met. I wanted her the moment I saw her and made no secret of it."

Masters spoke in a soft monotone. Shane understood. Masters hadn't just lost his girlfriend and unborn child that day; his entire life had gone to hell and Shane was stirring up painful memories. Masters kept his eyes on the road, stoic aside from the tick in his lower jaw. Shane waited patiently.

"It was my day off and I took her to lunch. She told me the night before that she was pregnant and we argued about it. I wasn't ready to be a parent, but she was. I had planned to apologize over lunch, but on the way to the restaurant we were interrupted by Luke. He was my partner at the time and called to tell me the suspect we'd been after for years had been located. The man was wanted for killing his daughter's boyfriend. He had barricaded himself inside a warehouse using his victim's mother as a hostage. Luke told me to get there quick because SWAT was preparing to raid the building."

Masters stopped speaking to clear his throat.

"I was in a hurry and didn't take Elizabeth home first. I drove straight to the site and told her to wait in the car, which she did. Luke and I, along with several other officers, followed SWAT into the building. It was a huge space and the asshole managed to slip by us. I was right behind Luke, walking out of the building once we realized he wasn't inside anymore, and that's when we heard a car start. We all ran to the street just in time to see the sonofabitch drive off in my car...with Elizabeth still in the passenger seat. I guess he thought he could beat the train–"

Masters's voice cracked and he swallowed convulsively. His fingers tightened and released on the steering wheel. Shane reached over and placed his hand over Masters's fist, diligently keeping his gift boxed up and the contact short in duration.

"Slow the car down," Shane said softly.

As Masters shared his story he had gradually pressed on the accelerator until they were driving nearly twenty miles per hour over the limit. Masters eased off the gas pedal to apply pressure to the brake. Shane pulled his hand back when Masters's grip finally loosened on the wheel. They shared a brief moment of eye contact before Masters returned his attention to the road.

"I never told her I loved her. Never told her I was okay with becoming a father. Never told her...so many things. The only justice I will ever have is the knowledge that the asshole who killed my family killed himself, too."

Shane's heart ached. He now understood the guilt that had pervaded Masters' memory. He had left his pregnant girlfriend in a car that ended up in the hands of a murderer. Shane wondered how desperate someone had to be in order to play chicken with a train. Or was death his end goal? It was entirely possible Elizabeth's death had been the result of a murder-suicide, rather than an accident. He was overwhelmed by the enormity of what Masters had been through.

"My god," Shane murmured and rubbed his eyes with his palms. "How can you talk about this without showing any kind of emotion?"

"Practice."

"How did you become a private investigator?" Shane asked. Since Masters appeared to be in a sharing mood, he would take advantage.

"I went kind of nuts after Elizabeth's death. Got a little trigger happy, acting like I had a death wish. I certainly didn't care whether I lived or died. Truth be told, the grief was so blinding I didn't know what I was doing half the time. Kept putting fellow cops in danger and eventually got my ass fired. I was good at investigating, but I wasn't too keen on working for anyone else at the time, so Luke suggested I become a P.I."

"And Masters Private Investigations was born."

"Yep."

Arriving at Shane's apartment, Masters parked the car in the lot. Crimson Moon Gifts was already closed for the day, so the lot was empty except for Kennie's sedan parked at the far end and that's when it hit him.

"Shit! My car is still parked in that paid lot," Shane said.

"I'll stop by on my way back and pay to leave it parked overnight," Masters said.

"Thank you."

Masters nodded as he got out of the car. Shane opened the door, got out, and pulled his jacket tighter around his body. The sun was beginning to set behind the mountains, slowly dropping the temperature. Shane grabbed Bella's leash and then walked to the service door. He had just slipped the key into the lock when a car backfired, making him jump in surprise. He screamed as Masters slammed him to the ground, pinning him beneath his body. White hot pain flashed up Shane's arm into his neck. Bella pressed up against Shane as much as she could, snarling and barking toward the street.

"Stay down," Masters shouted as he pushed himself off Shane and ran around the corner of the building toward the front of the store.

Shane reached out to pull Bella close to comfort her, but intense pain in his left shoulder had him yanking his arm back, cradling it against his body. He struggled to catch his breath as spots floated through his vision. He leaned back against the wall and yelled out in pain when his shoulder hit the brick. Despite the cold air, he was sweating and trying hard not to vomit. Every little movement caused the pain to spike. He did everything he could to remain completely still, which was hard to do with an excited German Shepherd licking at his face. The heavy service door opened and Kennie stepped out into the lot.

"Did I just hear a gunshot?" Kennie glanced down where Shane was leaning against the wall and gasped. "Oh my god, Shane, you've been shot. Bella, inside."

Kennie shoved Bella through the service door and then knelt beside Shane. He stared at her in confusion, white-hot pain radiated through his shoulder and back. He couldn't think through the fog descending around him. Something cold and wet slid over his hand. Shane looked at the redness covering most of his arm, watching numbly as the blood dripped from his fingertips to the asphalt. His gaze was drawn to Masters as he trotted around the building, rejoining them at the door.

"Kennie, what the hell are you doing out here? Do you want to get shot, too? Get your ass back inside."

"Shane's hurt."

"I've got him. Go."

Masters bent down and lifted Shane into his arms, carrying him into the building behind Kennie. He stopped inside the foyer where he lowered Shane to the floor. Masters pushed Bella away, telling Kennie to keep the dog away, as he pulled his phone from his pocket. Shane watched everything through a spotted, foggy haze, the sounds around him increasingly muffled and less important. Even when Masters grabbed Shane's arm directly over the bullet wound and squeezed, Shane didn't have the energy to scream in pain. Instead, he closed his eyes and let the fatigue of the day drag him under.

Shane woke to a cacophony of voices, beeping, and the stench of ammonia. He blinked against too bright lights, attempting to clear his vision. He felt oddly detached from his body; his limbs weighed more than they ever had before. A dull ache throbbed in his left arm while his right hand was encased in something soft and warm. The warmth of his ability pulsed through his veins unchecked, but there were no intrusive memories. Nothing but a sense of soothing calm. Shane smiled and glanced to the side.

Kennie held his right hand between both of hers, pumping good vibes into Shane's mind much like the IV snaking from his hand was pumping fluid into his body. The two of them had stumbled onto the technique of deep relaxation and revival years ago when Shane had been lost to a memory. Kennie still found opportunities to employ the trick – like now. Shane's mind was fuzzy and he was confused about how he ended up in the hospital, but he was immensely grateful to his best friend for the assistance. Kennie gradually loosened her grip as Shane woke up one tiny increment at a time.

"This helps him wake up slower and more calmly," Kennie said. "I don't know if you've noticed how he jerks awake."

"I have noticed," Masters grumbled.

Kennie smiled at Shane, gave his fingers a squeeze, and then let go completely. Fully awake and more aware of his surroundings, Shane rolled his head to the left so he could see Masters sitting in a plastic chair that looked uncomfortable, arms crossed over his chest and the usual scowl on his face.

"I hate when you pass out," Masters snapped.

Thanks to the deep relaxation and calm Kennie had shared Shane was able to ignore Masters' biting tone. As far as Shane was concerned, he had good reason to pass out this time; he'd been shot. His left arm was in a hard splint and rested across his body in a sling. He wiggled his fingers but then stopped when the dull ache started to burn. Masters stood up and reached for something at the foot of the bed.

"What are you doing?" Shane asked.

His voice was scratchy and his tongue felt thick and swollen. Without answering, Masters lifted a remote and turned on the TV that hung from the wall. The volume was too low, but the closed captioning was on so Shane could read what was being said. Masters scrolled through channels until he found a news program. The leading story was of the forest fire burning near Crystal Creek Hotel. The current visuals were being broadcast from a helicopter flying over the scene, staying far enough away from the flames to show the beautiful mountain backdrop to an otherwise devasting event. It was only a matter of time before any potential evidence inside the hotel was burned to ashes.

Kennie leaned in close and whispered, "Rein your power in before one of the nurses touch you."

Shane grinned before diligently shoving his ability back into the mental box. Masters mumbled something unintelligible before returning to the plastic chair. He placed his elbow on the edge of the bed and pinched his bottom lip as he stared at the television. Anxiety pulsed off him. Shane had the overwhelming desire to reach out and caress his shoulder, but Masters sat on Shane's injured side. Even so, touching was inadvisable on the best of days.

"I'm sorry I upset you," Shane said. He draped his good arm over his forehead dramatically, ignoring the tug of the IV tubing. "All this excitement is simply too much for fragile, little ole me," he drawled.

"Good grief," Kennie said, thumping Shane's elbow.

Shane giggled and watched Masters fight his own grin. Masters shook his head, but never looked away from the TV. When the news program moved to the next story, Masters sighed. He spun in the chair to face Shane.

"I'm sorry I put you in danger. This was supposed to be an easy case of find the millionaires. Shootings and *fragile* psychics weren't part of the plan. I never should've allowed Luke to bring you in."

Shane scoffed. He pushed the button on the railing to lift the head of the bed upright. The movement was slow but still caused quite a bit of discomfort on his left side. He looked at the bandaging holding the splint against his arm from his armpit to his palm. He remembered feeling pain and seeing blood, but not much else.

"Where exactly did I get shot?" he asked.

"A little below the shoulder. Considered a graze, but it left a nice gouge. Few inches over and it would've hit your lung or heart."

Masters closed his eyes and pinched the bridge of his nose. Shane wondered if Masters blamed himself for the shooting, even though it wasn't his fault. The fault was with the person who pulled the trigger. Masters was a man with a steel shell but then all squishy, attractive, and caring beneath it.

"If you're blaming yourself, please stop."

Masters held Shane's gaze for a moment before grunting in response, turning back to stare at the television.

"How long was I out?" Shane asked.

"Long enough to miss the sexy pieces of ass strutting around here," Kennie answered. Masters snorted. "No, seriously. The EMT was insanely hot and the doc who stitched you up was quite yummy, although he might be too young for you. Probably just graduated high school. Oh, oh, and the two cops who want to question you? Wow! You won't think Masters here is so drop dead once you get a peek of those two."

Kennie fanned herself, but Shane's cheeks heated with embarrassment. It was one thing to put his foot in his mouth when it came to Masters' appearance, but it was quite another when Kennie pointed it out...right in front of the man himself. Masters looked at Kennie, who waggled her eyebrows at him.

"Lansing is married and Gates is straight," Masters said.

"Doesn't like competition, does he?" Kennie asked Shane with a teasing smile on her face.

Masters muttered to himself as he stood up and went to the window. He was antsy and something in the back of Shane's mind said it wasn't the shooting or being in a hospital room that was bothering him. Until now, Masters had been pushy, rude, and insulting, but he hadn't been anxious or twitchy. Deciding to keep Kennie from filling the silence with more of her meddlesome teasing, Shane changed the subject.

"Masters, have you ever been shot?"

"No."

Shane scowled. How was that fair? Masters was an ex-cop who faced all kinds of bad people and dangerous situations, but he'd never been shot. Most days, Shane minded his own business and stayed within the walls of the Crimson Moon building, but he'd been kidnapped, raped, beaten, stabbed, and shot, all within the past decade. Seriously! What the hell? Kennie's voice broke Shane's moody thoughts.

"Hate to break up the party, but I need to get back to the store. With the parking lot cordoned off and cops crawling all over the place, I had to close for the day, but Alison was sticking around to watch them and give them access to whatever. If I leave her alone for too long, she may never come back to work. Call me when they discharge you and I can pick you up."

She gathered her belongings and blew Masters an exaggerated kiss as she passed him on her way out the door. Masters sighed, turned away from the window, and sat down in Kennie's vacated seat. At least that chair was cushioned. Masters' anxiety was slowly eating away at the serenity Kennie had infused Shane with. Masters's usual composure had noticeably slipped.

"What's wrong? I've never seen you so fidgety."

"Everything."

"Can you be a little more specific?"

"First, Holmestead isn't answering his phone. Tracy says she hasn't heard from him since this morning. Second, you've been shot by someone who was not at all deterred by the fact that it was broad daylight, you weren't alone, and you had a German Shepherd next to you, a breed known for being attack dogs. Didn't even think twice. Third, that damn forest fire has gotten dangerously close to Crystal Creek Hotel and I can't help but think it might be a blessing for the damn place to burn to the ground."

"Are you thinking the fearlessness of the shooter is possibly due to him being a cop?" Shane asked, remembering Paul Grant's accomplice had been an officer of the law.

"Yes, I do. Holmestead was right about me making you a target, but damn Paul moved fast. Why were you the only one shot and not me? I'm the bigger threat."

Shane wondered if the reason the bullet only grazed his upper arm versus hitting him square in the chest was because he *wasn't* the target. Maybe that bullet *had* been meant for Masters but missed the mark? One thing Masters was correct about was that Paul had moved fast. Too fast, considering his health condition which made Shane question if it was Paul who'd set up the hit in the first place. Luke and Masters had been working the case and interviewing people long before they brought Shane in so it was entirely possible that they'd already questioned the accomplice and set things in motion long before Shane was involved.

"Paul can't be the only one who's feathers you've ruffled," Shane said.

"No, but the accomplice angle is new since you came on so until now we didn't consider that we might be interviewing someone involved in the disappearance. We strongly suspected Paul and didn't want him tipped off so we made him the last person on our list to speak to. In fact, we would never have considered the possibility of an accomplice at all if it weren't for you reading people's minds."

"I don't read minds." Shane suppressed a yawn and adjusted his injured arm into a more comfortable spot. "If you've questioned everyone else the way you questioned Paul, it's entirely possible it wasn't the accomplice who shot me. Maybe it was just someone who was worried you would pin Robert's death on them whether they were guilty or not. Happened to be a bad shot. Hit me instead of you."

He certainly liked that idea better than being the true target of a homicidal maniac. Masters shrugged.

"Maybe."

"Or maybe it was the accomplice and he panicked when you showed up at his door asking questions."

"Possibly."

Shane stared at Masters. Something was off. The man was being way too agreeable.

"There's something else bothering you. What is it?"

Masters sighed and turned the chair so they were facing each other. "Paul was found murdered this morning. Shot once in the head. Gates told me when I suggested he interrogate Paul about your shooting. I pressed both Gates and Lansing for more information but they were either unable or unwilling to share. Someone is cleaning house."

"I was never in the 'house' so why try to kill me?"

Masters' phone beeped and he yanked it from his pocket. He scowled at the caller ID and then shoved the phone back into his pocket without answering it.

"Where the hell is Holmestead?" Masters muttered, tone heavy with worry and irritation. "This isn't like him. Tracy is due any day so he checks in with her frequently. It's been nearly eight hours since he last contacted her. He should've been home to have dinner with the girls. I know he said he wanted to run down a lead, but it shouldn't have taken him this long. And then there's the way he reacted to the idea of you being a target so when I texted him you'd been shot, he should have been here by now handing me my ass."

"What time is it? I want to go home." Shane's fear spiked. He couldn't put words to what was scaring him; he only knew that he needed to be out of the hospital.

"It's around eight in the evening." Masters leaned in close to Shane and looked directly into his eyes. "I'm sorry, Shane. You can't leave but I need to. I'll call Kennie to come back. She should be here by the time the doctor comes in to check on you. Do me a favor–" Masters cupped Shane's cheek "–once you get home, lock up and don't leave."

Shane swallowed hard. The tender affection Masters was showing was comforting and strange, and Shane liked it. Before he could answer, Masters kissed his forehead and then left the room, leaving Shane alone with his jumbled thoughts and emotions. He lowered the head of the bed to get more comfortable but his pain level steadily increased no matter which position he settled into. Finally admitting defeat, he hit the nurse call button to request some pain relief.

The nurse came in with pain medication that she injected into Shane's IV. As the throbbing burn eased away, he drifted off to sleep. He was vaguely aware of Kennie returning to the room, followed closely by the doctor stating he wanted to admit Shane for observation overnight but Shane insisted on going home so the doctor reluctantly discharged him under Kennie's care. Shane roused himself enough to get dressed in the throw-away scrubs provided and somehow managed to walk to the car. Kennie drove them home, cursing the entire way about Shane being stubborn and leaving the hospital at an "ungodly" hour. She took Bella out to pee while Shane changed into his comfy pajamas and climbed into bed. He had no idea what time it was when Kennie finally left his bedroom. He fell asleep with Bella's large, warm body pressed against his back.

CHAPTER TWENTY-EIGHT

Shane woke to Kennie gently nudging him toward consciousness. He pushed himself upright with his good arm, wincing in pain as injured muscles protested and his stitches pulled. He swung his legs over the side of the bed and waited for the discomfort to ease. He was still a bit loopy from the pain medication which caused the room to tilt and waver. Kennie sat beside him and handed him a glass of water. She wasn't her perfect, polished self having foregone makeup and leaving her hair up in a messy bun with loose strands hanging around her face. Even in such a state, she was beautiful, but it wasn't normal.

Shane sipped the water. "Thank you. You look like you slept for shit."

Kennie flopped to her back on the bed and stretched. "I slept on the couch in case you needed anything during the night. I didn't sleep as deeply as I could have because I thought every little sound was you."

"I'm sorry."

"No worries. You would do the same for me." Kennie sat up and rubbed Shane's non-injured shoulder. "Are you in pain?"

"Some, but I don't want any more pain meds. I feel fuzzy-headed and I want to be alert when we drive to Crystal Creek."

Bella bounded into the bedroom with her ball and dropped it on Shane's lap. He tossed it out of the room and Bella darted into the living room after it. Kennie sighed heavily, drawing Shane's attention back to her.

"For once in my life, I'd say 'no, we're not going back there,' but you would just go without me, wouldn't you?"

"Yes, I would," Shane answered honestly. He wasn't sure how he would manage to drive that far with his arm in a sling and pain shooting into his fingertips, but he knew he would undoubtedly make the attempt.

"Stubborn mule," Kennie mumbled. "And what exactly are we going to do once we get there?"

Shane thought about that, but didn't have an answer. He had no idea what to do once he arrived at the hotel; he only knew he had to go. He supposed he would head to the south side of the main lobby to see if he could relocate the memory of suffocation and perhaps the room the missing people died in. It was the only thing he could think to do.

"I don't know," he finally admitted.

"I need a strong drink."

Kennie went to the kitchen while Shane used the restroom and got dressed. The entire feat took three times longer than normal, thanks to the bandages and pain, and ended with Shane's frustration level shooting through the roof. He ran a brush through his hair to corral his messy bedhead but gave up quickly when his energy reserves tanked. He joined Kennie in the living room. She had placed two mugs of coffee on the low coffee table beside a plate of muffins.

"When you said you needed a strong drink I expected alcohol of some kind," Shane said as he sipped his steaming hot coffee.

"If I had pulled an all-nighter, I would've gone for whiskey. Unfortunately, I slept so my brain knows it's too early for alcohol."

"Didn't realize time of day made a difference."

"It didn't used to, but I'm turning into my mother which is just pathetic."

Shane laughed. There was nothing remotely similar between the Goth chick sitting next to him and the ultra-conservative Catholic woman who'd given birth to her.

"That's one thing you'll never have to worry about. I promise."

"You were shot," Kennie blurted out. "What do you hope to accomplish by giving that guy a second chance to kill you? Haven't you faced death enough for one lifetime?"

Shane took a scalding gulp of his coffee to buy a few seconds to get his anxiety under control. He and Kennie often fed off each other's emotions and her nerves were stretched thin.

"Paul was murdered yesterday morning." Shane said. "Masters told me before he left the hospital last night."

"It doesn't make sense. If Paul was already dead, then who shot you? This is scaring the hell out of me."

"His accomplice, I assume. Paul had a cop helping him who I think played a part in stalling the original investigation. Masters thinks the accomplice killed Paul and then came after me. We need to go back because that fire is burning really close to the hotel. If the wind shifts, that place is gone. Which might be a good thing, honestly."

"Shit. Things keep getting worse, but I guess the darkness the cards warned me about is beginning to make sense."

"Can I trust you with a horrible thought I can't shake?"

"Of course."

"Paul's accomplice was a cop and last night Masters couldn't find Luke. What if Luke is the accomplice? I don't want to believe that he could shoot me, but the bullet did only graze me so what if–"

"Stop." Kennie slapped a hand over Shane's mouth. "Luke is far too protective of you. You're family to him. He would never hurt you."

Shane pulled Kennie's hand away. Neither of them was clear headed and he didn't want to accidently read her.

"It might be why Luke was angry when he found out Masters took me to read Paul's memories. He thought I'd be able to identify him and he was pissed that Masters put him in the position where he had to kill Paul...and me."

His voice cracked at the end. Thinking about Luke turning on him was painful enough but voicing it had him close to tears. Aside from Kennie, Luke was his closest friend. He didn't want to believe Luke was capable of something so heinous, but Shane had been fooled before and the suspicion wouldn't go away.

"He would never hurt you," Kennie repeated. "Why are you suspecting him like this?"

"Twelve years ago, around the same time all of this happened, Luke had an affair. He told me he had considered leaving Tracy. So...knowing about the affair and then seeing how angry he became about me reading Paul followed by his sudden unreachability makes him look...bad."

Shane's speech became faster with each word so he forced himself to take a deep breath. Bella picked up on his inner turmoil and came to lean against his leg. He rubbed her head to comfort her and ground himself. Shane had known Luke for years. He had saved Shane's life and thinking of him negatively bothered Shane to the core. He hated that he suspected Luke of such horrible things when Luke had never done anything amoral or dishonest during their long friendship. But everyone had secrets.

"Did you tell Masters any of this?" Kennie asked.

"No. He left too fast, presumably to search for Luke. Masters said Luke was chasing down a lead, but no one had heard from him for hours. Not even Tracy."

Bella whined and Shane realized he was squeezing her ear a little too hard. He let go and rubbed Bella's chest. Kennie drained her coffee and then refilled her mug. By now, the liquid had to be lukewarm at best.

"These last few days have been hell," she said. "There is one hole in your theory about Luke being the accomplice. Luke was a rookie back then. I don't think he would've had the authority or the connections needed to mislead police or persuade them Paul wasn't a viable suspect."

"Maybe."

Kennie's observation didn't make him feel better but he was desperate to latch onto any small nugget of hope. He finished his cold coffee and rubbed his injured arm. The ache grew more noticeable as time went on without pain medication but he steadfastly refused to take another pill. Narcotics put him to sleep and he had to search Crystal Creek again. He had to be one-hundred percent to navigate that death trap disguised as a hotel. Shane wanted to find the missing people, not join them in the grave.

The accomplice's voice drifted through Shane's mind. There was a nagging sensation that he should recognize the voice, that he knew who the accomplice was, and that the voice belonged to Luke. He was uncomfortable with the idea but he coulnd't let it go.

"I need to go back to Crystal Creek...now."

Shane walked to the front door and grabbed Bella's leash. He struggled getting the fastener to catch onto her collar one-handed, but he eventually succeeded.

Kennie sighed. She collected the breakfast dishes and carried them to the kitchen. "I suppose it can't wait a few hours so I can take a nap and shower, huh?"

"There's a fire burning up there. We may not have a few hours."

"So damned pushy. Give me a minute." She sidled past Shane and Bella to go to her apartment.

Shane took Bella downstairs to wait. Without the pain pills muddying his thoughts, he was scared to open the heavy metal door leading outside.

He couldn't shake the fear that someone was waiting around the corner to finish him off the moment he showed his face. He leaned against the cold concrete and focused on his breathing. He would not let himself tip into a full-blown panic attack right now. He looked up at the sound of Kennie's clicking footsteps on the stairs. She had changed into black pants, knee-high boots, and a dark purple blouse that matched the streaks in her hair. She wore her hair in a loose braid that fell down her back. Pushing aside all reservations, Shane followed Kennie out the door.

"I cannot believe I'm driving into a forest fire for you," she said, unlocking the car doors.

Kennie was backing out of the parking spot when a red VW bug whipped into the parking lot like a bat out of hell and parked beside them. Masters got out of his car and climbed into the back seat of Kennie's sedan with Bella, grumbling when he came face to face with the German shepherd. Shane and Kennie shared a glance before she resumed backing out, choosing to ignore Masters' sudden arrival. Shane twisted in his seat until his injured arm protested and he faced forward again.

"Why are you here? What's wrong?" Shane asked.

"I thought I told you not to leave the house?" Masters said.

Kennie scoffed. "You obviously don't know him very well."

Several minutes passed with nothing but Bella's panting before Masters spoke again.

"That's it. Pull over and let me drive," he said.

"Why would I do that?" Kennie asked.

"You're driving too slow and if I have to sit back here with this damn dog another second–"

"Just do it," Shane interrupted. "He won't shut up until you do."

Kennie pulled to the side of the road and the three of them switched places. Shane climbed into the back with Bella while Masters got behind the wheel, adjusting the seat and mirrors. Kennie sat in the passenger seat, glaring at Masters as she clicked her seatbelt. As Masters gunned the car back into traffic, Shane suffered a moment of conflict. Having Masters behind the wheel meant they had a fifty-fifty chance of getting to their destination faster or dying in a fiery crash. Masters took a corner too fast causing Shane to bite out a few curse words as Bella was thrown against him and his injured shoulder met the car door, sending pain lancing down his arm.

"You're driving like a madman," Shane said.

"Do not wreck my girl because your whities are in a bunch," Kennie added.

She had a tight grip on the armrest of the door and the middle console. Bella was probably the calmest soul in the car, sitting on the backseat and panting happily. Masters ignored all of them, seemingly lost in his own head.

"What was that damned idiot thinking?" Masters muttered. He'd spoken softly, as though the question was rhetorical.

"Who?" Shane asked, leaning toward the middle console so he could see Masters's profile. As usual, the man's face gave nothing away. "Masters?" Shane prodded without response.

Gaze bouncing between mirrors and the front windshield, Masters executed several racetrack-worthy maneuvers as he weaved through traffic, zigzagging his way through the morning rush hour. Shane was pleased to see Masters was at least paying attention to his surroundings, but the ongoing silence made Shane nervous.

The car in front of them hit their brakes and, without losing an iota of speed, Masters zipped onto the shoulder, passed the slower vehicles, and then swerved back into the lane. Kennie cast a concerned glance over her shoulder at Shane. Choosing to push the boundary he'd set early on, Shane reached around the seat to touch Masters's shoulder where his palm met taut muscles.

Shane gently squeezed. "Dom, what's wrong?"

Hearing his first name spoken with such casual familiarity finally brought Masters out of his head. He seemed to have forgotten there were other people in the car. Shane expected him to be annoyed, to order Shane never to touch him without permission, or even to admonish the use of his first name, but instead, he did nothing. Masters glanced into the rearview mirror, making eye contact with Shane long enough for Shane to see the raw emotion. Masters' blue eyes swirled with anger and sadness. Shane squeezed his shoulder once more before pulling his hand back.

"I was able to gather some intel on Holmestead's possible whereabouts," Masters finally said.

"Ok," Shane said, keeping it short and sweet so Masters would continue talking.

"I think he knows the identity of Paul's accomplice and arranged a meeting with that person at the hotel. Whenever Holmestead and I interrogated suspects, I was the aggressive *beat the shit out of 'em* cop while he always took the stance of *I don't care that you killed them, just tell me where the bodies are.* Never once thought about the crime committed or how dangerous the criminal was. All he wanted was to bring closure to the families."

He pounded a fist against the wheel and then gripped it in both hands, shaking it like he was trying to yank it off the steering column. The amount of anger displayed made Shane nervous, especially while Masters was driving. Shane twisted in his seat until his back was to the door to survive another sharp turn at the on-ramp to the highway. He really should have remembered how terrible Masters' driving was when he got into the back seat. If he'd taken the seat behind Kennie, his shoulder wouldn't be taking such a beating.

"Please calm down before you kill us," Kennie said.

"God damned idiot," Masters yelled.

Shane reached forward once again and rubbed his hand over Masters's shoulder and then up to his neck, squeezing the tense muscles to ease his stress. Kennie's knuckles were white where she gripped the console, but she otherwise appeared calm. Shane glanced over Masters's shoulder at the speedometer and cringed.

"Relax and breathe," Shane said as he continued his one-handed massage over Masters's shoulders.

He wasn't sure if he was telling Masters to calm down or himself, but he tried to take his own advice. Masters always made Shane nervous when he was driving, but his anger added another level of recklessness. Shane squeezed the tight muscles at the base of Masters's skull.

"Dom! You need to slow the fuck down before you wreck the car or get arrested. We'll never get to Crystal Creek if that happens."

Masters gradually eased off the gas pedal and their speed decreased to just ten over the limit. He took a deep breath and let it out while uncurling his fingers from the steering wheel. His neck and shoulders were still incredibly tense, but at least he was trying. Masters reached up and covered Shane's hand with his own, squeezed, and then pushed him away.

Shane sat back in the seat properly, rubbing his injured arm. The wound itself didn't seem to hurt but there was a throb radiating down to his fingers. He adjusted the sling and then started rubbing Bella's head. He'd been able to restrain his ability long enough for the brief contact he made with Masters, but the pain was eroding his control bit by bit.

"I was thinking Luke might be the accomplice," Shane admitted. He'd spoken softly but was easily heard in the silence blanketing the car.

"He's not." Masters looked at him in the rearview mirror. "Stop rubbing your arm or you'll make it bleed again."

Shane hadn't realized he was massaging his arm again and dropped his hand to Bella's back. "It hurts."

"Of course, it hurts," Masters snapped. "You were shot yesterday. You shouldn't even be out of the hospital yet."

"He bullied the doctor into discharging him," Kennie tattled. She opened the glove compartment, pulled out a bottle of grocery store pain reliever, and tossed it back to Shane. A bottle of water from the middle console followed. Shane obediently took two pills and drained the water.

"I'm aware of what he did. I went to the hospital first."

CHAPTER TWENTY-NINE

The drive up the mountain was spent in uncomfortable silence. Shane was waiting for the over-the-counter pain medication to take effect and wondered if Masters would ever call him out for using his first name, but Masters was preoccupied with other concerns. Kennie was uncharacteristically quiet. The interior of the car was thick with anxiety and anticipation. The highway narrowed to two lanes indicating they were nearing their destination. An eerie, sickly orange hue tinted the low-hanging clouds, dimming the sun. Shane and Kennie craned their necks to glance up at the sky through the windows.

"Smoke," Masters said.

"The fire is that bad?" Kennie asked.

"It's that close," he answered.

Shane's stomach knotted as he glanced at Masters' concerned expression in the rearview mirror. Kennie twisted in her seat to glance at Shane. Fear darkened her eyes and tightened her facial features. Shane nodded as he gripped Bella's scruff. Without warning, Masters hit the brakes, swerved onto the shoulder, and then a few dozen feet down the road made a sudden turn onto a dirt road that disappeared into the forest. The road wasn't well maintained, with bumps and holes scattered everywhere. Shane leaned forward in his seat, cradling his arm against his body so the rough terrain didn't jostle him too much. The position was hard to hold and only helped marginally.

Suffering pain from his wound was one thing. Getting lost on some mountain back road with a forest fire bearing down on them was something else entirely. How long before his heart gave out from adrenalin or he went crazy?

"What are you doing?" Shane asked.

"I'm going around the road blocks. There's no way we'll get past the authorities blocking the highway," Masters answered.

At least Masters seemed to know where he was going. The longer they drove, the darker it became forcing Masters to turn on the headlights. Ash began falling from the sky and dark grey smoke floated around the car like fog. There was a small fire burning in the distance where flying embers had ignited the dry leaves and underbrush. Shane was lost the moment Masters had pulled off the main highway so he had no idea how close they were to Crystal Creek Hotel but he was bothered by the fact they were encountering flames. He really didn't want to be in the middle of a forest fire.

"Do you think the hotel is still standing?" Shane asked.

When they set out on this trip, he was filled with urgency and determination, but faced with the very real danger the fire presented, he was second-guessing his decision. He had hoped to revisit the hotel and be gone again before the fire reached it but that wasn't happening. If there was a change the hotel had already burned down, he wanted to turn around.

"I don't know," Masters answered tightly.

They bumped over a cow guard and hit a deep crevice in the road that jarred them all. Kennie cursed under her breath as the front bumper of her car thunked against the ground followed by a similar thunk when the back bumper did the same. Shane yelped in pain as his shoulder collided with the door again.

"Sorry," Masters said.

He reached back between the seats to squeeze Shane's knee. Shane wondered if the heat from the fire and his pain levels were causing him to hallucinate that Masters had touched him, but the sly grin Kennie gave him said differently. Shane gave his best friend a small smile.

A short time later Crystal Creek Hotel came into view, looming above them through the hazy atmosphere. A horror movie come to life. The swirling smoke, falling ash, and eerie orange glow gave the decaying ruin a sinister appearance that gave Shane the creeps. What made the entire scene even more bothersome was seeing Luke's sedan parked near the entrance.

As Masters parked alongside Luke's car there was a loud crash. Shane turned to look out the back window toward the highway to see Thunderhawk Motel engulfed in flames. One of the cabins had collapsed. His heart sank and renewed fear kicked his heartrate up. The fire was way too close and Shane no longer cared about finding a group of people who disappeared more than a decade ago. He wanted to find Luke and get the hell off this mountain before they were all burned alive. Masters and Kennie got out of the car. Shane grabbed Bella's leash and got out at a slower pace. The air was hot and acrid and burned as he breathed.

"Fuck," Masters muttered.

Shane followed Masters's line of sight. Another vehicle was parked along the side of the hotel, near the caretaker's cottage. Despite the heat surrounding him, goosebumps exploded all over Shane's body. Did that car belong to the accomplice? What was going to kill him first? The murderer waiting inside the hotel or the fire about to burn the place down?

Masters pulled a revolver from his ankle holster. "Stay here," he demanded before running up the stairs and disappearing into the hotel.

Kennie turned toward Shane. Her eyes were red and watery. "We can't stay out here," she yelled. The roar of flames was louder than Shane had expected.

"No," he agreed.

He needed to get Bella out of the smoke. She would need a vet visit to check her nose and lungs if they survived long enough to get off the mountain. A nearby tree cracked open, sending sparks flying. Shane watched an ember land on the roof of the caretaker's cottage. Smoke immediately began billowing from the rotting shingles and within seconds flames could be seen dripping like rain through the windows.

Thick, black smoke rose into the sky from behind the hotel and Shane was certain the building was now burning. He coughed and, pain shot through his arm. His chest felt tight and burned with each breath. Kennie grabbed his hand over Bella's leash and pulled him toward the hotel. He followed reluctantly because that was the last place they should be going.

"People die from smoke inhalation. We have to get out of this," Kennie yelled.

At this point, he didn't have a better plan and Bella was starting to hack. He'd been stupid to bring her into such a dangerous situation, but he had every intention of coming into contact with ghosts and he couldn't do that without Bella. If he got lost to a memory now, he would most certainly die. Shane was perfectly aware of his own idiocy, walking into a burning building that also held a mass murderer, but it was too late to turn around. He was going to visit a psychiatrist if he managed to live through this ordeal because this level of insanity needed to be treated by a professional.

Shane stepped into the lobby behind Kennie. The roar of flames outside was muffled somewhat when they closed the door. They stood side by side and took deep breaths of surprisingly smoke-free air. It wasn't exactly clean, fresh air, but it was better. It was only a matter of time before the entirety of the hotel was filled with lethal smoke so Shane didn't waste time. He crossed the lobby toward the gentleman's room where the servant staircase ended.

Masters had stated he believed the missing party was in an underground room on the south side of the hotel. As he drew near, he noticed thin, orange-brown smoke snaking and swirling from beneath the double doors. Shane put his palm to the wood and found it still cool to the touch. The air around him grew warmer and the smoke began swirling up around him, taking on frightening shapes that vaguely resembled faces. The prolonged inhalation of smoke combined with his obvious insanity were playing games with his head.

Bella whined and pressed against Shane's leg as Kennie shuffled up behind him. He pushed open the door and the three of them filed into the room. The smoke was thicker inside and moved in a way that it appeared like a group of people were milling about. Shane blinked several times but the images didn't change or fade. His brain was only beginning to register what he was seeing when Bella took off across the room, yanking her leash free of Shane's grasp and disappearing into a cloud of smoke.

Shane yelled Bella's name just as Kennie screamed. He spun around in time to see a man slam Kennie against the wall. Her head hit the doorframe hard and she slumped to the floor unconscious. Shane was already injured and weak and in no shape to take this man on. He turned to run after Bella, hoping to hide amidst the smoke, but the man moved too fast. Shane was grabbed around the waist and yanked back against a body gone soft with age, but despite his soft middle, the man was strong. He squeezed so tightly Shane couldn't breathe. Pain lanced through his shoulder and radiated into his neck, back, and hand. What little air Shane managed to gasp in was hot, dry, and stung. His eyes watered and cool tears slid down his cheeks.

The smoke in front of him coalesced into a face and he jerked back against his captor. The face rapidly dissipated into the swirling atmosphere. Hot, hard metal pressed against his cheek. Shane closed his eyes, instantly going still. The man's tight grip never let up, forcing Shane to gasp shallow breaths. That, combined with the pain shooting through his arm, made him increasingly lightheaded.

He knew the man pressing a gun to his face was Paul Grant's accomplice, but he still didn't know the man's identity. Shane hadn't seen his face clearly through the smoke. This man had already shot Shane once so Shane knew he wouldn't hesitate to shoot him again if provoked.

"I don't who you are," Shane ground out. "Didn't your face. You can let me go."

"I can, but I won't. He has feelings for you and that's enough for me."

Shane went numb with a small burst of panic as the voice from Paul's memory filled his ear. Thankfully, his breathing was inhibited and his heart was already pounding so he didn't drop into a full-blown panic attack.

"That son of a bitch is going to pay."

Shane shrank away from the hot breath blowing across his face. "Who?"

"Dominic. He took them away from me so I will take you away from him."

"What?"

Shane's left arm throbbed while his head pounded to the rhythm of his heartbeat and his lungs burned. He was dizzy and his thoughts were becoming fuzzy. He couldn't make sense of what the man was saying. Even if Shane didn't get shot, he was fairly certain he was going to die anyway. The smoke surrounding them thickened, pressing in from all sides, and taking on the distinct shape of people crowding in close to them. Shane blinked a few times before he realized he was seeing ghosts. Were they only visible to Shane or could his captor see them, too?

He's coming. He'll save you, was whispered in his ear by several ghostly voices.

Shane was half carried, half dragged farther into the room. The dark ghostly vapor dissipated as they moved through it and he was able to see the massive fireplace and the door to the servant stairs. Shane was being taken exactly where he wanted to go but he stumbled when he saw Luke lying on the floor, bloody and unmoving.

Shane's heart squeezed in his chest and his body went limp as pure anguish thundered through his veins. At Luke's feet, Shane was released and he dropped to his knees. He immediately scooted closer to Luke, pushing strands of blood-soaked hair away from the gash at Luke's temple so he could assess the injury. He was no expert on head injuries, but the wound didn't look good.

A tear tracked down Shane's cheek as he mumbled, "No, no, no."

The accomplice squatted next to Shane and fisted Shane's hair.

"Such a shame."

Hot breath blew across Shane's ear and he twitched in discomfort, trying to pull away but also not wanting to leave Luke. The man thumped Luke's wound causing fresh blood to flow.

"Taught this boy everything I knew. Took an over-excited rookie and turned him into a damned good cop, but then he went and made nice with Dominic who turned him against me."

"How could you do this?" Shane croaked.

He wasn't just referring to Luke, but to Megan, who this man had claimed to love, as well as the fourteen other people who suffocated alongside her. Shane felt the man's shrug against his right shoulder. His left arm was strangely numb but he could also feel the chilly wetness of blood slowly soaking through his shirt sleeve. At some point, the gunshot wound had reopened. Shane was pushed down toward Luke with a hard shove to his head.

"Fucking faggot. It was quick."

Shane couldn't process what was being said; he couldn't think clear. He was in physical contact with two living beings - and Luke *was* still alive, thank God – and who knew how many ghosts wisping about the room. The result was too many piecemeal memories and disembodied voices floating through his mind. He shoved the man away and pushed to his feet. Once upright, he turned to face the killer. He tucked his injured arm against his chest, forcing himself to look at the man's face. He was familiar but Shane couldn't place where he'd met the man before.

The swirling smoke coalesced into ghostly figures so clear Shane could recognize identities. Robert Grant, Megan Granger, and several others Shane had encountered in memories were all there. All fifteen missing people were in the room, surrounding Shane and the man who killed them. They dissipated and reformed as Masters stepped through them, gun raised. He must have been heard because the man grabbed Shane's injured arm, yanked him against his chest once again, and pressed the barrel of his gun to Shane's temple.

Shane cried out in pain, struggling to stay conscious. Too many emotions and too many memories along with the real-world danger he was in crashed into each other in his brain. Bella had run off and Shane was at risk of dropping into any one of the many memories scratching at him without a tether. When his eyes finally focused, Shane found himself being held as a buffer between a murderer and Masters's bullets.

"Let him go, Ted," Masters said with deadly calm.

"I don't think I will."

Ted.

Recognition dawned, followed closely by a deep sadness. Another tear slid down Shane's cheek as he held Masters' gaze. The man holding him hostage was someone Masters considered family. Elizabeth's father. The betrayal Masters must have felt in that moment wasn't visible on his face or in his actions, but Shane knew it existed. Luke had probably felt the same when he realized Ted was the accomplice. It explained why Luke had chosen to confront Ted alone; he had been Luke's first partner.

Shane flashed back to the photographs hung on the landing of the staircase showing Ted and Luke in their dress uniforms, Masters and Elizabeth sitting on a porch swing, Ted flanked by Luke and Masters pulled close in a fatherly embrace. Ted squeezed Shane's wound causing spots to dance in his vision. Burning heat spread through his shoulder. Shane went limp in Ted's hold and Ted released him. Shane slumped to the floor in a boneless heap. He rolled to his back and watched Masters face down a man he'd once admired. Ted kept the barrel of his gun aimed at Shane.

"I will kill him right in front of you," Ted threatened.

"Why?" Masters asked brokenly, voice laced with sorrow.

Shane's heart broke for him. He understood all too well what Masters was going through. Shane had suffered the same pain when Brent had attacked and tortured him.

"Why? How dare you?" Ted bit out. "How dare you move on when no one else can? You're just like her."

Masters inched closer. "What are you talking about?"

"You killed my daughter and then hooked up with a fucking slut and a fag to boot. God-damned two-faced son of a bitch. Megan was the same. He's mine, you know. Jacob. I'm the one who got the bitch pregnant but she had the audacity to leave me for that rich bastard. Well, I got the better end of that deal, didn't I? I got the kid *and* the money. Megan and Robert can rot in hell, right alongside that backstabbing ex-partner of mine and your disgusting little cock-sucking tramp."

Shane cringed as Ted waved the gun in his direction maniacally. One slip or twitch of the trigger finger and Shane was dead. Masters tensed and pointed his revolver at Ted's head.

"What money?" Masters asked.

Both Ted and Shane were thrown by that question. Out of everything Ted had said, it was an odd thing to ask about, but Shane assumed Masters had chosen that particular fact to focus on for a reason.

"What money?" Ted repeated as though Masters was the densest person he'd ever met. "The two million dollars Robert gave Megan when he found out she was pregnant because he wanted *his* child to be taken care of."

Shane blinked rapidly, trying to focus on the living men in the room, but the thickening smoke and partially formed ghosts were making that increasingly difficult. His hazy brain tried to make sense of what was happening around him. Megan and Robert moved closer to him, drifting through the physical bodies in their way. It was a terrifying sight. Shane remembered how he'd felt when Robert walked through him and wondered if Masters had felt anything. He didn't act like he'd felt anything, but the man's composure was incredible. Both ghosts knelt beside him, their mouths moving silently. Other smokey specters coalesced between Shane and Ted, obscuring his view of both men.

You must move, a female voice whispered in his ear.

The door, said a man's voice and Robert pointed toward the fireplace. *Save yourself.*

Shane pushed himself up using his good arm, biting his tongue to stop from crying out in pain. His left arm and hand were wet with blood and his shoulder felt dislocated, hanging limply at his side. The thought of moving it hurt. He was slow and unsteady, but he managed to get his knees.

"Why shoot Holmestead? He was like a son to you," Masters asked.

"Because he turned on me. Asking me to meet him here, telling me he knew everything. Little shit tried to arrest me. All because of you," Ted answered. His voice rose in volume with every word until he was screaming.

"No. He turned on you because you murdered sixteen people and tried to kill Shane," Masters yelled back.

Their voices were clear enough, but the smoke between them was too thick to see through. Shane realized the ghosts were doing it on purpose to cover his escape. He didn't want to leave his friends now that the soft orange glow of flames could be seen licking the wall across the room. Neither Kennie nor Luke could protect themselves. Crystal Creek Hotel was burning down around them and they needed to get out before they burned alive. The roar of flames was growing louder and the room was rapidly becoming an inferno. Shane got to his feet and stumbled over to the fireplace.

CHAPTER THIRTY

Here. We're here, several voices spoke at once.

Shane bit back a startled yelp when something solid bumped into the backs of his thighs. He spun around and breathed a sigh of relief. Bella had found her way back. Behind her, Robert lifted a ghostly hand to point at one of the carved adornments on the fireplace. Robert somewhat dematerialized as he mimicked a downward pulling motion. Shane hooked the loop of Bella's leash around his wrist and leaned against the fireplace surround, head right below one of the massive lion-head features on the mantel. It took far more energy than Shane expected to reach upward.

He gripped the lion head but couldn't get it to pull downward. The smoke surrounding him moved to his hand and solidified. The strength of fifteen ghosts and Shane's strong will to live resulted in the lion head finally moving. Haltingly, but eerily silent, the back of the fireplace swung open. A foul odor whooshed out of the opening making Shane gag. He looked back toward Masters.

The apparitions parted to allow Shane to see Masters still pointing his revolver at Ted, who was also still pointing his gun toward the floor where Shane had fallen when Ted released him. If he hadn't heard the two men talking to each other, Shane would've thought time had stopped because the only one who had moved was Shane. Masters made the briefest eye contact with Shane before quickly returning his attention to Ted.

"How dare you choose this disgusting little cock-lover over my sweet Elizabeth," Ted screamed.

"Elizabeth is dead," Masters said. "She died years ago."

"Because you killed her. You killed my baby girl."

Without warning, Ted pulled the trigger. The bullet tore through the smoke and ghostly miasma drifting around them and embedded into the wood flooring where Shane had been sitting moments before. Masters didn't hesitate before he aimed at Ted's chest and fired. Ted grunted and fell to the floor, gasping for breath. Shane clamped his hand over his mouth and turned away as the pool of blood beneath Ted spread across the floor. Flames licked along the wall behind Masters and spread rapidly to the ceiling overhead.

The old wood structure was nothing more than kindling to feed the blaze. Choking black smoke rolled in thick waves throughout the room. Remembering his elementary school days of Stop, Drop, and Roll, Shane slid down the fireplace surround to the floor where somewhat cleaner air could be found. Memories of burning alive in a fire outside of Masters' apartment door overwhelmed him and he fought the panic building in his chest.

Masters ran to Shane and knelt in front of him. He took the leash off Shane's wrist and then lead Bella into the smoke toward the door that connected to the lobby. When Masters returned, he no longer had Bella with him. Shane wanted to scream in terror but he didn't have the strength. Masters gently lifted Shane into his arms.

"Bella, lead," Masters yelled.

Bella reappeared with a groggy and unsteady, but living Kennie shuffling behind her. Masters carried Shane into the fireplace and through the large metal door at the back. On the other side was a small chamber big enough to fit three to four people. Kennie stumbled in after Bella as Masters lowered Shane to the floor. Bella immediately laid across Shane's legs and Kennie eased down to sit beside him.

Masters disappeared through the opening, but returned seconds later dragging Luke's body into the alcove with them. Once Luke was inside, he got behind the metal door. He grunted with the effort it took to shove the door closed and Shane wondered how it had opened so easily in the first place.

Shane didn't have much time to think about it because smoke billowed into their tiny room and the orange glow of flames was growing brighter. He hated how useless he was panicked to the point of paralysis, even when faced with his own death and that of his closest friends. His fight or flight response was horribly broken. The ambient light in the room dimmed as Masters successfully moved the door inch by inch until it finally closed with a thud, plunging them all into a deep, dark abyss.

Shuffling footsteps came towards Shane and then he felt a hand on his shin. Masters eased to the floor beside him, draped an arm over his shoulders, and pulled him against his chest. Shane's arm was partially numb but he still cried out in pain as his wound bumped into Masters' chest.

"Sorry," Masters murmured against Shane's temple. "I never meant for you to get hurt."

One of Masters' hands gripped Shane's shoulder while the other caressed his hair and then slid down over his ear to cup his jaw. Before Shane's pain-muddled brain could process what Masters was doing, soft lips touched his in a gentle kiss. Shane closed his eyes to savor the warmth and tenderness of the kiss, knowing it would be his last. He couldn't see any possibility that the five of them would survive. The only way in or out of this alcove was the closed metal door with a fire raging on the other side of it; a fire Shane was convinced would still find its way to them.

Masters kept the kiss brief but continued to hold Shane against him. Bella whined and Shane tiredly rubbed one of her ears while Kennie reached over to pet the top of Bella's head. When their hands met, Shane grabbed hold of her fingers and squeezed. Kennie squeezed back. No words were needed. Shane's gaze was drawn to a soft grey light emitting from the metal door near Luke's feet that slowly materialized into Robert Grant's ghost. He looked down at all of them with sadness in his eyes.

"Please?" Shane's throat was raw from the smoke.

Bella lifted her head with a whine and looked right at Robert's ghost. Kennie whispered "shhh" while Masters pressed his lips to Shane's temple. Neither of them knew that Shane and Bella were seeing something that could potentially save them. From the beginning, Robert and Megan had shown that even after death they were aware of their surroundings and had actively interacted with the living.

"Show me," he pled.

Robert pointed, stepping forward until his ghostly aura illuminated a doorway half obscured by a tattered curtain. Stamped into a gold plate above the entry were the words *The Shot*. Robert floated through the door where he stopped over a serrated metal floor. Shane sat up straighter as it occurred to him what he was seeing. The original owner of Crystal Creek, Julian Pastori, had been a gangster who'd made the majority of his money moonshining and bootlegging. Shane had wondered where all that alcohol had been made and stored, and he still didn't know specifics, but he knew he was looking at how the booze had been sold. *The Shot* was a hidden speakeasy.

Luke groaned, rolling to his side sluggishly and pressing a hand against the left side of his abdomen.

"Luke?" Shane called out.

Masters released his hold on Shane and fumbled his way through the dark to Luke's side. "You doing okay, Holmes-y boy? I guess he didn't actually shoot you in the head."

"Fucker tried. Grazed my temple. Hit the mark with my gut, though."

"I'd offer more help but I can't see a damned thing," Masters said.

"I can," Shane said. "Some ghosts give off a dim light."

"There's a ghost in here with us?" Kennie asked. She sounded tired but stronger, her face still pinched with pain.

"Robert Grant."

"How does my wound look?" Luke grunted, pushing himself up to a seated position.

"I don't see fresh blood," Shane answered, though he really couldn't make out much. When he said "dim light," he meant it. Moonlight was brighter.

"I am sadly not reassured," Luke grumbled. "What's burning?"

"Everything," Masters answered.

"We need to move," Shane said.

The only smoke in the room was from when they'd entered, but the door was metal and Shane imagined it would soon glow orange-red with heat. Megan materialized next to Robert, adding a bit more illumination to the tiny entry.

"Where exactly would we move to?" Masters asked.

"The ghosts are showing me a doorway behind Luke."

Shane stood up, thankful his legs weren't as shaky as before, and then helped Kennie to her feet. He wrapped Bella's leash around Kennie's wrist so the dog could lead her through the darkness. Shane placed his uninjured hand on Masters's shoulder.

"Bella will lead Kennie. I will lead you and Luke."

"Can you walk?" Masters asked Luke as he assisted him to his feet. Masters hooked one of Luke's arms over his shoulder and looped an arm around his waist. Luke leaned heavily against Masters but was able to move his feet on his own.

"I think so," he said after a couple of small, shuffling steps.

"Bella, follow," Shane commanded.

Because Masters had his hands full helping Luke, Shane grabbed the hem of Masters's shirt and tugged the pair along behind him. The ghosts floated a few feet ahead of Shane, illuminating the metal landing and serrated-metal steps that led downward into a deep, dark hole. He heard the click-clack of Bella's nails against the metal mixed in with the timid, shuffling steps of the humans carefully finding their way through the darkness.

On one side of the metal staircase was a concrete wall. On the other was a thin, metal railing with vast nothingness behind it. The entire staircase looked dangerously old and questionably attached to the wall, but Shane knew they would be going down. As he shuffled closer to the first step, more ghosts appeared, illuminating the steep staircase with their eerie glow. They were the ghosts of the fifteen missing people still trapped in this god-forsaken place. Unfortunately, the stairs were not the only thing their ghostly auras brought to light. On the landing, just inches from Shane's feet, was a mummified body. Bile burned the back of his throat as he sidled past the corpse to take the first step down.

"There's a metal staircase heading down that we're going to take. Steep and shallow steps. There's a railing to the left and a concrete wall to the right. Als0" – Shane swallowed down a wave of nausea – "there's a body right here against the wall. Be careful."

"So, we found them?" Luke mumbled.

Shane grunted in response. His chest was tight and his lungs still burned. If this *was* the place the missing people suffocated in, that meant the air quantity and quality, wasn't good so talking a lot or moving too fast would work against them. Shane took the first step down, and then turned around to place Kennie's hand on the railing. He patted Bella on the head before putting Masters's hand to the rail, as well.

"Use it as a guide, but don't put weight against it. It doesn't look safe."

Shane turned and began the descent, one careful step at a time. The lower they went, the colder it became and the more claustrophobic Shane felt. He whispered his gratitude for the light to each of the ghosts as he passed them. At the bottom of the steps, they encountered three more bodies slumped against each other. The darkness was oppressive, the silence terrifying, and the air stale, thin, and damp. *The Shot* had once been a place of celebration but it had become nothing but a tomb. Not even the sound of their shuffling feet carried more than a few inches, suppressed by the aura of death coating the walls. Shane hated this room.

The final step down was met with a splash as Shane's shoe broke through the glass-like surface of water on the floor. The water wasn't deep, only one or two inches, but Shane was confused by its presence. He didn't remember seeing water in any of the memories he'd received.

"Is that water I heard?" Masters asked.

"Yes. Maybe an inch or so deep," Shane answered. He turned around and grabbed Masters's hand. "One more step but stay close to the railing. There are bodies against the wall."

Masters and Luke took the last step down with a splash. Once Shane was certain both men had decent footing, he reached for Kennie. Bella stopped to sniff the skeletons and then the water before she was forced to follow by the tug on her leash. Shane kept hold of Kennie's hand, uncertain what to do or where to go next. They were trapped in an underground, concrete tomb with a fire raging over their heads so his uncertainty didn't matter. They'd be doing nothing and going nowhere. He felt completely defeated. Yes, they'd found the missing people, even learned the identity of their killers, but what was the point when they were going to die themselves?

Shane squinted as light unexpectedly flashed on beside him. Kennie had turned on the flashlight app of her cell phone, sending a beam of light ahead of them that reflected off a massive mirror. The mirror was mounted behind a mahogany bar, cracked and broken, with large shards missing, but there was enough glass remaining to send Kennie's light back into their faces. Shane blinked as he eyes adjusted and sighed.

"Kennie?" he asked.

"Yeah," she answered. She seemed to understand Shane's unspoken question because she immediately moved the phone's light off the mirror and spun around to get a quick look at their surroundings.

"Why did no one think to do that when we were coming down the stairs?" Luke asked.

Shane and Kennie glanced at each other, dumbstruck, and then simultaneously turned to look at Masters.

"Don't look at me. I have my hands full."

"And I'm too weak," Luke added.

"You still could've thought of it and said something," Kennie said.

"So could you," Masters pointed out.

"I did think of it, obviously. It was just a little delayed, is all."

"How's your battery?" Shane asked.

Kennie glanced at the screen of her phone. "Eight-seven percent."

The raised stage Shane had seen in Megan's memories was across the room from the bar, looking like an island floating a few inches above the water. Masters shuffled Luke over to it and eased him down. Luke pulled his feet out of the water, scooting back to lean against the wall the same way Megan and many others had twelve years before. Their skeletal remains were scattered across the stage mixed among concrete dust, torn fabric, and other crumbling debris. The sight sent shivers down Shane's spine. Would the five of them die the same way? He pulled Bella closer, seeking comfort from her warmth.

Once his hands were free, Masters pulled his phone out and then grunted. "Fifty-three percent for me. Luke?"

"Lost my phone somewhere."

Masters glanced at Shane. "Yours?"

Shane reached into his back pocket to grab his phone. He thumbed it on and sighed when he saw the screen was cracked. At least it still turned on and had a good charge.

"Ninety-six percent but no reception."

"That's not surprising but still use them sparingly. We don't know how long we'll be stuck down here," Masters said.

Kennie joined Luke on the stage where it was dry and then turned the flashlight app off. The soft glow of the screen lit their faces for a few seconds before darkening again. Shane wanted to look around so he thumbed through his apps in search of the flashlight. Masters turned his on and then covered Shane's hand to stop his movements.

"You have the most battery. Don't waste it."

Shane nodded and then followed Masters as he moved around the room. While Masters was interested in examining the skeletons, Shane found himself fascinated with the speakeasy itself. A massive gilt-framed mirror hung in pieces behind a hand-carved, mahogany bar that was cracked and decayed. The corners were adorned with dirty metal rods that matched the barstool poles. Shane turned in a circle, taking the room in. The velvet drapes, the bar with its broken mirror, the chandelier – it was all exactly as it had been in Megan's memory, except for one very big difference. One thing that gave Shane a sliver of hope that he and his friends might not die in this hole as he'd originally thought.

"Where did the water come from?" he asked.

Loud cracks from above drew their attention up toward the exit. Masters aimed his light in that direction but it didn't reach far enough. It wasn't necessary anyway. A sickly orange glow could be seen through the doorway and seconds later the tattered curtains hanging around the frame caught fire. A thunderous boom was accompanied by plumes of smoke that rolled along the ceiling. Masters leapt into action. He handed his phone to Shane and then went to the bar and began snapping the weakened wood away from one of the metal corner posts.

Shane watched him for a second and was about to ask what he was doing when Bella started barking. The ghosts of those in the speakeasy with them were materializing over their remains. All of them pointed at a female ghost who was on the floor weakly hitting the wall with the spiked heal of her shoe. The apparition herself appeared to be caught in a memory loop but her actions were important.

"Everyone start searching. If water can get in, we can get out. Hurry," Masters said. He placed his hand on Shane's lower back, pushing him into action.

"Over here," Shane said as he rushed to the damaged part of the wall.

Bella sniffed the skeleton as Shane reached around the female ghost to drag his fingers across the cracks in the cinderblock. There were several darkened streaks running from the broken block down to the floor. His fingertips came away dry but he was convinced this was where the water had gotten in.

"I think the river is on the other side of this wall," Shane said.

"Move," Masters demanded and Shane backed away, pulling Bella with him.

Masters lined up the end of the metal pole with the already-damaged section of cinderblock and rammed it into the wall. Pieces of cinderblock fell to the floor in a cloud of dust. Masters started breaking through the wall with rapid fire strikes. Shane wanted to help but he only had one useful arm so he stayed out of the way and kept the light pointed at Masters. He kept Bella close and his back against the wall, his attention bouncing between Masters and the fire burning brightly at the top of the stairs.

"Will the ceiling collapse?" Shane asked.

"Not waiting around to find out," Masters grunted as he continued his assault on the wall.

The smoke rolling over their heads thickened to the point the chandelier was barely visible. Shane squatted, hugging Bella close to him, and contemplated how he'd ended up in this place, with these people, facing death for the second time in his short life. A rush of hot air filled the room, sending the cloud of smoke rolling even more and the fire at the top of stairs flared brighter. Shane glanced at Masters but all he saw was Masters's lower half. The rest of him was in the hole he'd created. The place really was crumbling around them if Masters had been able to put a hole through a concrete wall so easily. Masters shimmied out and motioned toward the hole.

"Everyone out," he said. "But be careful. It opens to the ravine off the side of the highway. You're going to drop headfirst into the river."

Shane stared at the hole in the wall that was barely large enough to fit Masters and rubbed Bella's side. Kennie was the first to climb through and then Masters assisted Luke through with a firm shove. Faint splashes and cursing could be heard as each of them cleared the wall and plunged into icy water. How far was the drop? Would Bella be okay after the fall or would she be injured? How was he going to get her through the hole in the first place? Masters hooked his arm around Shane's waist and urged him to his feet. Shane allowed himself to be led to the hole but he couldn't stop the fear crawling up his throat.

"No, no, no. I can't leave her," Shane said.

"Kennie is already out."

"Bella. I can't "

"You first." Masters pushed Shane down toward the hole.

Shane pushed back, trying to straighten up and clutching Bella's leash to his chest. "I won't leave Bella."

Masters cupped his face. "Shane, please trust me and go. I promise not to leave her behind."

A tear slid down Shane's cheek as he handed Masters Bella's leash and crawled into the hole. The cinderblock surrounding him was two feet thick, but hollow and crumbling which explained why Masters had been able to dig through it so quickly. His head and shoulders were out of the hole on the other side while his feet were still in the speakeasy. It was an odd shuffle out but he was thankful to see the drop to the river was only a few feet. He wouldn't break his neck, at least.

His injured shoulder protested every move as he dangled headfirst toward the river, struggling to work the rest of his body free. When he felt himself start to drop, he held his breath, fell into the frigid water and jolted painfully from the shock. The heat from the surrounding fires combined with the icy water made him dizzy but he had to stay alert for Bella. Shane looked up to a terrifying sight.

Not only was Bella's head and front paws peeking out of the hole, the whites of her eyes visible, the overhang of tree roots and branches dangling at a precarious angle above them were on fire. The spot they escaped the speakeasy through had been undercut from decades of elevated water levels from spring snowmelt and heavy summer rainfalls. The foliage and surrounding terrain had created a tiny cave-like area that was completely invisible to anyone standing on the riverbank. Except for an unevenly exposed two-by-four-foot expanse of blackened concrete, the speakeasy walls were still buried beneath the ground.

Bella whined as she was pushed sharply from behind by Masters. Shane struggled to keep his feet under him, standing unsteadily on the slippery riverbed with icy water swirling around his legs. Bella flailed as she fell, but Shane was able to wrap his arms around her upper half before he was knocked backwards into the water. While he was grateful he managed to cushion her impact using his body, it was a fight to keep both their heads above water as Bella kicked all four legs in fear.

They bobbed in the water while Shane tried to catch his footing on the slick rocks and fighting to keep Bella's head above water even when he was dunked under. Shane had no idea how long he'd been fighting his dog in the water before Masters grabbed him and dragged them onto the riverbank. He clutched Bella to his chest with numb arms as more people joined them on. A woman in uniform with a friendly face and soft voice managed to work Bella loose from his grip so two men with stethoscopes could address his many cuts and bruises. From the bleak look on their faces, he must have looked close to death.

"Where...my friends...help them," Shane gritted out between chattering teeth.

"Your friends are nearby. They're being checked out, too," one of the men said.

"Bella...my dog...where?."

The EMT glanced around before answering. "Your dog's in the back of a squad car. She's safe."

A wave of dizziness hit Shane and he struggled to stay upright. Shouted commands and questions directed at Shane erupted all around him. He couldn't make sense of the words or see details of face anymore. He'd been sucked into a tunnel that was hard to see through, gradually growing darker by the second until everything went black.

CHAPTER THIRTY-ONE

Shane sipped coffee on the patio of his favorite small coffee shop, Deja Brew, less than a mile down the road from Crimson Moon Gifts. On days when the Colorado weather was pleasant, he would walk Bella the short distance, order an espresso, and then sit outside, people watching and leisurely rubbing the dog's fur. It had been a regular thing until three months ago when he'd answered that call from Luke. Shane had longed to get back to his predictable life at the time, but he hadn't realized just how much he'd missed the little things like coffee outside until this moment.

Despite the perfect temperature, the bright sun, the cloudless sky, and everyone going about their normal days, Shane was nervous. To anyone looking at him, he appeared to be a man relaxing with his dog and enjoying the morning, but he wasn't. The Grant party investigation had lasted mere days but had resulted in months of Shane and Kennie sitting through interrogations, dealing with constant interruptions at work when detectives dropped into the shop or called with "additional" questions which were really the same ones asked in different ways repeatedly.

The cops were convinced they weren't getting the full story and kept revisiting the same topics trying to wrap it all up with a neat bow inside their heads. As frustrating as it was, Shane understood. He and Kennie *were* keeping something from the authorities; they were diligently keeping Shane's psychic ability to themselves. No matter how many times he was asked or how many times the cops brought up that Crimson Moon Gifts advertised psychic readings, Shane would deny he was truly psychic. Luke and Masters had worked hard to keep that out of their files, and as far as Shane knew, neither of them had mentioned using a psychic in their investigation.

Shane's cell phone vibrated on the wrought-iron café table and he grinned at the name on the screen. He set his coffee down and answered with forced cheerfulness.

"Good morning."

"Morning" Luke said, tiredly, a tiny cry in the background. Shane loved Tracy and the girls, but hearing that newborn wailing made him thankful to be gay. "How are you doing today? Any more unexpected visits?"

"I'm doing okay and no visits in the last week or so. They're more into the phone calls now but even that seems to be slowing down."

"That's good to hear. Dom has been downplaying your involvement and trying to divert their attention away from you."

"Really? How so?" Shane asked.

He hadn't seen Masters since they'd been separated by the authorities at the hotel. He hadn't visited Shane during the days he'd been in the hospital, either, and they'd not crossed paths on the many trips Shane had made to the police station. Even Luke found the time to visit or call, and he had a newborn baby at home, so the fact Masters hadn't made the effort stung.

"Basically, he's playing the "I forced my boyfriend to go with me" card. Keeps telling them you only knew the most basic of details."

"That might be why the cops don't believe what Kennie and I are telling them. Masters tells them I don't know anything but then I go in and contradict him."

"It's fine. They'd probably be more suspicious if our stories matched up perfectly. Different people experience different things in different ways and all that." Luke yawned loudly and then sighed. "Anyway, wanted to check on you but I need a nap something fierce."

"Yeah, okay," Shane responded distractedly and disconnected the call.

His attention had been claimed by the man who took the chair across the table from him. The coffee in his hand was from Deja Brew and Shane wondered how he'd missed Masters going inside. The table was only a few feet away from the entrance. He had so much to say, so many questions, and a boatload of emotions he didn't know what to do with but not a single word came out of his mouth.

Instead, he stared into Masters's blue eyes and waited. For what, he didn't know. Masters held his gaze for a long moment as he took a drink. He lowered the cup to the table and licked his lips, the sight of which completely shut down Shane's brain. How had he forgotten how attractive this man was?

"You're looking better than I expected. The way Luke tells it you're at death's door, barely holding onto life, wasting away into fragments of your former self."

Shane rolled his eyes. "Such an overly dramatic lie."

"Maybe" Masters reached across the small table and ran his thumb under Shane's eye "But you do have dark circles and your eyes aren't as bright."

Shane swallowed thickly. When he was sure he could speak without croaking, he asked, "Where have you been?"

Masters seemed overly distracted by Shane's face, his hand preoccupied with cupping Shane's cheek, but he answered. "Surveillance. Small business owner thinks an employee is stealing."

"And?" Shane pressed, hoping to divert his mind from the sensation of Masters's palm caressing his face, warming his skin, and making him long for something he couldn't have.

Masters let his hand drop and leaned back in his seat. Shane tried not to let the disappointment show on his face. He picked up his coffee and took a sip, taking a few seconds to hide behind the thick paper cup. Masters was back to business instantly as if the past few moments hadn't happened at all.

"He's definitely stealing. Gave the photo evidence to the business owner so my part is done."

"And the Grant case?"

"Our part is done, Shane. We did what we were hired to do. The rest is up to the police."

"But the cops keep calling"

"They will for a while, but there's nothing more you can offer. Nothing more you can do. Let it go and move on."

"I'm trying but it's not that easy."

"I know."

"What about Alyssa and Jacob?" Shane asked.

Ted hadn't survived the encounter with Masters. He had bled out from his gunshot wound before Crystal Creek Hotel was completely destroyed by flames. His charred remains had been found several days later. When Alyssa heard from police what had transpired, she'd broken down, screaming at anyone who would listen that they had it all wrong. Ted wasn't a murderer. He had nothing to do with the disappearance and death of her sister. She was convinced everything Shane, Luke, and Masters had said about her husband had been fabricated. Lies up on lies to ruin a good cop's reputation.

Even as more evidence came to light that Paul Grant had orchestrated the deaths of his brother and fourteen of his colleagues with Ted's help, she refused to believe any of it. Alyssa had maintained civility until after Ted's funeral, which Luke and Masters had attended, and then she'd severed all contact with them. According to Luke, her hostility was mostly aimed at Masters. He supposed that made sense since Masters was the one who'd shot him. Shane knew being cut off from family so hatefully had devastated both men, but they hid it well.

"Nothing has changed," Masters answered.

They sat in silence, each drinking their coffee and mulling over their own thoughts, until Masters spoke again.

"Why don't we take our minds off it?"

Shane lowered his brows in suspicion. "How, exactly?"

"Another case."

"What?"

"Luke has retired from P.I. work and I have a case that could benefit from your unique ability so...what do you say? You in?"

Was Masters serious? Shane was surprised he wanted to work with him again, but he was secretly elated. He didn't know what kind of case Masters would bring him in on, but he liked being asked. Even with all the doubt, taunting, and arguments Masters had thrown his way, Shane loved the idea of helping him again. He felt good after solving the disappearance of Robert Grant and his friends and was excited to do it again.

And if he were honest with himself, he loved the idea of spending more time with Masters. Not that he would ever admit it out loud to anyone other than Bella, but he had missed Masters horribly over the past few months and now he was offering Shane the chance to see him on a regular basis. Shane smiled and his insides warmed when Masters smiled back.

"I'm in."

About the Author

Kay is an omnisexual/polysexual who lives in Colorado with her poly-family. Her house is overrun with cats and dogs. Family is important to her so there are daily texts, frequent visits to her parents, and constant banter with her brothers. She happily suffers an addiction to coffee and Mexican food. She loves to read and write and can easily become consumed by it for hours, much to the dismay of others. On occasion she can be convinced to venture out into the world of the living despite being annoyed with the sun shining in her face.

Email (public address): kaydohertyauthor@gmail.com
Facebook: @kaydohertyauthor
TikTok: @kaydohertyauthor
Website: kaydohertybooks.com